A Dang

P each P assion
P ublications

A
Dangerous
Love 7

The Price Of Love

JPeach

JPeach

Email: j.peach0509@hotmail.com, peachpassionpublications@hotmail.com
Facebook: Peach Johnson
Facebook Like Page: JPeach1088
Facebook Reading Group: JPeach's Spot
Twitter: JPeach1088

Acknowledgement

DaJah & Da'Vion, my heart, my two babies. If it wasn't for you two I swear I would not have the determination to continue to beat these keys as hard as I am. You two are my motivation!!
I LOVE Y'ALL SO MUCH!!

I want to dedicate this finale to all my readers/supporters. Thank you all so much for sticking with me through this all. To all my readers who are still with me from 2013 when this story was first created Thank You All For Rocking With Me ON This Journey!!
You all truly don't understand how much your constant support means to me! I promise words can't begin to describe this feeling!!
Thank You All So Much!

A Dangerous Love 7: *The Price Of Love*

JPeach

Prologue

Peaches

"Peaches, come on, baby girl. Get up." I heard Blaze over the loud car alarms.

My eyes blinked rapidly as I felt the immediate throb from my head when I hit it on the ground. Once my vision cleared, I looked up at my burning house and cried. I bawled harder as I imagined what would've happened had Blaze not called us back to him.

Even after the beating I received from Le'Ron, I realized these fatal threats were never going to end. They were really trying to kill me, us. I clung to the front of Blaze's shirt crying, as I silently thanked God that we were alright.

Blaze made it to the truck and thrusted me into the backseat where Blake sat screaming. Hearing his cries caused me to cry harder from the fear I knew he felt. I grabbed my little man and pulled him into my chest.

"Peaches, is he good?" Blaze asked once he hopped into the front seat.

I didn't answer him because I didn't know. I was so shaken from the explosion that all I could do was rock my baby and cry.

"Peaches!" Blaze yelled, causing me to jump hard and Blake to cry even harder. I could tell from his tone of voice that he was pissed. "Peaches, I need you to calm down and check to make sho' he's good." Blaze yelled once more as he jumped a curve.

With shaky hands, I sat Blake on the seat and began to look him over. His face was dirty, and blood ran from the right side of his head.

I had to pull myself together. My hands frantically wiped at my tears before I pulled up his shirt to inspect his small body. There was a big bruise on the right side of his shoulder besides that I didn't see any other marks.

I reached in the hatchback and grabbed the duffle bag. Opening it, I pulled out the wipes then cleaned around the cut on his forehead to see if it was deep.

It was.

"Blaze, he has a split on the side of his head and a bruise on his shoulder. He needs to go to the hospital." I told him over Blake's screams.

"Fuck!" Blaze yelled hitting the steering wheel before he ran a red light.

"Blake, baby, you're going to be okay. I promise. Shhh," I pulled him back into my lap. I held him tightly against my chest. His body bounced fast from my legs moving frantically. I was trying to calm myself down for him but that didn't change the fact I was terrified.

"Aye, King, meet me at my crib and call the twins over. I'll be there in about ten minutes and I need y'all there," Blaze instructed him.

I could tell from the way his hands squeezed around the steering wheel that he was having a hard time controlling himself.

"The mothafucka just blew up Peaches house!" He informed him. "Yo, don't ask me shit else. King, shut the fuck up and just meet us at the crib." Blaze threw his phone into the passenger seat as he continued to speed all the way to his apartment.

***

When we made it to Blaze's place, King and the twins were waiting on us. Blaze had Khyree stitch the side of Blake's head. I wanted to protest but Khyree was gentle with him. Blake fought at first until Khyree numbed the area. Once he finished, he gave Blake some medicine that put him to sleep.

"If I fuckin' knew who did the shit, I wouldn't be fuckin' sitting here!" Blaze yelled at King before he punched the wall. "Yo, that mothafucka called me and said I better enjoy our time because it wasn't gon' last long. This mothafucka just tried to kill my son and Peaches. And I don't know who the fuck it is. How the fuck am I supposed to do shit?"

Blaze flipped over the glass table in the living room, causing the glass to fall onto the floor and shatter.

His action caused Blake to jump. I held him tighter to me and shushed him. I continued to rock him back and forth, trying to calm him.

Blaze noticed and glared at me. "Get him the fuck outda here. Go put him in the room."

I didn't say anything smart to him. Instead, I got up and took Blake into the spare room.

Blaze had lost all cool once we walked through the door, he flipped and couldn't control his anger. He wanted to know who was behind this, but the people we knew that could've given us answers were dead.

We couldn't bring Le'Ron back to ask him anything and Blaze was pissed because he didn't know where to start looking. What he did know was that someone knew a lot about us, and he didn't like it. For them to be able to get to us so easily wasn't sitting well with him.

I watched Blake for a second longer before I left out the room. My fingers swiped at my eyes not believing what just happened. We all could've been dead.

As I walked back into the living room, there was a knock on his door.

Blaze was the first to grab his gun. He cocked it and so did everyone else.

"B, it's me." Bellow's voice came from the other side of the door.

Blaze waved his gun and Khalil opened the door for him.

"I done talked to everybody on that block and nobody saw shit. They said nobody came or left that house after y'all bounced. But the garage was rigged to blow once the door closed. So somebody had to get inside that house to set it up." Bellow flopped down on the couch. His hand ran over his face before he loosened his tie.

"We're still blind to whoever did this. That mothafucka got full control over everything. Even so, I don't think they'll make a move just yet, especially after this. But B, you have to capitalize on this. They don't know the outcome of the bombing just yet. You got to get lil' man and Peaches out of here. If those mothafuckas ain't scared to rig her place, those mothafuckas ain't fuck'd up about you, period." Bellow told him before his eyes glanced up at me.

King let out a heavy breath. His frustrations showed on his face, but he was doing a good job holding it in. His head shook, "B, Bell is right. They can't stay here. They know where yo heart at now, so they not gon' come for you no more. They gon' try everything to get at her and if they find out you got a kid, they gon come for the both of them. They got to get the fuck up out of here tonight. We can't sit on this. We need to move now."

"Fuck!" Blaze snapped again. He looked at me, I saw it in his eyes that he knew they were right. "We'll leave out and go to The City tonight and I'll figure something out in the morning." Blaze rubbed a frustrated hand over his head.

"B, you can't go with them. Wherever you go, they gon' follow." Bellow head shook. "It's obvious you're not hard to get at for them. They'll be quick to find you and once they do. Peaches and Lil' man gon' be pulled right back into this shit."

"I ain't letting them go by themselves. Hell n'all! Fuck that bullshit. Where they go, I go—" Blaze started to go off once again.

King cut him off. "Blaze, you ain't got no choice. Don't let yo stubbornness over cloud what you know is right. B, the mothafucka put a bomb in Peaches' garage. This mothafucka ain't gon' stop and we don't have time to sit around here going back and forth about this bullshit when you know we're right." King was pissed off.

Blaze punched the wall again. "Fuck!"

"The City ain't a good place to go. That's right next door. Hell, half the mothafuckas in Gary is from Chicago. Everybody know everybody so that's not a smart move," Khyree chimed in.

"They not going far. They not leaving Indiana if that's what y'all hinting at." Blaze told them.

"They don't have too. Indiana got a lot of cities. Matter of fact, I got a friend out in Lafayette that can hook them up in a low kept spot. It'll be safe for them because don't too much of shit happen out there. That's nothing but a two hour drive but the decision is all yours." Khalil sat on the couch next to Bellow.

"What you gon' do?" Khyree asked him.

Blaze said nothing else to them as he walked out. He grabbed a hold of my arm as he did and pulled me into the room then closed the door. "Peaches, I'm sorry about all of this shit." He took a deep breath as he began to pace the room.

I couldn't blame him, to me it wasn't his fault. "Blaze, you don't have to apologize." I sat on the bed, thinking about what the boys were saying, but after what just happened, I didn't want to leave his side.

"Peach, they right. As long as the two of you are around me, shit like this is going to continue to happen until I end this bullshit."

I grabbed his hand and pulled him next to me. "Blaze, I don't want to leave you—"

"Do you think I want this? I don't, Peach. But we don't have a choice. It's what's best for you and Blake. Peaches, it's not gon' change shit between us besides location. I'mma set y'all up at a hotel until we find y'all a house out there—"

I started to cut him off, but he waved his hand at me and my mouth shut.

"I don't need you to disagree with me, just know I'm making the best decision for y'all." Blaze pulled away from me. "Go pack what clothes y'all have here and get ready to leave out in a half hour," Blaze didn't say anything else as he walked out of the room, slamming the door shut.

He ended our conversation and made the final decision he thought was best for us.

Present

Five Years Later

My eyes tore away from the photo of Blake, Cherry and I at the park five years ago. Tears filled my eyes as I stared at Cherry, my first baby, knowing I would never be able to hold her again.

I placed the picture back on the banister. It was five years to the day that I lost my Cherry from my house blowing up.

Every year, this day would hit me hard, so I tried every year to do something special with my son knowing I could have lost him behind some bullshit. It was now a tradition that we lived this day to the fullest.

"Ma, you ready to go?" Blake asked as he came into the living room where I stood.

"Yeah, let's go."

Blake came and stood next to me, he looked at the picture I had just been staring at. My eyes glanced to the scar on the right side of his head.

"Ma, come on. You do this every year. We good, now let's go. I can't wait to play laser tag." Blake squeaked out excitedly.

I laughed at my little man and his excitement. "Come on, boy. And yo black butt bet not shoot me." I grabbed my purse off the table then headed to the front door.

Blake was right on my heels following me out of the house. "How you gon' say *don't shoot you*? What's the point of going then? We should've went paintballing."

I looked at him like he was crazy. "If you ever shoot me with a paintball, I'm gon' beat you."

He started laughing. "No, you won't, you love me too much."

"Boy shut up and put on your seatbelt." I laughed at him as I pulled out of the driveway and headed to Steradian in West Lafayette for a day of outdoor fun.

Chapter 1

Peaches

"Rashad, get your little butt back here!" He stopped in his tracks and glanced back at me. Blake let out a heavy, irritable breath. At eight years old, he looked even more like his father with the attitude to match. It seemed like the older he got the more like Blaze he became.

"Little boy…" My tone warned him not to play with me.

Blake straightened up and slowly made his way to me. "Ma, I was just about to run and get some Cookie Crisp. We ain't got no mo'." He replied, sounding just like his daddy.

"It's, *we don't have any more.*" I corrected him.

Blake's eyes rolled at my correction and I slapped him upside his head making him laugh. "Ma, stop, I just got my hair cut."

Laughing at him, I pushed my little man away from me. "I'm going in that aisle once I leave out of this one."

Blake shrugged before grabbing his blue basket with his junk food in it. "Then I can meet you over there, hurry up." After that, he took off running into the next aisle.

"Rashad!"

"Ma, I can hear you. Stop yelling, ghetto ass!" He yelled back over to me.

I dropped the bread into the buggy and left out of the aisle to go find him. *He done lost his mind.* Once I made it to him, Blake started laughing.

"I was only playin', you know how we do." Taking in my hard glare, he straightened up. "Mommy, I love you."

Laughing at him, I shook my head. "I don't know nothing but what I do know is you better watch yo mouth before I pour dishwashing liquid down yo throat—"

"*Your mouth, your throat.*" He suddenly said after putting his basket back in my buggy.

"What?" I asked confused by his reply.

"The word is *your*, you said yo—"

"Little boy…" My voice broke as I laughed. "Yo little butt gon' make me hurt you. Now I dare you to correct me again."

Blake gave me a cheeky smile. Only a handful of us really got to see his playful side. Other times, he was serious about everything and quiet, just like his dad. Blaze had cursed my poor baby. He was most definitely his father's child.

Blaze and my relationship was pretty much non-existent, which was crazy seeing as we had Lil B. Yet, after the explosion at my house, we kind of drifted apart.

That same day, Blaze moved both me and Blake from Gary to Lafayette, Indiana, which was only two hours away, but it was far enough away from Blaze and we couldn't build our relationship.

I understood Blaze didn't want to risk putting Blake and I in anymore danger, so the move was necessary. A part of me now saw that the move was a big mistake because here it was five years later, and nothing had happened that would harm us. Only thing that really ended was our relationship.

I could also blame myself for our distance because in order to not think about our situation, I registered for school at Purdue University in West Lafayette before I got a job at the hospital. And once I got into routine, I began to drown myself with my studies, working on top of taking care of Blake.

I missed Blaze. I couldn't lie. I missed how we were after we stopped dating, our late night conversations and the crazy sex. Hell, everything that was him.

"Bae, what do you want to get your dad for his birthday?" Leaving out the cereal aisle, he turned toward me shrugging.

"Shid I don't know—"

"Rashad, watch your mouth."

Sighing, he started his sentence over again. "I don't know. I asked him and he just said whatever I get him. Uncle King said I should just get him two hundred ones."

My brows rose at that. "Why?" The word slowly left my mouth, as confusion set in my body.

His *duh* facial expression messed me up. "Why you think? They ass taking him to a strip joint with them big booty girls." Before I could stop myself or think, my hand shot out, slapping him hard in the mouth. "Why you hit me? That's what Unc told me. Damn, hit him not me."

"Oh, I'mma hit him but what I tell you about your mouth? Rashad, it's not cute. I don't care how yo daddy talk it's not cute or cool." I chastised him.

I sometimes hated for Blake to be alone with his dad and uncle for this reason right here.

"It was something you had a baby by him." He shot back.

My mouth opened and then closed before a glare covered my face. My lips pursed tightly together as I bit my tongue. "Give me yo phone."

"Look I'm sorry—" He began to say, sounding so much like Blaze.

"Blake, don't play with me give me yo phone." I glared hard at him.

He reached in his pocket and gave it to me.

I snatched it from him and put it in my purse. "Don't think for a second you got a slide either, you just wait until I get you home."

"Man, for real?" He questioned with a pleading expression. "Ma." Taking in my facial expression, he shut up.

This damn boy done lost his mind talking to me like he crazy. If we wasn't in this store, I would've whooped his little ass.

"Walk up there and get a gallon of milk, you better come right back." Bumping the buggy, he walked down the aisle. "Kids, I swear." I mumbled to myself while pulling out his phone to call King.

"Tell me about it, I got a little boy about his age."

I looked away from Blake's phone to the voice. I laughed not realizing someone had heard me.

"Yeah, they're a handful."

"I'm Derrell." Taking in the dark skin man in front of me, my eyes went to his out stretch hand.

With a smile, I took it. "Peaches—" Derrell's side suddenly hit the buggy as he was pushed from behind. I didn't even see Blake come back, let alone walk behind Derrell.

"And I'm her son." Blake told him before turning back to me, putting the milk in the buggy. "You ready?" he asked nonchalantly as he turned the cart around and stood in front of Derrell like he was never there.

I couldn't believe he just did that, then again, I could. "Blake, say you're sorry, right now."

At my words, the look of shock covered his face. "For what?" he asked in a serious tone.

"Don't play with me, Rashad, you just pushed that man, now say you're sorry." I pointed to the man.

He glanced at Derrell then looked back at me. "I ain't push him, but why he standing here looking stupid for? Long face ass nigga. Get on." Blake said, waving Derrell off.

"I am so sorry—" I started apologizing only to be cut off.

"Fuck you apologizing for, that nigga better get on before I call my daddy up here. Homie, yo ass ain't getting none over here."

Grabbing Blake by the back of his neck, I held it tight and started dragging his little ass to the front so we could checkout.

"Ow, Ma, that hurt. Let go." He whined out, trying to pry my hand from the back of his neck.

Holding it a little tighter, I walked faster to self-checkout. Once there, I pushed him in front of the buggy. I hurriedly rung up our food and then bagged them. After paying, we left out of the grocery store to my white truck.

"Blake, why would you do that? You are a child. You don't talk to grown folks like that..." Blake made a noise in the back of his throat, which had me slapping him again. "Rashad, do you hear me?" This wasn't the first time he had done that to a guy that approached me.

At first, I figured it was only because he wanted Blaze and I to get back together. When I asked him if that was the case, he said that wasn't it and the guy just looked like a creep. But that was with every guy.

"I'm sorry, Ma. He just looked weird—" he went on to use that same excuse.

"Blake, everybody looks weird, creepy or something to you. You pushed that man and cussed at him. Rashad, we don't do that. Do you hear me?" I fussed at him already knowing it was falling on deaf ears.

"Yes, I'm sorry—"

"You're grounded, no phone, TV, Xbox, PlayStation, iPod, iPad nothing."

"Hell no! Just call my daddy on me. Fuck that! Man, you trippin." He snapped.

Quickly, I grabbed his forehead and before he could react, my hand slapped him repeatedly into his mouth, at least ten times.

"I'm trippin'? Oh, I'm gon' show you how much I'm trippin', get yo ass in the truck." After pushing him in the backseat, I put the food in behind him and slammed the door. *"I'm trippin'? This little boy done lost his gotdamn mind. Who does he think he's talkin' too?"* I mumbled to myself.

I hopped in the driver seat then glanced back at him to see his cheeks puffed up as he bit into his lower lip. He was mad but so was I.

"Put on that seatbelt. Oh, and I'm gon' call yo dad after I whoop yo ass."

"Man, I ain't even do nothing." He muttered with an attitude.

I looked back at him, but Blake's eyes shifted out toward the window. "That's what I thought." Throwing the truck in drive, I pulled out of the parking lot. "Blake, why do you do this? Is it because you want me and your dad back together?"

"No," he stated simply, as he reached in the front and grabbed my purse.

"Then why? And don't even give me that crap about them being a creep or weird." When he didn't say anything, I glanced back at him through my mirror only to see him with his cellphone. "Put it back in my purse and put my purse back in this seat."

Glancing up he let out a heavy breath. "Here, I don't want that phone anyway."

I didn't know what had gotten into my little man and his mouth. But he was crazy as hell if he thought he was going to talk to me like he did his dad and King.

I chewed on my bottom lip and my head nodded as we drove silently the rest of the way home.

***

I pulled up on our street just as my phone started ringing and once again, Blake reached into my bag, grabbing my phone and answering it.

"Hello? What's up, dad…pulling up in front of the house now… right here…hell yeah… shid, I don't think so…yeah, I did… she's mad… yeah… hell yeah, she took my damn phone… that shit ain't funny." Blake told his dad with an attitude.

I quickly pulled into the driveway and threw the truck in park. I turned in my seat and Blake quickly jumped in the rear back seats.

"Give me the phone and bring yo butt here."

Blaze's laughing voice soon came through the line as Blake put him on speaker. "Blake, she gon' whoop yo ass doing all that damn cussin' and shit. Fuck wrong with you, man?"

Where he does think he gets it from?

"Listen how you talk to him, Blaze. That's what's wrong with him," I replied to him.

"Shid, I ain't got shit to do with that. I told his ass about his mouth. I'mma beat his little ass, though," he assured.

My lips smacked at that and Blake laughed.

"I'm about to whoop his little butt because of his mouth."

"Man, I said I was sorry that man looked like a freakin' creep. Dad, that man looked like a damn gargoyle." Blake lied through his teeth.

Blaze burst out laughing into the phone. Whereas I stared at Blake' lying little self with parted lips.

18

Blake was cheesing hard as ever. "His teeth were yellow and he smelled like a skunk." He lied again, making Blaze laugh harder.

"Blake, why are you lying?" I asked him, not believing he was sitting here telling lies.

He shrugged his shoulders and took Blaze off speaker.

"You still in trouble, Rashad, I'm not playing. Start taking this food in and don't touch nothing. Let me talk to your dad." He climbed back over the seats and he handed me the phone then got out once I gave him the house keys. "Your son is a liar and I'm about to tear his little butt up." I told him.

Blaze stopped laughing and cleared his throat. "Man, leave him alone. He just tryna look out for you, is all. You can't blame him for that, Peaches." He took up for Blake, like always.

I smacked my lips.

"Get on with that shit, man. Fuck you smacking yo damn lips for?"

I couldn't help but laugh at that, remembering what Blake said to Derrell. "Blaze, that's embarrassing as hell to have my baby out in public and he's clowning like he did. Then for him to tell that man he ain't *getting none over here* is embarrassing as hell, B—" I was cut off by Blaze's sudden burst of laughter. I couldn't help but laugh along with him. "That's not even funny, to have people hear this and start looking at us crazy. I tell him, he's grounded and he like *hell n'all, call my daddy, you trippin'.*"

"Wait, he said what to you?" That stopped his laughter. Blaze laughed at pretty much everything Blake did until it came to me. If he was disrespectful in any shape or form, Blaze was on him.

"Exactly, but you can't get mad. Blaze, he hears how you talk to your momma and think it's cool when it's not. When he's with you, B, y'all have to be careful of what you say around him because then he thinks it's okay to bring that shit back here, when it's not. So, don't get hot when you learn the slick shit, he says to me. Blake's only acting how he see you do—well he's worse than you. He's eight and cuss like a sailor." This was falling on deaf ears. Like father like son.

"I hear you, but aye, you coming to my party?"

Deaf Ears.

"Yeah, I'mma stop by, I'm going to be super late, though. I have to work, and I don't get off until eleven-thirty, so I should make it there around one or one-thirty somewhere around there."

Blaze hummed into the phone and was quiet for a few seconds. "That's cool and invite who you want i'ight?"

My brows rose at that. That was the first time he told me to invite whoever I wanted to. My girls were an automatic invite, so I wonder what he was implying.

"You mean like a dude?" I asked for clarification and again he hummed.

"Yeah, a nigga. What the fuck else I'm talkin' 'bout?"

Smacking my lips, I got out of the truck and made my way into the house. "No need to get smart. Why are you saying I can bring someone?" He didn't reply back, so I laughed. "You must have a bitch you're bringing. Blaze, you can bring your little girlfriend. I have no problem with that—hold on—Blake, go lock the truck and pull your bike into the garage and whatever else you have in the yard bring it in too."

"Okay, when I finish, can I go to Eric's house?" He put those pretty light brown eyes of his on me.

My eyes slanted at him.

"When I come back, you can ground me. I promise. Please, Mommy, please. I love you."

Laughing at his whiny face, I shook my head.

"Thanks, I'll be back before the streetlights come on!" He yelled running past me. The screen door slammed hard behind him.

"I didn't say yes, Blake!" I yelled after him, but he was already gone. *That child of mine.* I shook my head and left the front door open then walked to the kitchen.

"I thought you was beating his ass?" Blaze chuckled.

I put the phone on speaker and started putting away the food. "I am when he gets back so don't worry about it. Now who is this chick you bringing to yo party? I heard you had a girlfriend." I lied, biting into my bottom lip to stop myself from laughing.

"You a gotdamn lie, boss. Yo ass ain't heard no bullshit like that," he replied.

"Okay, I lied. Hey, you can't blame me, I mean with you suddenly saying I can bring a dude to your party." I pointed out, then soon heard ruffling in his background. "Are you busy?"

"Nah, you good. But shid, I got a little chick that's riding with me and I ain't want yo ass to be feeling no type of way."

Rolling my eyes, I laughed. "Man, whatever I'm not going to feel no type of way. I'll be solo coming to your party. Thanks to our son, every man that looks my way, he runs off. Oh, and why do my baby need to give you two hundred ones?"

Blaze broke out laughing. "Boss, that's yo damn brother. He's a bad influence on Blake's ass. So, yell at that nigga, not me. But shid, I just wanted to give you a heads up on this chick that's coming. Peach, don't be tryna beat her ass when you see her on me, i'ight?"

Smacking my lips, I laughed already knowing what he was referring to. "For real, get on with that. That bitch jumped on me first, Blaze, I simply hugged yo little triflin' ass. That bitch came outda nowhere, pulled me off you and started hitting me first. And that was like two years ago, so let that shit go. I mean if that's the bitch you're bringing, then it's a different story. I'm gon' beat the shit out that bitch with absolutely no hesitation. You and these damn hood rats, I swear."

A small laugh slipped through my lips as I began to think about that time, I ran into him at the courts a couple years back. Blake and I had come to Gary to visit for the weekend. I had dropped my baby off at Mom B's house, then went to the courts to meet up with the girls and the guys.

When I got there, I had just given Blaze a simple hug that lasted for a second. When all of a sudden, some chick came snatching me away from him and started hitting me, claiming I was fuckin' with her man. I'm not going to lie, the bitch had me in the beginning until Blaze pulled her off of me and I turned around and beat the shit out of that girl.

"No, it ain't that bitch. Aye, let me hit you back, though, i'ight?"

"Okay, bye." My phone screen lit up, indicating he had hung up.

Already knowing I wasn't going to talk to him until his birthday, I tried pushing him to the back of my mind, but I couldn't. It never failed. Whenever I talked to him, that giddy feeling always returned, full force. If we were still in the same city, it would be nothing to roll up on him or have him come over to me.

The move was most definitely a big mistake. I now knew that.

I missed him like crazy.

Chapter 2

Peaches

"**B**lake, come eat!" Sitting his plate on the table, I passed Kimmy one.

"So we need to go shopping when you get off tomorrow, I honestly don't know what I'm wearing. Hell, if I'm going for that matter," Kim said, sighing.

"Mike must be coming?" I shook my head at her.

"Peach, don't do that, okay, because wasn't nobody judging you when—" Kim trailed off as Blake came running into the kitchen.

"Hey, Aunt Kim." Walking over to her, Blake gave Kimmy a hug.

"Hey, babe," she returned his hug and kissed his forehead.

He pulled away then went to the table and started eating.

Kim looked back at me and started whispering. "No one judged you when you had Ron and B."

Smacking my lips, I rolled my eyes at her stupid statement. "I wasn't with neither of them and I wasn't fuckin' both of them at the same time. Plus, they're not in the same circle so I wasn't at risk of being caught. Besides, that was years ago. I'm not messing with either now. And what Ron and I did wasn't sex, well a few strokes that's it. So, there was no reason for me to be judged." Shrugging, I grabbed my plate then went to the table, sitting next to Blake.

"So, what, you thought about letting him finish those strokes." Kim shot back.

Laughing at her comeback, I just shook my head. We had been telling Kim for years now to leave one of those men alone and that she was playing a dangerous game. But Kim, being her, didn't listen so for the past five years she had been sleeping with Bellow behind Mike's back. And even though Mike was still a hoe, that nigga was crazy when it came to Kim and he was going to flip the fuck out once he found out.

I must say she was smart about how she was going about doing it. She would use our visiting time to meet up with Bellow at their apartment they had out in Lafayette. She would come here twice during the weekdays and then spend some weekends as well.

They had their own little life together. I didn't know how much longer Bellow was going to take with doing this. He had been pushing her hard as of late to break it off with Mike or he was going to do it for her.

I just hoped she got smart soon and made a choice. The right one.

"Thinking, doing and really, really, really wanting to is three different things," I said with a dreamy sigh making Kim laugh.

"Bitch, you stupid."

"Kim!" I yelled at her.

Her mouth formed into an *O* as she looked at Blake who was just cheesing hard.

"It's cool, Momma, she good." Blake said, stabbing his macaroni then eating it off of his fork. He turned to look at me and I already started shaking my head *no*. "You don't even know what I'm going to say, though."

"I don't care, Blake, I know you all too well and my answer is *no* to whatever it is."

"Please—"

"No, Blake, so forget about it." I put a fork full of macaroni in my mouth.

"You don't even know what I'm going to say," he stated in an annoyed tone.

Rolling my eyes, I gave him a pointed look. "So, what, my answer is still *no* to whatever it is." Stabbing the string beans, I ate them then looked back at Blake.

"But, Momma—" he whined out.

"No, Rashad." My tone was firm and my words final.

26

"Forget it, damn, I ain't even hungry." He pushed away from the table, then got up and stomped out of the room.

"You bet not touch my purse, either!" I yelled after him already knowing he was about to get the phone to call his dad.

"I wasn't!"

Looking at Kimmy, I started to laugh. I already knew he was lying from the defensive tone of his voice.

"Why you picking on my boy?" asked Kim. Shaking my head, I told her what he did in the store earlier today. "No, he didn't?"

My lips pursed together as my head nodded. "He did, I was so freakin' embarrassed, Kim. I don't know what done got into that boy, but his whole damn attitude has changed. It has gotten so bad I can't even bring him to work with me anymore because he's constantly being disrespectful to the male nurses or doctors. Girl, he has gotten so many whoopin's these past few months it's ridiculous, but they're pointless because they're not doing anything." I pushed my plate away completely losing my appetite.

I just didn't understand what was really going on with my baby.

"Did you talk to Blaze about his attitude?" Kim asked.

Rolling my eyes, I let out a heavy sigh. "You know I did, but all he's saying is that Blake's just looking out for me or he laughs it off saying he's going to talk to him. Today he was worse. You should've just heard how he talked and looked at that man. I could've seriously beat his ass. Shid, I had planned to once we got home."

"I would've tore his little ass up, hell I'd probably still be whooping his ass. What stopped you from tagging his grown butt?" She leaned forward on the table fully engaged into our conversation.

Feeling embarrassed for my reason, I just shook my head. I didn't want to tell her talking to Blaze had distracted me. "I don't know, Kim…" Not being able to lie to her fully, I just sighed staring straight at her.

"Sweetie, it'll work itself out so don't stress it. All little boys are like that. He could simply be trying to keep them away hoping you and Blaze will get back together," she suggested.

"Maybe, but he says it's not—" Kim suddenly broke out laughing, hitting the table. "What?"

"It must be really hard. Yo thunder cat probably lonely as hell, aching and all. Wait, what's that noise?" Her eyes squinted and her head tilted slightly as if she was listening to something.

I got quiet trying to hear the noise. "Kim, I don't hear anything. What it sounds like?" I asked.

"Do I hear whining?" She leaned toward me.

I pushed her away. "Bitch, fuck you. Get yo ass out my house." I stared at her as I shook my head, laughing. "She do be purring, though, but thanks to Blake running every man off, I can't feed her." Looking at each other, we broke out laughing. "Shut up! That's not funny. I do need to get some." It had been

28

a long time since I last had sex. Three years to be exact. But I'd been so busy with raising Blake, work and school, I had no time to play.

"Don't worry we gon' find somebody at this party to break you in good. Somebody to have yo ass bowlegged as hell, coochie swollen, walls missing—"

"Girl, shut yo ass up before Blake walk in here. Kim, you stupid. Walls missing really, though?" I laughed at her as we left out of the kitchen going into the living room where Blake laid stretched out on the couch. "Rashad, get yo feet off the couch."

He sat up straight running a hand over his head then down his face. He seemed so frustrated.

I smiled at my little man then walked over and sat beside him. "You look just like your dad doing that." Blake let out a sigh, which I returned. "What is it, Blake?"

"Don't worry about it. I already know the answer…" he mumbled leaning back into the couch.

"Hey, Peach, I'm about to go. I'll see you tomorrow, okay." Kim grabbed her purse.

Nodding, I got up to walk her to the door. "Okay, I'll call you."

"Bye, Blake." She gave him a hug then kissed him on the cheek. She then followed me out of the living room and to the front door. "Alright, Peach, I'll message the girls and let them know what's up."

"Okay, boo, call me when you get in." With a wave, she walked out of the house to her car.

Once she pulled off, I closed and locked the front door then went back to Blake.

Blake and I sat on the couch blindly watching the TV. He probably thought I was going to nag him about telling me what was up with him. He was wrong. I was going to make him break first. I knew my son all too well. Once I opened the door for him to ask his question, he knew it was a possibility of me saying *yes* so he was going to crack.

Glancing at me, he quickly looked away.

"Alright, night, sweetie. I'm tired, so I'm going to bed." That did it and he let out an even bigger sigh.

"Okay, Eric's birthday is this weekend and they're going to Great America on Saturday. I know I'm grounded but can I please go? His mom got extra tickets for the party, so you don't even have to pay," he pleaded.

To send Blake off with someone was a no go. He didn't leave my sight if he didn't have school or I didn't have to work. Unless he was with his dad or nana. So, Blake going to Great America, which was two and a half hours away from me, was a *no*.

"You'll have to ask your daddy because you're with him on Saturdays," I told him, making a mental note to call Blaze.

"I know. I want all of us to go, though. We ain't did nothing together in a long time and since you don't have to work Saturday and I'm with my dad we can all go," he informed me with a serious face.

My lips turned up already knowing what he was doing. "Don't try to use a family day just so you can go to Eric's party and don't be puffing up either—"

"I'm not using a family day to go to the party. We just don't do nothing anymore," he stated with an attitude.

My mouth popped open at his lie. "Blake, we don't do anything? Seriously? When I'm off and you get out of school, we're always doing something." I stared at him in disbelief not believing he was saying this.

"I mean us. Me, you and dad. We don't do nothing anymore like we used to. Y'all don't even talk like that unless I do something, or I call him. Other than that, y'all don't talk. Just forget it, I'm going to bed." He got up off of the couch and stormed out of the living room. Blake stomped up all thirteen stairs until his door was slammed shut.

Groaning, I got up and went after him. I didn't know what to say to him. What reason did we have for not talking as much as we used too? We really didn't aside from the distance, my schooling and my work schedule. Those were the only reasons why we stopped doing so much together.

I pushed his room door open and leaned against the frame. I watched as he played *Call Of Duty*. I knocked on the wall to get his attention, but he didn't even glance up.

"Babe, you're right. We don't do things as a family like we used too and I'm sorry for that. Blake, this shouldn't be an excuse but with me having to go to work and school, it was sometimes hard. I was honestly tired with doing everything all at once. Babe, even though we may have stopped doing things together, don't make us any less of a family.

Baby, you know that. We're always going to be a family regardless of how much time we spend together." Rubbing the top of his head, he paused his game.

"You don't have school no more. Can we start doing stuff like we used to, again? It just don't be the same when we do different stuff. It don't be all that fun, with just dad and me. We don't do nothing but play basketball, go shopping or stay at nana's house. We don't go to the park, carnivals none of the fun stuff, but when we all used to get together, we did, but now…" Frustrated, his hand went over his head then down his face.

"Baby, where is all this suddenly coming from?" Blake had never been a *complaining* or an *I want* kid. He was always so Blaze like. Nonchalant about everything with nothing hardly ever bothering him. He always went along with whatever and with no complaints. So, for this to suddenly be coming out his mouth meant something was seriously wrong.

"Just forget it—"

"No, I am not going to forget it. Baby, talk to me." Sliding off of the bed, I sat on the floor next to him. "Blake, start talking."

"Eric, his mom and dad always doing stuff together like we used to. When he tells me the fun stuff they're always doing, it pisses me off because I can't say what we do. All my friends' moms and dads do stuff with them except for you two," he explained with an attitude.

32

A heavy sigh left my mouth, knowing he was right. "You're right, we don't but now that I'm done with school. We can start doing all that again, I promise. I'll even talk to your dad about Great America and we can stay the whole weekend. Summer break starts Friday, so we'll stay there from Saturday to Tuesday. How about we do that?" Again, he shrugged. "Blake—"

"Do you love my dad?" He suddenly asked me.

His question caught me off guard even, so I slowly nodded my head. "Yes, of course, baby. That should never even be a question. Blake, I love your dad, too much, *way too much*." I found myself laughing at that. Doing so, made him look at me.

"What's funny?" His brow furrowed with his head tilted sideways. He looked just like his dad.

I shook my head and laughed again as I thought back on how I fell in love with that psychopath. "Have I ever told you how I met your dad?"

Blake head shook at my question. "No, but I asked him, and he said you used to stalk him, standing outside his apartment all day."

"What!" *That lying nigga.* "I stalked him? Seriously? Of course, he would say that. Your father is a liar. He stalked me, forced his way into my apartment, beat up my then friend and fought my brother, Uncle King. Your dad was crazy. He still is but he was good to me in his own way. I honestly don't think love could really explain how I feel about him. What we had or have is beyond that four letter word. Those feeling grew even bigger the moment he gave me you." My smile was wide, and my head shook.

"Blake, just because we don't do family things like we once did, doesn't change a thing. My love for him, his love for me, and our love for you, none of that changes and it never will. So, don't ever question our feelings because we're not like your friends' parents. Okay?" My hands rubbed over his wavy hair before I pulled him to me.

"Yeah, you're right. So, dad beat up your boyfriend?" Blake asked, laughing, which I joined in on.

"Yes, he did. Your dad was obsessed with me. I'm not tryna brag but yo momma had it goings on, baby. Had your daddy drooling like a bulldog."

Blake burst out laughing. "So how y'all meet?" Before I answered his question, I pulled him off of the floor and walked to his full size bed. I laid against his headboard and patted the spot next to me.

Blake kicked off his house shoes and climbed in the bed next to me. Once he got comfortable, I started rubbing his head, like I've done since he came into my life.

"Your dad had just gotten out of jail—"

"Jail?" He cut me off.

Laughing, I nodded. "Yep, he was fresh out. That night, him, Uncle King and Sam came to the club where your aunties and I were at…"

Chapter 3

Peaches

I sat at the restaurant with my girls, not paying attention to what they were saying as I picked at my food. I couldn't let go of the fact that Blaze told me to invite whoever I wanted to his party. It was really bothering me, and I needed to talk to my girls about that.

A heavy sigh slipped through my lips and I looked up at my girls. "Y'all, B, told me I could bring somebody to his party." They all stop mid bite or drink to look at me.

"Like a date? With another man?" Angel asked, dumbly.

My head nodded. "Yep."

Missy snapped her fingers, then waved a hand at me while she swallowed her food. "Nuh uh, don't do it, Peach. That's a setup. He's just trying to see if you slickly giving his wet-wet away."

Looking at Missy, I started laughing. "Miss, seriously? You so damn stupid."

"Bitch, I'm serious. Niggas slick like that." She pointed at me. "Watch, once you walk in there with a man, Blaze's crazy ass gon' knock him the fuck out."

"Missy, shut the fuck up, with yo silly ass." After a few chuckles, I became serious. "No, for real, I don't think he was playing. Blaze said he didn't want me to feel left out or alone because he's bringing somebody with him." Saying that got Ebony's attention and her eyes quickly snapped to mine.

"Is it serious?" she asked.

Humming, I shrugged. "He says it's not, but you know B, he'll tell me anything to make sure I'm not uncomfortable. Even if that's the case, it's his business—"

"Bitch, shut the fuck up with yo dumbass. Now you know if you see him walk in that thang with a sexy chick on his arm, you gon' be feeling a certain type of way. Be it jealousy, insecurity or self-consciousness and let's not think about if the bitch pretty." Angel chimed in, making me groan.

I couldn't lie to my bitches no matter what, I just couldn't. "Ang, I know! Y'all know we used to hook up after his party so for him to tell me he gon' have a bitch on his arm." I paused for a second. "Ugh, this is kinda bothering me. Man, I don't know. I mean for B to tell me he's bringing a chick makes me think it may be serious, like he's actually feeling this girl."

"Peaches, I get it trust me I do. But, babe, you done cut that man off, you hardly ever see him. What you expect him to do? Wait for you when you had already stop giving him play? Babe, you have a habit of cutting a nigga off without any explanation. You just slowly let him fade off. That's exactly what you did to Blaze. Weekends was y'all thing, which you suddenly stopped. You had just started dropping little man off to him and it's been like that ever since." Kim saying that brought me back to my conversation with Blake last night.

It was true I had done just that. But given everything I was doing on top of driving back and forth from Gary to Lafayette, messing around with Blaze, then our family outings. Doing all that became tiring. That one weekend three years ago, was only supposed to be just that, a onetime thing but with the sleep I had gotten on that day. My body seriously needed. I had slept fourteen hours straight into the next morning. After that I really needed those two days for myself, my body was so over worked.

But now that I was through with school, I was going to start back setting up our family weekends like we used to have.

"I know. Rashad brought that up last night. I feel like shit now. It wasn't intended to last this long, y'all know that. I was doing entirely too much. So, by the time I had that one weekend to myself, it was like a breaking point. At that moment I really needed that time. Now I feel so bad. My baby actually asked me did I love his dad after he finished comparing us to his friends' parents. My body was just freaking tired." I explained that to them and they nodded their understanding.

"Did you ever explain this to either one of them?" Ebony questioned.

My mouth opened but closed, I couldn't reply because I didn't explain it to Blaze or Blake.

"Exactly, how was they to know what you were feeling if you weren't talking to them? Yeah, you talk to us, but you're not fuckin' neither of us nor do you have a kid with us that you're taking care of. Little man is a smart dude. I'm sure he would've understood. B? Umm, I can't speak on his persistent ass, but Rashad he would've got it with his little grown ass." A glare soon covered Ebony's face as she said that, pointing her fork at me with slanted eyes as she shook her head.

"What?" Angel, Missy, Kimmy and I chimed in unison. Looking at each other, we laughed.

"For real, E, what's the look for?" I didn't like that look on her face. He had to have done something.

Her eyes rolled into her head before she shook it. "That little boy of yours. Girl, I almost whooped his ass the other day."

That got my full attention. "For what?" Not knowing what he could've done to make Ebony want to whoop him. Blake loved his aunties to death and would never do anything to make them mad.

"Girl, the other day when I dropped Keema off to King's, Blake was with him. So, he asked me to drop him off at Mom B's house. Fine, cool. We caught a flat, so I had to pull over. Just so happens,

Sean was passing by in his pick-up and came to help change my tire." She informed us.

"Once he finished, we stood there talking, you know, catching up or whatnot. Tell me why Blake's little grown ass gets out the fuckin' car, came on our side, looked at the changed tire. He glanced at Sean, then to me and back at the tire. After checking everything out, he gon' say, *Why the fuck you standin' here conversing with this mothafucka. He done his damn job. Pay his ass and let's go.*"

My eyes were wide as was my mouth.

"Yep, that was my exact reaction. Then he looked back at Sean and said, *Yo ass out here smiling hard as fuck. Nigga, make me call my Unc out here. He gon' fuck yo ass up. Now gon' get the fuck outda here.* Peach, I was so fuckin' embarrassed. Then to emphasize that shit, he pulled out his cellphone and started calling King's ass. He put the phone on speaker and everything. I hurried up and dropped his ass off to Bianca. I was so pissed that he did that. You know I ain't fuck'd with King's ass since I had Keema." Ebony stressed.

The mention of my five year old niece made me smile as what Blake did seemed to fade.

It was true. Ebony stopped messing around with King five years ago. She was serious about being done with him until one drunken night when she slipped up, which resulted in her fourth pregnancy. But unlike the other times, she wasn't with King to stress over him and ended up having a healthy, beautiful baby girl.

"I'mma whoop his ass for real, now. This shit is getting ridiculous with him. But for Blake to do you like that is not acceptable." Shaking my head, I looked at her, but she ended up laughing, which had us joining in. "That's not funny. That shit is embarrassing as hell."

Ebony nodded while laughing. "Bitch, I know. Sean called me later that day asking was my guard gone. He actually found Blake's reaction funny. He said, *he was just looking out for his auntie. That's what a little man supposed to do, but he need his mouth washed out with a gallon of soap.*"

That had my brows raising. Since Shawn helped get my mom's car fixed for her so many years ago, they clicked. But it never went anywhere especially not with King's ass around.

"So, my son actually snagged you a guy?" I teased, laughing.

Ebony rolled her eyes as she forked her food. Her cheeks slowly started to turn red.

"This bitch is not getting red in the face?" Kim said, nudging Ebony.

"Y'all she is. So, what the dick was like?" We burst out laughing at Missy's question.

"Bitch, we didn't..."

"Oh, my damn. You hoe! You fuck'd him?" Angel asked loudly, drawing attention to us. Ebony turned redder.

"Wow, E. Well, how was it? Did he blow yo back out? Did he have you crying? He wasn't like a minute pumper, was he? He probably tore that shit up." Missy babbled.

"Missy, shut the fuck up and let her get a word out, damn." Laughing at her, she stuck her middle finger up at me.

"Y'all childish. Now, E, what happened?" Kim asked, just as curious as we were.

"Nothing. I mean, we started to. But then King called for me to come get Keema. I don't know what happened, but he was pissed, so we had to stop." Ebony shrugged as if it was nothing.

That didn't make sense. If something happened when King had Keema, he would have called Blaze to take care of whatever it was. Or he'd drop Keema off to Bianca's.

"Did he say what happened?" I asked her.

She shook her head not looking up at us. The girls and I looked at each other before staring back at Ebony who still hadn't looked at us.

"E?" I called her name. Glancing up, her eyes quickly dropped back down to her food.

Again, the girls and I shared a look before we broke out laughing.

"You hoe! For real, E? Damn." I couldn't do anything but laugh. "That's why King's ass was pissed. He swooped up on yo ass and saw that nigga car parked out front."

Glaring at me, she rolled her eyes but didn't say anything at first. We laughed harder.

"That shit ain't funny. Don't nobody have time to be playing with Ha'Keem's triflin' ass. But I did slip, though," she whined. "Y'all, I really tried to stop him and put his ass

41

out, but King wasn't leaving. He knew what he was doing. He started that argument then tried to jerk on me. One thing led to another and then we were on the living room floor, naked. We woke up the next morning with Keema jumping on his back yelling *Daddy*." Covering her face, she groaned loudly.

"Wait. If he told you to come get Keema, how y'all end up at yo place?" I asked.

"Girl, once Sean ass left, that mothafucka came knockin' on the door, with a sleeping Keema in his arms. That's what really had me thinking it was some serious shit happening. But once we got her off to bed, that mothafucka turned on my ass and went clean the fuck off. Talking about some, I'm having niggas around his baby when Keema wasn't even there. Matter of fact, it was the same damn day I picked up Blake." She exclaimed with a roll of her eyes.

"After I dropped Keema off to King and Blake to Momma B, I went home, and Sean called. We were talking and I invited him over. You know we had become really cool after I left King but once I got pregnant with Keema, I kinda brushed him off. So, seeing him again was nice. Nothing was meant to happen like that. It just did."

"Oh, shit! Y'all think little man really called King once he made it to Mom B's house?" Missy asked, seeming convinced he did.

"I don't know. Blake wouldn't do that—"

"Doesn't he call Blaze whenever he run niggas away from you?" Angel asked.

"I mean, yeah. Oh, my God! Y'all think Blake told King?" Their heads moved up and down. "No," though I said that I couldn't help but laugh.

"Yep, Blake a snitch. Don't he know what happens to snitches?" Angel asked, laughing. "Then again, they ass probably got his ass watching y'all, though. I wouldn't put that shit past King's ass. But Blaze. I don't think he's child-ish to do that."

I wouldn't put that past Blaze either, to be honest. Keeping my thoughts to myself, I changed the subject.

"So how Keema's grown ass been doing?" I took a sip of my drink, before looking at her.

"Bad as ever just like her damn daddy. That little girl makes my ass hurt. I swear she's so much like that man it makes no damn sense. But Mom B got her now. She called me last night and told me to drop Keema off over there. Bianca got her little ass spoiled. All she talks about is her nana." Ebony laughed.

Bianca had basically become a second mother to Ebony. Having her in Ebony's life was an amazing thing and I honestly thought that gave her the strength to be done with King. Hell, she was a mother to all of us. She was the strong female figure we needed in our lives, something neither of our mothers were. Even though Keema wasn't blood related to her, she didn't love her any less. She treated her just as she did Blake.

"I was thinking about inviting Shawn to B's party, but I don't know," Ebony said, looking at us.

I'm sure my facial expression matched the other girls. Ebony was trying to get Shawn hurt. Especially after she done gave King some wet. That wasn't going to end well for either of them.

We left the conversation at that as we continued to eat silently for a few minutes. None of us were willing to speak on the stupidity Ebony was talking.

"So, how are you feeling about Blaze's friend?" Kimmy spoke, breaking the silence that fell upon us, causing the girls to look at me.

"I really don't know how to feel, to be honest. I mean he says it's nothing serious and she's just a chick. So, I don't know and probably won't until I see them together. But Blaze is grown. His life shouldn't have to stop because of me. So, whether I like it or not, I'll keep it to myself and be happy for him." *Bullshit!* From the expression on the girls' face they called the same thing. "Fuck y'all, okay! I thought that sounded very convincing."

"Bitch, it didn't." Angel laughed, shaking her head. "I guess I gotda bring my knuckles 'cause some shit 'bout to go down." She joked, making us laugh.

"No, I'm going to be good. I promise." Although I spoke this, I didn't know how true it was going to be.

Chapter 4

Peaches

"Blake, let's go!" Looking at my phone, I sighed. I wasn't ready to take that two hour drive to Michigan City just to have breakfast with Blaze for his birthday.

"I'm coming!"

"Get your gift off of my nightstand! Hurry, Blake!" I yelled again. After a few long seconds, Blake still hadn't come down. "Rashad!"

"I'm coming, I'm coming. Dang!" he responded, bouncing down the stairs with his duffle bag that looked heavy.

"Why do you have that?" I scowled him. He acted as if he didn't hear my question and tried to walk past me. "What do you have in the bag?" I made a grab for him, but he jumped back out of my reach. I glared at Blake.

"Ma, we're going to be late. We'll talk in the truck, let's go." Blake simply smiled before he kissed my cheek.

He had my eyes rolling up into my head. He was most definitely his father's child. "Boy, let's go, slow butt." I popped him upside his head as we left out of the house. "Don't forget to hint to your dad that you have a bigger surprise for him tomorrow."

I never did call Blaze as I promised. Instead, I figured since he was a big ass kid anyway, we would make Great America a surprise. We were going to pick him up in the morning and just take him there.

"I know, I know it's a surprise, but I don't know, Ma, I might slip. You know money can keep my mouth shut, though," Blake stated, rubbing his fingers together.

"And you know I have to drive us there, right?"

His face fell as a thoughtful look covered his handsome features. "Damn— ow, why you hit me?"

"Watch your mouth. Now what do you have in that bag?"

Blake smiled his cute little grin. "Just my games—"

"Blake, what part of grounded don't you understand? You can't have no games, nothing. So, you know you're leaving that bag in the truck." I fussed at him and he groaned loudly.

"Momma, I'm grounded at yo house, not at nana's or my dad's, that's what they always tell me. What goes for yo crib don't bring it to theirs." Blake told me as he let his seat back. He then pulled out his Wii U and turned it on.

"They said what?" Why was I surprised by that was beyond me? Blake was spoiled, yes. And a lot of times, I would let stuff go when I really shouldn't have. It seemed like I was the only one who disciplined him, though.

Blaze would fuss at him, but grounding and taking stuff away from him didn't happen. Hell, the only time Blaze really got in his ass was if he said some disrespectful shit to me which he hardly did.

"You bet not take that bag out this truck, I know that. Give me that." Taking the Wii U from him, I put it in the back on the floor. "I don't care what your dad or nana say you're grounded. I will be sure to take every game console from both of their houses. The TVs I can't do nothing about, but I promise you will not play a game." I told him and I could tell he didn't like that because he grabbed my purse.

"I was just playing."

"No, you wasn't. Blake, I know when you're lying, and I know you're freakin' dad and nana. So, you can gon' 'head and text yo daddy and tell him I'm taking your stuff?" His fingers stopped moving across the screen when I said that, making me laugh. "Like I said, I know you, baby. You gotda do better. You're not slick, Rashad. And don't be roll-ing yo damn eyes either, I will pop them out. You're getting to grown for yo own self"

"Your," he stated, making me glance at him. He caught the mean slants to my eyes and laughed. "You said *yo* and it's *your* own self." Reaching over the seat, I slapped him upside his head before laughing.

"If you ain't yo father's child, Lord have mercy."

"You love me, though, so can I get my game back?" He smiled.

Shaking my head, I turned up the radio and ignored him as I drove. After a few seconds, I peeked over at him and watched as he reached in the back, grabbing his game. I chose not to say anything to him, which was probably why he thought he could get away with a lot. Even though I got on his ass sometimes, I was still weak when it came to my little man.

He was my baby.

***

"Dad!" Blake called out as he ran over to Blaze, hugging him.

"What's up, man?" Blaze pulled away from the hug and he shook up with Blake.

Seeing that, I rolled my eyes.

"Fuck you doing that for?" Blaze asked, coming over to me.

Smiling, I gave him a hug. "No reason. Happy Birthday."

He kissed the top of my head and then let go of me. "Thanks." Blaze gave me a once over. A smiled graced his lips before his tongue swiped over his full bottom lip.

Already knowing what was on his mind, I pushed away from him.

"Don't you even, Blaze." I turned away from him. My eyes rolled as my lips formed into a small smile from the giddiness that began to grow in the pit of my stomach. "Come on, Blake." I wrapped my arm around his shoulders and led us toward the back of the restaurant.

I tried to ignore the heavy gaze I felt on my back, so much so my hips moved faster and harder as my pace quickened to find us a spot. When I found a table for us, temptation had gotten the best of me and I glanced back. Sure enough, he was staring at my ass. His eyes had lowered, and a crooked smile found its way to his lips.

With a shake of my head, I laughed. "You are ridiculous."

"I ain't even said shit, yet." He laughed, knowing he had been caught.

I hummed and my eyes rolled. "You was thinking something, though."

"Mhm. I'm thinking yo ass wearing the hell out those jeans," he said, and Blake agreed.

"Hell yeah! I told her they was too damn tight. Niggas be looking at her butt and stuff. She always wearing tight stuff like that." Blake said and Blaze slapped him upside his head.

"Watch yo damn mouth." He told him before moving closer to Blake's side. "Niggas be looking at her booty, though?"

Laughing, I hit him. "Don't nobody be looking at me. Thanks to Blake," I glared at him.

He simply smiled at my look. "You're welcome. Dad said I'm supposed to look after you and keep creeps away." Blake informed me, then he high-fived Blaze.

"Looking after me and scaring dudes away isn't the same thing. He done scared off so many of the male nurses at work they started telling everyone about my crazy son. I'm lucky if one man at my job talk to me. The doctors don't even speak no more. They simply nod." I said with a slight attitude.

Blaze started laughing before he gave Blake dap, making me hit him again.

"That's not even funny." I snapped at Blaze.

"Shit if it ain't. That's what's up, though. He's doing what he supposed too. I was the same way." Blaze shrugged as he pounded Blake's fist again.

I wanted to tell him their situations were different but chose not to.

"So, you tryna date?" Blaze asked, taking me by surprise.

My brow rose at him before my eyes slid to Blake, who was staring dead at me. Why would he ask me something like that in front of Blake when he knew his nosey ass listened to everything?

My baby may not want to admit it, but I knew he hoped me, and Blaze would get back together one day. All kids wanted their parents together. With our

50

history, I didn't think I was ready just yet. Sometimes it got lonely, but I dealt with it because Blaze was poison. Being with him was literally a drug to me.

"Are you?" I threw his question back at him.

Even though, I grew up since we've met, that didn't really change anything. Simply being with Blaze for an hour could send me back to that place where nothing mattered, and all rational thoughts were gone. I honestly wasn't ready for those emotions yet.

When Blaze didn't respond, I looked back at him only to see he had taken off his snapback and was now rubbing the back of his neck.

"Oh…Blake, let's go make your plate." That was all I could think to say. Blaze liking someone else was something I never expected to happen so soon. And I honestly didn't know how to feel about it. I wanted him to be happy, I couldn't be selfish and have him waiting on me forever. It had been five years so maybe it was time.

I went to turn around, but Blaze grabbed my arm, stopping me. "Hold on. Blake, you gon' 'head. We're right behind you."

He looked from me to Blaze, then turned and started walking away. Once Blake was far up, he started talking.

"It ain't what you thinking. I'm not fuckin' with no bitch like that but I'm kickin' it with this one babe. A friend from back in the day. It's nothing serious, though." He explained as his head lowered a bit so that he was staring me in the eyes.

Grabbing his hand, I began to pull him toward the buffet. I didn't respond at first. I didn't know how to.

"You mad?" he asked, pulling me to a stop.

Laughing, I shook my head and turned to face him. "No, I'm not mad, B. You are a grown ass man. I don't have no control over your personal life unless it involves my baby. Other than that, babe, you can do what you want. But I do gotda check this bitch out, though. To make sure she's what's up."

Laughing, Blaze's hands went to my waist and I was pulled against him.

"You gotda check her out? That's the new saying to see if she's touching you, huh?" he questioned with a knowing look.

My teeth sunk deeper into my lower lip as I tried to keep a straight face. While doing so, my eyes rolled up basically telling him I wasn't worried about the bitch's appearance.

Regardless of how any chick Blaze fuck'd with looked, whether she was big, small, tall or short, they didn't hold a torch to me giving our history. So, appearance wise, I wasn't worried about no female. But him opening up to another chick was all together a different story.

Catching my look, Blaze laughed.

"Oh, so you ain't fuck'd up, huh? You think you in? You got it like that, huh?" He laughed.

My lips popped as the tip of my tongue pressed against the bottom of my top lip. "I'm not saying I do, but umm, you know what's up." That made him laugh as his hands slid into my back pockets.

"Nah, I don't think I do." Blaze licked his lips as his hands seemed to tighten. The pit of my stomach clenched as heat crept up my neck and goose bumps sprouted down my arms. "You gon' show me what's up?" His face moved closer to mine.

My cheeks went hot as my mouth opened then closed. I was stuck, at a loss for words. My lips parted, but I didn't know what to say as my eyes moved from his lips to his eyes.

"Oh, shit! Blake, yo pops still got it. I got her yellow ass speechless and red as fuck!" Blaze called out loudly, grabbing the people closest to us attention.

Now I was embarrassed.

"Get off of my momma." Blake squeezed in between us then pushed Blaze away from me. "Move back. Come on, Ma. I told you he was a creep too."

My hand covered my parted lips and I started laughing.

"Damn, B, it's like that? I'm a creep now?" Blaze looked at Blake shocked.

He grabbed us a plate and handed me mines then looked at his dad. "Hell yeah! Yo ass been a creep, fuck you mean?" Blake cussed.

My mouth opened in surprise, but I didn't say anything. I just looked at Blaze to see how he was going to react to our eight year old cussing like he was grown.

"How the fuck I'm creepy?" he asked, following Blake to the counter.

Quietly, I followed them and listened.

"You be looking at her booty. I told yo ass about staring at her butt. You just be gawking like you want her good stuff. But my momma ain't giving you none." Blake informed him in a serious tone.

Now I knew this was the moment Blaze was about to go off on Blake for saying some grown shit like that.

"How the hell you sound? I was all in her good stuff, fuck you mean. That don't make me no damn creep, though. Hell yeah, I check yo moms out, she sexy as fuck. When you find yoself a little shorty that looks like yo moms with good stuff, I bet yo ass ain't gon' think I'm a creep no more," was Blaze's reply.

My mouth dropped. *What the hell was he teaching my damn baby?*

Blake stopped making his plate to look up at his dad with a questioning look. "Like that one cute babe that was at the courts. She was ten, talkin' about I'm too young. That's why I pushed her black ass off the swing. She gon' have me pushing her then tell me I was too young for her. I should've slapped her ass." Blake explained to Blaze, looking upset.

I was shocked to hear my eight year old talk like this.

"That's why that little girl was crying? Hell n'all, yo ass didn't?" Blaze laughed steady putting food on his plate like he wasn't talking to a kid.

"Yeah, I did. She said she was gon' get her big brother to beat my ass. But they ain't never come back. I told her I'd beat both they ass, though. After that, she ran off. I think her friend like me because she was smiling at me before running off with them. Fuck them girls, though. Unc said his girl got a daughter and that he was gon' take me over there to meet her." Blake smiled as he nodded his head excitedly.

Blaze hummed as a thoughtful look covered his face. "Nah, you ain't kickin' it with Unc and his bitches. They crazy. Yo little ass don't need to be worrying about no little ass girls anyway. You need to stay focus on school, basketball and boxing, that's it. Liking these little ass girls now ain't gon' do shit but fuck up yo head and when you get sixteen/seventeen, you gon' be too focus on they ass and not on yo work, you know. Their girly parts is what's gon' always be on yo mind. You gotda be smart, man. Them parts ain't gon' make yo ass no money and you damn sho ain't gon' be living off yo moms and me." Blaze schooled him and I completely agreed with everything he was telling our son.

Regardless of my agreement, I was ready for him to say something about Blake cussing. But I didn't, I stayed quiet and continued to listen to their conversation.

"These bitches gon' always be here. A career ain't. You like basketball, Blake that's a one shot thing. Think about it like this, if you stay on track, 'bout time you sixteen, yo ass gon' have scouts looking at you wanting you to go to their school because you better then Jordan, you know. Or boxing, you love that shit. By eighteen you could be better than Mayweather, knocking niggas out, undefeated. But if yo ass lose that focus and turn it on liking some girls, you might as well forget about everything else because it's gone." Blaze explained as they sat across from one another.

"So, when you were my age, you wasn't chasing these chicks out here? Is that why you got so much money?" Blake asked.

I could tell from Blaze's facial expression he wasn't expecting that question.

"Umm…" For the first time since they had been talkin', Blaze's eyes finally slid to me.

Hell, I shrugged. He had everything under control, so he could answer that question.

"Yeah and no, but our living situations were different. When I was yo age, I had to grow up fast. I ain't have what you got now. To have caring people around and all this fun shit. I didn't have that. Everything was different. Nana was good but she wasn't like yo momma. She didn't have the funds we have for you." He told him.

"You got a pops, I ain't have my dad growing up. I was daddy, husband and all that shit in my house. Just being a kid was something I never got to be. So how I was at yo age don't apply to you because yo ass got it good. Spoiled ass. But yo momma she wasn't like that. She was wild as hell, going to strip joints, dancing on bars…" I punched him in the arm. "Gon' now, Peaches. Damn!" Blaze laughed, leaning back as I tried to hit him again.

"Don't be lying to him. I was not wild. I was a good girl who got involved with a bad boy, one I couldn't get rid of." Pursing my lips together, I looked directly at Blaze, making him laugh.

"Because you had me." Blake chimed in.

My lips stretched into a big smile. "Yep! Because we had you but before that I tried to get rid of him and he was just like a—"

"Bulldog drooling." Blake finished my sentence but said the wrong thing.

I started choking as Blake said that.

"Like a bulldog? What's that about?" Blaze asked and Blake opened his mouth.

"Nothing," I quickly said as I laughed. "Oh, so I used to stalk you?" Blaze looked at his son and I started laughing. "Don't look at him like that with yo lying self. Oh." Turning toward Blake, I slapped him in the mouth then reached over the table, punching Blaze. "I bet not ever hear you cuss like that again or I'm gon' tear yo little ass up, do you understand me?" When he nodded, I turned to the adult behind my baby's bad mouth.

"What I tell you about yo language when you're with him? He be with you and cussing then thinks it's cool to bring that crap back home with him. Blaze, he is not your friend. He's not King, so you can't talk like that when you're around him. He don't need to know anything about big booty bitches, or slapping girls…" I then turned to Blake. "Which by the way, if you ever do, I'm gon' kick yo butt. You understand me, Rashad?" I stated with my eyes locked with his as Blaze groaned.

"Oh, shit! She done said yo middle name." Blaze mumbled, rubbing his head.

"She been doing it since the other day." Blake tried to whisper over to his dad.

They knew I only called them by their middle names when I was serious. My mom used to always do that to us when King and I were younger. When she did, we knew we were in trouble.

I turned my glare back to Blake. "*She's* right here, I'm serious. B, you need to stop that. You too, Rashad, it's not cute."

"You cuss, too. Every time you talkin' to my aunties you always call them bit—" Blake started to reply back smartly but was cut off.

"We got it. Ain't that right, Blake?" Blaze cut in with a hard glare at our son. I thought that was it until Blaze reached over and grabbed the front of Blake's shirt and damn near pulled him on top of the table. "If I ever hear some slick shit like that leave yo mouth again when you talkin' to yo momma, I'mma put my hands on you, understand me?" He stared my baby down hard.

I felt bad for my little man, but I was glad he said something because as of late, Blake's mouth been more and more like Blaze's.

"Yes. Sorry, Momma." Blake apologized.

Hearing his sad voice, I glared at Blaze.

"Shut yo ass up. Don't say shit." He told me, catching my look.

I couldn't do nothing but laugh. "Don't talk to me like that. You have one kid and I'm not him so watch who you talkin' to."

He reached over the table and muffed my head back. "Or what? You gon' beat my ass, Peaches? Huh?" He muffed me again.

I slapped at his hand but ended up laughing. That was the reason I tried to keep my distance from him. In no time, Blaze could have me feeling like that love struck twenty-four year old all over again, instead of the thirty year old woman I was.

"Gon' somewhere, now. You too damn old to be playing like this. Leave me alone, Blaze, with yo creepy butt." I glanced at Blake and he gave me a cheeky smile, making us laugh.

Turning away from him, I continued to eat my food while I slickly took glances at two of the most important men in my life.

Chapter 5

Peaches

Breakfast went by smoothly with us joking and laughing. Blake and Blaze argued about nothing at all, which had me bursting into fits of laughter at their craziness. Especially Blaze's, it was comical to see him arguing with his mini self and lose.

"Blake, I'll beat yo little ass. You better shut up." Blaze suddenly threatened him.

I hit the table, laughing harder.

"Now you wanna whoop my ass because you know I'm right—" Blake stopped talking to Blaze and looked at me with wide eyes. "Momma, look, it was me, Dad, Unc, Bell and Auntie Kim at the courts. Unc was on my team against Dad and Bell, right. So some babes—" My brow rose at his use of the word babes, *Yeah I was going to have to start monitoring their weekends together,* "— had come up there to watch us play. Cute babes, too. Dad had tried to show out in front of them but failed when I shook his old ass and broke his ankles. Man, it was funny when he fell. But, Ma, tell me if this right. Before the game, we made a bet. Everybody had to give two hundred dollas—"

As soon as that last bit left his mouth, my hands started waving. I cut him off. "Wait, wait, wait you had to put up two hundred dollars? B, you don't have my baby out there betting? Y'all still do that crap?" I asked not wanting to believe this.

"You know it, so why you ask that dumbass question? Anyway, the bet was if they won, we pay. You know how it goes—"

"Dude, we won!" Blake yelled loudly, jumping up out his seat as he cut Blaze off. "What the fu—"

"Rashad." I yelled, his lips snapped shut and he glared at Blaze.

Blaze laughed as he started talking. "Y'all won the game, yeah, but our bet you didn't win that. You ain't shake me, my shoes weren't tied, and I tripped—" Blaze started saying which seemed to piss Blake off more.

"Bullshit! I broke yo old ass, made you fall and everything. Fuck you saying, man? You can ask Auntie Kim, she was there!" Blake snapped.

"Why the fuck I'mma ask her ass for, so she can lie? I know what the hell happened. Yo ass ain't shake me, so you don't get paid, baby. You can try again tomorrow if you want." Blaze told him.

My poor little man was hot. Blake's cheeks puffed up and his shoulders moved up and down from his heavy breathing.

Blaze didn't know but he was about to get it. Once I saw my baby's mouth open, my hand quickly covered it. I already knew his next words were going to get him in trouble.

"Baby, calm down. B, you gon' make me hurt you. Don't be having him out there playing if you gon' cheat him out his money. How much was the bet for?" I asked a cheesing Blaze.

He was taunting my baby on purpose. "Three bills, but he lost."

I let out a little laugh as I got out of my seat, then walked over to Blaze.

"I'm sorry, Rashad, but I gotda agree with yo dad on this one. You can't play a big man's game if you gon' whine and cry about it later. You gotda man up and comeback twice as hard next time. Especially now that you see yo daddy play dirty," I told him as I held out my hand so Blaze could give me a high-five. Once he did, I grabbed his wrist, then quickly unsnapped his black and blue diamond watch. I took it off him.

"Peaches, what the fuck you doing?" He made a grab for me.

Hurriedly, I jumped back and sat in my seat. "Watch your mouth, Blaze." I put the watch on my four fingers and stared at it before I turned to my little man. "What you think, babe? You like?" I asked Blake and his eyes lit up.

"Yeah, that thang shining." He said, making me laugh.

"So, here's the deal, you lost the three hundred dollars but you got a trophy. Since I know you shook your daddy out on the court, you get a trophy. From now on, when you're playing ball with them, don't play for money, play for trophies. You understand me? If they aren't willing to drop an earring, a chain, bracelet or pinky ring, then you don't play. Three hundred dollars ain't nothing compared to what they wear, so tell yo daddy to keep his money. You'll take this." Grabbing my baby's wrist, I slid the watch on him.

"No shit! I can have this?" he asked with wide eyes.

"Hell no—" Blaze started to say until I cut him off.

"Yep, that's all you, baby. And you don't take it off for nothing or nobody. You understand me?" Blake's head bobbed up and down as he stared at his new watch. "If somebody try to take it, you throw hands to them, no exceptions." I said, looking at a confused Blaze.

"Hell no! B, gon' take that off. Yo moms trippin', real shit. Gon' run that back." He told Blake, waving his fingers but my baby wasn't giving that up.

"Nope. You lost fair and square. I got the trophy now." Blake started waving his wrist around.

I broke out laughing as I looked at Blaze.

He bit into his bottom lip and Blaze started his famous head nod. "Gon' 'head and keep that. It looks nice on you."

Knowing Blaze all too well, I turned to Blake. "Baby, gon' give it back. I'll buy you a trophy."

Blaze started laughing. "Nah, don't do that. He won it. So don't even sweat it." Licking his lips, he turned his slanted eyes on me.

"Blaze, gon' for real." My warning made him laugh.

"I ain't done shit," He said with a sexy crooked smile.

"But you're thinking about it, so stop. I don't have nothing to do with what you and Blake have going on." I tried to get out of whatever he had planned.

His head tilted and his brow rose. "You say what?" He licked his lips waiting on my reply.

I bit into my bottom lip to keep myself from laughing. "Blaze, for real, I don't have time for you." Looking away from him, I glanced at Blake who wore a confused look. I let out a nervous laugh as I focused back on Blaze.

"What y'all get me for my birthday?" Blaze finally asked, which got Blake excited and me relieved.

I couldn't take no more of his look. I knew I was gon' get it for taking that watch. I just didn't know what he was going to do or when. Grabbing my tea, I took a drink.

"I asked momma for two hundred ones like Unc told me to, but she said no." Blake shrugged.

Covering my mouth, I broke out laughing as I started to choke which caused the tea to spill from my mouth. Blaze quickly grabbed some napkins covering my hands as him and Blake patted my back. My eyes burned from tears, as my throat ached.

"You i'ight? Damn, you spitting all over the food and shit." Blaze laughed.

Looking at Blaze with teary eyes, I hit him before pushing his black ass away from me. "Shut up, Rashad, you gon' get yo little self hurt. The both of y'all. See…" Biting my tongue, I just shook my head already knowing whatever fuss I was about to do was falling on deaf ears. "Give him his gift."

Blake was all too eager as he grabbed my purse and pulled out the small square box that was gift wrapped. He then grabbed the two bigger ones before he reached in his pocket and pulled out an envelope. One I didn't know he had.

"Here, open this one first." He told his dad, sliding him the envelope with a wide smile.

"What's that?" I tried to whisper but Blaze heard and raised a brow in Blake's direction.

"Dang, you nosy. Gon' this is man business." Blake brushed me off with a serious look.

I slapped him upside his head as a laugh slipped through my lips. "Boy, you ain't no man. Rashad, stop talkin' to me." Shaking my head, I watched Blaze open the white envelope.

Once he looked inside of it, he broke out laughing. "Damn, who you rob?" Blaze asked as he pulled dollars out and started counting it.

"Rashad, where you get that money from?" I know damn well my baby wasn't stealing from folks. I haven't given him any money so seeing that caused confusion to set in my body.

"Nana and Pops gave it to me for cleaning up around the house. I told them I wanted to get my daddy something without asking you for the money, so they paid me to clean up." He explained just as Blaze whistled.

"Shid, what did they have you doing?" Blaze looked at him.

As they were talking, I grabbed Blaze's coke and started drinking it.

Blake shook his head at that. "You don't even wanna know. Just make sho' you spend that on a pretty girl with a big booty."

Again, I started choking. This time pop burned my nostrils as it came out. God, this little boy was going to be the death of me.

"Rashad!" Blaze had tainted my son and it was nothing I could do. "Blaze, we gon' talk about this," was all I could really say on my baby's behavior.

Blaze went to grab the last box and Blake smacked his hand away.

"Open this one." He gave him the small box first, then looked and smiled at me before his gaze fell back on his dad.

Blaze picked it up and shook it by his ear. "Making sho' it wasn't no change. Them strippers complain about that shit."

I grabbed a piece of ice from my cup and threw it at him. "Shut up and open it."

He tore the wrapping paper that covered the tan colored box from Diamond & Co and his brows rose before opening the box. "Oh shit!"

Blake started laughing at his dad's reaction. He took out the 10K solid gold, black rhodium plated, diamond pinky ring.

"This how y'all do it?" Blaze asked excitedly as he put the ring on his pinky finger. After seeing it was jewelry, he quickly grabbed the next box and ripped it open, making us laugh at his eagerness. It wasn't a secret Blaze liked his diamonds. He wasn't one to show off, but he had a lot of jewelry.

After opening the matching bracelet and watch, Blaze tried to give it back.

"Man, I can't take these. Don't get me wrong, this shit is hot as fuck, but I know you came off too much to get this, Peach." He looked at his gifts then back at us.

"Babe, it was nothing. It's your birthday and price doesn't matter around this time. Plus, Blake really wants you to have it."

"Yeah, keep it, I picked everything out." Blake lied. My hand rubbed over his waves and I kissed the side of his head. "Ma, gon'," he whined, shrugging me off him.

I muffed his head to the side, then pushed away from him. "Forget you, too, watermelon head punk."

"Thank y'all, man. Y'all ain't even have to get all this." Blaze got out of his seat with his arms stretched wide. Blake quickly followed suit as he hopped up to hug his dad. "Come on, Peaches, don't sit yo stuck up ass right there. Get yo ass up, this a group hug."

Laughing, I stood up and pressed my front against Blake's back and wrapped my arms around Blaze's waist. I held them tight. We didn't see each other every day, but we were every bit of a family.

"Y'all squishing me." Blake started to wiggle, trying to get loose. "It's hot in here." He complained

Blaze and I laughed at his dramatic self and we broke apart. I didn't get a chance to walk away as Blaze grabbed my arm and pulled me back to him. "Good lookin'."

Smiling, I nodded my head. I wasn't trying to look into his eyes for too long as my stomach became tight. "As long as you like them, that's all that matters." His hands soon slid into my back pockets. "You need to stop before you get yoself in trouble."

Blaze bit into his lower lip as he made his famous hum. "Mm, is that a promise?"

Pushing away from him, I laughed. "I'm not about to go there with you, Blaze. We gon' be good." I knew where his head was at. Apart from the last three years, we would always end up together, around this time, until the sun came creeping through the curtains the following morning. "Tell me about your little friend."

68

"You'll meet her tonight." He smiled.

Smacking my lips at his reply, I let it drop knowing I wasn't going to get nothing out of him.

"Whatever, Blaze."

Even though it came off jokingly, I hope the chick was up to par for her sake.

More importantly, I hope I didn't come off like the jealous ex.

Chapter 6

Peaches

Once we left the restaurant, we drove forty-five minutes back to Gary to meet up at Mom B's house like always. Every year she would buy him a cake and we all would go over there to eat it.

"Can we eat cake now?" Blake asked as he flopped down on the couch next to me.

"Once your papa get back, we can." Bianca sighed heavily.

Blake seemed to ask that question every thirty seconds or so and it was frustrating her. My baby groaned and stomped out of the living room making me laugh.

Blaze walked into the living room and sat down next to me with a cup.

"Ooh, give me some." I asked him as he was about to take a drink. With the cup still to his lips, he glanced at me before taking a drink. "Blaze, don't drink it all."

"Yo yellow ass don't even know what it is and you begging." He fussed before drinking some more.

"B—"

"Here with yo begging ass!" He gave me the cup with just a little bit in there. "Yo ass bet not say shit, drink it."

"Don't talk to me like that with yo black ass." I laughed before drinking the rest of his Sprite. "I hope you ain't been doing nothing with your mouth."

"Ain't that some shit. You gon' think about it after you done drunk it. Shid, yo ass done tasted whose ever coochie I had in my mouth this morning." He licked his lips, then rubbed his chin. "Might as well kiss me now. Come here." Blaze leaned into me.

"Yo ass is so childish. Let me find out you been eating some chick's box, we gon' fight. I don't care if we're together or not. We eat and drink behind each other. I ain't got time for that." I was so serious about every word that left my mouth.

Blaze's brow raised before he broke out laughing. "Shut the fuck up, I ain't worried about yo short ass. You know I ain't ate no chick's box. But shid, I should start because you ain't trying to spread yo legs and let me eat—"

"Why momma gotda open her legs for you to eat?" Blake asked his dad as he sat on the floor by our feet.

My mouth opened and closed trying to think of what to say. "Umm, I have to go to the bathroom." I hopped up so fast and left out the room.

I swear sometimes Blaze could be reckless to the mess he says. He never thought about who was around and what could be overheard. My face was so hot from embarrassment.

Once I made it to the bathroom, I closed the door and leaned against the counter. I looked in the mirror at myself and started laughing. "That damn man, I swear." My head shook as I went to use the restroom. I was in the middle of washing my hands when the bathroom door opened.

Blaze walked in. His eyes were slanted as his lips stretched into a little smirk.

Before he could say anything, my head was shaking. "No, get out. We're at your momma's house. Blaze, gon' now. Stop looking at me."

"I can't stare at you now? Why not?" he asked, leaning against the door.

"Because I know you—"

"What you know?" Blaze pushed off of the door, then locked it. He walked toward me. "You know I missed you, is that what you know?" He walked me into the counter and leaned into me.

I bit into my bottom lip trying to hide the stupid smile that caused my lips to quiver. But I couldn't deny him or lie to myself. I had missed him. "I've missed you too. I'm not going to lie but we're not going there."

Blaze let out a laugh. "*Psst,* we going there. You brought it here when yo ass decided to take my watch and give it to our son. Baby girl, you got to pay for that, and I don't want yo money." He licked his lips before rubbing a hand over his mouth, then down his chin.

No, he wasn't.

"Are you serious right now?" He nodded his head. I laughed. "You can't do that. You owed him and you know that! But to try to make me have sex with you because of your bet, Blaze, that's messed up. What the hell kind of bargain is that? Man, bye." I couldn't take him serious right now.

"Baby, ain't no bargain. You jumped in something that had nothing to do with you." Again, he licked his lips as his finger hooked the inside of my jeans. He rubbed the button before undoing it.

My eyes moved to his hand, watching as his thumb and index fingers pulled my zipper down. "Come on, Peach, stop playing. You know you want it; I can tell. So, let me play with her." His hand slid into the front of my pants.

"You get on my nerves, Blaze. We can't do it in here." Once those words left my mouth, he was pushing my jeans and panties down my hips. "B, we can't. Let's go to the truck." I knew my mouth, there was no way I could be quiet, and it's been a while for me.

Even with my thoughts and my semi resistance, my hands had a mind of their own. My fingers made quick work with his button and zipper. "Blaze, we can't be long, and you have to be quiet." I told him as I kicked off my gym shoes to pull my jeans off.

His movement stopped. "I gotda be quiet? Really?" He reached on the side of me and grabbed a hand towel from the rack. "Here just bite on this when you get loud."

Grabbing the towel, I hit him with it and laughed. "You are such a fuckin' asshole."

Blaze sat me on the counter, stepping between my legs. He pulled my shirt off and dropped it to the floor. He freed my breast then cupped my titties in his palms, bringing them to his mouth.

My lips parted as he sucked on my right nipple, then the left, making them erect. My back arched, pushing my breasts more into him.

He pulled back. "But you love me, though."

My arms wrapped around his neck and I pulled up on him. A smile stretched across my lips. I couldn't deny it and he knew that. My smiling lips pressed against his as my hand grabbed his soldier, placing him to my opening. "I do, I love you."

Blaze lips covered mine as he pushed inside of me.

We both let out a moan/groan as we met each other's movement. Blaze hips thrust forward, and I came down.

I pulled our lips apart and buried my head into the side of his neck. My mouth opened and my teeth gripped his skin in order to muffle my sounds.

"Damn, Peach." His grip tightened and his pelvis moved faster against mine.

"Ahh! Ahh! Ooh, ooh! Mmm!" I moaned as my nails dug into the nape of his neck. "Sss! Ooh, shit, Blaze."

His hand held my ass in a vice grip. Blaze stopped my movement as his hips smacked into mine.

Trying to keep quiet was no longer an option as my head went back. My lips parted. "Ooh, Oh, my God!" I moaned loudly as he grunted.

Blaze laid me sideways on the countertop, he placed my left leg on his shoulder and began to pound harder into my body.

"Ooh, shit, baby! I'm about to cum. Shit, harder Blaze." I grabbed his hip, letting my nails bite into his skin.

"Let that shit go." He pumped faster as his fingers came to my clit. He pinched, then rubbed my pearl. Blaze leaned into me as he grasped the side of my neck, pulling me up. His lips came to mine, he sucked on my top then bottom lip before his tongue slid through my parted lips. "Damn, bae, I missed the fuck outda you." Blaze mumbled against my mouth.

I've learned a long time ago not to take offense whenever he said *he missed me* while we were having sex. It was his own way of expressing his feelings both sexually and emotionally. Besides at this moment, I didn't care which way he meant it. My body had desperately missed his. The way my inner muscles gripped and sucked on him as well as my loud moans told that much.

"Ma!" Blake's loud voice could be heard from the hallway.

"Shit!" my hand went to Blaze's pelvis. I was about to push him away.

"Oh no the fuck you don't," Blaze told me and I glared at him but my face soon dropped against the counter as he rolled his hips into mine. He pulled out only to push back in, going deeper.

I tightened my pussy muscles on his dick. I could tell from the way his nails dug into my thigh and his frantic thrusting he was about to nut.

Blaze's pace slowed down, and he tapped on my mound. "Bae, let up."

"Momma! Dad!" Blake yelled, sounding like he was a few doors down.

"I swear that's a cock blocking little mothafucka." Blaze grunted before he took the hand towel and brought it to my lips. "Bite on this."

I looked at him like he was crazy. I didn't know if that damn towel was used or not. When I pushed the towel from my face, he sat it down and rolled me on my back. He placed my thighs on his forearms and folded my arms together, gripping them both he lifted me up.

His thrusting started as did my bounce. Blaze brought me down to meet his pushing hips.

"Ahh, ahh, ahh! Oh, my God!"

"Peach, shut up," Blaze's hips moved faster.

I now regretted not biting down on the damn towel.

Blaze's thrusts once again became frantic as my muscles locked on him. My body shook and I came with a loud moan. Blaze followed after three powerful, frantic pumps he came with a grunt as he held me to him, filling me with his fluid.

"Damn." Blaze mumbled. He let my legs go and leaned against me, pressing me onto the countertop. His lips soon found mine and my arms wrapped around his neck, kissing him back.

We both moaned into the kiss and Blaze pushed his hips more into me and I felt him twitch.

I pulled back to look at him. "No, get out," I laughed.

Blaze joined me as he finally pulled out. "If it wasn't for Blake, I wouldn't have stopped." His expression was serious, so I knew he was telling the truth. He pulled up his pants and fixed himself into his jeans.

"Me either," I told him truthfully as I went to the toilet, trying to pee. Only a few drops dripped out and I silently cussed. *Damn, fuckin' with Blaze ass.* I didn't think to use a condom, that was the last thing on my mind. With a sigh, I got off of the toilet.

"Come here." Blaze beckoned me to him. With a warm towel, his hand came between my legs.

My cheeks immediately went hot. I would never get used to this Blaze no matter how much time goes by.

"Peach, don't be taking no damn pills, man. I wasn't thinking 'bout a condom either or pulling out. If it happens it does." He lowered his head to level his eyes with mine.

My thoughts quickly reverted back to what happened five years ago with my first pregnancy.

"Peaches," Blaze touched my chin.

I mentally shook my head from wondering further into the events that led up to my miscarriage. "I hear you. Blaze, you know I wouldn't do that." I mumbled, fixing my bra and pulling on my shirt before I pulled on my panties and jeans. Once I finished, I quickly washed my hands.

Blaze's front soon pushed against my back as his hands went to the counter. My eyes rolled and I bit into my lower lip to suppress my smile.

"What you smiling about?" he asked as he pulled the tie from my hair.

"I'm not smiling." I glanced at him through the mirror and laughed. "Whatever, man." I turned around to face him. My arms wrapped around his waist.

"What you thinkin' about?" His fingers ran through my hair. My shoulders shrugged and he let out a heavy breath. "Peach, don't do that. Baby girl, we're past all that hiding shit. So, tell me what's up?"

He was right, we were past keeping secrets but with sudden thoughts of my miscarriage, I didn't want him to think I was living in the past.

"The miscarriage is what I was thinking about. I don't know if I'm ready, if we're ready. I mean we aren't even together for one and you were just telling me about this chick you're seeing. This is so backwards, B." My hands slid into his back pockets.

Blaze's free arm wrapped around my waist and he lifted me up and place me on the counter. The hand in my hair tightened and he pulled my head back. His lips pressed into mine. That giddiness filled the pit of my stomach and my lips stretched into a smile as I kissed him back.

He pulled back from the kiss. "You ain't got to worry about shit, I got you, Peaches, so don't even start rethinking about that. As I told you then, it wasn't our time. We don't even know the outcome of this right now, so we shouldn't be worrying about you being pregnant—" Blaze stopped talking as the door burst open.

"You're pregnant?" A look of shock covered my baby's face before disappointment graced Blake's handsome features.

"Baby no—" I started to explain myself, but Blaze cut me off.

"Did yo ass knock on that gotdamn door?" Blaze's face contorted into a mean glare as he stared at Blake.

"I was looking for Momma—"

Blaze cut him off. "I know I locked that damn door." A puzzled look covered his face.

When he said that, I'm sure my expression mirrored his. I looked at Blake only to see him putting his hand behind his back. The silver object in his hand had my mouth parting.

"Blake, you broke in the bathroom? Really? Little boy—"

Blaze once again cut me off. "I'm about to beat yo little ass. You done lost yo damn mind! And you gon' question her? Fuck is wrong with you?" He fussed before he made a grab for Blake.

Blake jumped back then ran out the bathroom, he dropped the knife as he made his escape. My hand covered my mouth as I stared at it.

"Fuck is you laughing about. He does this shit because of yo ass." His finger pointed in my face as he turned on me.

My brows rose before I bit at his finger. "Don't point in my face. I don't have anything to do with that. Blake is you in every way, shape and form. Baby, you're the reason he's like that." My arms crossed over my chest as my hip cocked to the side.

"Shut the fuck up." He muffed my head to the side before grabbing my arms so I wouldn't hit him. "Gon', Peach, I'm just bullshittin'. Gimme kiss." Blaze kissed me.

I laughed as my lips parted and my head tilted, kissing him back.

"Ugh, Ma, don't kiss him and Nana said come on. She's ready to cut the cake." Blake peeked back into the bathroom. He was about to walk out but stopped to stare at me. His eyes moved from me to his dad then back to me. "Ma, why your shirt inside out?" As if he knew the answer to his own question, my little man mugged Blaze hard before he grabbed my arm and pulled me with him out the bathroom. "Didn't I tell you he was a creep? Stay away from him. Dad you better stay away from my momma. Damn!" He fussed.

I looked back at Blaze to see that flirty smile on his face.

"Shid, tell yo moms to stay away from me. B, she was all over me. I tried to fight her off." Blaze picked at him.

Laughing, I rolled my eyes at Blaze. "Man, shut up. Blake, we were just talking. My shirt probably been inside out." I shrugged as if it was nothing, but Blake didn't seem to buy it. My eyes soon drifted to his duffle bag in the hallway. A glare covered my face. "Matter fact, I was fussing at him about telling you *what goes for my house doesn't go for his.*" They both stopped walking then.

"Here I come, Nana!" Blake let me go and ran off.

I turned my glaring face to Blaze as my arms crossed over my chest.

He licked his lips before rubbing the back of his neck.

"Blaze, now you know—"

"Here I come, Ma!" He mimicked Blake and left me in the hallway.

All I could do was laugh at those two crazy fools. I couldn't help but love them.

Chapter 7

Peaches

I stood in the full length mirror that hung from the bathroom door. Glancing at myself, I took in the sexy, purple, floral backless lace bodycon dress I had on. Standing on my tip toes, I looked at myself sideways into the mirror, smoothing down the dress.

My eyes soon shifted down to the suede, purple Red Bottom platform pumps on my feet. Satisfied with my look, a smile stretched across my lips as I pushed my mid back length hair over my right shoulder. I continued to stare at the peekaboo lace dress that hugged my curves like a second skin.

I had picked up a little weight over the years, not that much, but my stomach had a cute pudge to it. My thighs and hips were thicker but even so, the extra pounds fit my five foot three frame perfectly.

I walked away from the mirror and went to my dresser. I grabbed my black chain, where my purple brass knuckle hung from, putting it on. I then slid my black oval shaped ring on my index finger.

Grabbing my holster for my purple and black custom made .380, I then pulled up my dress so I could hook it to my boy shorts. I smooth my dress back down and over my hips. With the tightness of my dress the slight bulge was very noticeable. But there was no way in hell I would leave without my babies. I grabbed my LCP Ruger and put it in my handbag.

After I slipped on my black leather jacket, which covered the bulge on my hip. I swiped my lips with a coat of clear gloss, then headed for the door to make my super late entrance at the party.

***

I parked across the street from Prestige. Once I got out of the truck, I hurriedly ran across Broadway to get to the night club. Folks stood waiting outside, trying to get in as the line slowly moved.

Going to the front of the line, I slowed down my fast pace, stopping at the tall bulky man in front of me. "King?" I saw him against the front door, holding some chick's arm while whispering in her ear.

Hearing his name, he looked up and his eyes fell directly on me. "Fuck you doing here? Yo ass should be at the crib. It's passed yo bedtime." He joked.

Hitting his arm, I rolled my eyes at him. "Don't you even start, okay." He gave me a hug. "Where yo boy at?" I asked, catching ol girl's slight mug. I ignored her and my focus stayed on my brother.

"He in there. Peaches, don't go in there starting no shit." He warned.

I already knew he was talking about whatever chick Blaze was in there with. I wasn't fazed by her, not in the least. "King, now you know I don't be on no mess so don't come to me like that. I'm too grown for petty shit. So gon' somewhere."

"I ain't playin', Peaches. Don't go in there starting shit."

Why would I start something? I never started anything so for King to repeat himself twice. He probably thought I was going to be on some jealous ex type shit but that wasn't my character at all.

"Whatever, I'm going in."

"I'll walk with you." He said, grabbing my arm.

Linking my arm with King's, we started to walk away but ol girl he was with cleared her throat, bringing his attention back to her.

"Oh, shit, baby girl, my fault. Come on."

Typical King, I swear. Shaking my head at his foolery, I said nothing. I just let him lead me through the doors into the club.

The club was packed as expected, seeing this caused a small laugh to leave my mouth. I bet Blaze's ass was somewhere in a dark corner scoping the place out.

"Oh, there he go." King pointed at the bar.

Breaking out of King's hold, I quickly made my way over to where he stood. Once I was close to him, I pinched his side, getting his attention.

"Happy Birthday." Blaze smiled at me as I wrapped my arms around his waist, giving him a hug. As I held him, he brought his mouth to my ear.

"Yo ass late. I ain't think you was coming." He joked.

"I told you I was going to be late. I had some last minute shopping to do." I had to get the rest of our stuff together for the trip to Six Flags.

Blaze hummed into my ear before he stood up straight.

I released him from my hold and shrugged off my jacket.

"You wearing that dress, ain't you?" He commented while running his hand down my left side.

Laughing, I rolled my eyes at him. "So, you like?" I smiled at his roaming eyes before they met back with mine. His serious face said it all. "I'm not even messing with you, so gon' somewhere."

When Blaze and I were together it was always crazy and if he had a female friend as he claimed, we needed distance between us. If earlier proved anything, it was that our chemistry was still heavily intact.

Blaze ordered me a drink and handed it to me. He then grabbed my hand and began to lead us to the back tables, but we were stopped midway as Missy stood in front of us.

"Hey, mami." She pulled me into a hug, then released me. Her eyes glanced over to Blaze and she smiled. "Hey, Blaze." Missy waved then looked around. Her brows furrowed and she pulled me closer to her. "Where the bitch at?" She loudly whispered in my ear.

I couldn't help but laugh at her silly self. My arms wrapped around her neck and my mouth went to her ear. "You are so stupid, but I love yo ass. Girl, I don't know. I'm about to try and find her too, so just see where we sit. She'll pop up." I told her.

Missy's head shook and she pointed to Blaze. "I'm about to steal her for a second. Give me a few minutes and I'll have her back to you. I promise." She didn't give him a chance to reply as she started dragging me away from him.

"I'm so sorry give me a sec, please." I yelled to him.

We walked back over to the bar area where my girls were. And from the looks of things they were all lit. "Babes!" I called out to them loudly.

They looked at me smiling. "Peaches!" My name chorused from their lips, making me laugh.

"I see y'all didn't wait for me." I pointed out to the shot glasses.

"Bitch, you was taking to fuckin' long and I needed this drink." Kim rolled her eyes.

"What's wrong with you?" I sat next to her.

Again, her eyes rolled. "Me and Bell done broke up."

My eyes widened. "What? Why? When?" I was shocked to say the least. I knew he had been making threats, but I thought it was just that, *talk*.

"Because Mike's ass showed up here. You know him and Blaze ain't really cool or whatnot, so he said he wasn't coming. But his ol' dumbass popped up here anyways while I was chilling with Bell. Mike flipped out, him and Bellow got into a fight. King and Blaze broke it up. Then Blaze put Mike's ass out. So, he pulled me outside with him asking what the fuck I was doing with that nigga." Kim stopped talking and took a shot before waving the bartender over.

"And what did you say when he asked you that?" I waited on her reply.

Kim gave me a blank stare before her eyes rolled. "What the fuck you think I told him? I said it wasn't like that and we were just cool. Bell overheard it, he said *fuck me* and *we were done*. Now this nigga all over there with some bitch. I'm ready to go over there and whoop his black ass. Like, Peaches, he's being hella disrespectful right now."

She was wasted.

My head shook and I rubbed my forehead.

"Don't you do that, Peaches. I promise, don't. I know I should've broke it off with Mike a long time ago but I just thought he would get his act together—"

"Girl, get real! Mike was born a hoe and gon' die a hoe. If he ain't changed by now, it's obvious he's not going to or you're just not his one—" Angel harshly began to lay it to Kim.

"Ang, damn, seriously?" Disbelief couldn't begin to describe how I felt about her words. Angel was known for being brutally honest but at that moment she had crossed the line.

"Don't *Ang* me! We all knew this was going to happen, including her. So now that the shit done hit the fan, she wanna cry? Bitch, get real and capitalize on this shit. It's already out that something is going on between the two of you, so why not make the shit known now? Fuck crying about it. That ain't gon' do nothing but give you and us headaches. I don't have time for that shit. Man, the fuck up and either go get your man or run yo ass back to Mike's dog ass. You bitches stresses me out with all this crying over these no good ass niggas. When y'all got a good one, you wanna fuck it up. If you don't go get him then no better for yo ass, Kim. With yo smart dumb ass. I'm about to go dance before y'all fuck up my buzz." Angel threw her shot back as well as Kim's and Missy's drinks before she walked off.

"Bitch!" Kim yelled at Angel's back. "I hate her." Kimmy's face frowned and she glanced back over to Bell. "I hate when she's right. I need to calm down before I go over there." She called for two more shots.

"She don't need them." I waved the bar man off then grabbed Kim's hands and pulled her off of the stool. "Let's go dance." I grabbed Missy's arm, then patted Ebony on the shoulder, waving for her to follow. We all made our way to the dance floor and started to dance with each other.

It didn't take long for different men to start coming our way. I made no complaints as I started dancing with one of them. I looked over at Ebony, Kim and Missy to see they were grinding all over brothers of their own. We were having a blast. Every so often we would look at each other and start to laugh for reasons unknown.

"Ooh." Ebony's mouth formed into an *O*.

My brows raised when she tried to discreetly point to my left, but I caught on too late and was suddenly pulled away from the guy I was dancing with.

"What the fuck is you doing?" Blaze snapped at me.

My mouth opened then closed, I was confused by his attitude. "Dancing," I slowly replied. "Why you seem mad? Don't tell me you're jealous?"

"I ain't jealous about shit. You mothafuckas might as well be fuckin' with the way y'all was going. Don't ever do no bullshit like that again. Fuck is wrong with you?" Blaze was not happy.

"Aye, what's up? You good, ma?" The guy I was dancing with approached us.

Blaze rubbed his nose before he pulled up his jeans. "My nigga don't worry about her. Now homie, I'mma tell you this once. Turn yo ass around and walk the fuck away!" He pushed dude hard as hell, making him bump into some-one.

"I'm sorry, he's sorry." I apologized to the dude. "B, it's not even that serious. Come on. Damn." I stepped in the middle of them and pushed Blaze back.

He didn't look at me at first. Instead, he was staring at the guy smiling.

Same old Blaze. "Why would you do that?"

"What the hell you mean, Why? Peaches, why the fuck you out there fuckin' that nigga?" He snapped at me as he grabbed my forearm and started pulling me with him.

I didn't want to fight with him on his birthday, so I said nothing as he pulled me with him. I was beyond tripped out. *Wasn't he just telling me the other day I could bring somebody to his party?*

"We weren't fucking. My ass was barely touching him, Blaze. Besides, didn't you tell me I could bring somebody?" I stopped walking and stood face to face with him, waiting on a reply.

"Peaches, shut the fuck up. I don't give a fuck what I said. Yo ass ain't have to be all over that nigga like I ain't in this bitch, though. You disrespectful as fuck." He fussed at me.

My head tilted to the side and I let out a laugh. I stepped closer to him and wrapped my arms around his neck, bringing his head down. My mouth went to his ear. "So, you think because I gave you some wet-wet things done changed? Huh?"

Blaze's head reared back, and he laughed. "That's exactly what the fuck it means. I'm tryna be low tonight and yo ass on some other shit. I'mma fuck around and have to beat a nigga's ass because of you. So, sit the fuck down all night, no dancing unless it's with me." He yelled into my ear.

I pushed him away from me and started laughing. "Man, whatever. Don't you have a bitch around here somewhere?"

He rubbed the back of his neck, then shrugged. "That's different, though. Come on." He took my hand and led us off the dance floor.

He had a lot of nerves by telling me not to dance unless it's with him. When he had a whole ass bitch here for him. But that's *different*? I truly didn't see how it was.

Once we sat down, Blaze handed me a cup. I crossed my right leg over my left knee and took a sip of my drink, then focused back on him. "Are you enjoying your party?"

Blaze nodded. He looked around the club, then back to me. "It's i'ight." He shrugged, making me roll my eyes.

He was crazy if he thought I was going to be cooped up in this area all night without dancing. I stood up and held out my hand for him to take.

He looked at my outstretched hand and then back to me. "Fuck you going?"

"We're about to dance, come on. I ain't come here just to sit down beside you and look pretty." My hand waved over myself to emphasize the word *pretty*.

Laughing, he grabbed my hand and let me pull him up. Just as he stood, my body jerked forward from someone bumping into me.

"Damn—" I started to snap but was cut off by some chick apologizing.

"I'm sorry, those drinks and these damn heels." She claimed but the bitch didn't have a drunk slur to her voice. She looked behind me and a smile stretched across her face. "Hey, bae."

Being the stupid person I was, I looked around to see who she was talking to. Catching my action, Blaze hit me in the back slightly, trying to be hush with it. I looked at Blaze and gave him a confused look.

"What? I'm trying to see who she's talking to. She's kinda drunk and I don't want her falling into the wrong man's arms, you know." The slight glare to his face had me rolling my eyes. *I already didn't like this bitch.*

Peaches, breathe. She ain't even worth it. Petty bitch. You're here for B only, no silly ass bitches. Breathe...

She walked past me and went over to Blaze, giving him a hug before going in for a kiss. Blaze's eyes met with mine and my brow raised. Seeing that, he pulled back before their lips could touch.

Hell no. I wasn't gon' make it. I was jealous. Breathe, Peach...

Ol' girl took his withdrawal without saying a word, as her smile stayed plastered on her face. "Bae, who's your friend?" I asked not thinking too much of the word *bae*.

"Peach, this my friend, Keisha. Keisha this Peaches." He introduced us and immediately the wheels started to turn as I remembered hearing her name before.

"Bae?" She questioned, looking at Blaze, then to me.

My eyes slanted as I pretended like I didn't hear her.

"Roz' daughter?" I asked confused. I didn't understand why out of all people it was her that he was with.

His head nodded *yes* and I sized her up.

She stood 5'6 maybe. Keisha's long blonde and black weave complimented her mocha skin complexion and her heart shaped face. The girl was cute, I had to give her that. My eyes then drifted down to the tight red dress that hugged her breast and curvy figure like a second skin. Her protruding hips that balanced her big healthy ass seemed to be stretching the dress to its limits. Even so, it looked good on her.

I remembered Blaze told me she was the second bitch he had sex with when he was fourteen. My mind was made immediately, *I didn't like this bitch at all.* Why the fuck did it have to be her?

"Hmm." I mimicked his hum, causing him to look at me funny.

"Peaches, don't make me beat yo ass in here." He threatened.

I didn't take his warning to heart. I sized her up again. *I could still probably beat her ass.* "What?" I rolled my eyes at him with a laugh. I already knew what he meant. I was going to try and put my childishness to the side. "Whatever, B." I put on the fakest tight lip smile I could muster up. I looked and nodded at her. "It's nice meeting you."

"Same here, so you two are friends?" she asked, pointing between us.

I licked my lips before I sat down on the couch. I crossed my legs and grabbed my drink. I took a sip, then looked back at her. "We're best friends to be exact. Real close. Have a seat." Holding my hand out toward the couch, I gestured for her to sit down.

"I think I'm about the only consistent female in his life. The rest be here for a second..." my fingers snapped "... and be gone like that." I brought my glass to my lips taking another sip, while avoiding Blaze's stare. "Not saying you're not different, you probably are. I mean, given your history—then again, given your history you should know." This bitch made my skin crawl. I did not like her and the way she clung to Blaze's arm was pissing me off.

"It's funny because he never mentioned you at all. I mean, I've met King, Sam, Bell—Well, you know his other friends." She stated with a slight twist of her lips as she took me in.

Glancing at Blaze, he wasn't paying any attention to us. He was too busy scoping out the place.

Laughing at her statement, I shrugged as my head nodded. "It's very funny, indeed, because I'm just finding out about you too. I mean that y'all are friends again." Glancing at Blaze this time, he caught my eye and I stopped talking. He didn't know but he just caught my tongue because I was sure about to say some foul shit.

"What you do?" he asked right off bat.

Shaking my head, I laughed. "Nothing. Just trying to get to know your friend, is all. We'll talk later," I said loudly, making sure she heard. "So how long has it been since y'all linked back up?"

"Shid, I don't know. It ain't been that long." Blaze simply shrugged while grabbing his cup of Hennessey. Whereas Keisha popped his arm with a giddy laugh.

"For real, Blaze, not that long?" she asked, smiling way too hard for my taste.

"Shid, it ain't been that long." He replied nonchalantly.

Same old Blaze. That nigga ain't never gon' change.

"I swear, just like a man. We linked back up a few years back but sadly he was with someone at the time, so our contact was limited. Then last year we ran into each other again and started kickin' it and things kinda started to get heavy a few months ago." She explained and had the nerve to be too happy.

I started choking from my laughter as this morning events at Mom B's house popped into my head. *Poor thing*, she looked so sincere about what she was saying while rubbing his arm.

"I need another drink. This shit is not strong enough for me." I grabbed Blaze's Hennessy bottle and poured some in my cup. Taking a long gulp, I rubbed my chest from the heated sensation.

"Hey, Peaches." Bellow smiled as he came over to me.

Standing up, I gave him a hug as he kissed my cheek. "What's up, Bell? Damn, it seems like forever since I last

95

saw you." Even though Bellow and Kim had been messing around, I didn't see him as much. It had been well over a year, if not longer, since I've last seen him.

"I know. You wearing that dress, ain't you?" He held me at arm's length, and he looked me over.

"You staring too fuckin' hard, ain't you? Peaches, sit the fuck down." Blaze snapped at Bellow and then me.

Bell and I looked at each other first and then at him, laughing.

"Same old, B. Nigga, don't nobody want her crazy ass. Damn, I'm just sayin' she looks good. I know she's you. Shit, breathe." He looked back at me smiling hard. "I see you still got my nigga pussy whipped." Bellow spoke loudly and my hand went to my mouth.

These niggas didn't care what they said or who they said it in front of. And at this particular moment I didn't even care. I stared at a confused looking Keisha.

"Blaze, what is he talking about?" She asked him.

Blaze glared at Bell before looking at Keisha. "He ain't talkin' 'bout shit." Was all he told her as he looked back to Bellow. "Nigga, fuck you. She ain't got me shit." Blaze took a swig from his cup. Turning toward me, he began to fuss. "I don't know why the fuck you came out here with that little shit on. Sit the fuck down, Peaches. I ain't gon' tell you no damn more."

Smacking my lips, I waved him off. "Bell, he ain't talkin' 'bout shit. Gone, Blaze, damn! You play too much." Laughing, I moved on the other side of Bellow as he got up.

"Y'all still the same, B. When you gon' lock it down? Peach, if he on that bullshit, I got a brother that like crazy chicks like you."

"Get fuck'd up, Bell. Folks, you gon' get yo brother hurt. She's good." Blaze replied for me.

Wasn't he just telling me earlier to bring a date? I couldn't help but find his reaction funny.

"I mean, if she wanna get with his brother that's on her. You don't have a say in that." Keisha spoke up. "Hey, Bell."

"Oh, shit! What's up Keisha? You sitting over there quiet. I ain't even see yo ass." Bell laughed before looking at the both of us. He shook his head.

Keisha waved her hands to get Bell's attention. "Which brotha you talkin' bout Wayne or Pint? She might like Pint."

Blaze head turned toward ol girl. "Keisha, shut the fuck up. Ain't nobody ask you shit. Bell, get the fuck from over here. Where yo bitch at? Go find her ass."

My brows rose as I looked at him like he was crazy. "You don't mind if I steal him for a minute, do you?" Not really caring for her reply. I grabbed his wrist ready to pull him to the dance floor to check him about his attitude.

"Where y'all about to go?" she asked him with a slight pout to her lips, making me roll my eyes.

"The birthday boy owes me a dance, so I'm about to collect on it," I replied.

"Bae, you gon' leave me here?" She whined.

This bitch was pissing me off. "You'll be good for a few minutes." That time I didn't give her a chance to reply back. I grabbed Blaze's wrist tighter, then pulled him away from her and onto the dance floor. Once we got in the mix of folks, I turned toward him.

"You wrong as fuck for that bullshit. Why yo ass being extra?" Blaze whispered in my ear once I was facing him.

Laughing, I started dancing. He had his nerve. "Me? You just snapped at her. Plus, I was just testing her." *Lie.* "And she failed. But she seems nice, though." I told him with a roll of my eyes. "You know that bitch bumped me on purpose. I was about to shoot that bitch." I joked.

Grabbing my waist, Blaze turned me around. He pulled my back to his front and slowly, his hands began to roam over my body. It didn't take him long to find the gun on my hip. Feeling it, he laughed in my ear.

"Damn, how I ain't notice that thang with this tight ass dress you got on?"

"Because you only noticed my girly parts." I spoke loud enough so he could hear me.

He placed his arm around my waist as his head went to my neck. A hum left his mouth. The action caused the pit of my stomach to tighten. Entwining our fingers, my hips began to roll against him as I pushed my body more into his.

Blaze's lips touched my neck, causing me to bite into my lower lip as my hand squeezed his.

"Blaze, you better stop. I'm sho' yo girlfriend is lookin' over here." I mumbled not sure if he could hear me or not.

Blaze moved our entwined fingers down to the hem of my dress. My hands grasp his tight. I knew what he was about to do, and I didn't want that to happen there. Even so, I really didn't want to stop him. My hand tightened into his as he bit into my neck harder while sucking at the skin.

My teeth sunk harder into my lower lip. "B, not here." It came out as a whisper over the blaring music, so I knew he couldn't hear me.

"Let me just play with her." He whispered into my ear.

Glancing at him over my shoulder, I couldn't stop the slight twitch of my lips at his seriousness. Realizing how close our face was, my eyes dropped to his lips, then back to those light brown orbs I loved so much.

Unlocking our hands, I laid his palm against my lower stomach before slowly moving it down my pelvis. With my hand pressed flat into his, I slid our hands into my boy-shorts, then pushed his middle finger through my slit. My eyes lazily closed for a second, loving the feel of his rough callous hand touching me.

"Come home with me." As soon as the words left my mouth, Blaze stopped playing with my clit and moved to my opening. My mouth parted as my chest heaved, shakily anticipating the invasion of his fingers.

My stomach tightened; my legs widened instinctively waiting for his move. My pussy contracted around the tips of his fingers while my tongue played with his lips. "I missed you, we missed you. You gon' take care of us?" Turning in his hold, I pushed both his index and middle fingers into my pussy while locking our lips together. Our tongue started their sexual dance as I grinded myself against his hand.

My free hand slowly moved to the crotch of his jeans. I undid the zipper, then slipped my hand inside, taking hold of his erect dick.

"This still mine?" Licking my lips, my lustful eyes peeked at him from underneath my thick lashes.

"It's yours." He kissed me again.

A wide smile came to my lips. "Then give it to me—"

"Is you drunk?" he suddenly asked.

The question caught me off guard. "No, I only had one drink and a shot of Hennessy. Are you drunk?" I questioned.

Blaze pulled his hand from my panties. "Kinda, you gon' take advantage of me?"

Laughing at his craziness, I stood on my tip toes, grabbing the nape of his neck, I kissed him. My tongue slid into his mouth as his hand slid down to my ass. Taking a handful of my booty, he squeezed it. I broke the kiss, then pressed my forehead against his chin as my eyes closed. I was enjoying being so intimately close to him again. Pulling back, my eyes locked with his.

"I missed you," I told him truthfully. After tonight, I honestly didn't think I could be without him. "I really do, we missed you." That time I was referring to Blake and myself. Spending another day without him wasn't going to get it for me.

"Does Peaches love Blaze?" He questioned with a playful smile. That carefree look was back in his eyes, one I haven't seen since the night of my graduation. "Because Blaze love Peaches." His arms held me tight as his head lowered.

"I love you too—" As soon as the words left my mouth, a loud shot rang out and Blaze's body jerked twice as more shot started going off. I grabbed the gun from my hip and handbag, I started shooting blindly as Blaze did the same. Grabbing his two twin Desert Eagles from his hip he let it rip.

Neither of us knew where the shots were coming from. My eyes were jumping in every direction, trying to find the source.

"Go!" He yelled, pushing me toward the back. Blaze short distraction to warn me to run, he didn't see the man with the .9mm pointing at him.

Grabbing the front of his shirt, I jerked him down as hard as I could. I started shooting toward the man. I kept shooting until the gun just clacked.

"Peaches, get the fuck out of here!" Blaze snapped, pushing me toward the back exit.

"No! Not without you. Now, come on!" Grabbing one of his guns, I pulled him up.

Blaze pushed me in front of him as we made a quick dash to the door. Once outside, I started looking around to make sure no one was out there. The constant screams from bystanders and party goers were so loud in the mid-morning air as everyone tried to get out safely and away from the flying bullets.

"Ah shit!" Blaze cursed.

My eyes snapped to him as he leaned against the building. I checked the area once again to make sure everything was clear, and no one was behind us. Not seeing anyone I turned back to him.

"I parked across the street. Come on before the police show up."

Blaze fell into the dumpster and I quickly ran to his side.

"Shit!" I could see he'd been shot through his right shoulder. "Come on, babe. We can call King on the way to the house." I tried not to freak out.

"Just go get the fuckin' car." He pushed me away from him.

I fell to the ground hard. "Blaze, I'm not leaving you! Now come on." He could yell, fuss and cuss at me all he wanted, but I wasn't leaving him out there by himself. Standing up, I pulled at his left hand trying to get him to stand up.

"Ah shit!" He cursed again, grabbing his leg. Once I got him up, the back doors of the club came flying open. My eyes locked with a tall, lanky, dark

102

skinned man before they drifted to the barrel of his gun.

My mind didn't process what was happening as my body hit the ground hard, causing the gun to fall from my grip.

Chapter 8

Peaches

B laze's body knocked into mine before he fell on top of me, knocking the air from my lungs. He covered my body with his as both Blaze and the man started shooting at one another.

I couldn't see a thing. All I could do was hear the thundering sound of their gun fire. It wasn't long after that more shots followed from another direction.

"Peaches!" I heard King call after the last shot went off. Relief quickly filled my body.

"Blaze, get up." I grunted, trying to push him off of me but he didn't move. His body felt heavier than it did before. "Blaze..." I shook his shoulders again, but I didn't get a response. "King!" I screamed for my brother as loudly as I could.

"Oh shit!" King cussed as he rushed over to us. "Bell, help me get him up!" He frantically demanded. Once they got him off of me, King pulled me to my feet. "Peach, you straight?"

Snatching away from him, I went to Blaze's side only to see his eyes closed. I pulled his shirt up, there were two holes in his chest. I broke down. "Blaze, get up!" I cried, trying to pull him up. "Come on, baby. Get up! We're going to get you to a hospital." I pulled his head into my chest as my tears ran rapidly down my cheeks.

"Peach, we can't stay here. Baby girl, I need you to go get your car and come get us." King instructed as he pulled at my arms. "Bell, call the twins and tell them to meet us at the house on fo-9."

I couldn't leave him. I didn't want too. I felt if I did, something worse was going to happen. "Blaze, come on—"

"Peaches, go get the fuckin' car!" King snapped at me as he yanked me up.

My vision went blurry and my chest shook violently. I couldn't leave him. "Not without Blaze."

"Baby girl, I need you to get it together. I need you, Peach, now go get your ride." He turned me away from Blaze and gave me a push.

With a nod of my head, I took off on shaky legs toward my car. Hearing sirens in the background, my legs moved faster.

***

We pulled into one of King's low kept houses on 49th Avenue. The twins were already there. Once they saw my truck, they quickly rushed to the back doors where Blaze and King were.

He pushed the back doors opened and hopped out. After I threw the truck in park, I jumped out as well.

"Peaches, go opened the door." Catching King's keys midair, I hurriedly ran to the front door fumbling them in the door. "Peaches, open the fuckin' door!" King yelled at me.

I jumped hard and drop the keys on the ground. I quickly picked them up. I fumbled with them for a few seconds with shaky hands. "I'm trying!" Finally, I found the right key. The moment I stuck it in and turned the knob, I was pushed inside of the house.

"Put him on the table," King told them before his focus turned on me. "Peaches," he grabbed my arm and pulled me back outside of the house. "I need you to get yoself together, right now. I'm about to ask you to do me a favor."

I wasn't trying to hear shit he was saying. Blaze was in there stretched out on a damn table bleeding to death. "King, I can't leave him."

"He'll be good."

"King, you don't know that! He lost a lot of blood. I have to make sure he's okay." I tried to push around him so I could go inside of the house to see what they were doing to Blaze. I needed to make sure he was going to be okay.

My emotions were getting the best of me and no matter how many times I silently prayed or chanted in my mind that he was going to be okay, a part of me felt it was a lie.

"Ha'Keem, move! Damn, get the fuck out the way!" My voice shook with the last word as that lump grew thicker in my throat, causing a burning sensation. "King, I have to know that he's going to be okay. Just let me check on him. There was so much blood. Just let me make sure he's okay, please. Let me check on him." I constantly repeated as tears fell rapidly from my eyes.

King shook me hard. "Baby girl, I'mma need you to put yo fuckin' emotions away right now, i'ight? Lose those mothafuckin' tears. Ain't no time for crying." He shook my body harder as his firm, demanding voice barked at me.

The bass in his tone got my attention and I focused on him through blurry eyes.

"I need you to clean out that truck. Wipe that mothafucka down, inside and out. Then park it in the back of the shop and leave it. Peach, you gon' have to clean these burners for me. Strip them, then toss them in the sewers, i'ight? Can you do that for me?" He asked in a calm tone of voice.

Realizing I couldn't break right now, I nodded my head. "Yeah, yeah, I can do it."

King led me to the white truck he bought me five years ago as a graduation present. He opened the door and handed me a pair of gloves from his pocket while he pulled out his phone to make a call.

"Start taking everything out. I'll be right back." He turned away from me. "Yo, Ron, I need a favor." I heard him say before he disappeared into the house.

I didn't know why he was calling Jerron but at that moment, I could care less. The back of my hand rubbed at my eyes before I blindly started doing as I was told. All the while I tried to keep my mind off of Blaze.

***

"You good?" Bellow asked, getting out his truck and coming to me.

"As good as I'm going to be." I told him while tossing my keys to Sam. "Here, we'll meet you back at the house." My eyes felt swollen and I was worried sick thinking about Blaze. All I could do was pray that he was going to be alright.

"You straight?" Sam repeated Bellow's question.

As bad as I wanted to yell at them both and tell their dumb asses *hell no,* I kept my cool, even though I was anything but that. I was beyond pissed that somebody would start some bullshit like that at Blaze's party. Then the mothafucka had the nerve to shoot him. I was hurt and pissed the fuck off!

"I'll be better once I get back to see how he's doing." My tone was neutral, and I gave him a nonchalant shrug.

Sam didn't buy it. Instead, he pulled me into his chest holding me tight. It was at that moment I felt myself starting to crumble, but I couldn't let King down. "I'm good, Sam. Seriously, I am." I lied as I shook out of his hold.

"You know he gon' be good. He's too stubborn to die by somebody else's gun. So, don't stress yourself out too much worrying about him," Sam reassured me.

Giving him a small smile, I pulled back and then got in Bellow's truck.

"Peach, you know that dread head bastard is right. That man of yours is too gotdamn stubborn. Plus, he not gon' leave you and little man by y'all self." Bellow awkwardly patted my hand.

I simply nodded at his words, knowing he was right. Even so, it still didn't change the ache in my heart. I had to clear my mind; I needed a distraction.

In an attempt to keep Blaze off of my mind until I got to him, I turned the radio up and leaned back in my seat trying to get comfortable. But the constant images of his blood covered body kept invading my thoughts.

"Bell, do you have an extra shirt and a bag in here?" I asked while looking around trying to find something to wrap myself in so I could rid my body of my dress. "I need to get this off of me." I gestured toward my blood covered clothes.

"Look in the back seat, I have a shirt back there and Kim keeps a box of wipes under the seat." He reached in the back like he was trying to find something. A few seconds later, he handed me a shirt.

For some reason a smile came to my lips at the thought of them. *This was the distraction I needed.* "Y'all nasty ass. I'm not touching that backseat. I'm not about to sit on yo dried up nut or her juices. I knew it smelled funky in here."

Bell broke out laughing before muffing my head to the side. "Shut the fuck up. We clean the seats, *sometimes.* Shid, that be yo girl, though. A nigga ain't complaining. Real shit! I love that damn girl, man."

My smile kind of dimmed from the shine in his eyes as well as his smile. I could tell he meant it. "You really love Kim?" Kim was stupid if she didn't leave Mike alone and make things right with Bellow.

"What?" His brows rose as he stared at me dumbly like he hadn't expected the question.

My brows furrowed as I took him in. *Did he not realize what he just said?* "You said you love her." I repeated his words as he turned down Clark Road.

Bellow stared at me for a second before looking away and turning up the radio, ignoring me completely.

A heavy sigh left my mouth as the conversation died; the silence allowed my mind to wonder back to the shooting. Mentally I shook my head, trying to rid myself of those thoughts. However, once my eyes closed my mind quickly went to Blaze. He just had to be okay. I didn't know what we would do if he didn't make it through this.

I couldn't fathom what life would be like for myself or Blake without Blaze. My fingers wiped at my cheeks, brushing the tears away as I sniffled.

My body suddenly jerked forward as Bellow's truck swerved off to the side of the road and smacked into a tree. My forehead hit hard against the dashboard. A groan left my mouth as my head snapped back against the headrest. My vision blurred and my hand went to my aching head, as I felt blood run down from the side of my forehead to my eye.

"Peach, you good?" Bellow's voice seemed just above a whisper as I began fading in and out.

A groan left my mouth as my head laid back against the passenger side window.

"Come on, baby girl. You gotda stay awake for me. You hear me?" I felt him slap me on my cheek.

My eyes drifted from him to a red beam that soon appeared on the dashboard. Bellow was too busy focusing on me that he didn't see it. With the little strength I had, I quickly jerked him down to me. I pulled him to me just as his window shattered.

A scream tore from my throat as the bullet missed the back of Bellow's head and lodged into my shoulder. That was the first of many shots that started flying into the truck.

Last thing I remembered before everything went black was the hot bullet tearing into my flesh.

Chapter 9

Peaches

Two Weeks Later

I walked out of the hospital's bathroom from just taking a shower. I couldn't wait to get the hell out of there so I could see my baby and Blaze. I knew Blake was fine, but he was worried sick about me.

I looked down at my right shoulder to the patched up bullet wound before my eyes went to my side where a bullet grazed through my skin.

The shot to my shoulder had just missed the main artery but the bullet that had lodged inside of me was still close to a blood vessel. The doctors didn't want to risk the bullet moving and wanted to do an immediate surgery to remove it.

Now that everything was fine, and I was cleared by the doctor I was ready to get the hell out of there. I needed to see Blaze. I hadn't heard from him and no one was telling me anything, not even Bianca would let me know how he was.

I'd been in the dark for too long trapped in the hospital and I couldn't stop my mind from thinking the worse.

Blaze was dead.

That had to be the only reasonable explanation as to why they wouldn't tell me anything. A lump formed in my throat as I thought back to that day. Tears ran down my cheeks as flashes flickered through my mind of our moments together on his birthday.

He couldn't be dead. Blaze wouldn't leave us. We needed him.

Why wasn't anyone telling me how he was? My eyes burned and I thought about Blake. He couldn't be without his dad. *I* couldn't be without his dad.

My chest tightened and I fell against the wall. Tears fell rapidly from my eyes as the pain in my heart grew. I didn't know how we were going to get through this without him.

"Peaches pull yourself together, you can't break now. You have Blake to think of." I chastised myself. My tone was thick from the lump in my throat. Hearing my own words only made me cry harder. How was I going to be able to look at Blake without seeing Blaze?

I've called Blaze's cell so many times but never got an answer. That only confirmed my thoughts.

How could he leave us?

He promised he would always have me.

He can't be gone. He wouldn't leave us.

"Peaches," Jerron's deep voice echoed through the room.

I didn't even have the strength to move or reply. All I could do was cry.

"Peaches, what's wrong?" He picked me up bridal style and carried me to the bed. "Hey," Jerron pushed the hair from my sweaty forehead and cupped the side of my face. "What's wrong?" His concerned filled eyes stared deeply into mine.

I sniffled, trying to calm myself down but I couldn't. I just couldn't shake the feeling of him being gone. "I—Blaze—I," a loud sob tore from my throat and I cried, that was all I could do.

Jerron's lips touched my forehead before he pulled my head against his chest, allowing me to cry.

"Peaches, it's gon' be okay. I promise you. Let's get you out of here and it'll be good."

How was me getting out of here going to be good? Regardless if I was confined to a hospital bed or out on the streets it wouldn't change a damn thing. I just wished I would've planned our trip to Great America on his birthday where he would've been safe with us.

"Come on let's go." He helped me into my clothes.

Once I was dressed and signed the discharge papers, we left the hospital. We had been driving for a half hour and the ride had been silent the entire time. My mind couldn't stray away from thoughts of Blaze. My heart was heavy, and my head pounded painful from my crying. Sniffling, I wiped the lone tear that escaped my eye, then another.

Jerron's hand grasped my knee and gave it a slight squeeze. I glanced at him with a neutral look. I couldn't give a pretend smile, even though I was truly grateful for him being here with me. He just wasn't who I wanted to be around at that moment. I wanted Blaze. I needed him.

My eyes burned, my lips trembled, and my chest shook violently. I couldn't hold in the sob as I once again broke. The flood gates to my tears opened.

He couldn't be gone, he wasn't dead. Not after everything we've been through. He just couldn't be.

Jerron brought the car to a stop on the side of the road. He reached over the seat and tried to hug me, but I hissed out in pain as he leaned against my shoulder.

"I'm sorry. Peaches, everything's going to be alright, okay."

Him repeating that pissed me the fuck off and I snapped. "How is everything going to be okay when Blaze isn't here? Jerron, nothing is ever going to be okay again. Why couldn't I just take him away like we planned? God!" I cried. My feelings were so hurt.

"Ron, it wasn't supposed to be like this. We weren't supposed to end like this. I had just gotten him back and now he's gone. This can't be our end." I ranted as I cried hard. "Jerron, tell me he's okay, please. Just tell me you saw him and he's okay. Please tell me that." The pity that showed in his eyes clarified my painful thoughts were true.

I watched as his mouth opened then close followed by a sigh. "I promise everything is going to be okay."

Jerron saying that pissed me off. I moved his hand off of my knee and stared out the window. He let out a heavy sigh before he started back driving on the highway.

All I did over the past two weeks was cry and I was tired of crying.

I watched the trees for a long while before I closed my eyes and forced myself to sleep. I just couldn't stand the pain.

Chapter 10

Peaches

A Week Later

I sat on the front pew looking at the casket with blurry eyes as I cried hard. My body shook violently, and I clung to King's arm. It wasn't until I stared at the gold casket that I realized Blaze was everything to me. He was my first, my first love, my soulmate. Blaze was the father of my first child and even though it didn't survive, he gave me another in its place. I loved him with every fiber of my being.

But now he was gone. I could never tell him how much I truly loved and appreciated him.

Thoughts of his morning birthday. The breakfast we had as a family. Our time at mom B's house then at the club that night. I should've told him then, I tried to tell him. Now there will never be a later on where I could lay back on him and express myself.

I wasn't there when he took his final breath.

King held me tighter as I sobbed loudly. My chest heaved as I felt bile raise up into my throat. I hurriedly jumped up from my seat and ran out to the restroom. I burst through the door going straight to the toilet and emptying everything in my stomach until I began to dry heave. The veins in my forehead felt as though they were going to burst.

The feelings of him actually not being here was becoming too much to bear.

I couldn't do this.

"Peach, sweetie are you okay?" Kim came into the stall with me. She pushed my hair to the side of my face and began to rub my back soothingly. "Here, babe." She handed me a piece of tissue.

I wiped my mouth then sat up. After I flushed the toilet, Kim helped me out of the stall and over to the sink. "Kim, I can't do this." I told her after I rinsed my mouth out.

"I know, Peach, but babe you're going to be okay. I promise." She pulled me into a tight embrace.

I hugged her back and broke down crying harder.

"It's going to be okay, babe." She soothed as she sniffled. "You know we're here for you. I know it hurts right now, but it'll get better. I promise it will." She squeezed me one more time before she pulled out of the hug. "Come on, let's get you cleaned up." She grabbed some paper towels, wet them and then handed them to me.

I had just finished cleaning my face when the bathroom door opened.

"Shit, I thought I locked that damn door." Kim fussed as she turned toward the person.

From the change of her posture I knew it was something. I glanced over my shoulder and saw it was Tishana who had walked in.

"We'll be done in a minute. Can you give us a sec?" Kim rudely dismissed her.

I didn't know why but from the moment Kimmy met Tish, a few years back, she didn't like her. "Kim, it's cool. I'm finished." I dabbed my eyes once again and sniffled.

"I saw you run out and I was coming to check on you. Are you okay, sweetie?" Tish moved closer to me.

Kim stepped in front of me and tossed her towel paper in the trash before turning toward me. Without looking at Tishana, she responded to her. "No, she's not but she will be." Kim grabbed our purse then my hand. "Come on, babe." Kim said nothing else as she led us out the restroom.

With the way I was feeling at that moment, I couldn't bring myself to say anything smart to Kim about her behavior or apologize to Tish for it. That was something I would have to do later on.

Once we were back inside, I took my place beside King and Bianca and zoned out as grief consumed me.

***

We all were gathered at the cemetery. The pastor had just finished saying his prayer. Bianca, Brittany and Marcus were the first to walk up and drop their flowers down on top of the casket. Brittany was crying so hard, the pain in her sobs shook my soul. I just wanted to hold her and tell her everything would be okay, but I couldn't.

After the girls and I dropped our flowers, I needed to get away from everybody. Everyone's emotions was beginning to take its toll on me. Especially Brittany's constant screaming and crying for her brother.

She didn't want to leave him alone.

I couldn't stand there any longer. My heart and soul was weeping. I couldn't do this, I needed to get away from them. I needed to see him so he could tell me everything was going to be okay.

"Hey, hey, aye!"

I heard from behind me. I didn't know the person was talking to me. I was going to ignore him until he grabbed my arm.

I pulled out of his hold and turned to face a tall brown skinned man dressed in a nice black suit. My eyes squinted as I stared at him. I didn't know why but he looked so familiar. I sniffled before taking my tissue and dabbing underneath my eyes.

"I'm sorry. Can I help you with something?" My voice was thick from my crying. I cleared my throat, as I tried to get myself under control.

"I'm sorry for your loss. I was trying to make sure you were alright. I saw you at the church, but I didn't have time to check on you." He explained.

I sniffled and wiped my eyes once more. "Thanks. And I'll be fine." I couldn't put my finger on it, but I just didn't know why he looked so familiar. Then again at that moment, I didn't care to know. I just wanted to get out of there.

"Sorry, I'm so rude. I didn't introduce myself. I'm Joseph." He stuck his hand out for me to shake.

I shook it slowly, still not recognizing the name. "I'm sorry, but am I supposed to know you?"

He gave a faint smile that didn't reach his light brown eyes. Staring into his eyes, Blaze immediately came to mind. My heart broke.

I had to get out of there.

"It was nice meeting you, but I have to go." I was about to haul ass out of there and go home. But the man's next words stopped me.

"I guess I shouldn't be surprised he never talked about me. I wasn't the best father a person could ask for. I'm Joseph Carter, Blaze's father."

My mouth opened and closed before my eyes squinted. I literally didn't know what to say. He was right. Blaze had never mentioned him, so I was under the impression the man was dead.

"Can we go somewhere and talk?" He asked.

My eyes glanced over to the grave where Bianca, Brittany, Marcus and everyone else still stood.

Did he not want to say his final goodbyes to his son?

"I'm sorry for your loss. You don't want to go up there? I'm sure it'll be fine." I guessed.

"I'll wait. I don't want to start a scene and knowing my ex she'll do just that. She damn near kicked me out the church, so I'll wait. I'm just trying to pass time." He looked like a heartbroken man who was on the verge of tears.

My eyes welled up again because I knew his pain. "Yeah, we can talk."

I started walking toward the parked cars but shortly came to a halt.

"What's the matter?" Joseph asked.

"I forgot I didn't drive here. I rode in the limo with the family." I embarrassedly admitted, given I was just about to leave but with no way.

"That's fine you can ride with me," he offered.

Again, I looked back to the grave site. With everything going on, walking off should be the last thing I did. "I'm sorry. I don't think this is a good time. Maybe—"

"I understand you don't know me." He gave a faint smile, which didn't reach his eyes. He began to walk off but stopped and looked at me. "I wasn't the best dad to him. I was hooked on drugs bad. The pipe and needle was my best friend for twenty-five years. When I got clean and didn't relapse, I tried reaching out to my son. These past five years I've tried through his momma, his friends, everybody. But he didn't want to see me. The night of his birthday, I went to the club to see him and he threw me out." His eyes turned red as tears filled them.

"He told me he had no problem with me, but he didn't fuck with me so he didn't want to see me and that I should move the fuck on. And now," tears ran from his eyes. "I saw you with him a few times. I just wanted to know how he was and you're the only person that could tell me that."

My heart ached for him. He wasn't able to make amends with Blaze, and I could only imagine his pain. Although Bianca's dislike for him was understandable it truly didn't help his situation.

"I'll ride with you." I told him as I quickly texted King, letting him know I needed to get away. I told him I had a ride and he didn't need to worry about me.

"Thank you." He led me to a beautiful 1962 pearl colored Lincoln. He opened my door for me then went to his side and got in. He looked at me. "Thanks again. Are you hungry?"

"I can eat." I really wasn't hungry; food was the last thing on my mind. I truly just wanted to go home and pretend today didn't happen.

***

"Blaze was about five at the time and I was in the streets heavy. I started dabbing in powder, you know. One night, I came home high and I carelessly sat my pistol on the side table in the living room. I had passed out. It seemed like I had just closed my eyes when I heard a loud *POW* go off." His head shook.

"That was the scariest moment in my life. Blaze's little badass had grabbed my damn gun and shot it. I was sure I had been hit. I jumped up checking myself and him, but he shot through the wall. The bullet had missed his momma by a few inches. We both got our ass beat that day. Bianca's ass didn't play." He told the story with glazed over eyes as if he was there in that moment.

I couldn't help but laugh because I could see Bianca trying to whoop a grown ass man. "I'm sorry but I don't blame her. You needed your ass beat for that. Both of y'all needed it but you more so then him."

"I admit I was careless. And yeah, Bianca went crazy on our asses. But that taught Blaze something because he never touched my guns again. If he saw one of my guns, he was telling. We were good up until I fell off." He cleared his throat, then took a sip of his drink. "You knew him personally something I never got the chance to do. How was he?"

I didn't know how to answer because Blaze was a dick. *But should I tell his father that?*

"Be honest with me. As a man, how was he?" Joseph asked.

"Blaze was a great protector and provider when I allowed him to be. He had his issues, of course, but that didn't change anything. I loved him with everything in me. Blaze wasn't an expressive person. So, it was hard in the beginning. Even so, I can honestly say he felt the same way about me." My eyes began to water as I thought about everything Blaze and I been through.

"I feel so cheated, you know. The night that every-thing happened I was in the middle of telling him that I wanted him to come home…" I wiped my eyes with the pad of my thumb and sniffled. "I'm sorry." I apologized for getting emotional.

"No, you're fine. Believe me I know how you feel. I just wish he could've told me he forgave me for everything I put him, his sister and mother through. His forgiveness was all I needed. We were bonded at one point in time and I wanted that back. He was my boy, my first born, my only son. And to lose him this way—" he shook his head and his own tears began to flow swiftly down his cheeks. "I needed to know he didn't hate me. I wish I had the chance to apologize, let him know I was sorry."

I reached across the table and took ahold of his hand and gave it a slight squeeze. "I know this may not mean the same coming from me, but I can tell you he didn't hate you—"

"How would you know when he never spoke about me?" he questioned.

"Because that's not Blaze. He would never hold onto anything painful. For him to hate you would give you some form of control over him. He won't allow that at all. I don't know what he does exactly, but he lets it go. Blaze is harsh as hell, he doesn't know how to be expressive, or sensitive. So if he told you he had no problems with you, that was the truth." I explained to him.

"Blaze, saying he doesn't fuck with you is his way of saying he doesn't trust you. If he don't then he truly wouldn't deal with you because he wouldn't know what to expect from you. You know, he never talked about his childhood with me. His mother did. Blaze is the definition of harsh literally." I shook my head remembering all the harsh stuff Blaze had spat at me in the past.

The sudden added pressure to my hand caused me to glance down at Joseph hand holding mine. I forgot I covered his hand in a form of comfort.

"But you loved him?" He looked up at me. His light brown eyes bored into mine.

The way he looked at me had my brows slightly raising. The look was so familiar. It was one Blaze used on me numerous times before. I looked down at our jointed hands and pulled mine from his. Joseph's stare made me feel uncomfortable. Regardless of my feelings, I didn't show my discomfort. I gave him a smile and shook my head.

"Yeah, it's crazy, I know, but I love him and he loved me." I explained, thinking about the playful times Blaze and I had.

"I wish I could have known that side of him. How did y'all meet?"

I laughed at the question before I jumped into the story of how Blaze and I met.

***

By the time I was done with the story we had finished our food and Joseph was looking at me like I was crazy.

"I'm still stuck on the part where you locked the both of you in your room. Was you not scared that he would hurt you?" The disbelief in his voice made me laugh.

"A part of me was terrified but I would never show it. Blaze was tall and big naturally but when he got pissed, he seemed somewhat bigger. I'm talking about The Hulk big—"

"But that didn't stop you." He stated factually.

Again, I laughed. "No, B was so used to everyone being scared of him and getting his way that he kinda expected it from everyone including me. But I grew up around the hood. You know, so I was somewhat used to his type. Plus, my mother and father didn't raise no push over. I was far from a punk, so scared or not I always stood my ground." I laughed before I shrugged.

"Our relationship wasn't perfect." I shrugged. "It wasn't terrible either, though. We had our moments. We both had a lot of growing to do. With Blaze, I actually think I brought the best out of him and that was something he didn't expect. Blaze could never look outside of a hood mentality. I kinda think he thought that's where he belonged, so he never looked outside of that. I think I kind of made him see that there was more to life in a way, so he pushed me away. Blaze was an asshole. But I understood him so we kind of worked."

"Given his upbringing, I understand that. It's hard out here and coming from those projects it's harder to see anything outside of that." He tried to justify his son's actions.

I shook my head at that because he was wrong. "But he did. Blaze went to college twice and has gotten his bachelor's degrees. If he truly wanted to see past all of this, if he wanted it bad enough, Blaze would've changed his whole prospective on life." That was how I truly felt about it. Blaze's problem was that he was afraid of change because he had adapted so well to the hood environment.

A thoughtful look came over his face. "My son went to college. That's true?"

"Yeah, he did." I smiled at him as a small laugh left my mouth. I still didn't understand how Blaze had managed to go through college twice when he really didn't like people.

Joseph let out a sigh and a sad look covered his face. "Are you ready to go?"

I nodded my head, and he waved the waiter over. He requested the bill. Once the bill came, he rejected my money, but I insisted I pay for my meal. He ignored my request and he paid for us both. Once he did, we left the restaurant.

Chapter 11

Peaches

"I wish I had a moment to tell him I'm sorry. Just a second to talk to him again. My boy." Joseph cried as we stood at Blaze's grave. He had fallen to his knees as he sobbed hard.

I felt so bad for him that my heart cried with his. I wished I could tell him, but I couldn't. The way he was bawling I wish he had those moments with Blaze.

I didn't know how to comfort him any further. What other words could I say? I had no idea, so I kept my mouth shut and kneeled down beside him. My arms wrapped around his shoulders in a consoling embrace as I cried with him.

I felt so bad because I knew I'd be at peace with today, but he never would, thinking his son was forever gone.

As I thought that my mind went back two weeks ago to the moment I was now regretting as I held his grieving father.

Two Weeks Earlier

I woke up with a painful groan from the agonizing ache to my shoulder. I rolled on my back and looked up at the ceiling, watching the fan spin until my eyes slowly started to drift back shut. The realization that I had been staring at a fan in a bedroom instead of trees out of a window caused me to sit up straight. My fingers rubbed at my eyes, wiping the sleep away before I looked around the dimly lit room.

It was a decent sized room. A few dressers and a TV decorated the tan colored room. There was nothing at all noticeable in there, so I still had no clue as to where I was. Even so, I didn't feel the need to panic. If Jerron brought me there, I had nothing to worry about.

With a yawn I got out of bed and lazily walked to the door. I left out of the room and stood in the unfamiliar hall. There were two other doors on the floor as well as two different openings in the hallway. I looked from one side to the other, trying to figure out which way to go.

"Jerron!" I finally called out to him. I didn't know how long I had been asleep, but I felt so

drained. All I wanted to do was go back to bed. "Jerron!"

The last door down on the right soon opened and I groaned as one of the twins looked out.

"I can't believe him." I mumbled to myself before I rubbed my forehead. "Khalil? Khyree?" I couldn't tell which one it was. "I don't know why King has you here but I'm fine—"

"I'm Khyree and it's good to know that you're fine. But we're not here for you. Your friend should be downstairs." He pointed in the direction to my left. The closest end to where I stood. With that, his head retracted back into the room and he closed the door.

My brow furrowed. If he wasn't here for me, why the hell was he here? I honestly couldn't find it in me to care either. Hell, knowing King it could be anything. I shrugged it off and headed down the hall to a set of stairs.

I ended up in the living room. Jerron sat on the couch watching basketball. I walked over to where he was and sat beside him. Doing so, got his attention and he sat up straight.

"Hey, how you feeling?" He asked as his hand rubbed the back of mine.

My shoulder moved up then down before my head laid on the back of the couch. I didn't know how to answer his question at that moment. I was feeling numb.

"Peaches, about Blaze—" he started to say.

My head shook and my hand waved, cutting him off. "I don't wanna talk about what happened. I understand—"

"No, you don't understand. Peaches, it's not what you think—"

"Jerron, I don't wanna talk about it, okay, please." My voice cracked as the lump quickly formed in my throat. My eyes began to water as my lips started to quiver. I was trying hard to hold back the tears, but I was failing miserably. My eyes rolled up and focused on the ceiling. I cleared my throat before I looked back at him. I tried to give a faint smile but I'm sure it didn't reach my eyes.

"I never did thank you for that night. If it wasn't for you, I probably wouldn't be here either." He opened his mouth to interrupt me, but I held up my hand, stopping him. "Let me finish. Thank you so much for always being here for me. I don't know what else to say or do to show you just how grateful I am to have you in my life." Tears ran down my cheeks as I thanked him.

If it wasn't for Jerron showing up on time the night someone shot up Bellow's truck, both he and I would've died that night.

King didn't really feel comfortable about sending me off to do anything. But since Bellow hung back at the club in hopes of overhearing someone talk about who started the shooting. And with Sam being unreachable until the very last minute, he had no one else so he asked me. He also called Jerron telling him what went down and asked him to follow me until I met up with Bellow.

Jerron did as he was asked. Even when I got with Bellow, he continued to trail us until he got cut off by a stop light. But apparently that didn't hold him too long because whoever hit our trunk didn't do too much damage, thanks to Jerron's interference.

They managed to shoot Bellow twice on his left side, but it could've been a lot worse had Jerron never caught up to us.

Blake popped in my mind; he had already lost his dad. I needed to see my baby. I hadn't seen him since Blaze's birthday. While I was in the hospital, all I could do was talk to him on the phone or video chat with him, which wasn't the same. I needed to see my son. I needed to hold him and see how he was doing.

"Peaches," Jerron's fingers snapped in my face, pulling me from my thoughts.

I blinked a few times before I glanced down at his hand that covered mine. I turned my hand up and entwine our fingers together. If it wasn't for him, I wouldn't be here for my baby. "Thanks so much." I kissed his cheek, then hugged him.

Jerron returned my hug as a heavy sigh left his mouth. "Peach—"

The front door opened, grabbing my attention and cut Ron off. He let out an irritable groan which I ignored. I pulled back away from him and looked at the entrance to see King and Bellow walking through the door. I stood up from the couch and made my way to my brother.

King hugged me then kissed my forehead. "How you feeling?"

I shrugged, "Giving everything, I don't know. Hey, Bell, I'm glad to see you're good." I gave him a faint smile as I let my eyes drift to his side.

"You know ain't no bullets gon' get me down." He joked while he hugged me. "How my man doing?"

I looked back at Jerron and shrugged. "I mean, I guess he's good." I didn't understand why he was asking me about Jerron when it was clear he was fine. Bellow was weird anyway, so I brushed him off.

My main concern was my baby, Blake. I needed to see him. Taking ahold of King's arm, I pulled him to the side. I didn't want Jerron overhearing my conversation about Blake. Even though Jerron and I kept in touch when I moved to Lafayette, he still didn't know about Blake. Blaze didn't want him to know, so I kept it from him.

I pulled King into the dining room. "How's Blake doing? Is he okay?"

"Yeah he's at Mom B's crib. I told him we'll be down to get him next weekend but right now I need to keep the two of you low until we can figure this shit out. And with B not up and running like usual, my nigga can't handle shit so I need him here until he can move on his own." King explained.

My brows furrowed at what he just said replayed in my head. Blaze was here? "Wait, wait Blaze? What?"

With no one willing to tell me anything about him, I had assumed he was dead. Every time I brought him up everyone would beat around the bush and wouldn't tell me anything. King, Bianca, Bellow hell even Jerron wouldn't even speak his name.

King's head tilted as he looked at me. "Ron ain't tell you?" The tone of his voice wasn't a questioning one instead it sounded more factual.

My head shook. "Didn't tell me what? King, talk to me. Is Blaze alive?"

King's head snapped toward me so fast. "Who the fuck said he was dead?"

"King, don't fuckin' play with me. Blaze isn't dead?" My tone sounded harsher than I intended it to be.

Khyree being in the room popped in my head and I quickly pushed King out of my way and ran to the stairs. My side hurt like hell as I took the steps by two, but I paid the pain no mind. I came to the last room in the hallway.

I pushed the door opened and Khyree jumped up from his chair. I paid him no attention as my focus shifted to the bed. My body froze, I couldn't move. I couldn't believe I was actually looking at him. I thought I had lost him.

"Yo ass gon' stand there looking stupid or you gon' come over here." Blaze licked his lips as he gave me a crooked smile.

I shot to the bed so fast to him. I didn't think about his wounds nor mine. I just lunged myself on top of him with my arms wrapped tight around his neck.

"Ah! Fuck, Peach! Damn!" Blaze groaned out.

His grunts didn't bother me any. I still pressed my lips to his and once again as if a faucet was turned on, tears fell from my eyes. I couldn't stop them even if I tried nor could my lips stay off of him.

"Baby girl, you hurting me. What's good, Peach? What's up? Why you crying?" He spoke between my constant kisses. With a grunt leaving his mouth, his hand gripped the back of my head, tilting it backwards. "What's up?" His face contorted into a look of confusion.

I didn't want to talk, all I wanted to do was hold him. I leaned into him again and kissed him.

Just like before he kissed me back, but he didn't get into it. Blaze pulled his head back. "Peaches."

How could he even ask me what was wrong? "I thought you were dead, I didn't know—"

"Hold the fuck up. Who told you I was dead?" His eyes tore away from mine and focused behind me. A mean scowl covered his face. "Who the fuck told her I was dead?" He snapped at everyone that was in the room.

"They wouldn't tell me anything. For two weeks, I asked how you were. Where you were. And everybody just seemed so depressed. They wouldn't talk about you. I didn't know what to think. Everybody just told me it'll be good. But I didn't know." A laugh suddenly left my mouth as more tears poured from my eyes. "I'm so glad you're okay. I didn't know what I was going to do without you here. Now I don't even want to think about it. I love you so much."

My lips were back on him as my arms held him tightly around his neck. I bit into his bottom lip then sucked on the top. My mouth parted, allowing his tongue to slid through the slit of my lips and tangle with mine.

A moan left my throat as the kiss grew intense. I tried hard to merge our bodies as one. I needed to be close to him, feel him. I had to know this was real instead of a dream.

136

Blaze's head pulled back as a painful groan left his mouth. "Ah fuck! Peach, baby, you killing me."

"Yeah, Peaches, his body ain't healed. You probably done busted his stitches." Khyree came and stood next to us. He gave me a look that told me to move.

I glared hard at him before I got up and pushed him back. "Yo ass could've told me he was in here when I saw you in the damn hallway. You get on my damn nerves." I snapped at him before looking at the others in the room. I opened my mouth to yell at them but Khyree started talking.

"I didn't do nothing to you. Hell, I didn't know you thought he had died. You were calling him," he pointed to Jerron. "So how the hell was I supposed to know?" He questioned.

He just had to get smart, but he was right, no less. So, I turned my attention to the other two idiots who knew. "King, every day I asked you about him and you told me nothing. You didn't even give me so much of a fuckin' hint that he was alright—"

"Bae, calm down." Blaze told me.

I was anything but calm. I couldn't calm down. My chest raised and fell hard from my erratic breathing. Did they not know what I went through those past two weeks? How much my body, heart and soul hurt with thoughts of thinking he was dead?

I was pissed the fuck off but happy at the same time.

"No! For two weeks I've cried. Not knowing how we were going to get through this with you being gone, only to find out you're still here and these assholes knew! And you want me to calm down? How the hell am I supposed to,

Blaze?" I yelled at him. I wanted to hurt both King and Jerron. "You two fuckas knew and didn't tell me shit!"

"Peaches, we couldn't talk at the hospital or on the phone." King explained as he walked to me. "I ain't wanna hurt you and I hated to see you tore up like that. Peach, if you had of known you wouldn't have been able to fake those emotions. Right now, it's best if people think he's dead. The shit that's going on is wild." He explained to me.

"We don't know shit about the shooting, which is crazy because we have hella eyes and ears around, but nobody can tell us nothing. So, I moved B out to the City to lay low for a minute. Sooner or later somebody gon' slip and I'mma catch that shit. Until then, Blaze being alive have to be quiet. I'm sorry, Peaches, but I couldn't risk it." King seemed frustrated as he spoke.

After hearing his explanation, I understood his reason.

"Regardless, someone could've gave me a hint." I looked at Jerron.

He raised his hands before pointing at me. "I tried to tell you downstairs, but you wouldn't stop talking. You kept cutting me off. I didn't tell you in the hospital because the night you got your surgery, we caught someone leaving out your room. We found three bugs. We didn't remove them because we needed folks to think your dude was dead and with your reaction it helped."

They both had great explanations as to why, but it didn't change anything. They could've written me a damn letter explaining everything. Not have me going weeks thinking my man was dead. Sighing, I shook my head before I made my way back over to Blaze.

My adrenaline slowly started to fade once my body calmed down. Once it did the pain in my shoulder and side became noticeable.

"Peach, you're bleeding." Jerron stopped me from walking past him.

I jerked away from him. I understood his position and the decision that had to be made. Regardless of that, a part of me still felt as though they could've found a way to secretly tell me Blaze was still alive. The pain of thinking he was gone was one I never wanted to feel again.

I looked down at my shirt and saw the small spot of blood. I pulled my shirt down and looked at the wound. I had busted a stitch. It was nothing serious in my eyes. All I wanted to do was layup with Blaze and just talk to him. What about? That didn't matter as long as he was talking.

After Khyree finished with Blaze, I asked them all to leave us alone. King wanted to talk about what was going on, but I felt as though it could wait. He already made it clear they didn't know anything, so I didn't see the point in wanting to discuss the situation.

Blaze must have felt the same way because he told them to leave. Once everyone left, my insides became jittery.

"So, you was worried about a nigga, huh? Did you cry hard?" His face was straight for all of a second before he started laughing.

My eyes rolled up in my head as I laid against the headboard next to him. "B, that's not funny. My damn soul was hurt. I still feel like crying." I confessed.

Blaze licked his lips as his head nodded. His demeanor broke and he started laughing again.

If I wasn't afraid of hurting him, I would've punched his childish ass. I didn't see how he saw my pain funny. "Blaze, you're a fuckin' dick. That ain't even funny, like seriously."

"I'm sorry, Peaches, but you dumb as hell."

I hit him on the arm. "How the hell am I dumb?" I was beyond confused.

"Ah, Peach. Damn, man, chill the fuck out." He fussed but ended up laughing.

My brow raised at him. He stared back mimicking my look. All I could do was laugh. "You so stupid." I leaned over and pressed my lips to his. I just couldn't imagine him not being here with us. A sigh left my mouth and I pecked his lips once more. "I love you. Don't ever get shot again. We should go somewhere, anywhere. Me, you and Blake could just pack up and leave. No one would have to know where we are." My lips pressed against his again.

Deep down I hoped his mind was in the same place as mine and he wanted to leave everything behind. But from the way his lips barely moved I knew he wasn't thinking the same.

"You wanna run? That's what you want to do?" His head reared back as he stared at me.

"If that's what you want to call it, then yeah. B, it's never going to end unless you're dead or you stop hustling. What part of that don't you understand? It's been five years and they're still hung up on you. Bae, I don't think this has nothing to do with territory anymore. Maybe at one point in time, yeah, but not now. It's not going to stop." I explained to him.

Blaze wasn't looking at me and I knew whatever he was thinking his mind couldn't be changed.

"Baby, it's not that simple. I'm not running. Ain't nobody about to run me from my city. Fuck that! Its gon' stop once they're dead—"

"Or you're dead. Blaze, how many second chances are we going to get before they run out? Why stay and fight a fight that doesn't need to be fought? If they want territory, give it to them! It's not like you need the money—"

"It's not about the fuckin' money, Peaches! I don't give a fuck about no gotdamn territory! None of that means shit to me. Baby, this ain't never going to end whether we run or not and I'm not letting this bullshit go." He snapped pissed off.

"You don't fuck with me and mine then think I'm not gon' do shit. Peaches, they could've killed you. Do you not understand that? And you want me to run? Hell nah, man, fuck that. Baby, I'm only giving them what they want." Blaze grabbed my arms and tried to pull me closer to him.

I lightly pulled my arm from his grasp. I couldn't even look at him. After what went down, I wanted to take him, and Blake then get as far away as possible. A part of me knew he was right about one thing. It was never going to end until Blaze was dead.

"Peaches, don't be like that." Blaze let out a sigh.

The sound was heavier and longer than usual. I knew it was something else. I turned to look at him. "What now?" I was dreading his reply.

"I need you to do me a favor." He raised his arm, but he stopped with a grunt. "Shit!"

I bit the inside of my lip so I wouldn't say anything smart. He was so stupid sometimes maybe this pain was good for his dumbass. Hopefully, this would make him realize he wasn't invincible.

"You find something funny?"

"No, I just wish you'll let this go, but I guess you're not. B, what you want me to do?" My eyes rolled hard up into my head. I hated that I was giving in and was going to do whatever he asked of me.

"I need you to plan my funeral in a week." He stared into my eyes. I didn't find a trace of a lie. He was serious. "Peaches, I need you to pull off the best gotdamn service. Pick me out a nice ass casket. And that pain you felt these past two weeks, keep it. I need that exact reaction. Baby, everybody gotda think I'm dead. Blake will be here with me so don't worry about him. Peach, I promise once this is over, I'm done. But I gotda finish this." His head tilted as he stared at me trying to read me.

Again, I looked away from him.

"Peach—"

I moved closer to him and took his face into my hands. "Blaze, I'll do it only if you promise me I won't be planning a real funeral no time soon."

He shook his head. "I can't make that promise."

"Then no, I can't do it. If you can't look me in the eyes and promise me, I won't be planning one for you no time soon, then the answer is no. I can't do it." I couldn't pretend if he couldn't sincerely make me that promise. I wasn't about to practice for his death. Hell No!

Blaze took ahold of my face and pulled it closer to his. "I'm not going anywhere no time soon. Peaches, you're not losing me, I promise," he spoke so sincerely.

I believed him. "I'll do it. Blaze, I swear if anything happens to you—"

"Peaches, it won't. Nothing is going to happen to me. You and Lil B is reason enough for me to push through anything. I'm not leaving y'all. You hear me?"

I nodded my head. "I love you."

Blaze kissed me. "I love you, too, i'ight? Now I want you to go out and get me a nice ass casket, then plan the best gotdamn funeral you can. Will you do that for me?"

"Yeah, I will."

Chapter 12

Peaches

Present Time

The ringing of my phone pulled me from my thoughts. I pulled away from Joseph and stood up. I wiped my eyes, then brushed off my knees before I grabbed my phone out of my handbag.

King's name flashed across the screen before it stopped ringing. A few minutes later a text came through. King sent me a text asking if I was good. I quickly shot him one back. I told him I was and that I'd be at my hotel soon.

Since I no longer lived in Gary, which was where the funeral was held. I've been staying at the Radisson Hotel for the past week.

"Is everything okay?" Joseph asked.

I put my phone away and focused back on him. "Yeah, just my friends checking on me. How are you?"

He dropped his flower into the open grave and nodded his head. "I'll be okay. I have no choice. Thanks for being a listening ear." He held his arm out for me.

I gave him a polite smile and linked my arm through his.

"I can see what my son saw in you. And why he was having a fight within himself. I sincerely think you were great for him and I'm thankful he had you." He spoke kindly.

A smile came to my face and my cheeks heated. "Thank you. He was the same for me." Blaze was really my everything and I was his.

"Come on, let me get you home before someone starts a search party." He let out a faint laugh.

I ignored my ringing phone and let him lead me to the car. Once we both were inside, he pulled out of the cemetery. I told him where I was staying, and he drove me to my hotel. The ride there was silent.

***

He pulled to the front door and I got out. "Thanks for the ride and it was really nice meeting you. Though I wish it was on better terms that we met."

"The same here. Wait, before you go can I ask you a serious question?" He turned in his seat to face me.

"Yeah sure."

"Why did Bianca wait two whole weeks to bury my son?" he asked.

"Because I was in the hospital and she didn't want to bury him without me being there. Plus, she couldn't plan it alone and with the state Brittany was in, she couldn't handle it. So, Bianca waited for me." I explained.

"Why was the casket closed?" He asked.

My brows raised at his question, but I guessed it wasn't an odd one. "Bianca didn't want anyone to see him like that. We don't know exactly what they did to him, but it just didn't look like Blaze. His face looked a dark purple. I couldn't have that be the very last image folks saw of him. So, we decided to have it closed plus it was best for Brittany." I shook my head as if I was remembering a bad image.

"I understand that. Here, I would really appreciate it if you kept in touch." He wrote his number on a piece of paper and handed it to me.

"I will. I'll talk to you later." I closed his door, waved at him then made my way into the hotel. I went straight to the elevator and rode it up to the third floor.

Once I made it to my room, I overheard King talking.

146

"She's good, B. Damn...Bell been following her... I don't know who ol' dude was... Obviously, she does... Hold on she just walked in the room." A look of relief covered King's face once he saw me. "Calm this nigga down." He pushed me the phone, then walked into the kitchen.

"Bellow was following me?" I asked no one in particular as I put the phone to my ear.

"Where the fuck have you been?" Blaze's demanding voice boomed through the line.

I pulled the phone from my ear to look at it.

"Peaches!" He yelled again.

"Blaze, why are you yelling? Bae, I'm about to FaceTime you." I pushed the video button only to be met by his scowling face. A few seconds later my baby's face appeared next to his dad's.

"Hey, Momma. What's up?" Blake asked with a cheeky smile.

"Nothing, baby, just getting in. What have you been doing? You haven't been working your dad's nerves, have you?" I sat on the bed, then pulled off my heels, tossing them to the floor.

Blake took the phone and moved away from Blaze. "No, I haven't. He been working mine, though. Telling me everything to do. When are you coming here?" Blake didn't hide the fact he wasn't having fun.

"I'll be there sometime in the morning. Rashad be nice to him. You know he's not feeling good and he really needs your help. Remember when you were sick, and I wasn't there. Your dad took care of you so it's your turn to look after him." I glared at him through the screen.

147

"I know but, Ma, he worrisome as hell." He started to go off.

I cut him short. "Blake, you better watch your mouth. You don't think you work my dang on nerves? Now you know how it feels. Give your dad the phone and go play your game or something. I love you, baby."

He let out a heavy groan before doing as he was asked. Once Blaze's face appeared on the screen, I couldn't contain my smile.

"Hey, baby. How you feeling?" I asked him.

"Where the fuck have you been, Peaches? Yo ass know the bullshit that's going on. Yo black ass just up and left my funeral with some random motha-fucka without nobody knowing shit. Peach, what the fuck is wrong with you?" He snapped at me.

I couldn't blame him or snap back at him. I was wrong, I knew it wasn't right, but because I felt so bad for Joseph I didn't really think.

"Bae, you right I shouldn't have left. But I seriously wasn't thinking. Are you alone?" I asked him while going to lock the room door. I powered on the TV turning the volume up then went into the bathroom to make sure I wouldn't be overheard.

"Yeah, I am, Peach. Where were you?" he asked again.

"Joseph came to the funeral—"

"Wait, Joseph? My dad?" His brows rose.

"Yeah, your dad came. B, he was just so sad I didn't feel right leaving him alone like that. So, when he asked me could I talk, I went with him—"

"Peach, what the fuck was you thinking going anywhere with that nigga? Do you know him?" He snapped at me.

"No, but—"

"Fuck a *but,* Peaches. What you thought because that nigga told you he my dad and shed a few tears you can trust that bitch ass mothafucka? Peaches, is you stupid?" He yelled at me.

My mouth opened then closed. Not once did I think he'd be that pissed about me comforting his father. "No, I'm not stupid and don't fuckin' yell at me. You have no idea what I've been through today. So, yes, I fell for a few gotdamn tears! Yes, B, I thought just that. You didn't see him! How tore up he was knowing he couldn't make up for leaving you." I explained to him as I felt myself getting emotional.

"You didn't look into his devastated eyes as he cried. I did! You didn't have to look at none of these people as they sobbed over you. All day, I had to think about how life was going to be without you just like everyone else! So, yes, I became vulnerable to him. I felt bad." My fingers quickly wiped the angry tears again so he wouldn't see me cry.

Blaze let out a breath before rubbing his head. "Peach, don't cry. I ain't think about how hard this could've been on you. But, baby girl, you can't go running off with anybody that shed tears and give you some sob ass story. Maybe he was sincere about everything he said to you. I don't know that, though, and I'm damn sho' not gon' chance yo life to find out. I don't trust that nigga. Peaches, I want you to stay away from him. If you see that mothafucka, go the other way. I'ight?"

It seemed like déjà vu with him warning me to stay away from someone. Unlike last time, I was going to do as told and if I came across Joseph again I was going to haul ass the other way.

"Okay, if I see him, I'll go the other way. I won't say anything to him. I promise."

"Peach, I'm serious, man." He warned in a stern tone.

"I know and so am I." I propped the phone against the bathroom mirror then grabbed a hair tie from my makeup bag. I tilted my head to the side closer to my bent arm to keep myself from raising my arm. I messily put the tie in my hair then proceeded to take off my dress.

"Mmm." Blaze hummed, getting my attention. "Pack up and come back tonight." Blaze told me.

"Why?" I unhooked my bra as I slowly asked.

"Because I wanna see you. Plus, I'mma worry all night about you," he said.

I wasn't even looking at him and knew he was only telling me half the truth. "Is that why you really want me to come home?" I glanced at the phone screen while I pulled off my panties.

"Yeah," he lied.

"Are you going to try and have sex with me?" I turned on the shower, changing it to a light spray.

"Mhm, you already know I am." A hum left his mouth, followed by a grunt as he pushed himself up against the headboard.

"Bae, you shouldn't be moving around." Even though I said that I couldn't contain my smile. "Were you cleared to have sex?" I leaned on the counter, making sure he had clear view of my breasts.

Blaze tilted the phone as if doing so was going to give him a clearer glance at my naked body.

I was most definitely about to tease the hell out of him.

"B, what are you doing?" I bit the inside of my bottom lip in order to hide my smile.

"Peach, why the fuck you playing with me?" His face contorted into a glare.

Again, I had to contain my laughter as I pretended to be confused. "Bae, I'm not doing anything. Do you want me to call you back or are you going to shower with me?" I didn't wait for his response as I walked to the shower. I laid a towel on the floor before I stepped in under the warm spray.

I left the shower curtains opened and grabbed my sponge. I poured my lavender body wash on it, getting it soapy. Squeezing the sponge in the center of my breasts, I glanced up at him. I bit into my lip giving him a flirty smile.

"Peaches," Blaze called loudly.

I ignored him and continued to rub the sponge down the center of my chest before moving it over my left breast then to my right. Coming back up, I ran the sponge over my neck. I stepped under the spray, letting the water rinse off the soap.

Getting back in his view, I turned my back toward him and bent over more than needed as I spread my legs wide apart. I slowly moved up my legs, washing them both longer than necessary. I stood up and got under the shower head, rinsing the soap off of my legs. Once it was off, I rinsed the sponge and then added more soap. I leaned against the wall spreading my legs and began washing my inner thighs.

"B, you know this would be so much better if you were here doing this for me." My tongue swiped over my lips as I stared at him.

"That's why you should come home tonight." His head stayed tilted the entire time.

I rinsed myself, then turned off the water. I stepped onto the towel and wiped my feet. Sexily, I made my way to the propped up phone. "Or you could watch me." I told him as I walked back into the room.

"Yo ass think this shit funny, Peaches. It ain't." He glared at me through the phone.

"Babe, I don't think it's funny at all. I'm just giving you a view of what to expect when you're all better. Baby, all this is yours and you can do whatever you want to it." I bit into my bottom lip as I laid on the bed.

152

"Peaches, stop playing with me and get yo ass back here."

"So, you don't want to watch me? I'm pretty sure I can give you a good show." I grabbed the pillows and laid them in the middle of the bed and then propped my phone up against them.

"You know when I get you, I'm fuckin' yo shit up." Blaze warned.

A moan left my mouth as I leaned against the headboard "Mmm, baby, don't tease me." I sucked on my pointer and middle finger as I spread my legs. Blaze had a clear view of my pussy. My fingers parted my lips then ran through my fold.

"Baby, that pussy pretty. Fuck! I need to be there. Peaches, come home." Blaze licked his lips. "Damn, Peach," he groaned.

My fingers pushed at my opening as I imagined it was Blaze playing with my pussy. "Mmm," my fingers stroked my inner muscles as I played with my clit. My eyes slid closed as I began to lose myself in the feeling.

"What the fuck is you doing?" King's hands covered his eyes as he hurriedly left out the room.

My eyes shot opened. "Gotdammit, King! Don't yo triflin' ass know how to knock! Shit!" I quickly grabbed a pillow and covered myself as I yelled at him.

"What the fuck is wrong with that nigga?" Blaze snapped.

"I don't know but it better be important." I was too pissed off.

"I'm not even gon lie. Man, King my motha-fuckin' nigga. I'm glad that mothafucka walked in there. Yo ass was killing me." Blaze admitted with a laugh. "My damn stomach hurt and my nuts tight as a mothafucka. Yo, wasn't no jackin' gon' get this nut off. Tell that nigga to bring yo ass home now. Matter fact, I'll call you back." He gave me no time to re-spond as he ended the call.

"Well, I'm pissed the fuck off. I could've still gotten mine. Shit!" I snapped at the black phone screen. I fell back on the bed, covered my face with a pillow and let out an irritable scream.

Letting out a heavy breath, I got out of the bed and threw on a tank top and some jogging capris. I walked to the door only to find it locked. How the hell did he get in if the door was locked? Knowing my ass, I probably didn't close it all the way. Espe-cially since I was in such a rush to tell Blaze about Joseph.

I walked into the living room of the hotel to see King throwing back shots. He looked at me and shook his head before taking another.

"I should beat yo ass." He pointed his finger at me.

"No, you should beat yo own ass for just walking into someone's bedroom without knock-ing." I stated in matter a fact tone.

"Shut the fuck up." He tossed back another shot.

"Blaze said bring me back now." I informed him.

King glanced at me then waved toward the room. "I know he just called. Go get yo shit ready. We're leaving in fifteen minutes and don't go out the lobby go through the side door on the far end." King instructed before he tossed back another shot. "Hurry up." He said then left out the room.

I was hella embarrassed about King catching me. Even so, I bet that taught his ass a lesson about just walking into a room when the door is closed.

"Stupid ass." I mumbled to myself as I walked back into the bedroom and started packing my stuff up.

Chapter 13

Peaches

Two Weeks Later

"**B**lake Rashad Carter! If I see another controller on this floor, I'm throwing it in the trash!" I screamed up the stairs, pissed that I had stepped on another one of his damn toys. Picking up the remote, I put it on the TV stand next to his console.

"Ma, that wasn't me. Unc played the game last!" He shouted back down to me.

I couldn't see how someone could live in the house with all males. These niggas were starting to get on my last damn nerves, including Blake's little hardheaded ass. Sighing, I continued to fix up the living room before starting on the kitchen.

Two weeks had passed since Blaze's funeral and everything was slowly returning to normal, somewhat anyway. With Blaze still injured from being shot in his legs, he wasn't able to do much, which made his boys not want to be too far away from us just in case something happened. We had moved three times since I left the hospital. We went from Chicago to Indy and now we had settled in Muncie, Indiana.

Bellow found a nice big house out in Muncie, which was pretty much a damn hick town. I didn't like it out there at all. The cell phone reception sucked, and you had to drive damn near an hour just to get to a supermarket. I wanted to go back to my home in Lafayette. I missed my comfortable little spot and I missed talking to my girl's every day.

After I finished the dishes, I started on dinner. We were having catfish, spaghetti, macaroni & cheese and cornbread. I took out the tilapia and ground beef earlier, so it had already thawed out. Blaze woke up craving that specific meal.

"Hey, Peach." Bellow walked into the kitchen with his arms full of groceries.

"Hey, Bell. You can sit them on the dining room table. I'll put it up in a bit." I waved toward the table, while I stirred the spaghetti noodles.

"T'ight. Does Blaze's beers go in the garage fridge or in here?" He asked.

My brows raised as I glanced back at him. "Blaze don't get no beers—"

"Why the hell not? Bell, toss me one of those." Blaze's voice came from behind Bellow.

I peeked around him to see Blaze standing in the doorway on crutches. I turned the burner on the stove down. "Blaze, you should not be out of bed. What the hell are you doing?" I asked as I walked over to him.

He didn't say nothing at first, he simply walked around me with Khyree and King behind him ready to catch him if he fell.

"Y'all give us a minute," he told them. After King and Khyree helped him in his wheelchair, they left out. "Come here," he beckoned me to him.

Slowly I walked to him. Once I was close enough, he grabbed me by my waist and pulled me into his lap. I freaked instantly. "Blaze, what the hell? Let me go. I don't wanna hurt you." I tried to get up, but he held me tight.

"That's a good thing," he said.

He confused me with his reply, but I stopped moving. "You want me to hurt you?" I asked dumbly, not understanding.

"Hell no! This hurts but I can feel it. I couldn't before." He let out a sigh.

"What?" I didn't want to believe what he was telling me.

"When I was shot, I lost all feeling in my legs. I couldn't feel shit. About two weeks ago the feeling started to come back. Before you get mad, I told them not to tell you. I wanted to but when I was going to say something about it, I started to feel the pain in my legs. I wanted to make sure I wasn't imagining it.

158

I knew I wasn't, when I got an erection." He smiled big and that made me laugh.

Even so, I was pissed. "Blaze, don't joke. If you couldn't feel your legs, you should've been in the hospital. Not having Khyree looking after you and you should've told me." They put too much trust into the twins.

"I know and I've been to the hospital. When you and Lil B go out with Bell. King and Khyree been taking me to the hospital. The twins got an uncle who works at a hospital out here. Moving here wasn't a coincidence. A Femoral—"

"A femoral nerve dysfunction. The bullets damaged the nerves in your legs. Blaze, you still should have told me. I'm glad the feeling is coming back. Did they give you medication? Do you have to go to physical therapy? Is the doctor actually qualified for this? I think I should meet him—" I started to rant.

"Peaches, shut up. Baby, you don't need to do nothing. We got this. Yes, its therapy. I go for an hour. Plus, Khyree been helping me out. Bae, this the reason why I didn't want to tell you because I don't want you to worry. I'mma be good and I need you to believe that. So, stop worrying. All I need you to do is make sure Lil B is good, I got food and..." he stopped talking as he pressed his tongue against the inside of his jaw.

"What's that?" I asked, pretending I didn't know what he was implying.

"Don't play with me. You know what that mean—"

I didn't hear his last words as I jumped off his lap and ran to the bathroom. Hurriedly, I lifted the toilet seat and released the little fluids that was in my stomach before I began to dry heave. Once there was nothing left, I rolled off some tissue and wiped my mouth. Panting heavily, I sat on the tub trying to regain my breathing.

"You i'ight?" Blaze asked from the doorway.

Clearing my throat, I nodded at him. "Yeah, I'm alright." I wiped my mouth once more then tossed the tissue in the toilet before going to the sink and rinsing my mouth. I reached in the drawer and grabbed a new toothbrush to brush my teeth.

"You sure you're i'ight?" His tone sounded as if he didn't believe me.

Once I finished, I walked back to him. "Yeah, I'm okay. So, don't worry. Are you going to help me cook?" I pushed him away from the door while I leaned into him, pecking his lips.

"No, but I'll watch." He kissed me once more before pulling back. "Gon' 'head so I can watch you walk."

I started laughing. "Damn perv."

"You already know that." Blaze rolled up closer to me and grabbed my ass. "You gon sit on my lap?"

I burst out laughing. "See, I'm not about to play with you. Yo ass need to stop before Blake walk in here."

"Don't even speak his cock blocking ass up." Blaze looked out into the hallway to make sure Blake wasn't around. "You gon' ride?" He grabbed my ass again.

"No. Blaze, stop. I'm not about to deal with you." I laughed at him. Moving away from him, I got the pot out to start boiling the macaroni noodles.

***

"So, tell me this, when I was giving you a show at the hotel, was that real or you was playing?" I asked Blaze, trying to pinpoint when the feeling in his legs returned.

"That was real. I told you I got an erection. My dick was so hard, my shit just stopped aching yesterday." He grabbed his crotch and squeezed it. "Mmm," His eyes lowered.

Laughing, I moved away from him. "B, stop playing. I'm being serious right now."

"I'ight, I quit. Yeah, that was real. If yo ass wasn't playing around when you got home, I would've been all in that shit." He sounded amped as if imagining having sex with me that night.

My lips pursed together before I cleared my throat, trying to get rid of my laughter. "Babe, not trying to deflate your ego but umm what was you gon' be in when you can't move?"

The flirty look left his face and he glared at me. "Fuck you, Peaches. Yo ass foul for that shit, boss. Yellow ass trick." He fussed.

"Damn, bae. You got real mad fast, huh?" Laughing, I took a fork full of spaghetti and held it out to him. "Taste this."

161

He hummed and his head nodded. "Yeah, that shit good."

"Okay, here." I got some macaroni and had him taste that.

"Damn, keep cooking like this and I might have to make this official." Blaze popped the elastic of my shorts.

"Dude, whatever. This is already official. I don't know what you're talking about." I wasn't paying his ass no attention. This was beyond official.

"Who the fuck you think you is? Yo ass think because you almost my height right now you can talk shit?" His head tilted to the side as his brow raised.

"You are such an asshole. You didn't even have to go there. My height, though? That's low." Blaze opened his mouth to say something but stopped once I held my fork toward him. "I am making your plate remember that."

"I got it." Blaze licked his lips. laughing. He didn't say nothing else to me. He just watched me.

After I set the table, I made everybody's plates, then sat three different pitchers filled with Fruit Punch, Pepsi and Sprite in the center of the table.

"Blake!" Blaze called out loudly. "Blake! Get down here!"

I turned to look at him. "You know he don't hear you."

162

"What's up, Dad?" Blake came bouncing into the kitchen. "It smells good in here." He rubbed his stomach before reaching over into the macaroni.

I opened my mouth to say something, but Blaze beat me to it.

"If you stick yo dirty ass hands in that pan, I'mma break them. Gon' wash yo hands and come eat."

"I was just gon' get a little." Blake mumbled under his breath as he walked past us.

"What you just say?" Blaze asked.

"Nothing!" Blake ran out of the room and into the bathroom.

Even though Blaze was in a wheelchair, Blake hadn't lost respect for his father. But my son wasn't dumb. He must have known his dad don't forget anything and once he got better, he would get in that ass.

"You're a great father. You really are good with him." I complimented before kissing him.

"Now that you see this, you gon' give me my team? We have to work on six more."

My eyes slanted at him. "You always have to mess something up. Don't talk to me." I laughed, walking away from him.

"Shid, I'm serious. You need to stop playing. It's getting to quiet around here. B, you want some siblings, don't you?" Blaze asked Blake as he walked back into the kitchen.

He shrugged his shoulders as he sat next to his dad. "Yeah and no. I don't want to hear no crying baby but having a little brother will be cool."

"Lil B wants a brother. Give it to him. Tell her, Blake." He pointed at me.

I glared at him. "You get on my nerves." I rolled my eyes at him. "King, Bell, Khyree and Khalil, come eat!" I called to the others. I could hear them coming before I saw them. "And don't bring your damn phones, either!"

"Peaches, shut yo ass up. Everybody know by now not to have they phones at yo table." Blaze laughed. "Y'all gotda excuse her. She's sexually frustrated. She ain't had none."

I hit him upside his head then looked at Blake. Blaze didn't care what he said or who he said it in front of.

"Blaze, shut the fuck up." King snapped at him.

"Oh, you still mad because you caught her trying to be grown." Blaze broke out laughing, thinking about King walking in on me teasing him.

"Blaze, shut up and King watch your mouth. Y'all are so disrespectful. Blake, excuse them." They pissed me off, cussing in front of Blake like he wasn't a kid or around for that matter.

"Don't say y'all. We didn't do anything." Khalil jumped in.

I looked down at him.

"Khalil, shut yo creepy ass up. My momma wasn't even talking to you." Blake snapped at him.

I looked at Blaze.

"That's what the fuck I'm saying. Yo ass took the words right out my mouth." Blaze told him with a laugh. His eyes glanced up at me and his whole demeanor changed. "Blake, you better watch yo damn mouth. What I tell you about cussing?" Him and Blake shared a look and Blaze's head jerked toward me slightly.

"I'm sorry, Momma. My bad, Khalil," Blake apologized.

"We're good, lil man." Khalil and Blake bumped fist.

Blake looked up at me and smiled before he started to dig into his food.

Father God, help me with these men in my life. My son was going to be terrible because of them.

***

We all finished our food and we just sat at the table. Blake and I was silent as the guys talked about basketball. I rubbed my hand over my stomach as I took deep breaths while I swallowed. I was concentrating on keeping my food down. Closing my eyes, my chest raised and fell as I tried keeping my breathing at a steady pace.

"Ma, you okay?" Blake asked.

I jumped out my seat and ran to the bathroom and just like earlier, I release everything I digested.

"Momma." Blake came into the bathroom and began rubbing my back.

Once I was finished, I wiped my mouth then flushed the toilet. This time I stood hunched over longer as I tried to catch my breath.

"You okay?" Blake questioned again.

"Yeah, baby. I'm fine." I wiped my mouth again then stood up.

Blake put some water in the decorated cup and handed it to me. "You sure?"

Taking it from him, I drank the water and then let out a strained laugh. "Yeah, baby. I'm sure. I promise I'm okay." I kissed his forehead and pressed my head against his.

"Blake, come help yo uncles clean up the kitchen and then go get ready for bed." Blaze told him. He looked hesitant to leave my side at first. "B, she's good. Now gon' help them." He reassured him.

Once Blake was gone, Blaze came into the bathroom and closed the door behind him. He didn't say anything, he simply stared at me.

Ignoring his gaze, I went to the sink and started brushing my teeth. When I finished, he still didn't say anything. My eyes soon started to water, and I rolled them up in my head. My fingers swiped at my cheeks quickly wiping the tears away.

Blaze's fingers brushed against my waist. "Peach, come here." For some reason him saying that made the tears fall rapidly. "Peaches, why are you crying?" he asked. My eyes rolled harder as my head shook. Sighing, I glanced at him. "You got something to tell me?" His head tilted to the side as he continued to look at me.

"B, I don't know, and I honestly don't want to know." I told him truthfully. I sat on the tub and put my head into my hands.

"Are you pregnant?" he asked and I shook my head *no*. "Come on, Peaches. Talk to me. Damn!" Frustration was seeping into his voice.

"I don't know for sure. Blaze, I don't want to know if I am. I don't even want to think or speak about it." My head shook as if that was going to emphasize what I was saying.

"Why not?"

My head snapped up and my eyes locked with his. "Are you seriously asking me *why* I don't want to know if I'm pregnant? Why? B, look at you. Look at where we are! Blaze, I don't want to bring a baby into this chaotic world. It's starting to seem like every time something good happens tragedy is never too far behind." My head shook as I told him that.

"I can feel it. That's why I'm not trying to acknowledge this." I hated to admit that, but I didn't think now was our time. The first time I had gotten sick was at his memorial service. I didn't know for sure then but now I was positive of it. Even so, there was a slight hope inside of me praying that the vomiting was all stress related.

"What are you saying, Peaches?" he asked.

I shrugged. "I don't know."

"What? You thinking about an abortion?" He questioned me.

I heard the disbelief in his voice. I didn't even have to look at him to see it cover his face.

"I don't know—"

"What the fuck you mean yo ass don't know? Peaches, don't fuckin' play with me." Blaze's tone raised, causing a slight echo in the bathroom.

I wasn't expecting his anger, or his deep bass filled voice to shout at me, which made me jump.

"Were you even going to tell me?" He continued to question.

"Blaze, I don't know. I wasn't trying to think about it. Every time I did, the whole thing with Le'Ron popped up. I don't want to go through that again. I can't lose another baby. I hadn't thought about an abortion but maybe it's just not our time—"

"Peach, you not the only mothafucka that lost a fuckin' baby! You a selfish ass bitch to even think to say some shit like that. *You can't lose another baby.* Yo ass wasn't the only one who lost something. No, shit ain't the best right now. Shid, fuckin' with me, nothing is ever going to be a perfect time. What happened in the past, you gotda let that shit go. Peaches, I don't give a fuck, you not having an abortion. So, if you thinking about that shit, you might as well lose those thoughts." He said in a final tone.

That pissed me off. "You're selfish to even ask me to bring a baby into all this bullshit! You want me to let shit go but how can I when bullets are flying? I don't want to bring a baby into this. Especially when I don't feel safe!" I spat out of both anger and fear.

I didn't want to bring my baby into this bullshit. What if something else happened and I lost it. An abortion was the last thing on my mind. Even so, I didn't know what I wanted to do.

Blaze let out a laugh. "You don't feel safe? What you think I'll let something happen to you? Do you think I won't be able to protect you, y'all? Is that what you saying?" The angry lines showed across his forehead.

"Blaze, I didn't say that—"

"Answer the fuckin' question! You think I can't protect y'all now? Why because I'm in a wheelchair? I can't do shit now?" He yelled at me.

"I didn't say that—"

"But that's what the fuck you're thinking! If you wasn't why the fuck don't you feel safe? Huh?" Blaze continued to yell.

"I didn't mean it like that." I tried to explain.

"Peaches, get out." He moved back so I could walk past him.

"Blaze, I didn't—"

"Get the fuck out!" He demandingly yelled angrily.

My mouth snapped shut but opened right back, nothing came out. He looked pissed and hurt. I never meant it in that way. Then again, I didn't know. Without a word, I walked past him and out of the bathroom.

"Fuck!" Blaze's yell was followed by the sound of glass clashing and breaking against the floor.

I stopped to go back into the bathroom, but King stopped me.

"Peach, give him a minute. Why don't you go check on lil man?" He instructed. I stared at the bathroom door for a long minute until King gave me a slight nudge. "Gon' 'head."

Sighing, I turned away from him and made my way up the stairs. I went straight into our room, sat at the end of the bed and tears just started pouring from my eyes.

I didn't want to hurt him but I couldn't deny the fact I was scared of losing everything that time. Not only our baby but everybody, Blake, Blaze and King. Deep down I knew it wasn't going to stop until everyone was dead. Who was to say it wasn't going to stop at Blaze? I didn't know and I felt it wasn't. Shit was going to get crazier.

I didn't want to risk the life of our unborn child, hell our living son over that bullshit. Blaze had made it perfectly clear he wasn't going to run so sooner or later; folks were going to learn he wasn't dead and more bullets were sure to come followed by more death.

"Momma…" Blake knocked on the bedroom door.

Sniffling, I wiped my eyes with the back of my hands. "Baby, go back to your room. I'll be there in a minute."

"Are you okay?" he asked.

Tears ran down my face again. *My little protector.* He loved his momma and I loved him with everything that was me. Wiping my face, I went to the door and opened it. I gave my baby a tearful smile. "I'll be fine. Come on, let's go watch a movie." I wrapped my arm around his shoulder and led him to the family room that was on the same floor our bedrooms were on. "You pop the popcorn and I'll find a movie. Okay."

"Put in Transformers." Blake said from over by the microwave.

That boy knew he loved his Transformers. Laughing, I put the first movie in and then got comfortable on the couch. Once Blake had the popcorn in a bowl, he came and sat next to me.

"Are we leaving?" Blake suddenly asked.

His question confused me. "I don't understand what you mean." I'm sure my confusion showed on my face.

"I heard y'all downstairs fighting. I don't wanna leave. I like us together," Blake explained.

I hated that he overheard us yelling at one another. Blaze and I fighting was one thing I tried to keep from him. We had never fought in front of Blake and I wanted to keep it that way. I pulled him into my side and wrapped my arms around him.

"We're not going nowhere and we're always going to be together. I promise." Kissing the side of his head, I held him to me.

"Okay." Blake got comfortable against me and started eating popcorn.

We both fell silent and watched the movie. I pushed what happened between Blaze and I to the back of my mind, not wanting to think about it any longer. And I wasn't going to make any final decision until I knew for sure if I was pregnant.

Chapter 14

Blaze

"You're not hearing me. If she don't feel safe what the fuck is my purpose here? What kinda man can't make his lady feel safe? Who the fuck wanna be with somebody like that? Huh?" I snapped at King as he tried to explain that I had taken what Peaches said the wrong way. But I heard what she said loud and clear.

"B, she ain't mean it the way you taking it. You know how Peaches can be sometimes when explaining shit. She's scared, man, not only for her but for Lil B and you. Nigga, don't forget she thought you was dead for two fuckin' weeks. With this shit starting back up, you can't be pissed at her for not wanting to bring a shorty into this shit." King shook his head as he leaned against the doorway.

"I hear you but you not understanding me. She supposed to trust and believe that I got her regardless of the bullshit that's going on. You ain't see the look on her face, the

173

doubt in me. You ain't see that shit." My hand rubbed over my head.

The events that took place five years ago came rushing back to me. The pain Peaches went through from the beating she gotten from Le'Ron, the miscarriage. How she pushed me away.

She was right about one thing. Every time shit was going right, something fuck'd up happened.

"King, I can't lose her again. After that shit happened, not only did I lose my baby, but I lost her. It took Peaches five fuckin' years to come back to me. Do you know how hard it was not to be with her, to let her go? I can't do that again. I'm not losing her or my baby behind this bullshit. I can't." It was hard the first time to let Peaches and my son be away from me. That wasn't about to happen again. "First, I need to get the fuck out this chair."

That I was determined to do.

***

Ejecting the clip from my Desert Eagle, I slammed another one in, aimed it toward the target sheet and let my trigger finger go. A few days had gone by since the whole blow out with Peaches. To be honest, I was avoiding her. I couldn't bring myself to be around her or Blake knowing I couldn't make her feel safe. I felt helpless, less of a man knowing that. I couldn't stand to be around them while feeling like that.

For these past few days, I had been spending time in the soundproof shed. I had turned one side into a shooting range, while in the far back was where I had my exercise equipment.

The clacking of the empty clip brought me from my thoughts. The shed door soon opened and Khyree walked in.

Never had I ever trusted a person more so then I did King or Sam but over the years, Khyree had proven he was loyal. Never had shit ever came back to me when I dealt with him. Once I was shot, both him and Khalil stayed with me day in and out, making sure I was straight.

"Peaches cooked. She said come eat." Khyree informed me.

"I'll be in there when I finish out here." I sat the Desert Eagle down and grabbed the AK-47 from off the table.

"You know you're about to fuck this whole thing up because of your pride. She has every right to feel all of what she's feeling—"

"You don't understand—" I tried to explain but he cut me off, snatching the gun from my hands.

"I'm not the one who has to understand. You don't have a kid by me, nor do you plan on spending the rest of your life with me. From what I know about Peaches, you can only avoid her for so long before she come to you, which ain't gon' be good." Khyree shook his head with a laugh. "Maybe you forgot but um, yo girl hits and she hit hard. Trust me, if Peaches' pregnant like I think she is, don't let her walk out here. Yo ass just might need these guns." He laughed before he let the AK rip.

He was right about two things. Peaches' ass does punch, and she hit hard when she do. I really did need to talk to her. We were past all this bullshit. We had come to the point where we could talk about anything. My eyes slid to the wheelchair I still sat in and it caused that *less of a man* feeling to rise once again.

"Come on. Let's go," he nodded toward the door.

The feeling pissed me off. I couldn't go in there yet. "I'll be in there when I'm finished out here." I turned away from him and made my way to the walking bar. My legs really couldn't uphold my upper body just yet and walking was painful. But I had to get out that chair. I was going to push my body passed its limits until I was able to make Peaches feel safe.

I grabbed the bars using my upper body strength while ignoring the pain in my shoulder. Pain made me weak and useless, I couldn't afford to be or feel that. Putting pressure on my right leg caused my knee to go out from the pain shooting up my leg.

"I got you." Khyree caught me before I could hit the floor.

For most of my life, I never had to depend on no one for shit and now I needed someone to help me learn how to walk all over again. *Hell no!* I jerked away from him. "I got it."

I didn't have it and after a few failed tries, I wanted to give up but all I had to do was think about

Peaches and Lil B. The thought of losing them had me pushing through the pain.

I was determined now more than ever to get myself out that fuckin' chair and end all the bullshit.

***

"I'ight Blaze, you need a break." Khyree grabbed his bottle of water. He took a drink, then grabbed another one and held it out toward me.

"I'm good." I was tired I couldn't deny that. My body was in agony, but I couldn't stop. Not until I could walk to the end of the bar then back to where I started without slipping.

"Man, take the damn water. B, doing this isn't going to heal you faster. Your body is still weak, it's not fully healed. The nerves in your legs are still damaged and you don't want to push yourself to hard. On top of that, you're making yourself dehydrated, Blaze that's not going to help you." Khyree was frustrated, the redness to his face told that much.

I let out a heavy pant. "How long do you think it'll be before I'm fully healed?" I took in a deep breath as if doing so would cause the pain that vibrated through my body to stop.

He shook his head. "A month in a half/two tops and that's if you haven't caused any more damage to your legs. You're trying to do too much, and I don't think your body can handle all of that right now."

"I don't have two months. I need to kick this shit now." I had been cooped up long enough. I couldn't stay down any longer. I had moves I needed to make. "That's too long."

"It's not going to happen overnight. Blaze, you're just now getting feeling back into your legs. You don't want to fuck that up with putting too much on your body." Khyree repeated.

I wasn't trying to hear it. "That's a risk I'm willing to take. I can't sit around here and do nothing." With that, I took a deep breath, trying to block out the pain as I gripped the bars once more. Slowly but steadily taking one painful step after another.

One Week Later

"Don't hold it close to your face, that damn thing will jerk back and wack the fuck out of you. Loosen the fuck up, hold your arms out, grip the handle tight. Now pull the trigger." I instructed. He let off a shot and then another.

"This thang got a little kick to it."

I looked at Blake and laughed. "The fuck you know about something having some kick?" I brought in the sheet he shot at and then looked back at him.

"What?" he questioned.

"Yo ass don't have no aim, that's what. You get that shit from yo momma's side. King's ass ain't got no damn aim either. You need to work on that."

Pushing the button, the sheet went into the distance. "Go," I nodded toward the sheet.

Blake plugged his ears, then grabbed the .380 and started shooting.

Peaches had sent Blake out to the shed a few days ago to bring me my food and ever since then he had been sticking with me. It was stupid of me, but I decided to teach him how to handle a gun. For the first three days, I basically had him stripping the guns down and cleaning them before showing him how to turn the safety on and off. I knew Peaches was going to be pissed when she found out, but he had to learn sooner or later.

I rolled away from him, going back to the weights. Khyree was pissed and kept insisting I was pushing my body past its limits. I agreed with him all the way. I was risking everything by pushing myself. I just couldn't sit around and wait for my body to heal. I had to push past the pain so I could move around.

"Ah, shit!" I grunted as I pushed myself up to sit on the bench. I looked over at Khyree to see him shaking his head. "Shut the fuck up."

"I ain't said shit. I'm just watching yo stupid ass. Continue." He waved his hands toward the weights.

If I didn't need his ass, I would've put him out. "Get the fuck out. Don't wave at me, you whiny bitch."

"Whiny? We gon' see who be crying in a minute. Bitch!" He slapped his hand against my shoulder hard before walking past me laughing.

"Son of a bitch!" I grunted out then took a deep breath, trying to block out the pain. After a few seconds of deep breathing, my legs started to slowly lift the weights. Every time I pushed it up, a painful moan left my mouth. After the twentieth lift for my right leg, I massaged my thigh down to the calf before I started on my left leg. "Ah," I groaned out as I began.

"What the hell? Blake Rashad Carter, what the—if you don't put that gotdamn gun down!" Peaches yelled from behind me.

I looked back just in time to see her whacking him upside the head with her hand before she turned her angry glare toward Khyree.

"And you see him with this damn gun?" she screamed at him.

Khyree quickly pointed to me. "I was against it too, Ms. Peaches. That's your man over there. He done lost his dam mind. I said you was gon' be pissed but Blaze ain't want to listen to me. So, don't be mad at lil man, it wasn't his fault. Blaze told him he was gon' teach him how to look out for the both of you when he wasn't around." Khyree told her in one breath.

My head tilted, looking at him funny. Not believing that nigga done stood his grown ass right there and told on my ass like she was his momma. What the fuck was wrong with him?

"Blaze, you got him shooting guns now. Really?" Peaches turned her angry glare toward me.

My words got stuck in my throat. Shid, I ain't know what to say. Peaches was looking pissed and ready to swing. I couldn't hit back if she came at me, so I had to choose my words carefully.

"Y'all give us a minute and Blake don't think for a second that I'm done with you. Now go get cleaned up for dinner." She waved them off.

Both Blake and Khyree hauled ass out of the shed.

"Peaches, it wasn't shit but a little toy gun." I shrugged as if it was nothing. Although the gun was real, yet to me, however, it was only a little toy given the size of it.

She picked up the gun and aimed it at the target. Peaches let off two shots. "So, toy bullets just tore through that sheet is what you're telling me?" she said, walking over to me with the gun in her hand.

"Oh shit!" I lowly muttered to myself.

"That's what you saying? It has to be true because I know you're not crazy enough to give our son a loaded gun." She let out a humorless laugh. "It's such a toy that I could literally just shoot you and nothing would happen, right?" She laughed harder than before, pointing the gun at me.

What the fuck is wrong with her?

"Peach, baby, you good?" Hell, she was scaring me.

"Water would probably come out if I shot you seeing as the gun is just a toy!" Her hand went back before it shot forward and she slapped the fuck out of me. "Do I look fuckin' stupid to you? What would possess you to give him a loaded fuckin' gun? Have you lost your gotdamn mind, Blaze?"

She had me feeling little as hell at that moment. "Bitch, is you—"

Her hand shot out again cutting my words off as my face went to the side. "Call me another one! I dare you too!"

I rubbed my jaw and nodded my head. I was crazy but not stupid. This was a fight I wasn't going to win.

"Peach, don't hit me no damn more. I ain't even bullshittin'. It was stupid, I know, but with the shit that's going on, he needed to know how to handle one. I'm not saying he was ever gon' use it, but shid, we don't know."

Her brows rose. "Are you hearing yourself right now? Blaze, he's eight. There's no way in hell he should know how to handle a gotdamn gun. What is wrong with you?"

"Ain't shit wrong with me. I'm good." Grabbing the bar above my head, I pulled it down lifting the weights up. With each movement, a grunt left my mouth. Peaches stood in front of me with her face scrunched up into an angry mug. My eyes diverted away from her to the wall.

"You've practically moved out here, but nothing is wrong with you. Blaze, you have Blake handling guns and you're going to tell me there's absolutely nothing wrong with you?" She moved back into my line of vision.

Sometimes talking to Peaches was like having a conversation with a brick wall. She never heard what I was saying, which became frustrating to the point I wanted to choke the hell out of her. "I said

I'm good. Gon' back inside. I'll be there in a minute."

"You're dismissing me? Really?" Peaches arms crossed over her chest as her hip cocked to the side.

I didn't say anything to her. Instead, I continued my workout.

"You know what? Stay yo ass out here. I don't even care anymore. I'm not about to stay here only to be ignored. It's been almost two weeks and I'm not about to do this. Blake and I will be going back home to Lafayette tomorrow."

I let the weights go, then grabbed Peaches and quickly snatched her to me. "Yo ass ain't going nowhere and if you think you're taking my son, you done lost yo fuckin' mind. Peaches, don't threaten me especially not now."

"Let me go," she jerked out of my hold. "I'm not threatening you I'm telling you what we're doing. I don't need the stress and we're not staying out here when you're like this."

"I'm good. Ain't shit wrong with me—"

"Yes, there is and it's crazy you don't see it. Blake had to come out here and learn how to shoot a gun just to spend time with you. When was the last time you came in the house to play a game with him, watched a movie or done anything *with your son?* Hell, actually had a normal conversation with Blake? Sat at the table beside him?" She asked me but I didn't say anything to her.

"Blaze, when was the last time you talked to me? It's been damn near two weeks, that's how long it's been. You're so caught up in your own self loath that you're pushing us away. So, we're going." She reached in her pocket and pulled out a folded piece of paper. Peaches threw it in my face, then walked away.

"Peaches!" She kept going, not once looking back. "Peaches, yo ass bet not leave this gotdamn house." The shed door slammed shut. I picked up the paper and my eyes glanced over the words. "Damn," the paper confirmed she was six weeks pregnant. But the fact I missed her going to the doctor fuck'd with me.

I got back into the wheelchair and made my way inside of the house.

Chapter 15

Peaches

I stopped in the kitchen where Bellow sat eating the food I cooked earlier. "Bell, will you take us to a hotel, please?" As of late, any place I needed to go, Bellow had been there for me.

He did anything I asked of him with no problem, especially with King going back and forth from Gary to Muncie. Bellow was the only other person that was truly looking out for us.

"Yeah, I'll take you. Just let me know when you ready." He replied before he started back eating his food.

"Thanks, Bell." After thanking him, I walked into the living room where Blake sat on the floor playing his video game. "Blake, go in your room and pack a bag."

"Where we going?" He asked me.

I glared at him and pointed to the stairs. "Don't ask me no questions, don't get smart and you bet not stomp on those stairs. Just do what I just asked. Now go."

He let out a sigh and dropped his remote controller to his game and slowly walked up the stairs with me behind him. I went into the hall closet and grabbed two duffle bags.

"Here, you can use this." I tossed him the bag then made my way to my room. I immediately started throwing clothes inside the duffle. As I was stuffing my bag, the bedroom door came open. I didn't even have to look back to know it was Blaze.

"Peaches, you might as well stop because y'all not leaving this house."

Ignoring him, I went into the closet and grabbed my tote bag. I walked to the bathroom and got my body wash, then went back into the room, going to the dresser. I just started throwing my body sprays, oils, powder and deodorant into the tote.

"Peach, hold up. Damn!" Blaze rolled in front of me.

Glancing at him, I rolled my eyes and walked around him. "Now you want to talk? I ain't got shit else to say. So, go back into your shed where you've been."

Blaze snatched the tote out of my hand, making the content waste onto the floor. "You're not leaving so quit all this dumb shit."

"No, the dumb shit is you ignoring us—"

"That's your fault! Yo ass the one hiding shit and crying how you don't feel safe. But you want to blame this bullshit on me. What the fuck was I supposed to do, Peaches? Huh?" He asked me.

"What? You want me to lay up in the mothafuckin' bed and feel sorry because I can't make you feel like I can protect y'all. Or do you want me to get my ass up and do something? I'm not sitting around here waiting no damn more!" He yelled at me before snatching my bag off the bed and dumping everything on the floor. "And yo ass ain't going no fuckin' where!"

From his outburst, I now understood my mistake, the impression my words had appeared to him. I couldn't blame him for not wanting to be around me.

"Blaze, the other day, what I said I really didn't mean it the way it came out." A sigh left my mouth as I moved closer to him. "B, yes I'm scared but not just for myself. And trust me I want more than anything for you to get better but I'm afraid of what's going to come once you are. So, the safety of my family scares the shit out of me." I explained to him truthfully.

"Baby, I know you can protect us whether you're in a wheelchair or not. I never doubted that for one second. Blaze, I just had to plan a fake funeral for you, so yes, I'm terrified of something else happening. And once you're better, that fear is going to worsen. So how can you be pissed at me for feeling any of this? For not wanting to lose you?" The back of my thumbs brushed the tears from my cheeks, trying to stop the tears from falling.

"Come here, Peach." Blaze grabbed my hand and pulled me to the bed. He got out his chair and sat beside me.

"You're not going to lose me I don't know how many times I have to tell you this. I'll do it every day if I have to, though. Peaches, I wouldn't leave y'all, but you have to understand I can't hide either. What kind of life would we have if we're looking over our shoulders every day? Baby, that's not living and ain't no bitch in me. If I can't protect my family, what is my purpose as a man, as a father? Answer that."

I couldn't answer it. And I felt selfish to have even asked him to hide, given the type of man he is. "You're right and I shouldn't have put you in a situation where it'll question you as a man. Call me selfish but my mindset will never change. If it means, you'll be safe and don't have to go out there then I'm going to always look at the easier way out. And that's to leave everything behind and just go. Regardless of that, I'm not leaving you. I'll be here going along with whatever you want."

It was a foolish decision and every nerve in my body screamed trouble. I ignored it as I do a lot of things when it came to Blaze. I always found a logical reason behind his words. That time I really didn't need to. He was right about everything. I didn't want to be running for the rest of my life with my kids for nothing.

Blaze didn't say anything at first, he just stared at me. He looked from my right to my left eye as if he was having a hard time believing what I had said.

"Blaze, I love you, so I'm with you." My lips pecked his once then twice.

188

His hand came to the back of my head, his fingers tangled into my hair. He kissed me back, then pulled away. "I don't deserve you, but I'm selfish." His lips pressed against mine once more.

"You are and you really don't deserve me." My lips stretched into a smile as he leaned into me. My back touched the bed and I laughed at the grunt that left his mouth.

"That shit hurt." He complained but didn't stop kissing me.

My arms wrapped around his neck as my legs went to his waist, hooking at the ankles. One of my hands left from around his neck and went to his lower back, slipping under his shirt. My nails dug into his flesh as the kiss intensified. I quickly became lost into us that I forgot about him being hurt. I rolled us over and my lower body pressed down on his.

"Ah, shit, Peaches!" Blaze groaned out.

I quickly jumped off of him. "I'm so sorry. Let me see." I pulled at his shorts.

"Peaches, chill the fuck out. A little pain ain't gon' kill me. Now get back up here." He laughed at me before beckoning me back to him.

"I don't want to hurt you." I shook my head. His grunting scared me.

"Man, gon' finish pulling them shorts off, then get yo ass back over here."

I stared at his erection that pressed against his boxer briefs. "Blaze, no. Was you cleared to have sex?" I couldn't help but laugh at his mannish ass.

"I'm grown as hell. I don't need to be cleared, shid I just found out you about to have my baby and my dick hard. Baby girl, that's all the clearance I need. Now stop playin' and get over here. Come ride this shit. This yo dick, remember?" He pulled his soldier out and waved it at me. "You gon' come take yo dick?" His fingers wrapped around his shaft and he slowly began to stroke himself.

"Baby, I don't wanna hurt you. I can suck your dick—"

"You gon' do that too, but right now I want yo pussy to suck my shit. Peach, don't worry about hurting me. This shit right here hurt." He grunted stroking his dick. "You can just bounce on my dick. I'll hold you up. Come on, Peach. Baby, don't make me beg." His palm ran over his leaky tip before going back down his shaft.

My teeth gripped my bottom lip as I watched him. I was getting turned on with each stroke. My pussy muscles tightened when he squeezed his tip. *Fuck it!* My hands made quick work taking off my shirt and shorts. I tossed them to the side, then removed Blaze's shorts, boxers and shoes. My eyes slid to the bandages on his thighs and I started to rethink what I was about to do with him.

"No, the fuck you don't. If you don't get yo ass over here, I'mma fuck yo ass up I promise. Don't play with me, Peaches." Blaze glared at me. He must have seen I was about to change my mind.

"The first time you grunt, I'm stopping." I got on the bed and stood over him.

"Fuck you doing?" he asked with his brow raised.

Oh, he was crazy if he thought I was just about to jump on his dick. I was horny as hell, but we were gon' do this right. "Say ahh." I opened my mouth and stuck my tongue out showing him what to do.

Blaze started laughing. "Come on, mama. You can sit on my face." He licked his full lips as he beckoned me down to him.

I squatted down until I felt his tongue touch my lips. The thought of teasing him quickly left my mind once his arms hooked around my thighs and he pulled me down on him. My knees laid on each side of his head, I lend forward and kissed his pelvis as my fingers wrapped around his thick shaft.

"Mmm," My forehead pressed against his lower abdomen as a moan left my mouth. "Sss. Mmm, like that." My hips grinded against his face as he sucked on my clit. My lips pressed against his pelvis once more before I moved to his one eyed monster. My tongue licked around the rim of his mushroom shaped tip, then over the head. Tasting the salty pre-cum as it leaked out.

Blaze's hips bucked and his dick twitched. I smiled at his reaction. But it quickly faded as my eyes rolled into my head from the pleasurable sensation his mouth was giving my swollen pearl.

He licked from my opening to my nub. His mouth latched onto my pearl as he thrust two fingers into my soaking sex. My hips jerked as my inner walls contracted around his fingers. His mouth sucked on my clit as his fingers hooked my pubic bone.

"Mmm, Blaze." I moaned out loudly. My hips started to move in sync with his fingers before I turned my attention back to his dick. My tongue licked around the rigid rim before I sucked his tip into my mouth. I released him with a pop before taking him deeper into my mouth.

"Ah, Shit!" Blaze's mouth left my clit, and he let out a groan. His hand soon came down hard on my ass.

My cheeks sunk in and I moaned on his dick as I cupped his sack, massaging them as my head continued to bob up and down on his hard throbbing pole.

"Damn, Peaches! Shit!" Blaze's fingers moved inside of my pussy slowly as he enjoyed the pleasure, I was giving him.

My head continued to bob up and down as I massaged his sack. I released him and then spit on his dick. My fingers stroked up and down his man while I sucked then licked around his mushroom tip.

Blaze's fingers picked up its pace once again as his mouth went back to my swollen pearl. I felt the muscles in his legs tighten and he grunted from both pain and pleasure.

"Ma!" Blake yelled from the hallway.

My movement stopped. "Shit!"

Chapter 16

Peaches

"**S**hit my ass," Blaze pushed my head back down toward his erection.

"Blaze, stop—"

"Hell no! Fuck that! You better finish suckin' that dick." He grabbed the back of my head once again and pushed it down.

The doorknob jiggled.

"Blake, if you don't get yo black ass away from my door, I promise you I'm gon' fuck you up. Now gon' sit yo ass down some fuckin' where! We'll be out in a minute. Damn!" You could hear the frustration in his voice as he fussed at my baby.

I went to move but he pushed me back down. I looked back at him. "Don't be cussing at my baby, Blaze. I don't know who you—"

"Peach, shut the fuck up and finish suckin' my dick. Damn! Always fuckin' talkin'." His hand slapped my ass hard.

The sting had me about to snap at him, but my words were replaced with a moan as he went back to sucking on my clit and fingering my pussy like there was never an interruption.

"Sss, Oh, my God." My hips started their grind as I enjoyed the feel of his mouth and fingers. My fingers stroked his dick as I continued to fuck his face, feeling my orgasm approaching. I couldn't think to pleasure him from the amazing sensation he was giving me.

My inner walls milked his fingers, my muscles tightened, and my thighs started to shake as my orgasm shook my body. "Blaze! Oh, my God, Oh, my God!" I cried. My body twitched and he held me to him, savoring every drop that left my running sex.

My mouth went back to his standing soldier. I took him deep into my throat and moaned. Coming back up, I spit on his dick, stroking him up and down. My tongue swirled around his tip before my lips wrapped around it, sucking on him. One hand stroked his pole while the other massaged his balls, not once did my sucking stop.

"Ah, fuck, Peaches! Shit!" He grunted out. Blaze grabbed my ass, squeezing it before he slapped my cheeks hard.

The action caused my body to jerk slightly and moan, causing vibration around his dick, which had him squeezing my ass harder.

"Ah shit! Suck that dick." Blaze grunted.

I sucked, stroked and slurped all over his dick until I felt the muscles in his legs tighten.

Blaze hit my ass then grabbed a handful of my hair, pulling my head back. "Nuh uh, baby girl, get on that dick. I wanna cum inside that pussy. I miss that shit."

Immediately, I started to reject him. Doing this was enough but to actually sit on his legs was a different story. "B—"

"Peaches, don't do me like that. I need to feel my shit." He slapped my ass hard. "Gon' get on it." He stuck his fingers into my pussy and started to stroke my inner walls once again, quickly finding my sweet spot.

My hips started to grind and roll against his fingers. "Mmm, Blaze."

"Get yo ass up and ride that shit." He demanded, slapping my ass hard as hell, causing a yelp to leave my mouth.

Without having to be told again, I moved down toward his standing erection. I placed my feet flat on both sides of him and positioned myself on top. Taking ahold of his dick, I brought it to my opening.

Blaze gripped my hips, bringing me down. His eyes focused between my legs. Once his tip pushed in, his eyes moved to mine just as they closed from the sensation of him entering me.

He moved me down until he was deep inside my pussy before moving me back up, pulling out of me. My eyes opened only to find him watching his soldier move in and out of my sex. The gaze of his eyes caused my inner muscles to tighten around him and I started to move a bit faster. His stare turned me on more.

With my feet planted firmly on the bed, I grabbed his hands and linked our fingers, using his hands for support. I started to bounce faster on him while tightening my pussy muscles.

"Ooh, sss! Oh, my God! Ooh!" I squeezed his fingers tighter. My head went back, and my eyes closed.

"Oh shit! Fuck!" Blaze cussed.

I slowed down and rolled my hips. I put my weight on him, causing his man to go deeper inside of me. My hips slowly began to grind before picking up in pace. "Ooh, Blaze. Mmm, baby!" My hips rocked back and forth as my muscles contracted tighter around him. "Sss, ah, ah, ooh!"

Blaze let my hands go and grabbed my ass. His nails dug into my cheeks as he moved me faster and harder on him. His hips thrust up frantically before he held me to him.

"Ah, fuck!" He grunted out.

I felt the fluid leave his body and fill mine. The pain from his nails digging into my skin turned me on more and I began to bounce on him even more, bringing myself to yet another orgasm.

My muscles tightened and my body shook as I came with a long moan. I collapsed on top of him, panting hard.

"Ah shit! I'mma be sore as fuck." Blaze complained.

I didn't reply at first, I just laid on top of him trying to catch my breath.

"Mmm, you think you can go for another one?" he asked, grabbing a handful of my ass.

Again, I didn't say anything. I was too hot and thirsty. Hell no, I couldn't go another round.

"Blaze, you gon' clean me up?" I asked while I kissed along his chest. Coming to the bandaged wound on his right shoulder, I kissed it, then moved up his neck, slowly making my way up to his full set of lips. My tongue flicked at the bottom then the top lip before pecking them both. "I love you." I whispered. I stuck my tongue out.

Blaze laughed and shook his head. He stuck out his tongue and I pulled it into my mouth, sucking on it. "Mmm," he moaned. His hand tangled into my hair and he pulled my head back. "I love you, too." his tongue stuck out.

A big smile stretched across my lips before I licked his tongue.

"Yo ass crazy, man." He kissed me again then pulled me down on his chest.

My lips pressed against his chest once more as I got comfortable. A content sigh left my mouth and shortly after, I quickly fell asleep.

***

"Peaches," Blaze shook me.

I rolled over on my side, facing away from him.

"Peaches," he shook me harder.

I shrugged him off and pulled the sheet closer to my body.

"Peaches, wake yo ass up. It's important." His tone was loud as he shook me harder.

A yawn left my mouth, and I rubbed my eyes. "What's wrong?" I rolled over to face him.

"Come here," he motioned me to him. He grabbed my arms and pulled me on top of him.

My head tilted to the side looking at him, trying to figure out if he was serious but the very hard member poking me in my ass told me he was. "Dude, you didn't wake me up to have sex?"

"Peach, I'm horny as fuck. That's yo fault. You shouldn't have given me none." Blaze held me to him as he slapped his dick against my ass. "Lift up right quick."

My eyes slanted at him and I slapped his hands away from me. "You get on my nerves." I took ahold of his dick, running his leaking tip through my slit. I brought him to my opening. I teased myself by pushing the tip inside of my pussy until I became wet. My sex quickly started to throb. I slid down. "Mmm," I moaned.

Blaze's hands held my waist as he guided my hips in a back and forth motion. Once I was at the steady pace, he wanted me to go, he released his hold on my waist, reached up and grabbed my chest. His head raised and his tongue came out. He flicked his tongue over my nipple before pulling it into his mouth, giving it a hard suck. He pulled his head back until my little nub popped from his mouth. Blaze moved to the other one as his hands came back to my waist.

I gripped the headboard as my feet laid flat on the bed and I began to bounce on his dick. Repeatedly, he hit my sweet spot, which caused me to move faster so I could reach that pleasurable high that only he could bring me to. "Ooh, ooh! Sss! Mm! Blaze. Oh, my God! Ooh!"

Blaze's hands gripped my waist tighter as his hips thrust up, meeting my every bounce.

Our movement became too much, and I tried to slow it down, but Blaze continued his hard thrusting. My hand went to my lower abdomen as I tried to sit up and put some space between us, but Blaze wasn't having that.

"Where you going?" His grip tightened and his pumps became harder.

"Oh, my God! Ooh, ooh, ah, ah, fuck, ooh, Blaze!" My moans were loud and uncontrollable. "Oh, my God! Oh, my God!" I cried as my orgasm shook my body.

He didn't stop. "Turn around." He was already turning me into the position. "Ah shit." Blaze cussed from the pain of bending his knees. "Nuh uh, don't sit down. Stay just like that. Hold my knees."

I stayed in my squatted position.

Slowly, his hips raised and with each lift, he let out a painful grunt, but didn't stop.

"Blaze—" I was about to call it quits but the suggestion of him stopping flew from my mind as he started to pound into my body. "Ooh shit!" A yelp left my mouth, and I gripped his knees tight as my muscles tightened.

Blaze hit my sweet spot, showing no mercy to my still sensitive pussy. I bit the inside of my lip trying to quiet myself down but the pleasurable sensation he was wreaking on my body wouldn't allow it.

"Ah, ah, ah, sss! I'm cummin'. Ooh, Blaze!" My hips came down, meeting his frantic thrust.

"Let that shit go." His hand slapped hard against my ass.

The hit caused my inner muscles to squeeze around him. I let go of his knee and brought my fingers to my swollen clit. I rubbed and spanked my pearl as Blaze pumped faster. My toes curled, my ass muscles tightened, and my body began to shake.

"Ooh shit!" Blaze grunted out as his pelvis jerked against mine. He held me to him, his fingers dug painfully into my skin as he released his fluids into my body.

With my back toward him I leaned forward on the bed, with him still inside me.

"Ooh shit!" He shouted before his hand came down on my ass.

"Blaze, stop and be quiet before you wake up Blake." I said as I just laid there. I didn't have the energy to move.

Blaze laughed as his hands rubbed across my ass before he shook, then squeezed it. "Shid, he probably already woke with all that damn noise you was making. Screaming and praying to God, you should be ashamed of yo self." He slapped my ass.

I couldn't do nothing but laugh. "Dude, stop, stupid ass."

"Who the fuck you talkin' to? Huh?" His hand came down harder than before. "Damn, that bitch jiggled. I bet that mothafucka red as hell." He spread my cheeks and slapped my ass again before rubbing the sore spot.

"Dude, you slap my ass like that again and I'm going to slap the shit out of you." I threatened, knowing damn well I wasn't going to do nothing. My ass was tired as hell. I just wanted to go to sleep but I knew that wasn't going to happen.

"Peaches." he called, shaking my booty.

I didn't say anything. I just laid there.

"Peaches," he tapped my right booty cheek.

I don't know why but I ended up laughing. "Yes, Blaze?"

"Baby, I'm hungry as fuck. My damn stomach growling. That bitch feel like it's in my back." Blaze complained. I didn't say anything. "Baby, you gon' make me something to eat?" His hands rubbed along my thighs.

The soothing caress had my eyes closing and I slowly started to drift off to sleep.

"Peaches?" He shook me.

"What!" I snapped at him.

His movement stopped and he didn't say anything. "Who the fuck is you yelling at?" He snapped at me before slapping my ass hard. "Peaches, don't make me fuck you up. Get yo black ass off me."

I started laughing as he pushed my hips but didn't make a move to pull out. "Stop, dang. Bae, I'm sleepy."

"I'm hungry, though." He countered.

A moan left my mouth and I sat up. I felt him twitch inside of me. I moaned and began to roll my hips on him.

"Mmm…" He groaned as he took hold of my hips.

Laughing, I pulled him out of me and hopped off the bed. "What you want to eat?"

"Yo black ass play too damn much. Shit, you done woke his ass up. Baby, come sit on it." He grabbed his dick and waved it toward me.

I laughed at him while picking up his shirt off the floor. I slipped it on and then I threw on his boxers. "No, because you're hungry." I leaned over him and kissed his lips once then twice. "I'll be back. You want me to get you some lotion for him?" My fingers wrapped around his erection and I slowly began to stroke him. "Can I taste it?" I licked his lips as I gave the tip a slight squeeze.

"Hell yeah! This yo dick. You can sit on that mothafucka if you wanna." He pushed.

A wide smile stretched across my lips. I kissed his mouth, then moved to his chest. "You," I moved further down. "Telling," I pressed my lips against the spot above his naval. "Me all this," I kissed his pelvis. "Is mine," I kissed the head of his one eyed soldier before opening my mouth and taking him deep into my throat.

"Fuck yeah! All that's you." Blaze groaned.

I released him, making a popping sound with my mouth, staring him in the eyes as I did. "Okay, I was just making sure." I stood up straight and began to make my way to the bathroom.

"Yo, where the fuck you going?" He called after me.

"You're hungry, remember? I'm about to go make you something to eat, duh. Right after I brush my teeth."

"Yo black ass dirty as fuck, Peaches. That's cool. I'mma get yo ass back, believe that." He let out a humorous laugh as he talked shit.

I went into the bathroom and washed my face then brushed my teeth. Once I was finished, I left out the bathroom and looked over to the bed where Blaze laid watching TV.

"Bae, you are so damn sexy." I blew him a kiss.

"Fuck you, Peaches." He stuck up his middle finger.

Laughing, I walked to the door. "I love you." I blew him another kiss and walked out of the room laughing. I headed downstairs and started to make his breakfast.

My stomach tightened as that giddiness once again returned. My lips twitched before they formed into a smile. That man had me so gone over him. There was no way I was ever walking away from him again.

Blaze was my everything.

Chapter 17

Peaches

A Month Later

"Blaze, are you coming with us or you're staying here?" I walked out of the bathroom and into our room, only to find him the same way I left him, on the floor stretching his legs. He grabbed his bent knee and brought it to his chest. He held it there for a few seconds before stretching his leg back out. He repeated this action with the other leg.

He didn't answer me, instead he placed his hands behind his head and began to do his sit ups, while bringing his knees up.

After the whole misunderstanding was cleared up, Blaze had been working himself harder than ever to strengthen his legs. Regardless of the warnings Khyree and myself constantly gave him. Blaze paid them no mind, instead he continued to tell us how it was a risk he was willing to take. I found he was being selfish, but regardless of what I thought, Blaze did what he thought he had to do.

Blaze forced himself through the pain and him spending hours in the shed worked for him. The muscles in both legs grew stronger and he was now back to walking around. Even so, I could still tell some movements bothered him, though he tried to cover it up.

My eyes rolled into my head as I went to the dresser and got out my underclothes. After I had on my panties, I grabbed my bra about to put it on.

Blaze walked up behind me and wrapped his arms around my waist before his head went into the side of my neck. "B, move. I'm trying to get ready." I tried to shrug him off but that only made him hold me tighter, while biting into my neck. Laughing, I elbowed him. "You play too much." I turned around in his arms and puckered my lips up.

His face came to mine and he kissed me. "Yeah, I'm coming. Yo ass better kill that attitude you been having, too. You gon' make me fuck you up." His hand slapped my ass before his lips pressed against mine again.

"Then you shouldn't be ignoring me. You heard me talking to you, so don't wait until I get an attitude to say something back." I bit his bottom lip, then kissed it before I moved out of his hold.

Blaze slapped my butt as I walked past him. "Shut yo whiny ass up. I was counting. I would've had to start all over if I answered you." He took off his shirt, then threw it at me.

"Peaches, look in the closet and get my black jeans and white shirt out then iron it for me."

I paused from putting on my lotion to look at his back as he walked into the bathroom. With a roll of my eyes, I went to the closet, talking shit as I did. Not once thinking to whisper. "I swear his last minute ass get on my damn nerves. Black ass knew we were leaving hours ago. Stupid ass should've been had his shit out."

"What?" He yelled from the bathroom.

"I said do you want the plain white shirt or the polo shirt?" My lips pursed tightly together to stop my laughter.

"It don't matter!" he replied.

Once I had on my jeans, I pulled on my royal blue tank top then reached under the bed and grabbed the ironing board and iron.

As I was ironing Blaze's jeans, Blake knocked on the door before sticking his head in the room. My eyes squinted as I scowled at him.

"What I tell you about half knocking? If I don't say come in, then you are not to open that door." I fussed at him.

It had been too many times Blaze and I were about to get nasty and he came bursting into our room. He was lucky it was just me and his dad was in the shower. Blake worked Blaze's nerves walking into the room whenever he felt like it. Especially when he was about to get some. He was ready to hurt my baby.

206

"I'm sorry." He rubbed the back of his head and his eyes dropped to the floor.

He wasn't fooling nobody. Shaking my head at him, I laughed. "Yeah right, what do you want?"

Blake let out a sigh before kicking off his shoes and getting on the bed. He grabbed the remote, then stretched out. "Nothing, just wanted to see when we're leaving. I'm ready to get out this house. Khalil starting to be worrisome as hell—I mean heck."

"Make me hurt you, Rashad." I laid Blaze's jeans on the bed before I started on his shirt. I looked back over at Blake to see his hand was now under his shirt as the other laid above his head. My baby was most definitely his father's son. He looked just like him. "What Khalil do?"

"Getting on my nerves. He always telling me to do stuff for him." He complained.

Khalil and Blake had become cool since we moved to Muncie, since King was mainly in Gary and Khyree watched over Blaze most of the time. Bellow wasn't really into video games. Plus, he was always taking me places.

Blake didn't have any friends out there. Hell, he couldn't even leave the house, so Khalil was the only other person he could play video games with.

That was the main reason to go out today. I was tired of being locked up in this house with these men and I wanted to take Blake out to do something, anything. Blaze coming was just an added bonus.

Given all Blaze had been doing these past couple of months, was working out to build his strength. He was so determined to do that, playing with my baby was out. And I wasn't about to have him shooting guns just for him to spend time with his dad.

I laughed at him. "You got yo nerve. Now when you don't have anybody to play the game with who do you go to?" My head tilted to the side as I awaited his reply.

"Ma, but that's different—"

"Blake, get out my room with your crazy self." I couldn't do anything but laugh. The shower in the bathroom turned off and I pointed to the door. "Your daddy is about to get out the shower." I pointed toward the door.

"Why he can't get dressed in the bathroom?" he asked.

Blaze walked in hearing his question. "Because this my damn room. Now get yo ass out." Blaze had the towel tucked at his waist with a hand towel rubbing against his head.

Blaze was just sexy for no reason at all. My stomach tightened and I bit into my bottom lip. I wanted to play with him, going out was the last thing on my mind.

Blaze glanced over at me, then to the dresser before looking back. "B, you better go before you see yo momma get nasty. She got that *I want it* look." He licked his smiling lips.

He gets on my nerves.

"Blaze, shut up." I rolled my eyes at him.

"What's the *want it* look?" Blake asked, looking over at me.

I felt my face get hot. Covering my mouth, I laughed. My stomach was tight, and my inner muscles started to contract.

"Momma, you turning red." Blake pointed out.

Blaze broke out laughing. "Because she wants it."

"Blaze, shut up and Blake get out." Grabbing Blake's shoulders, I pushed him toward the door. "Go get your shoes on and take out the trash." I pushed him out of the room, then closed and locked the door. I turned toward Blaze. "You are such an asshole, stupid ass! I don't want shit." I cut my eyes at him.

He dropped his towel and grabbed himself. "So, you don't want it?" Blaze walked to me as he stroked his man awake.

"No, I don't." I lied, looking away from him to the bed. Damn, I wanted it bad. "Blaze, go get ready so we can go." I attempted to walk past him, but he stopped me.

"Come here. Where you tryna go?" He pulled me to him and grabbed ahold of my face, bringing his lips to mine.

My knees quickly became weak as I pecked his lips, trying hard to resist the urge to jump him. "Blaze, we can't. I'mma have to take a shower all over again and Blake is ready to go." My back hit the bedroom door.

Blaze wasn't hearing nothing I was saying. He grabbed the hem of my shirt and pulled it over my head, then made quick work with the button and zipper on my jeans.

"Blaze, for real. I'm serious." My lips moved against his as his hand slipped into my pants.

"Me too. I'll be quick." He pulled my left leg out of my jeans and picked me up.

Instinctively my legs wrapped around his waist. I was done. I couldn't fight it and there was no point in doing so. I sucked at his top lip, then the bottom before sliding my tongue into his mouth.

"You want it?" He suddenly asked as he moved my panties to the side. He placed himself at my opening and pushed the tip in.

Gripping his shoulders, I pressed down. My inner muscles squeezed around him.

Blaze let out a groan as he grabbed my ass tighter and lifted me up off him. "Do you want it?" His lips covered mine as he thrust deep inside me.

A surprise scream left my mouth and my nails dug into his neck as the heels of my feet pressed hard into his lower back. My pussy squeezed tightly around him, and I started to bounce but he pulled out of me. "Blaze, I swear—"

"Do you want it?" He repeated.

I was starting to get frustrated to the point I wanted to cry. Those horny pregnancy hormones were becoming too much for me. "Yes!" I snapped at him and again he thrust inside of me fast and hard. "Oh, my God!" My head hit the door before I bit into my lip trying to quiet my noise.

His hips slapped against my pelvis, causing me to bounce. "Fuck!" He cussed as he thrust faster.

210

"Ooh, Blaze." My lips parted, causing heavy pants to slip from my mouth. I held onto his shoulders and started my bounce, meeting his rough thrust.

Blaze took us to the bed and laid me down on my right side. He crossed my left leg over his right shoulder, his hips rolled before he started to dig into me slowly, building up his pace. Still with my leg on his shoulders, his arms reached up and took ahold of mine. His hips slapped against my ass fast and hard.

"Ah, ah, ah, ah, ooh, ooh, ooh. Ooh shit," My head fell on the bed as my fist clenched the sheets. "Blaze, sss, ooh, ooh." I was about to lose my mind from the pleasurable feeling his body was giving mine.

He repeatedly hit my sweet spot as his hand massaged my clit. My hips jerked and one hand went to his pelvis trying to push him back as the other tangled into my hair.

"Oh, my God, Blaze!" I cried. My inner muscles throbbed around his dick, squeezing tightly. The muscles in my legs tightened, causing my body to shake.

"There it is, baby. Let that shit go." Blaze egged on as his thrust became frantic. "Mm, fuck." Blaze spread my legs apart and held my thighs to the bed. His pelvis slapped hard against my ass three times. The final thrust he pushed deep inside of me and he held me to him as he came.

I could feel his dick pulsing inside of me. The feeling caused my sensitive inner muscles to clench tightly around him as my body shuddered.

Blaze's mouth covered mine as his hips slowly started to move once again.

One arm wrapped around his neck as my other went to his back. My nails moved down his spine to his lower back. I pressed my nails down harder. I felt his dick twitch. I bit his lower lip then sucked on the top. My tongue stuck out and Blaze's did the same. I licked his before pulling it into my mouth, sucking on it.

The action caused a groan to sound in the back of his throat. Blaze pulled back and kissed his way down to the center of my breast. He kissed the bow on my bra before biting the top of my right tittie. He sucked the skin into his mouth, no doubt leaving a mark. Blaze pulled my tittie out, his tongue played with the hard nub before he sucked it into his mouth.

My pussy reacted to the feel of him still inside of me as well as the suckling he was doing to my breast. My hands moved down to his ass. I held him to me as I began to roll my hips against him.

"Mmm," he moaned against my breast as he grew harder.

My inner muscles squeezed around him, milking his dick as he started to grind my hips.

"Momma!" Blake banged on the door hard. "Dad!" The hit was harder, louder.

"Damn," Blaze cussed but didn't pull out of me, instead he brought his mouth to mine.

"Is y'all ready! Dang y'all taking forever. I'm ready to go!" Blake yelled before pounding on the door. This time the bang was even louder.

Blaze's head lifted up and he glanced at the rattling door. "Did he just kick that mothafucka?"

"Uncle King's here!" He banged again.

"Blake, get yo ass away from my damn door! Shit!" Blaze fussed. I glared at him. "Shut the fuck up, black ass." He snapped at me. "Yo cock blocking ass son, man damn I ain't never gon' get none with his worrisome ass here." He fussed.

I broke out laughing. "Don't cuss at me and you always getting some with him here." I rolled us over and pulled him out of me.

"Ma!" Blake called sounding irritated.

"What the fuck I just—" Blaze started to fuss but my hand covered his mouth.

"Here I come, baby. Did you take out the trash like I asked?" I didn't wait to hear his reply as I looked down at Blaze. "You better stop yelling and cussing at him. That shit ain't cool at all. Yo ass on his fuckin' time. We were supposed to be taking him out, not be cooped up in the room fucking. So, you better get yoself right." I muffed his head to the side as I got off of him.

"Black ass done lost his mind. Cussing at my damn baby because you wanna be a horny fucka all damn day." I fussed as I walked into the bathroom. Blaze was starting to piss me off with fussing at Blake. Now if he did something, I could understand him getting in my baby's ass. This, though not so much.

I took off my bra and panties then turned on the shower and hopped in. I quickly washed myself, taking a whore's bath. After I rinsed myself out with the sprayer, I got out the shower. I grabbed my underclothes from off the floor then went back into our room.

Blaze caught me as I was coming out and pushed me into the wall. "You better watch who the fuck you talking to before I smack the shit outda yo ass." He glared down at me.

"Blaze, let me go. You ain't slapping shit but my ass." I rolled my eyes at him. My lips pursed together as I stared at him trying to match his glaring face. *I was failing.* Before my smile could give me away, I stood on my tip toes and kissed him. "Now go wash up so we can go. Somebody still have to tell Blake about the new addition to the family." I took his hand and moved it to my stomach.

That did it for him. "I can't stand yo ass." He laughed while rubbing my stomach. "Peaches, you know I love the fuck out of you, right?" Blaze kissed me, then moved down to my stomach and kissed it.

"I know. I love you, too." I rubbed his head as he kissed my belly once more.

"Damn," Blaze cussed. "This shit yo fault. If you wasn't pregnant, I wouldn't be horny as hell all the time. Shid, the thought of you having my baby get a nigga brick real quick. Peach, you might be having twins, boss, because my ass been extra horny lately." He explained with a serious face.

I couldn't do anything but laugh at him. "Blaze, get away from me. Ugh! Why would you say that?"

He laughed. "I'm serious as hell, Peaches, look." He pointed to his man standing up. "Shid, one nut and I'm good. Lately, it's like two nuts and I'm straight for a few hours before we got to fuck again."

"Blaze, shut up. Don't be jinxing me, shit." I snapped at him.

A serious look covered his face as his head tilted. "Who the fuck jinxing you? Shid, I'm telling yo ass so you can go get that shit fixed. We ain't ready for no damn twins. I can barely get some pussy with the one we got. The fuck you think I'mma be getting with two babies? New babies too? Hell no! I'mma have blue balls like a mothafucka." He exclaimed with a shake of his head.

"Hell no! Yo ass better start calling mothafuckas about merging them babies as one or give one away. Hell no! They ain't about to fuck up my pussy flow. Nope, not happening." His head shook as he stared at my stomach. "You need to make a doctor's appointment—" Blaze broke out laughing. "I'm bullshitting, man. Damn. Fuck you looking at me like that for?" He laughed.

I felt the muscles in my face loosen so I knew my facial expression was blank. Hell, I didn't know if he was being serious or not. You could never tell with Blaze's ass sometimes. My mind had gotten stuck on the part of merging two babies together.

"Hahaha," I started off with a real laugh before I stopped and gave him another blank stare. "Yo ass ain't funny." I went to move past him, but he stopped me. This time I laughed. "Blaze, gon' now. Blake is going to come back and bang on our door, so stop playing."

"I'ight, but I'm serious about twins. I'm telling you, Peaches. That team I want is coming," Blaze said excitedly.

I laughed at him. One thing that couldn't be denied was he wanted me to have his babies. That was a good thing but also a scary one. A part of me feared he was going to try and keep me pregnant. That was the only thing that put a damper on my excitement. I didn't want to have more kids if he was still going to be hustling.

Chapter 18

Peaches

"It took y'all long enough." Blake's attitude could be heard in his voice as well as seen on his face.

"Who the hell you talking to?" Blaze asked him.

I elbowed him in the side, then got in front of him. "Y'all don't start that mess. Blake, you better watch yo tone of voice before it get you hurt. Now let's go." I checked him.

"Sorry," Blake mumbled under his breath but loud enough so that we could hear him.

"Come on," I walked over to him and put my arm over his shoulder. I could feel Blaze staring hard at me, but I ignored it. We had to tell Blake he was having another sibling. Yelling and fussing at him wasn't going to help him accept it. Plus, he had been cooped up in this house, so I knew he was frustrated and wanted to go out and have fun.

"Blaze."

I heard King's voice come from behind me. I turned to look at him. I thought Blake was playing when he said King was here.

"What's up, Peaches?" King came over and gave me a hug, then kissed my cheek.

"What's up? I didn't know you were coming out here today." I stared at him confused.

King always called when he was coming to visit us. King just popping up unannounced, I knew something wasn't right.

I glanced over at Blaze to see him staring at King with a raised brow as if trying to read him. Blaze then looked over at me and his face straightened up. So, I couldn't read him.

"B, I see yo ass moving about. How yo legs?" King asked, jumping at Blaze.

Blaze bounced back as King swung. He dodged the blow then came forward. His fist shot out and King caught it. He laughed as he pulled Blaze into him. It looked as if they were giving each other a man hug. But the hold was a few seconds to long. I knew it had been a good month since King been here, but I knew damn well he didn't miss Blaze that much.

They pulled apart and they both laughed.

"Bitch ass holding me. You know I can still fuck yo ass up." Blaze joked, pushing King away from him.

"Yo bitch ass could try. You ain't fuckin' with me, crippled ass. I saw that slip, that's why I grabbed you." King talked shit back.

"King, I don't know why you didn't call. Are you coming out with us?" I asked him.

He glanced at Blaze then back to me. "No, I'm not staying long. I just had to pick up some shit I left here. I'm leaving tonight. You need to get back to Gary, though and check up on Mom B. You can't just have the funeral and disappear on her, Peach. Making it seem like you abandoned her, you need to get back there and soon." King explained to me before looking at Blaze and nodding toward the kitchen.

"Peaches, give me a second." Blaze said before he walked off with King.

I looked over at Blake and sighed. He let out a groan before walking into the living room and flopping down on the couch. He turned on the TV and started flipping through the channels.

When I heard the back door close, my curiosity had gotten the best of me. "Blake, I'll be right back. Start up the truck for me, please." He did as I asked of him.

I went into the kitchen to see Blaze, King and the rest of the men heading to the shed. I waited for a few seconds until they were all inside before I followed them out there. The shed was sound proofed, I couldn't hear anything. So, I opened the door and went in.

"Yo fuckin' youngin' out there wild as fuck. That little bastard out their wrecking hell on them niggas. He's bringing too much fuckin' heat to any mothafucka out there tryna serve shit. Niggas scared to setup a gotdamn meeting because of that little mothafucka. I'm coming to you because that's yo boy, but he fuckin' with my business. Little dude got heart, I give him that but when you fuckin' with my money, I take that shit personal." King snapped at him.

"Shid, Mac a go getta period. He gon' make his money regardless—"

"This ain't got shit to do with money, my nigga. I thought so at first, too. So, I stepped to his ass with a proposition, but he turned that shit down. That nigga said fuck me and my money. Money ain't got shit to do with it. He tryna figure out what the fuck happened to yo ass. Like I said, I'm coming to you because that's yo boy and he's loyal as fuck to you. So, you can either bring him in or I'm killing his ass when I touch back down. I ain't got shit against youngin' but his recklessness is fuckin' with my business and money." King told him. I could tell he was heated.

"Damn, don't kill him. Shid, he a hotheaded sonofabitch but he a crazy little mothafucka and if he already out there asking questions. He'll find something out before either one of us—"

King cut Blaze off with a disagreeable shake of his head. "Shid, how the fuck he gon' find out shit when that mothafucka killing niggas who ain't talking. A nigga ain't gotda know nothing and Mac killing that mothafucka. That nigga leaving a trail of bodies—" King stopped talking as if a thought came to him.

"That trail can be his calling card. If mothafuckas know he dropping niggas without a care, somebody bound to talk. Fuck! That mothafucka still fuckin' up my shit. Niggas want work and scared to meet up thinking this little nigga gon' come kicking in the fuckin' door. Shid, he done shook mothafuckas down on Bottom Side. He got niggas spooked."

"I knew I liked his ass for a reason. He ain't doing shit we haven't done. Only difference is, police ain't caught up to Mac ass yet. Shid, we make a move and they're on our ass. We just got to shape Mac's ass up and he'll be good." A thoughtful look covered Blaze's face.

"Ain't no we, that's yo boy. You shape that mothafucka."

"Stop acting like a bitch. I'll get at him." Blaze made me and King's head tilt to the side. I'm sure our facial expression was the same.

"How the fuck you gon' get at him?" King asked the question I was thinking.

"Because I'm going back to Gary with you." Blaze nodded as if he was still thinking on something.

"I'm about to leave once we done here. And you 'bout to ride out with Peaches." King reminded him.

"Damn," Blaze's hand ran over his head then down his face. "Let me go holla at Peaches right quick. Shit!"

My head was already shaking at him. I knew he wasn't about to blow us off to go run back to Gary and play hood again.

"I'm staying out here." Bellow told Blaze, shaking his head. Khyree, Khalil and King agreed on doing the same.

"We all might as well stay out here." I jumped in, still leaning against the wall.

"I'm going in the house." Bellow once again said. True to his words, he was the first to walk past me and out the door, followed by Khyree and Khalil. Neither one of them said a word to me.

I cut my eyes at my brother. "King, you might as well stay. I mean, you're the one who came with the news. Gon' talk, Blaze."

"Peaches—"

I held my hand up, cutting Blaze off. "What are you going to do, Blaze? Go back home, get with this Mac dude and shake the city, letting everybody know you're alive?"

"Peaches, I'm going to talk to the nigga. I ain't shaking shit. The fuck is you talking about?" His voice raised.

My head shook at him. "Blaze, who are you trying to convince that you're only going to talk to this dude? Damn sho' not me. King, you knew what yo ass was doing when you told him this. You two mothafuckas live for trouble. King, you're not dumb so I know you seen what Blaze saw in Mac when he turned down yo fuckin' offer. So, you came running to Blaze to get him on board with y'all. Blaze, yo ass stupid if you didn't see that shit. You're not going back to Gary." I fussed at him.

"If the dude been killing folks for months, another day ain't gon' matter unless he dies by then, which means his time ran out. Right now, though, we

222

have an eight year old son out there waiting to have a family day with us. And those plans aren't about to change because the hood in you wanna go run the streets. King, you can stay or take yo ass home, your choice. But Blaze ain't going anywhere today. He's not about to blow my baby off for this bullshit. We'll be in the car waiting on you."

I wasn't about to argue with Blaze about anything. My mind wasn't changing and if he knew what was best for his ass, he'd be in that truck driving us to the movies, the toy store and then out to eat. All that extra shit could come after family time. I left out of the shed and went back into the house where the others were.

"You need me to take you somewhere?" Bellow asked.

"No, Blaze driving us out today." I replied as I walked past them into the living room and out the front door. I got in the truck. Blake sat in the backseat with his cellphone in his hand, playing a game.

"Are we still going?" Blake asked.

"Yeah, we're about to leave in a minute. Sorry we've been slow all morning."

"It's cool." From the way it came out, I knew he didn't mean it.

I reached over to the steering wheel and started blowing the horn. A few seconds later, Blaze came out of the house. After he shook up with King, he made his way to the truck. Once he got in, I turned away from him to look out my window.

"B, you ready to go?" Blaze asked a dumb question.

"I guess," Blake responded. He didn't seem excited at all anymore.

Blaze let out a sigh as he started backing out the driveway. "Peaches, did you put the address into the GPS?"

"No, I forgot." I took out my phone and pulled up the address for Lights Out Putt & Play. I programed the address into the GPS then turned back to look out my window. I was most definitely in my feelings about what just took place. Even so, I didn't want to say too much because Blake was in the truck with us.

Blaze was seriously going to make me hurt his black ass. He better get his shit together or I was packing up and taking my baby back to Lafayette on his ass.

***

We were having so much fun, the three of us. So much so, I had decided to let the whole ordeal go about Blaze trying to go back to Gary. Eventually, he would have to go back anyways.

I was truly just trying to stall him from going back because of the drama it would bring us. Right now, though, I pushed it to the back of my mind as we had a family day out. Blake had fun at Lights Out Putt & Play. We played miniature golf and air hockey.

Once we left there, we went out to eat. Now we were at the mall and I was beyond tired. My feet were hurting, and I was sleepy.

"Boy, stop playing and come on now. My feet hurt." I complained, grabbing Blake and pulling him back to me.

"No, man, you heavy. Get on dad's back." Blake laughed as I tried to hop on his back again but he quickly moved out of the way.

"Forget you then, punk." I stood in front of Blaze, snapping my fingers as I held my arms out. "Come on, big daddy."

His brow raise before they fell to the bags in his hands. "Fuck you snapping yo fingers for? I ain't no damn dog. Hell n'all! I got all these bags. I'm not carrying yo ass too. Fuck outda here." He shook his head and walked around me.

"That's okay, y'all better remember this. Blake, who gon' feed you? Yo daddy can't cook. Blaze, who gon' feed you too? Blake can't make nothing but a hotdog. And what about your late night problem? You bet not wake me up at two/three in the morning. I bet you don't get my medicine." I hinted to him about sex.

"Medicine? Peaches, shut the fuck up. Shid, yo ass gone need my needle to give me yo damn medicine." He tried to come back but failed.

"Point exactly. I'm not using your needle anymore. I can go to the store and buy me some. Different color ones too. Can you get my medicine from anywhere?" My lips twisted into a smirk. He couldn't go to the store and buy pussy, but I could always get a vibrator and batteries.

"Fuck you, Peaches." He tried to push me, but I moved out of the way.

Laughing at him, I turned around and headed for the exit. "Ahhh!" A surprised scream left my mouth as I was suddenly lifted off my feet. I looked back at Blaze and started laughing. His ass wasn't stupid. The way he'd been wanting to have sex lately, he better had come to his senses. "Nope, put me down. I can walk now. Gon' now."

"No, I got you. I can't have my lady walking around with her feet hurting. What kinda man would I be if I let her walk in pain?" Blaze questioned.

"Dude, you gotda come better than that. You just trying to get some of her medicine at night." Blake jumped in.

Blaze burst out laughing so much so he had to lean against the door from laughing so hard. "Hell no! On what yo little ass gon' blast me like that? B, I'll knock yo ass out. But it's cool, though because you don't understand. Now when you get some girls' medicines you gon' be just like me."

"Blaze, for real? Don't be telling him stuff like that. I done already told you about that. Blake isn't getting no medicine from nobody." I rolled my eyes at him before looking at Blake. "Ain't that right, baby?"

Blake looked away from me to his dad, then he rubbed his hand over his head. "Yeah." He said before scratching the back of his head.

"Oh shit! Damn, boy yo ass cursed! You ain't never gon' get away with a lie doing that shit." Blaze started laughing as we reached the truck. "Damn, boy."

"I'm not lying. I'm not gon' get no medicine from anybody." His eyes slid to me and again he scratched the back of his neck.

Now I didn't know whether to be mad about the fact his telltale lies were just like his dad's or the fact he knew what I was talking about when I referred to medicine. Of course, it was the latter. Now I just had to figure out whose fucking medicine was he thinking about getting.

Once the truck was started, I turned toward the backseat to look at my boy. "Blake, don't lie to me—"

"Now he know to lie to you, Peaches. Stupid ass." Blaze stated.

I glared at him. "Blaze, shut up, with your real irritating ass." I cut my eyes at him before turning back to Blake. "Rashad—"

"Oh shit! She's serious now." Blaze cut me off once more. "B, just say I plead the fifth to whatever she says until I teach you how to lie."

I reached over the seat and punched Blaze in the arm. "You can't even lie to me, so how can you teach him and why would you want him to lie to me?"

Blaze licked his lips and glanced at me as he drove down the street. "Firstly, I'm a damn good liar. I just don't like to lie to you. Secondly, leave that man alone. If he wanna get some medicine from some chick, let him. He ain't no damn girl. I done already told you once before you not about to turn my son into no damn spoiled ass girl. He gon' be a man. Let him go out and poke his needle in some skins."

My mouth opened then closed. I looked back at Blake and then to his dad. My eyes squinted at him. Was this the type of foolishness my son had been around for the last few years when Blaze had him?

Of course, it had been. I seriously didn't know what to say at that moment. Was he really encouraging our eight year old son to go out and have sex with different women? My mouth moved in the motion of a fish. I was at a loss for words.

"See that, Blake? Cat got her tongue. Just say some dumb shit like I just did, confuse the fuck outda her and she'll be lost to the point she don't know what the fuck to say." Blaze told him before reaching in the back and letting Blake slap his hand.

No, this yellow bastard didn't.

"I wasn't at a loss for words. I was simply thinking of ways to whoop yours and his ass." I lied. "Blake, don't listen to your daddy. He's going to mess around and get you a whoopin'."

"You only got one kid in this damn truck and it ain't me. Fuck out of here." Blaze reached over the seat and muffed me.

"Gon' now, Blaze. You play too much." My eyes rolled and I ended up laughing.

"B," Blaze called to Blake and I saw his head nod toward me before he mouthed *this all you have to do.*

I was confused at first until I remember what started this. Blaze was good, I must admit. I thought about blasting him but figured I would let it go for now, just in case he tried to pull that mess one day.

***

When we pulled into the driveway, Bellow, Khyree and Khalil were sitting on the front porch. Blaze put the truck in park and Blake was about to hop out, but Blaze stopped him.

"Blake, hold up. We wanna talk to you about something real quick." Blaze turned off the truck.

"What's up?" He closed the door back and stuck his head between our seats.

I looked at Blaze waiting to hear what he had to say.

"Yo momma about to have another baby." Blaze put it plainly as if it was nothing.

I rubbed my forehead not believing that man. Why was I surprised he told him the way he did was beyond me? I shook my head at him, then tried to make light of the situation. "Blake, what do you think about having—"

"Like what I think really matters. But if you want to know, this some bullshit is what I think! Fuckin' bullshit!" Blake snapped before getting out the truck and slamming the door behind him.

"He done lost his gotdamn mind!" Blaze was right behind him, slamming his door as well.

"Oh, God." I didn't want to go in there. Mainly because I didn't want to interfere with the trouble Blake was about to get in with his dad. I was too understanding when it came to Blake, so I knew following behind them was only going to cause Blaze and I to get into it.

Blake had a right to feel anyway he did. He just shouldn't have cussed. Then again, Blaze could've been a bit more considerate about his feelings when he told him. My hand rubbed my forehead.

Let me go in there before he hurt my child.

I got out of the truck and headed inside. I could hear Blaze yelling from outside the house. By the time I reached the porch, Blake had ran back outside to me. Again, Blaze was right behind him.

"Blake, I'm not about to chase yo little ass. You wanna cuss like you grown and slam doors. So, I'm about to beat yo ass like you grown." Blaze snapped at him as he walked down the steps.

I had to roll my eyes at what he said. Blake's mouth was bad because that was how Blaze and his friends talked around him. He had no one to blame but himself for the way Blake talked at times.

"Blaze, just chill out for a sec, dang. I really don't feel like this right now. Blake, let me go." I tried to shrug him off but he was holding onto the back of my shirt tight.

"Hell no! Fuck that! He ain't 'bout to talk to me crazy, I'll fuck his little ass up." He fussed as he snatched Blake up like he was a rag doll.

I got offended. "Blaze, don't be snatching on him like that. You got yo fuckin' nerves to be pissed at him for the way he talks when he got the shit from y'all. And Khalil if you say one thing, I'm going to slap the shit out of you. I don't have time for your smart ass reply." My eyes slid to him. I had come to know him all too well. It never failed, he always had something smart to say back.

His hands raised in the air as if he surrendered. He didn't say anything.

I grabbed Blake and put myself between the two of them. "Blaze, let him go. You have nobody but yourself to blame for his mouth—"

"Yeah, it's your fault!" Blake suddenly snapped, jerking away from me.

From the hard, rapid pants of his breathing and the raise of his shoulders, I knew he was pissed.

"All of this is your fault. We out here in this nothing ass town because of you. I hate it out here. You ruined everything. I had friends and a life back home in Lafayette! I have nothing here but your fuckin' friends. You're too busy to do anything with me, all you do is shoot guns, workout and sleep with my momma. Now she's pregnant. How the fuck are you going to have another kid when you don't have time for the one that's here. I hate you—"

Blaze slapped the shit out of Blake. My mouth dropped as Blake's head jerked to the side.

Slowly Blake's head turned back toward his dad and the meanest glare I had ever seen covered his face. Blake hocked and spat blood from his mouth.

"Oh, my God." I grabbed his face to look at his mouth.

His head jerked back and out of my hold. "Don't touch me. I wanna go home." His eyes slid to Blaze as he walked past him, still mugging him hard as he walked by. "Move!" Blake snapped at Bellow before bumping past Khyree and going into the house.

Blake's words played inside my head. *Did my baby feel neglected?* Tears filled my eyes as his outburst repeated in my mind. "I'll go talk to him." I needed to explain something to Blake. I didn't want him to ever feel like we didn't have time for him.

"No, you stay yo ass right here. Don't bring yo ass in that house." Blaze walked away from me and went into the house, slamming the front door shut.

I wasn't about to let Blaze touch my baby. He was already upset about everything. Blaze should've been a little more considerate with telling him about the baby.

"Nah, Peaches, let that man handle that." Bellow pulled me back.

I jerked away from him. "No, I'm not about to let him beat up my baby."

"Oh, he gon' whoop his ass and it ain't shit you can do about that. Look, I get you see him as yo baby but, sweetheart, he gon' be a man one day. So, you got to see him as that right now. It's no way in hell he should've ever popped off like that to B. You

232

wanna blame Blaze for everything but you can't do that. Yeah Blake's mouth is us, ain't no denying it. But that extra flippin' shit he do is because of you. Yo ass always running behind that man, so he pops off knowing what you gonna do." Bellow pointed out to me with a shrug.

"Every time that man in trouble, you running to his rescue, which causes problems with you and Blaze. You gotda stop doing that. He ain't no damn girl, he's not going to be a woman one day. He's a little man and that's how we see him. You ain't his father, Peaches, B is. So, chill out and let B handle this." Bell leaned against the front door and crossed his arms, indicating he wasn't going to move.

I knew he was right, but I just couldn't do anything. My hand rubbed my forehead once again and I let out a breath. I thought about how Blake acted when it came to Blaze. Ever since he was two, I had always jumped in the middle of them. Bellow was right, I needed to let Blaze handle it.

I looked at Bell and sighed, "Is he going to hurt him bad?" I questioned nervously.

The three men laughed. "Oh, he gon' fuck him up." Bellow said with a head nod. "Just think about how yo pops was with King."

The images of King getting his ass whooped popped in my head. *Oh, hell no!* King was a boy, so my dad never took a belt to his ass. He fought King with his fist. "Oh, hell no! Bell, move! He bet not be in there fighting my baby."

"Peach, chill out. Yo pops might have boxed King's ass up but look how he turned out now?" Bellow tried to make me see reason in what he said.

"Bellow, have you not met King? He's not normal. That man is crazy as hell. *No! Move!*" Using King as an example was terrible.

"He's normal to me." Bell shrugged.

I gave him a blank stare. "Nigga, yo ass ain't even normal. Bell, what are you talking about?"

"She has a point." Khalil pointed out.

"Thank you, Khalil." My lips pressed together, and my head tilted to the side as I stared at Bellow.

He looked away from me to Khalil. "Shut the fuck up, Khalil. Yo ass ain't normal. Yo whole family fuck'd up. Shid, just look at y'all fuckin' names. Khalil and Khyree."

"Don't bring me into y'all shit." Khyree jumped in. "My pops is mixed, which is how we got our names. And we got our name from my grandfather and his twin brother, who died before we were born."

My eyes squinted. They didn't look mixed at all. "So, you two are half black?" I pointed between the twins.

They both nodded.

"That makes so much sense to me now. I simply thought y'all grew up in the hood." I exclaimed.

"We did. After my pops died, we couldn't afford to live middle class. My mom wasn't working, and her mother wasn't helping us out for the simple fact she got with my pops who was half black. So, she had to sign up for government assistance and Gary's low income housing. She found a place out in Ivanhoe. And like mostly everybody else that live out there, they become stuck. Our moms did, but we didn't, though. Khalil may seem dumb but he's smart as hell. I wouldn't let him fall off, we had to look after each other. School was the only way to do it." Khyree shrugged tossing a rock from off the porch.

My head nodded, I understood them wanting to leave the hood. "I'm not going to ask about the side job with the cleaning vans—"

"Khalil has a cleaning and plumbing business." Khyree informed me. "He can pretty much do some of everything when he's not being dumb. But he smokes too much."

I looked over at Bellow and he shrugged. "Yeah, they not normal at all."

They broke out laughing.

I didn't find anything funny. All these niggas were dumb if they asked me. Realizing what just happened, I glared at Bellow before hitting him. "It's been long enough. He should be done by now. Move." I told him just as the front door opened.

Blaze walked out, he looked highly pissed off. "Gon' in the room and pack some shit up. We going back to Gary, we're leaving here in about an hour. So, do what you have to by then."

I didn't move at first. I looked him over, trying to spot some blood on him. I didn't know what he did to my baby, but I was nervous to go see. I didn't want to have to fuck Blaze up, but I would if he had hurt Blake.

"Why the fuck you standing there for? Get yo ass in the fuckin' house and get ready." He snapped at me. My mouth opened but I shut up when he raised his hand. "Real shit, Peaches, not right now. I will seriously hurt yo ass. Now get the fuck inside."

I don't know what happened in the house but from the look on his face, I knew he was serious. I was far from a punk, but I knew when to choose my battles and this wasn't one, I wanted to fight. Not saying anything, I walked past him into the house. Once inside, I quickly took the stairs by two and went into Blake's room.

He was packing his clothes into a suitcase. "Blake, are you okay?"

His shoulders shrugged but he didn't say anything.

I walked fully into his room and sat on his bed. I peeked at his face, expecting the worse. Besides the mark from the slap Blaze gave him, there wasn't anything else, so I let out an easy breath. "Blake, talk to me."

"I don't want to be here no more. I wanna go home." He told me.

I patted the spot beside me. "Come here." He sat down and I grabbed his hand, pulling him into my side. "Blake, you know even though I'm having a baby it's not going to change anything between us, right?"

He shrugged me off of him. "Ma, it's not you. It's him. How is he going to have a baby when he don't have time for me? Ever since I been here, we've done nothing together. He's always with you or Khyree in the shed. Even when I went out there the only thing, he taught me was how to clean a gun and shoot it before he went back to working out. He didn't even shoot his gun with me, Khyree did. Now you're about to have another baby. I want to go back to Lafayette. I wanted y'all together at first but now I don't. At least we did stuff when y'all was broken up." He shrugged again. Before he went back to packing his stuff.

"Blake, you know your daddy loves you and will do anything for you. Baby, you have to understand that he was working out so much to build his strength back up for us. He might not tell you this, Rashad, but being in that wheelchair hurt him. All because he couldn't do anything for you while he was in it. It made him feel bad, like he was failing us. For the simple fact that he was in there and not able to walk." I explained to him. I just wanted him to understand what he couldn't see, what he was too young to grasp.

"Baby, I felt just like you did and lashed out on him the same way. He couldn't face us while in that chair. It made him feel less of a man and a father. But, Rashad, you can't jap out like you did. Regardless of how you feel, he is still your dad. Let that had of been my daddy that I snapped at like that. Y'all will still be looking for pieces of my face. Or Uncle King, my dad used to actually fist fight him." I told him.

"Rashad, you owe him an apology. I get you're mad but think about what your daddy had to be feeling not being able to do anything with you. Think about him having to be carried up and down the stairs, to the car, needing help to get dressed every day. He loves playing basketball with you and he couldn't even do that. And to watch you shoot guns with Khyree and play around with Khalil, I know that hurt him. Now think about all that he had to been feeling." Standing up, I kissed the top of his head. "Hurry and finish packing."

Once I stepped into the hallway, I had to hurry into my room. I burst into the bathroom and went straight to the toilet, releasing everything I've eaten. Once I finished, I rolled off some tissue and just sat on the floor. "I hate this." I mumbled to myself before I felt myself getting sick again. I leaned over the toilet once more and began to dry heave. I wiped my mouth again and laid my head against the side of the counter.

I didn't feel like moving. My eyes closed and I started to take steady breaths in order to keep myself from getting sick again. It wasn't long after I felt arms wrap around my waist before I was lifted up off the floor.

"Come on, baby." Blaze took me to the sink and turned on the water.

He held me up as I rinsed out my mouth and brushed my teeth. Once I was finished, he carried me back into the room. I wanted to tell him I could've gotten up off the floor and walked. It would've taken me a minute to do it, but I chose not to say anything. I was going to accept his help whenever he was giving it with no complaints.

Blaze laid me down on the bed and started to remove my shoes then clothes. He took off my panties and then un-hooked my bra.

I know he was not about to try and have sex with me, right now?

Even with my thoughts I kept my mouth shut. He took the sheet I kept folded at the foot of the bed and covered me up. He then walked away from me going back into the bathroom. My brows furrowed as I heard the water turn on in the tub. Blaze walked out the bathroom a few seconds later and left right out our room.

I was even more confused. He wasn't talking to me, so I didn't know what to think. A rude shit talking Blaze I could deal with but a quiet one. I never knew what to expect.

I slowly started to sit up until I heard the door open. Then I quickly laid back down and closed my eyes. I was about to play sleep just so we didn't have to talk.

"Peach," he shook me. "Peaches, here."

I let out a tiring sigh before I opened my eyes. "What's this?" I asked dumbly while staring at the paper plate with premium saltine crackers and the cup he held out for me. I sat up against the headboard.

"Ginger Ale and crackers? What the fuck it look like?" His eyes squinted and he looked at me like I was the one crazy. "Here suck on these." He sat the plate on my lap and the cup on the nightstand before he hurried to the bath-room to turn off the water.

I picked up a cracker and smelled it.

"What the fuck is you doing?" Blaze laughed at me as he walked back into the room.

239

"Smelling it." I replied as my stomach turned. I wanted to eat it but the thought of eating something right now had my stomach feeling queasy. "Thanks, bae, but I can't eat those right now. I'll sip on the Ginger Ale, though." I grabbed the cup and took a drink from it.

"And you'll eat those crackers. It'll help settle your stomach." He informed me.

I knew that but how the hell did he? "Who told you that?"

Blaze ignored my question instead he picked me up out the bed and took me into the bathroom, where he had ran a bubble bath for me.

I was really confused because just moments ago he was on the verge of hurting me had I said something else to him. On top of that he was determine on going back to Gary tonight. But now he was giving me a bubble bath.

Once my body hit the warm water all my confusion was forgotten as a moan left my mouth and my eyes closed. The water felt amazing against my skin. My head lazily moved to the side and I peeked up at Blaze to see him watching me. "Are you getting in?"

He shook his head *no.* "Nah, this all you." With my sponge in his hand, he got my body wash and got it soapy. Blaze kneeled down beside me and began to wash me up. "What? Why you looking at me like that?"

"I'm trying to figure you out. You always seem to surprise me with your actions. Like right now, I'm trying to understand it. You were just pissed off a minute ago and now you're bathing me. So, I'm just trying to understand what changed."

Blaze ran the sponge over my breasts, cleaning them. He dipped the sponge into the water, rinsing it off before he put more soap on it and started to wash me again. He cleaned down my stomach to my pelvis before he pushed my legs apart. Not once saying anything, he just continued to clean me.

He let the water out the tub then pulled me up and turned on the shower. Taking the spray off the hook he rinsed me off. Once Blaze finished, he grabbed the towel from off the counter and wrapped it around me.

I held my arms up and waved my fingers so he could pick me up. He laughed at my childishness but picked me up, nonetheless. My legs wrapped around his waist; my face buried into his neck as my arms held tightly around his neck. When we made it to the room, Blaze tried to lay me on the bed, but I wasn't letting him go.

"Peaches, come on, man." He tried once again to pull my arms from his neck.

"No, stop it and just lay down." I instructed.

He let out a heavy breath before laying down on the bed. "What's up?"

He knew me all too well, just as I knew him. "I don't know, you tell me. Babe, I know you and as much as you love me, you're not doing this just because. Now tell me what's up." Blaze helping me off the bathroom floor and rinsing my mouth was just him. The extra stuff, though, there was a reason behind it. I knew that much because he didn't try to have sex with me in the tub. Blaze was always trying to have sex on any given opportunity. But not this time.

My lips pressed against his neck before I pulled the skin into my mouth. I bit him then kissed the spot. "Bae, talk to me."

"It ain't shit—"

"Maybe not to you but it is to me. So, tell me." I sat up on him and grabbed the hem of his shirt. I pulled it off then tossed it to the side. I unhooked my towel and leaned into him. My mouth pressed against his, pecking his lips twice. I kissed my way down to Blaze's jaw, then his neck before my tongue trailed to his shoulder.

Lifting up, I pecked his lips again before I moved down his body so that my head laid on his chest.

Blaze's arms wrapped around my waist and he kissed the top of my head. "I overheard you talking to Blake a little while ago. You good with him. Man, Peaches, I can't get to him like you do. He won't talk to me like he do with you. We might fuck around on some bullshit, but Blake will never be open with me like that. Shid, if I can't click with my own son how the fuck I'mma do it with these babies? Shid, maybe we are rushing into this."

I knew it was something. "B, you click with Blake. Maybe not on a sensitive level but you two are like two peas in a pod. It's going to be times when

Blake come to you over me about some things and vice versa. I mean, Blake has never talked to me about girls before, but he does with you. Babe, you are amazing at what you do with him. Look, whether he comes and talk to me about something, that isn't going to change anything about y'all's relationship. Blake simply felt as I once had, which was ignored. Baby, if you don't talk to him, he's going to feel that way."

"Before the shooting, you and Blake was tight. Bae, to suddenly lose that connection with someone hurts, badly. For months it's been like that with him and after a while hurt turned into anger. That's what happened with Blake. Blaze, you have a tendency to shut folks out without intentionally meaning to or knowing you're doing it. That's what you did to us and if you don't talk and tell us what you're feeling all we have are assumptions." I explained to him.

"It's no telling what thoughts Blake was thinking. You have to talk to him, explain what you must and then, work to get back to where y'all were. And believe me if I didn't think you were capable of loving and taking care of our baby, then I wouldn't be having it. You are amazing with Blake, so I know you'll be just as great to this one."

Everything I said was the truth. Blaze was more than capable of raising a kid. He had to work on his communication skills a lot, but he was still an amazing father.

"Shid, I can't talk to him like you do."

I love that man like crazy. I would never understand why he could talk to me so easily, but not to anyone else.

"B, you don't have to talk to him like I do. Talk to him like you normally would. Baby, he's used to the way you are and how you talk. And I seriously think you would freak him out if you went to him the way I do. So be you. All I'm going to say is don't go to him first, let him come to you and apologize. The way he flipped wasn't cool and was hella disrespectful of him." I leaned into him and bit his bottom lip, then sat up again.

"Oh, I doubt he jump stupid like that again. I'm far from a bitch. I ain't taking shit from a nigga on the streets and damn sho' not about to have my own son jumping bad with me like he's one either. I fuck'd his ass up real nice. Don't fuckin' look at me like that. Hell no, mine ain't gon' pop off at me like he can whoop my ass, fuck outda here." Blaze stated.

I could tell just thinking about Blake's actions pissed him off. I wanted to know what he did to my baby, but I decided against asking. Hopefully Blake learned his lesson about jumping crazy with a crazy person, who happens to be his father.

"Blaze, I'm hungry." I rubbed my stomach actually seeing everything I wanted.

His hand came to my stomach and he started rubbing it too. "What we gon' name them?"

I rolled my eyes at him. "I'm not having no twins. And I don't know yet. We'll think about it later—"

"Yo ass just thinking about food, that's why you don't wanna talk about it, ol' hungry ass. What you want, man?" He laughed, still rubbing my stomach.

Again, my eyes rolled but mouth watered. "I want some waffles. Ask Bellow if he'll make his buttery waffles for me, please. I swear I can taste them." I bit into my lip just thinking about those buttermilk butter waffles dripping in syrup.

"Shid, the way you looking, I think I'm jealous of some gotdamn waffles." He laughed. "That's it?" He rolled us over, kissing me before he got off the bed.

"Wait, no that's not it. Bellow's waffles, eggs and some biscuits. I think it's some ice cream in the freezer. Ooh no, forget the ice cream. Look in the cabinet and get the Flamin' Hots then get the round pickles out the fridge also get the cheese *and* warm the cheese up. Umm…"

"Umm? The fuck you mean *umm*? Hell n'all! I ain't about to get all that shit. You better get yo ass up and come get it." Blaze looked at me like I was crazy.

My eyes cut at him. "I don't be saying that when you ask me to suck yo dick at three o'clock in the morning or when you wake me up to ride yo shit when I don't be feeling like it."

His expression didn't change. "Shit, we be in the same place and you ain't gotda carry shit—"

"Oh, my God. Are you serious right now, Blaze? I'll do it for you. Forget it, I swear you get on my damn nerves most of the times and I still deal with you. But now that I'm starving, you can't walk yo simple ass down a few stairs to get me something to eat? Ugh, man, I swear I don't know why I continue to deal with this shit." I fussed as I sniffled. My hands quickly wiped at my eyes before I snatched his shirt up and put it on.

"Peach, I was just bullshitting. You dead 'bout to cry, for real?" His brows were furrowed, and his head tilted. "Hell no. Yo ass straight went off because you hungry, though. Damn. Baby, what else you want?" His hand moved over his mouth so I wouldn't see his lips twisting up.

"Never mind. I'll get my own food." I lied. My ass wasn't about to leave out that damn room.

"Peaches, stop playin' and tell me what the fuck you want before I change my damn mind."

I let out a heavy breath and rolled my eyes as I walked back to the bed.

"Fuck it," Blaze said, coming back to the bed.

"Okay. Dang. I want everything I said. I got a taste for some garlic bread. No, forget that. I want some bread sticks and look in the bathroom and give me the Ajax—"

"Hell no! You tryna eat bathroom cleaner?"

My face went blank. "You're not funny, you ass. No, I'm not about to eat it. I like the smell of it. The smell help with the sickness sometimes."

"Hell no, and yo ass bet not be smelling that shit no damn more. The fuck wrong with you. Man, get those damn crackers until I come back. Yo ass crazy." He fussed at me.

"I'll get it myself." I mumbled. I was going to wait until he left out to get the Ajax.

Blaze walked into the bathroom. He returned a few seconds later with two cans of Ajax. "Don't

246

worry, I'm getting all this shit outda here," he said, walking out the room.

"Bastard." Sighing, I flopped down on the bed. My eyes slid over to the crackers and I sat up remembering something else, so I grabbed my phone and called Blaze.

"What Peaches?" he answered.

"Bae, can you get the salt and vinegar chips out the cabinet? That helps settle my stomach too. These crackers really don't work. And can you bring the Ginger Ale up here too? Ooh and can you make the eggs into an omelet, please?" I bit into my lip. I was nervous that he would go off.

"I'ight, Peach."

"Okay, thanks, bae. Aye, and can you bring the other stuff up now until the food gets ready, please? And some ice!" I quickly added.

"Bye, Peach." He hung up on me.

Oh, I was not about to be the only one going through this pregnancy by my lonesome. Nope, I wasn't. Blaze was going to be running like crazy for me.

Chapter 19

Blaze

Two Weeks Later

Bellow pulled two blocks down from Oak Knoll's apartments. "Pull right there." I pointed to the dark street. I looked around until I saw King's tinted, all-black Navigator parked further up the street. "Go to the end of the block and wait there." I pulled my hood over my head, then hopped out his car. Once the door closed, he pulled off and I made my way to King's truck. I tapped his back window three times before going to the back passenger door and slid in.

"Yo boy just went in there about ten minutes ago." King pointed to an apartment that was dark.

"Ain't shit happened?" I asked, looking at the house.

248

He turned around to face me. "How the fuck am I supposed to know what's goin' on inside that mothafucka?"

"Shut the fuck up, stupid mothafucka. Look…" I heard a gun go off followed by flashes of light coming from the front room's window.

"I told you that nigga was reckless. He don't give a fuck." King stared at the house.

The front door opened, and Mac walked out the house. He came to the end of the sidewalk and looked around. He stared in our direction for a long while before he turned and headed the way I sent Bellow. I pulled out my phone and text Bell, letting him know Mac was headed his way.

"What the fuck is he doing?" King mumbled to himself, but loud enough that I heard him.

Mac stopped halfway up the block under the streetlight. He looked back down our way before he turned around and headed toward us.

"Why the fuck you drive this big ass, noticeable ass truck. Yo ass could've got a toy car for this shit." I snapped at him while looking at Mac. His pace picked up and he was getting closer to us. "King, pull off."

He put the truck in gear but didn't move. "I know this nigga ain't that fuckin' bold."

Oh, he was bold as fuck. "Nigga, go—" as soon as the words left my mouth Mac started shooting. "That mothafucka!"

King reversed down the street. "Nigga, yo ass better shoot back. What the fuck is you doing?" King snapped at me.

I laid on the backseat laughing, not believing that little nigga was bold enough to walk down toward the truck and start shooting. Now if we were niggas trying to kill his ass, he would've been dead. Then again, he 'bout would've taken one of us with him.

"When I see that nigga, I'm fuckin' him up. Bitch ass mothafucka." King was pissed. "I don't see the comedy in this shit! That nigga could've shot us, and he hit my damn truck. I'mma stomp the fuck out that nigga. Tell Bell to follow his ass."

"Hell no. He'll notice Bell. Plus, his ass done cut through them houses. He gon' stay off the streets. We gon' have to grab his ass another time." I started to think about the different spot's Mac used to hang out at. He probably done dropped a few cribs. It was probably one crib he kept up.

"How the fuck you gon' do that when you not supposed to be out?" he questioned.

"Don't worry about it. I'll get him and be low." I told him as I hit the back of his seat. "Now take me to the crib. If it ain't too late, I could probably get some." I rubbed my stomach just thinking about Peaches.

"Oh, y'all good now?" King laughed.

I didn't find shit funny. It had been two weeks since I moved us back to Gary. Peaches ain't like that shit at all. She simply thought we were coming to visit my moms and go back to Muncie. She was pissed when she realized we weren't going back and that I had King find us a house out in Ogden Dunes before I was even walking.

I thought she would've liked the house. It was a nice two story brick ranch. It had five bedrooms, five bathrooms, a nice big living and dining room. A full basement, big kitchen and the crib had a pool. What really made me think she would love it was because of the waterfront on Lake Michigan.

A few years back, Peaches wanted a house on the beach. But now that I found her spot, she dreamed of having, she was pissed because it meant being back. So, she done spent more time with Blake, my moms and her girls than she had with me.

It was time to come home but her attitude told me she didn't understand that.

Muncie was just a low key spot until I was better and able to move around. Now that I could walk it was time that I handled business now and I knew that's what really pissed her off. While I was confined to the house, she could watch me. Hell, she knew my every move. But Peaches couldn't do that now and she was scared for me. I couldn't be mad at her for that.

"He'll nah, we ain't. Peach ain't gon' be good until this shit is over with." My hand ran over my face thinking about the shit that was coming. I know mothafuckas gon' regret coming at me. They done did too much. I was going to enjoy this to the fullest.

"You ain't getting shit, then. Yo ass better get used to that hand and some lotion." King thought that shit was funny. "Here, roll that." He tossed me a sack and a swisher.

It wasn't shit funny to me. I grabbed the weed and broke it down before I started to roll the blunt. "You don't know Peaches like I do. Yo sister a freak. She be wanting it just as bad as I do. It's been two weeks too? Oh, her ass gon' give that shit up tonight." I lit the blunt and inhaled deeply.

"Shut the fuck up."

That time, I laughed. Peaches couldn't resist it when I went for her all the way. I had just let her be mad for the time being but shid, it was time her ass got over it. We were there now and wasn't shit changing.

***

When I got in the house, I tossed my keys on the table in the hallway then made my way to the kitchen. It was a little after midnight and I could still smell the food Peaches had cooked. I opened up the microwave and just like every night this past week, my plate was in there. I warmed the lasagna, garlic and grilled chicken up. Once it was done, I quickly smashed everything on the plate then made my way to our room.

Blake laid at the foot of the bed watching wrestling on the TV. He loved that WWE shit. His ass had so many recorded shows on our TV, it didn't make any damn sense. When I stepped in the room, he looked at me and sat up.

"Why you in here?" I asked him as I walked to the closet. I kicked off my shoes, then took off my shirt. When he didn't say nothing, I peeked back at him to see he had gon' back to watching TV. "You don't hear me talking to you?" I walked back into the room.

"Yeah, but I didn't wanna miss this match." He replied before pausing the TV.

"And you couldn't have pause that mothafucka?" I asked him.

Blake laughed. "I could've," he shrugged.

"You gon' make me fuck you up. Now why you in here and not in yo own damn room? Shid, we might as well move yo bed in here with as much time you spend in this mothafucka like it's yours."

Blake laughed again. "Nah, momma was getting sick, so I came in to check on her. That damn baby be having her throwing up everything. Dad, that baby gon' be problems, I'm telling you." He turned and looked at Peaches, pointing to her. "Look at what it's doing to momma. She can't eat nothing without getting sick. She's always crying and fussing about something. Auntie Kim said its hormones. Well, they need to take them damn hormones out. That baby gon' be bad as hell, man." Blake's head shook before his hand ran over his head, then down his face.

My son had it honest. He took straight after me and a part of me was happy as hell he had no parts of Leslie in him. The other part was kind of nervous about just how much he took from me. Blake's ass was gon' be hell once he got into his teen years. My little dude was already sounding grown.

"You think so?" My head tilted to the side as I watched him.

"Hell yeah. With the way momma be acting, hell yeah. I bet it's a girl too." He looked over at Peaches and shook his head. "No boy is gon' have her like that."

I started laughing. "Yo momma having twins—"

"You better stop saying that. She be so mad. You should hear how she talks about you to my aunties. Oh, that Jerron dude told Auntie Ebony to tell momma to call him. He wanna check on her." Blake informed me.

"Oh, for real? What momma say?"

"Yeah, momma said *oh okay, I really need to talk to him. I haven't heard from him since we been in Muncie.* That's it. She didn't call him, though, unless she did when I was in the pool." A thoughtful look appeared on his face before he stared back at me with his hand held out.

In the past, when Peaches and I split apart, I had Blake looking after her. She couldn't talk to a nigga without me knowing. Hell, whenever a dude tried to holla at her or make conversation while Lil B was around, he was to run they ass off. Shid, I paid my son good money to look after his moms.

I didn't have time to be trying to take her away from no other nigga. And she damn sho' wasn't about to have a nigga around my son tryna play daddy either. That's why whenever he got out of line and became disrespectful toward a nigga, he called me, and I would always talk Peaches down before she could whoop his ass.

Hell, my little dude was so good at his job, King put him onto his girl, too. Blake was a little snoop. He heard and saw everything, then came back and told us about it.

"I'm tired. I'm going to bed." Blake got off the bed and stretched with a yawn. He was about to walk past me but stopped. "Give me my money." He held out his hand again, rubbing his fingers together.

Laughing, I reached in my pocket and peeled off two bills. "Here." I slapped it in his hands.

"Night, Dad."

"Night." I watched him walk out my room, I let out a sigh and rubbed the top of my head. I ain't know what the fuck I was going to do about that Jerron nigga? He looked out for Peaches when I was down and everything, which I appreciated to the fullest.

King told me if Jerron hadn't showed up when he did my baby girl and my shorties she was carrying wouldn't be here. But I needed that nigga gone if he still had feelings for her. I really needed to holla at him to see where the fuck his head was at when it came to Peaches.

Although I ain't like him, we shared a common interest. *Peaches.* With the shit going on and the heat that was about to come when mothafuckas found out I wasn't dead; Peaches was going to need somebody she trusted to look after her when I wasn't around. But first I had to talk to him, just in case I had to get rid of his ass before shit got crazy.

I took out my phone and shot King a quick text, telling him to setup a meet with Jerron later on tomorrow. I stood and went to my side of the bed, sitting my phone on the nightstand.

I then took off my jeans. I pulled the covers back, then leaned across the bed next to Peaches. My mouth went to her shoulder and I kissed my way up to her neck.

"Peaches," I pulled her skin into my mouth and sucked on it hard. "Peaches," my hand moved to the front of her shirt. I played with her nipples through her top. The small nub quickly became erect. She let out a moan and my dick grew harder. "Peaches, baby, you up?"

"No, I'm sleep, and you stink like weed. The smell is making me sick." She grabbed my hand and pushed it off her tittie. Peaches grabbed the cover and pulled it up to her chest. "Blaze, go shower before you get in this bed. I don't feel like running back to the bathroom." With that, she rolled over on her stomach.

"Damn, for real, Peach?"

She shrugged me off of her and pushed her face into the pillow. A sigh left my mouth as I got out the bed and went into the bathroom to shower. Peaches ass was trippin' hard, but I was getting some tonight, otherwise her ass was getting the fuck out. I looked down at my dick and shook my head. I wasn't about to jerk that mothafucka when I had a lady in the bed. *Fuck that.*

Once I finished washing myself up, I got out the shower and went to the sink to brush my teeth. When I finished, I went back into the room.

The room was dark. She had turned off the TV. *Man, her ass on some bullshit.* I didn't dry off or put on clothes. I just slid in the bed, grabbed Peaches and pulled her to me.

"Blaze, gon' now." She tried to pull away from me.

"Shut the fuck up. Why you still mad?" I managed to pull her on top of me.

"I'm not mad. I'm fine." She lied. The attitude in her voice gave it away.

"Peach, you know why we had to come back. And I wasn't leaving you out in Muncie. Let me finish. Damn!" I snapped at her as she tried to cut me off. She let out a loud breath but didn't say anything. My hands moved along her spine, down to her ass, then back up to her neck.

"I wasn't leaving y'all in Muncie or Lafayette, fuck that. Y'all being that far away from me would've had my head fuck'd up. I would've been worrying about who could've followed King or one of us out there one day. That's too damn far for me to get to you if some shit happened. So, if you're pissed at me for not wanting to separate us, then so be it, fuck it. I'm not taking no chances or leaving you alone. I'm not doing it *and* you pregnant. Hell no, I ain't chancing it again, Peach."

I was going to make sure someone stayed with them when I wasn't around no matter what. After the whole thing with Le'Ron went down. I knew that bitch he worked with was dirty and would try coming for Peaches again, hell, even my son. I wasn't playing with those mothafuckas anymore. I had too much that was important to me that I couldn't lose.

My hands continued to stroke along her back. For a while she didn't say anything. I started to think she had gone back to sleep until I heard her sigh.

"I know all that, but it doesn't change the fact that I didn't want to come back here. All that's here is pain and death, nothing else. I understand you have to do what needs to be done, but even so, that don't mean I have to like it. But I'm going along with it because you have to do this. So, I'm not mad at you, Blaze." She tucked her face into the side of my neck.

My head moved back, and I tried to look down at her. "If you ain't mad and you understand all this shit, why we ain't fuckin'?" I had to understand that.

"Why you always out until midnight with King? Huh? The same night we got here you dumped us at momma's house, left us there and didn't come back until three in the morning. Every day after that you've been home at midnight wanting to have sex. When I have to sit in this house horny all day. Fuck you and yo dick. Until you can be considerate and come home in the afternoon and give me some, then I'm not having sex with you. My pussy is closed until further notice." Peaches sat up, kissed my lips, then rolled off of me. She scooted to her side of the bed. Grabbing a pillow, she put it between us. "I don't wanna feel you poking me in my ass. Good night."

"Peach, you serious?" I hoped her ass was playing. She didn't say anything. "Peaches?" Again, I was met with silence. "Man, this that bullshit, boss. Ol stupid ass." I had every mind to push her ass off the fuckin' bed. "Stupid shit, man." I was pissed off. "This why niggas find hoes."

Peaches broke out laughing. "Damn, bae, you real mad, huh? You wanna find hoes now?"

"Peaches, shut the fuck up, real shit." My damn dick hurt. I was so fuckin' hard. But I wasn't about to beg her black ass. Fuck that.

"Okay, I love you, Blaze." She yawned.

I didn't say anything back to her. Instead, I rolled over on my side and forced myself to sleep.

***

The constant ringing of my phone woke me up. I glanced over at Peaches to make sure she was still sleep. She was. I grabbed my phone and put it to my ear. "Yeah?" My hand ran down my face before my arm covered my eyes.

"Yo boy on the move. I got my little dude on him now. Get up, I'll be there in five minutes," King said.

"I'ight, I'll be out in a minute." I disconnected the call and let out a yawn. I looked at the time on my phone. It was 4:45 in the morning. "Shit." I cussed lowly as I tossed the covers off of me. I got out the bed, then went into the bathroom and took a piss. When I was finished, I hopped in the shower.

Once I was done, I brushed my teeth then went back into my room, to the closet. I pulled on my boxer briefs, grabbed a pair of black sweats, a black beater and a black hoodie. After I got dressed, I stepped into my black forces then left out the closet. I went to Peaches.

Leaning over her, I kissed her cheek. "Peach," I shook her. "Peaches."

"Mmhm?"

"I'm about to make a run. I'll be back later on, i'ight?" My phone started ringing. Still leaned over her, I reached on the nightstand and grabbed it. "Yeah?"

"I'm outside, let's go." King hung up before I could reply.

"I'll call you in a few hours to see what's up, i'ight?" I kissed her forehead and went to sit up but she caught the front of my shirt.

"Blaze, y'all be careful out there. You answer when I call, okay?" Peaches grabbed the sides of my face and kissed me.

"I'ight, if I don't answer, it means I can't, and I'll text you. Now go back to sleep." She didn't let me go. "Peaches, come on, man." I let out a little laugh at her worrying ass. But shid, I really needed to go. "Peach, come on, baby girl. I gotda go."

"Okay, you be careful, Blaze. I'm serious. I love you." She kissed me again.

"Love you, too, Peach. I'll call you in a few hours." My lips pressed into hers once. I sat up and went to my side of the bed, reached underneath it and grabbed both of my Desert Eagles. I tucked them on each side of my waist band and left out.

I stopped in Blake's room before heading out of the door. When I went inside, he was damn near hanging off the bed. Little dude had to be tired. "B," I pulled him fully into the bed so he wouldn't fall off. "B."

"Yeah?" Yawning, he rubbed his eyes then sat up. "Hm?" he hummed, looking up at me through squinted eyes.

I sat on his bed. "I'm about to make a run so look after yo momma for me. Bet?"

"I'ight. I got you." His hand came out. We shook up, ending the handshake with a fist bump.

"I'ight, I'll be back in a few hours." I got off his bed and left out of his room, closing the door behind me. I grabbed my keys from the side table by the front door, set the alarm and left out the house. I hopped in King's truck and shook up with him. "What's up?"

"Yo youngin' making early moves. You see how that little mothafucka get around. If we could teach his ass some form of control, he'll be slick as fuck." King said as he drove down the street.

I looked over at him with a raised brow. "How the fuck can you teach a mothafucka shit when you can't control yo gotdamn self?"

We were a lot of things but when shit got heated, self-control was the last thing we had. That mothafucka was crazy, but he had a point. If Mac could chill the fuck out and evaluate shit before killing a mothafucka, then he'd most definitely be sweet. At that moment, though, his ass was just running around like a fuckin' hitta and ain't finding out shit.

"Fuck you. My dude said he ran into him out in Delaney last night. He said Mac was out there until this morning and he followed him out to a house in the Bronx." King parked and pointed up the street. "It's that third brick one from the corner. Here." He tossed me a pair of gloves and a black mask that covered from my nose to my chin.

I put it on and threw my hood on my head. "Circle the block." I got out the truck and cut through the yard he had parked in front of. Once I hit the alley, I made my way down to the house. I slid into the backyard and jogged to the back door. The door was slightly opened, and I shook my head. He was most definitely getting reckless. Once a mothafucka began to make dumb mistakes, their asses wasn't no good to anybody. It was no way that door should've been left opened.

I stepped into the kitchen and saw two duffle bags. Curiosity got the best of me and I peeked inside one. Bricks of powder filled it. The other bag was full of money.

What the fuck was he doing? Robbing those mothafuckas too?

I heard Mac voice come from the front room and I moved closer to hear what he was saying.

"A few months ago, my homie was killed at Prestige. Word around is it was over territory." Mac let out a laugh. "And it's crazy that once he was gone yo little crew tried to take over his corners. Shid, I can say them mothafuckas was loyal to yo ass. I had to kill half of those fuckas just to find you. Do you know how fuckin' pissed I am?" He let off a shot and a dude hollered out in pain.

"The next bullet going right into yo heart. Now tell me what you know about that shooting. I don't think you had anything to do with it. I believe you just jumped at the opportunity to take the areas.

But I think you know who might have sent the hit since ain't nobody came at you about those spots."

I was tired of hearing him talk to that mothafucka and was ready to kill him my damn self. But Mac's last question is what stopped me. He had a point. If he wasn't behind the hit and took over my areas with no problems coming his way, he knew who did.

"I don't fuckin' know—ah fuck!" He screamed as Mac shot him again.

Mac smacked him across the face with the gun three times before he cocked it. "Don't fuckin lie! I'mma ask you one more time. Who was behind the hit?"

"Okay! Rice and his bitch is trying to run shit. He gave me the areas for a profit. He's the one who told me I could get the spots." He blurted out.

I pulled my gun from my waist, cocked it and let off two shots into his forehead.

Mac turned around and started shooting my way.

Chapter 20

Peaches

"Ah! Blake, I'mma kill you! Stop, that's cold!" I screamed out a laugh as he sprayed me with his water gun. "Blake! Ang, get him!"

"Ah shit!" Blake shouted out as Marcus picked him up and tossed him into the pool. "Pops, you better run!" He grunted out before swimming to the end of the pool and getting out.

"Thanks, Marcus, but you better run." I laughed as he took off running from a wet Blake.

"Blake, gonna get him." Bianca laughed as she flipped brats on the grill.

"Ooh, y'all would never believe what I found out last night." I shook my head as I waved them into the kitchen. I turned to focus my attention on my baby and his pops as they played around. "Marcus,

Blake, can y'all watch Keema by the pool until we come out. Blake, you can pull her around in the float." I pointed to Keema's Disney princess ride on floaty.

"Okay, come on, Sha." Blake called to King and Ebony's baby girl. I didn't know why but he was the only one who called her *Sha*.

I stole a brat off of the grill and wrapped it in a paper towel before I went into the house. The girls and Bianca were in the kitchen. "Y'all come in the living room before Blake comes creeping his ass in here."

We all went into the living room. I sat on my folded leg and then unwrapped my brat to eat.

"Ooh, give me a piece." Angel reached over with her fingers already out.

"Girl, no. Go get you one. Shoot, ol begging ass." I rolled my eyes at her before biting into it.

"Stingy ass, you could let me get a small bite." She stood in my face waiting for me to give her some.

"Ang, sit yo greedy ass down somewhere. She's feeding for two now. Gon' somewhere. Damn. Now, Peaches, what you find out?" Missy pulled Angel away from me and onto the side of her.

"Thanks, Miss. Ebony, remember when you was telling us about your run in with Sean and how King popped up at your house later on that day?" I asked her.

"Yeah, why?" Her reply was slow as her head nodded.

"Blake's little creep ass told on you. I found out last night. Y'all know since we've been back, Blaze be out late with King and I can't sleep unless he's home. I always fake sleep when he gets here, last night was no different. Except, I hear Blake's ass telling him about Jerron wanting me to call him. Blaze asked what I said, and that little bug told him word for word—"

"No, nuh uh, Peach, he didn't." Kim's mouth parted.

My head nodded and I held up my finger. "Yes, he did, and the kicker was Blake said, *Where my money at*? Blaze's ass been paying him. Now I'm thinking Blake done ran off men because of Blaze's ass. Remember, I told y'all every time a dude tried to talk to me he would get disrespectful toward that man and before I could get in his ass, he had Blaze on the phone. He never got in trouble with B because he put him up to it. Y'all my baby been spying on us and then running back telling his dad and King everything."

Bianca burst out laughing. "Well, what did you expect, Peaches? Shid, I could've told you that. I thought you had something serious to tell us. I'm about to burn my damn meat." She stood up from her seat and started to walk out but stopped. "You seriously didn't know that?"

I shook my head. "No, I honestly didn't think Blaze would have him snoop on me." It was crazy to me to think Blaze would be that childish to have our son run men away from me. A guy couldn't look at me without Blake going off and embarrassing me. Now I know it wasn't just him.

"Peaches, knowing my son, you shouldn't be surprised at all. You think Blaze was going to actually let you start dating someone other than himself? If Blaze thought you were interested in a man, he would've ran back trying to make claim on you. He let you have a break from him, only. Y'all wasn't on break to see other people—"

"I was under the impression we were. Especially, when he told me I could bring a man to his birthday party." I pointed out.

Bianca laughed again. "The same birthday you got pregnant on? I mean that is when he knocked you up right?"

My mouth opened then closed and I rolled my eyes at her.

"Exactly, girl, Boon knew you wasn't gon' bring no man. If he thought for a second you did, his ass would've been all in yo shit. He's many things but stupid isn't one of them. I must admit, I had a lot to do with making you come to your senses. One thing a female hate is to see what she considers hers with some new arm candy. I told Blaze if he wanted you all he had to do was throw a nice bitch on his arm and in your face." She laughed again clapping her hands together. "Who was he going home with that night before the bullshit happened?" She laughed before she let out a light breath. "My point."

I felt stupid. Did I think Bianca was lying? Hell no. She wanted Blaze and I together. "So, wait. The girl he was with at the party, Blaze wasn't really seeing?"

"Oh yeah, he was, but it wasn't serious. I saw her around a couple of times with him. But he pretended he ain't know me when they were together, so I knew she was nothing but a time passer. If it was serious, I would've met her." Bianca waved me off.

"Wait, I thought you knew her because she's Ms. Rozlyn daughter." I was confused because I knew Blaze told me that his momma and Roz were cool at one point in time.

"I knew Rozlyn all of a year while living in Delaney before I stopped dealing with her. After I found out she was messing around with Joseph's nasty ass. From the small time I knew Rozlyn, her daughter didn't stay with her." She shrugged. "I have to check on my meat." Bianca walked out of the living room.

"That's a nasty ol bitch. She jumped from father to son." I mumbled to myself, but I guess Blaze's nasty ass was no different seeing as he hopped from mother to daughter. That was some nasty shit.

"Look at Peach over there thinking. Don't worry about that girl. He ain't thinking about her," Ebony said.

I laughed and waved her off. "I ain't worried about Blaze's ass going nowhere or fuckin' with no bitch. We are so past all that. Plus, if he just so happens to decide to revert back to his old self, I'm gone. I'm about to have two kids and I'm grown as hell. I'm not about to play those games with him."

"Shid, he just might have to because you ain't giving him no coochie." Missy laughed, slapping hands with Kim.

I couldn't help but join in. "And I'm not giving him none until he could walk into this house in the afternoon and break me off something. Y'all, I be so damn horny in the afternoons. My hormones be raging like crazy. I'll try to call his ass, but he won't answer, just text me that he'll be home later. I find that so inconsiderate. He don't even have to come home. He could just meet me somewhere and give me the dick in his truck. Damn. I can't even get that. But he wanna waltz his ass in here at midnight *after* I done got sick and shit. Talking about, *Peaches, baby you sleep?* Hell yeah, nigga, I'm sleep. I'm not about to bounce on yo dick when I'm feeling sick."

The girls laughed at me. Whereas I was being so serious.

"Damn, Peach, that is kinda messed up but shid, if he comes home horny and I ain't got none all day, I'mma bounce all on the dick. Bitch, split, cowgirl all that good shit." Kimmy added, making me laugh.

"I do be tempted but my stomach be so queasy. I hate this shit and can't wait until it's over." Even though I hated that part, I was excited about the pregnancy. I don't think excited could truly explain the feelings I had. I smiled as I ran my hand over my belly.

"What do y'all want? A boy or a girl?" Missy asked, rubbing my stomach. "What are you?" She cooed at it before putting her ear to my stomach. "Oh. Mmhm."

Laughing, I pushed her away from me. "You stupid. Move." I shook my head at her before looking at the other girls. "I don't know. I mean, I think I want a girl. Seriously, I don't think I could handle three of Blaze. Blake is all I need, and my poor baby can't help that he takes after Blaze to a freakin' *T*. No, I don't think I can handle another one."

"What Blaze want? Why are you rolling your eyes at me?" Ebony laughed at my sudden blank expression.

"Girl, that crazy ass man talking about I'm having twins. Gon' tell me it's because he's twice as horny than usual. I could've slapped his ass. Don't jinx me with no twins." I looked at my stomach. "It's not two of you in there, is it?"

"No, it's three of us, Mommy." Missy said in a childlike voice.

We burst out laughing.

"Missy, get yo irritating ass away from me. Ugh, why would you say that? Stupid self!" I pushed her away from me, still laughing.

"Peach, I feel as though I owe you an apology." Ebony suddenly said.

Confused, my brows rose. "Why?"

"Because of how I tried to make Blaze seem in the beginning of y'all's relationship. I just didn't want you to have to deal with half the bullshit I did with King. I can honestly say I misjudged him and I'm sorry for that. You look so happy and I hope he continues to make you feel this way. Otherwise, I still carry my nine which I have no problem using." She joked before turning back serious. "I'm glad I was wrong about him, though."

"Thanks, E, but you wasn't all that wrong. The shit I went through with that man and his hoe—"

"Peach, that was one girl, who he never had sex with. He only kept her around because of the feelings you brought out of him. Regardless of that, Blaze has seriously changed to be with you, Peach. It took him a minute but once he realized you wasn't playing, my nigga got right real quick. I like that he did because he'd rather lose that chick than you permanently. Girl, that man waited on you for five whole years. Bitch, bye. What hood about to do that?" She stared at me waiting on my reply.

My face turned hot. I had to agree, Blaze did change and that said a lot. Even though he had a couple of bedroom rumps with a woman during our split, I couldn't be mad about that. Especially when he was quick to drop her once I came to the realization that I wanted us to get back together.

"Yeah, that's my bae. I love him like crazy." I confessed. My cheeks pushed into my eyes from my hard smile. I couldn't control it. Blaze had me.

They laughed at me.

"Y'all shut up, for real. I misjudged him too, though. I must admit he ended up surprising the hell out of me. What I love most of all is he can talk to me now. He couldn't before, which is why he always did dumb shit and spat out harsher shit. Now it's so much easier. Don't get me wrong, he still have his moments when he kinda shuts me out and does him, but we work. It's crazy but I now know we can really overcome anything if it's what we truly want." My smile was still intact, but my eyes rolled up as I started to feel giddy.

"It's so crazy to see you like this. To see that you have fallen hard for a hood. Hell, in a relationship, period. Wasn't she the one always talking about how relationships were meant for disasters? And look at you now. My bitch done snatched herself up a hood. She's glowing, a mommy and pregnant. What!" Angel laughed as she hi-fived the girls.

"Shut up. Y'all stupid. I'm about to go check on these kids and that meat. My ass starving." I stood up from my seat and stretched.

"Yo ol' hungry ass. Not gon' lie, though. I'm hungry too. Bianca know she can throw down." Ebony rubbed her stomach following behind me.

We all went into the backyard and my niece ran to me. I picked her up and placed her on my hip. "What are you doing, little girl?" I kissed her cheek then ran my hands over her wet ponytails.

"Nothing." She looked over at the pool before grabbing my face. She brought hers closer to mine. "Blake put water in my face." She tried to whisper.

Keema was just too freaking cute, looking just like King. "Rashad, you bet not put no more water in her face. Otherwise, I'm going to beat yo butt!" I yelled over at him.

He stopped playing basketball with Marcus in the pool to look over at me. "What? Man, she's lying. I was playing basketball."

I opened my mouth to reply but Keema started yelling at him. "No, I'm not, ugly little boy.

That's why my daddy gon' knock you out." She fussed back.

I glanced at Ebony. All she could do was shake her head.

"Man, shut up." Blake laughed. "Yo daddy not gon' touch me."

"Say it in my face, then." She wiggled her little self out of my arms and walked over to the pool.

I don't know what he was supposed to be saying in her face, but I hope he didn't. She marched over there with a determine promise in each step to do something.

"Ebony, what the hell have you been teaching my niece?" I grabbed a paper plate and started putting different stuff on there. I got brats, chicken, corn on the cob and a piece of steak. I got some pink lemonade from the cooler then went and sat at the table next to Kim.

"Girl, I don't know where she gets that mess from. I had Britt watch her the other day while I was at work. Peaches, I came and got my baby the next day and she had a whole new attitude." She shook her head.

"Oh, Lord. Not Brittany. Girl, she done taught her that mess, then she gon' start picking at her just so she can snap off. Blake was already bad but that's how she would do him." Brittany was just bad with kids. She looked after them and took care of them like she was supposed to but her attitude was a mess. She did too much for my taste and thought the mess was cute. Oddly enough, she loved the kids.

"I wasn't bad. Gimme a bite." Blake's wet hands reached into my plate.

I slapped his hand away and looked at him with my face twisted up. "Boy, all that food you just bypassed and you gon' come over here asking for mine. No, gon' now." I waved him off.

"Ma, I don't want a plate. Just give me a bite, please." He pleaded.

My eyes rolled hard at him. I don't know why he couldn't get something, bite off of it then come back to it later on. "Here, boy." I held up my brat for him to bite.

He bit into it and then pointed to the corn. "That too."

My eyes cut at him, but I held it up for him. He took a big bite and then grabbed my lemonade and drunk it all.

"Blake, why would you do that? Now go get me some more, black butt *and* a bottle water out the freezer."

"I can't go in the house. I'm wet." He countered with a smirk, looking just like his daddy.

"Boy, you better take yo butt in that house and get my water." I returned his grin before I went back to eating my food. I was halfway through my steak when I realized Blaze hadn't text or called me to check in. He knew how I got when I didn't hear from him after so long. "Ebony, hand me my phone off of the chair."

"Girl, leave Boon alone. He's okay. He'll be home in a minute." Bianca joked.

I was serious. I needed to check on him; otherwise, I would worry like crazy. "E, give me my phone." I repeated ignoring Bianca.

She picked it up and passed it down to the girls until I got it. I checked my phone for any missed messages or calls. I had none. I called him. He didn't answer. I then remembered him saying if he didn't answer for me not to worry because he would text me. I waited twenty minutes, but I didn't receive a text or a call back.

I text him again and this time I left a voice message, telling him I was starting to worry.

Again, I waited twenty minutes to get a reply, but nothing came. I called him three more times only to get his voicemail each time. That was the shit I hated. Don't be out running the streets trying to find a faceless person and then don't return my phone calls or texts.

He could've shot a quick message saying *in a minute* and I would've been satisfied. But Blaze's ass had to make shit harder.

With a sigh, I called King's phone. The exact same thing. His damn voicemail picked up. "Oh, my God! They're starting to piss me the fuck off." I fussed, dropping my phone on the table. My hand ran through my hair before I picked my phone back up and tried calling them again. "E, let me see your phone to call King." I got up and walked down to her.

"Here." She handed it to me.

I called King from her line four times and didn't get an answer. "This the shit that pisses me off right here. Now what if it was an emergency? Then what? We all would've been—I don't know but something. And they asses wouldn't know shit because they not answering the phone or texting back." I flopped down on the chair trying to calm myself down. My leg bounced fast and I just felt like crying. I didn't know if something happened or not and the fact that they weren't answering had me thinking something had.

"Auntie Peaches, you want me to call him on my phone. Don't cry, I'mma call him." Keema pulled out her little princess phone and press numbers, putting it to her ear. "Hello. Uncle Boon, where you at? Auntie Peaches is crying. You need to come get her, okay?" She pulled the phone from her ear and then got into my lap. Her small fingers wiped my face. "Uncle Boon said him on his way so don't cry, okay?"

Through my tears, I couldn't help but laugh at her little grown self. "Okay, baby. I'm not going to cry."

"Okay, gimme kiss." Her small lips puckered up and she kissed the corner of my mouth.

Again, I laughed. She was most definitely Ha'Keem's daughter.

Chapter 21

Blaze

O nce I let off my shots, I ducked back behind the wall and dropped to the floor. I was already expecting Mac's move and I knew he was going to be shooting high. It was only so many bullets that was going to leave the chamber before it was empty. Once I heard the click, then the magazine hit the floor. I stood up.

"Yo young ass ain't got too many more times to shoot at me. Gotdamn!" I dusted myself down getting all the dry wall off of me. "If I come around this corner and you shoot me, mothafucka, I'm going to kill yo ass." I warned him before I came from out the kitchen.

"Nah, hell no!" Mac repeated shocked.

"Yeah and you been causing hell out here. Let's go before the laws show up." I turned around and picked up a duffle bag, but he didn't move. "Nigga, bring yo ass on." I

277

pulled on my hood and hit the back door hard, not waiting on him.

I was supposed to be dead. No way in hell was I waiting around for the damn laws to catch up with my ass. I hit the alley and without looking, I felt him behind me.

As expected, King was parked at the end of the alley. I hopped in the front with Mac jumping in the back. "Go!" I told him as we heard sirens. Both our doors were still opened when King pulled off.

"Nigga, what the fuck? It's like I'm seeing a fuckin' ghost right now? What the fuck? I saw them bury you," Mac said.

"No, you saw them bury a closed casket—"

"Hell no! Don't give me that shit. The way yo girl was crying and shit. You can't fake no shit like that? My nigga do you know how many mothafuckin' bodies I done dropped thinking yo ass was dead? Damn! Yo ass ain't dead?" Mac continued saying.

I could hear the disbelief in his voice. "I ain't dead. I got too much to live for. I was supposed to be low, but my nigga here rolled up on me one day talkin' about my youngin' out here causing problems." I looked back at him.

"Shid, that's yo fault. I thought somebody popped yo ass. I was grieving." Mac told me with a straight face.

I started laughing. "King, you hear this mothafucka. He was grieving so he went on a killing spree."

King nodded his head. "Yeah, I hear him. You shot my fuckin' truck last night. You could've shot me. So, when I stop this truck, get yo ass ready because I'm about to fuck you up."

"I got you," Mac replied to King before turning his focus back on me. "Why the fuck would you fake yo death and not tell me?" His sincere expression had me shaking my head.

"Shid, I ain't know who was who out here. So, I had to be cautious of mothafuckas. Money make mothafuckas turn and do some low down shit. Not saying you was one of them, but I couldn't chance it. I got too much to be gambling on a *what if*, you know?" I explained to him.

Shid, I ain't even want Peaches' friends to know what was up, but I couldn't keep her from them, and they would've eventually found out. It wasn't until a few days after the funeral that I told her she could tell them.

Mac was my little dude no doubt, but he was a hood nigga as well. And if it wasn't for the fact that he was out there dropping niggas left to right to find out what happened to me. I wouldn't have come and found his ass. He earned my trust by doing that. Shid, at his rate, my nigga was heading straight to a body bag within a couple of weeks. I couldn't let that happen.

"I hear you. Man, this shit crazy. What the fuck is going on that you gotda be low?" he asked a good question.

"Shid, all I know is somebody put a hit out a few years back. We killed the pawns but, on my birthday, other pieces came out to play. And supposedly, a bitch is behind all this bullshit. But shid, I don't know." Remembering what Le'Ron let slip, I'm starting to think it wasn't a slip at all. Maybe that nigga knew he was gon' died and just threw us off on purpose.

Shid, I ain't know and the bullshit was starting to piss me the fuck off.

"The little shit I did find out is it's over territory but that's crazy and I don't believe that bullshit. I mean, why give Doe the spot out in Ivanhoe? That nigga a pussy without his guns and boys. You saw how quick that nigga sung after two shots and a couple of hits knowing he was gon' die anyways." He hummed. "Rice? That name sounds so familiar. I don't know where from, though." Mac's face contorted into one of thought.

"I knew I heard it from somewhere too but it's not coming to me either."

"I'ight. Well, since we're all here. Real shit though, I was coming to knock on his door next." He pointed to King. "His ass was just too cool about everything. I mean, this nigga ain't slow his business down or anything. I was kinda fuck'd up about it. Real shit, I figured that was yo truck last night and that's why I started shooting." Mac told us before shrugging. "My bad, now I know it's because you knew this mothafucka wasn't dead. Shid, it's a good thing I ain't hit yo ass, huh?" Mac asked him with a straight face.

I burst out laughing but stopped. "Nigga, I was in the fuckin' truck. Yo ass just started shooting."

"Shid, that's y'all fault. That truck wasn't out there when I went into the house and all of a sudden it appeared. Hell n'all, I felt like I was being followed." He shrugged.

King stopped at a light and looked at him. "How the fuck you ain't know the truck wasn't parked at somebody's house?"

He had a good point. I looked at Mac waiting on his reply.

"Because that mothafucka wasn't outside when I got to the crib. Plus, the radio light was on. Now unless somebody drove someone to that house and they was sitting in the truck waiting on them, then aye, it would've been an accident. But I wasn't wrong. You two fuckas been following me. I personally got tired of you watching from afar and was just gon' holla and see what was up." Mac shrugged nonchalantly.

I looked at King. "Dude got a point and if it was either one of us, we would've noticed somebody following us and done the same thing."

"I don't give a fuck. That nigga shot my truck and I just got that mothafucka—" King started to go off.

Mac cut him off. "Actually, yo truck hit my bullets, but you don't see me pissed."

I fell out laughing.

King pulled the truck over to the shoulder of the road. "Get yo ass out. I'm about to fuck you up."

"King, come on, man, he just bullshitting. Damn, Mac, shut the fuck up, i'ight? I'm tryna get to the crib so I can get some. A nigga been out for two weeks. We can drop Mac off at the apartment then swoop him up later on." King was on some bullshit. I needed to relieve this damn nut. I was trying to make it home by twelve no later than one o'clock. "Aye, where the fuck Pooh ass at? That was like yo right hand."

"Shid, that nigga wasn't tryna get his hands bloody to find out what happened to yo black ass. I had to stop fuckin' with him because of that. Plus, he had his nose too far up some bitch's ass. I ain't chasing no pussy if one, it ain't making me no money, or two I wanna wife the bitch. Shid, it was like he was tryna hide that hoe for some reason. If he wanna be a cuddly ass nigga, so be it." He shrugged before he reached in his pocket and pulled out a blunt that was inside a baggy. He took it out, inspected it then lit it. He looked at me and shook his head. "Nigga, I thought yo ass was gone homie. Shid, it's a good thing you ain't."

"Why you ain't bounce off like Pooh? Why you come looking for trouble?" King asked, glancing at him through the rear view mirror.

That was a good question.

"Ain't no pussy in my blood, boss. And if I fuck with you, I ride with you, period. I fucks with B. My nigga looked out for me hard one time when I was out here without shit. You know, he ain't never clowned me or nothing like that. Instead, he stayed looking out for me. He hooked me up with some work and set me up in a nice little spot. I felt it was only right I looked out for him. It ain't like I got shit to lose." Mac hit the blunt hard before he held it out to me. "Man, I'm hungry as fuck."

I looked at the clock on the radio and saw it was already 12:45pm. "My girl cooked, so we might as well go there."

King and Mac started laughing.

"This big mothafucka tryna get some pussy. My nigga said fuck it just take me home. Damn, B, she been holding out?" Mac laughed.

King replied before I could. "Hell yeah, got this nigga over here with blue balls. All he be talking about is how he getting some tonight. I see this bitch the next day and he whining about how she was trippin'."

"Fuck you mothafuckas. Man, Peaches ass be on some other shit. I'm thinking she pissed because I moved us back here. But no, it ain't that. This mothafucka gon' say we ain't fuckin' because she be horny during the day and I ain't there to give her none, so until I can come home in the afternoon to break her off, we ain't never fuckin'. Man, I'm about to take my ass home and be all up in that pussy. A nigga about to go swimming in that shit. Shid, two weeks too fuckin' long for me. I'm addicted. I can't even lie. Peaches make a mothafucka need rehab." I rubbed my stomach. Just thinking about being buried deep inside of her guts had my damn stomach hurting. I was imagining that hard nut I was gon' bust once I got ahold of her.

"Shut the fuck up. I don't wanna hear that shit. You take shit too far. That's some nasty shit." King snapped.

"It might be nasty to you but I be in heaven. Hurry the fuck up and get me home." I rushed his ass. I was ready to go.

"Damn, B, the way yo ass sounding you might not last but a minute." Mac blasted.

"Shid, that's all I need is a minute." I wouldn't be surprised if I only lasted that long my damn self. Peaches had a nigga's head all fuck'd up right now.

***

The ride back to the crib felt slow as hell, while we passed the blunt between the three of us. Mac wanted to stop by the liquor store and King needed to make a few drop offs while we were out.

I was starting to get pissed off. I knew King had to handle his business but damn that mothafucka could've dropped me off first. Shit, that nigga wasn't moving fast enough for me.

"Damn, nigga, calm down. You too gotdamn antsy for me. Yo ass got me nervous. Sit still, damn." Mac pulled out a square and lit it.

"Fuck you, I'm pussy deprived. All I'm thinking about right now is putting that mothafucka in a pretzel and wearing her ass out. Yo ass won't understand until you find yo lady." I looked at the time. It was now one thirty. "I'm about to leave this mothafucka."

Mac started laughing. "Damn, homie yo ass straight whipped. She got you all fuck'd up in the head. You better go find yo ass some pussy if she ain't giving it up."

"That's how I know yo ass young—"

"Mothafucka, you was just young a few months back! The fuck you mean, nigga? Damn, shorty straight got yo head fuck'd up. Shid, wasn't you just fuckin' with that one bitch before shorty showed up at yo party?" He tried to clown me.

"Shut the fuck up! Ain't that a bitch? You gon' try to play me. Fuck you, nigga. Keisha wasn't shit important just something to do while my girl got her head right. She was a cool ass chick that could swallow a dick, but I couldn't fuck with her on no serious type shit." Peaches was the main reason I couldn't fuck with Keisha heavy. But also, she hung out with Tishana, Sam's sister, and I didn't like that.

Once Le'Ron disappeared, Tishana had started to act crazy so I had to distance myself from her. Otherwise, I would of fuck'd around and killed her ass.

She took him leaving hard. Shid, I knew they fuck'd around but I ain't know it was ever serious. I hardly ever saw them together so her reaction fuck'd me up. It wouldn't have changed his faith had I known still. Finding out she was crazy about his ass actually had me wondering if she knew what he was planning.

That's the other reason I kept my distance from her. If she knew what he was going to do and didn't tell me, I was gon' kill that bitch, remorselessly. Regardless of her being Sam's family, which I also considered mine. Peaches lost my baby behind that shit and it was only right everyone involved died.

And if problems came my way with Sam, so be it. I had to protect what was mine. That was why Sam didn't hang around as much and his people didn't know I was alive. They thought I was dead just like everybody else.

King hopped back into the truck as a thought came to me. "Aye, didn't Tish used to fuck with Blue?" How the fuck that shit slipped my mind was beyond me. I wasn't the type of mothafucka who believed in coincidences. How the fuck was it two niggas she fuck'd with ended up doing some shit to me? Hell no, coincidence my ass.

"Yeah, they was together for a couple of years. He had knocked her up and everything, but she ended up having a miscarriage a couple of months after he died." King informed me.

Learning she was pregnant shocked the fuck out of me. Shid, I never knew that. I knew about her being pregnant once when she was a teen. She came and asked me if I would help her take care of it. Shid, I told her ass then about fuckin' with those lame ass niggas, even so, I gave her a stack to get rid of the baby. I figured she ain't want nobody to know, which was why she came to me.

"When was she pregnant? How the fuck did you know she was pregnant?"

King shrugged. "I used to fuck with this bitch named Tammy. Her and Tish were cool but after Blue died, she kinda stopped fuckin' with her. I think she even left town or some shit. Anyway, I was with Tammy the night it happened because Tish called her crying. Shid, it wasn't my business. But she was cool the next time I saw her."

"Nigga, who haven't you fuck'd with in this gotdamn city? Yo black ass get around more than these hoes do. Gotdamn, and yo ass ain't never caught shit?" I had to say something. I couldn't let that shit slide.

"Nigga, fuck you! I ain't fuckin' these bitches raw. So, I ain't catching shit. These mothafuckas ain't even suckin' my dick. Man, fuck you, B. Don't worry about my dick. Why the fuck you asking about Tish for?" He changed the subject back.

"That bitch done fuck'd with two different mothafuckas that came at me. You know I don't believe in coincidences and I don't think this is one." *Damn!*

Mac made a grunting sound that caught our attention. "That's where I know that name from. Blue got an Uncle named Rice. He a mixed cat from The City. I tried to get some work from him before I hit you up and that mothafucka blew me off. Blue introduced us. Once his uncle said he wasn't gon' put me on, Blue stopped fuckin' with me. A month or so later, that's when he got killed."

If Tish and Blue was real close, I'm sure she met his uncle Rice. What wasn't making since was why Tish would be plotting against me to begin with. And why the fuck Rice ain't made an appearance just yet? What the fuck that Monica/Macy bitch had to do with it?

The questions that were running through my head suddenly stopped. Krystal replaced all of my thoughts. "Aye, turn this bitch around."

"Where we going?" King asked quickly busting a U-turn.

"To go see Krystal. Don't say shit right now. Just listen to the story I'm about to tell you."

As King drove to Krystal's house, I jumped into the story she told me years ago about her, Blue and his girl.

Chapter 22

Blaze

King parked in front of Krystal's house and killed the ignition. "This shit gets crazier the more we find out."

That was a fact.

"You think Sam know about it?" he asked me.

I shrugged, "Shid, I doubt it. I mean, he don't really fuck with Tish like that, though. He ain't never did no shaky shit so far to make me think his ass was on some other shit. Sam always look out for me." Even with some of the dumb shit I'd done over the years, Sam never flipped on my ass. His loyalty I never had to question. Tish, on the other hand, could most definitely be a snake. "Mac, go knock on the door and see who's inside her crib." My finger jerked toward the window, telling him to go.

"I'ight." He hopped out the back and jogged to the front door. He knocked.

"Krystal wouldn't know Tish by face, but she heard her voice. That's all we got to go on. Krystal said when she heard her at the shop, she thought it was Tish but with her working for me it was just too much of a coincidence. All these gotdamn coincidences is starting to piss me the fuck off. Boss, if I find out this bitch is behind everything, I'm going to cut her ass up." I was pissed.

The shit was starting to make sense now. Who else knew me enough to know where I be? To even know where the fuck to start looking for me at. That bitch had everything to do with that hit Jerron was given.

"You know that's gon' start shit with you and Sam." King tried to tell me.

"I don't give a fuck. I lost my shorty because of his sister. Now if that mothafucka don't see the logic in me killing that bitch because of that bullshit, then I'm going to kill his ass too. You don't touch what's mine and think I'm gon' let the shit go because of who a mothafucka related to. Yo, I don't give a fuck about no gotdamn relatives." I told him straight up.

"It ain't my gotdamn blood that started this bullshit. It was my blood that got spilt so I don't give a fuck how a nigga gon' feel. Anybody can get touched when you come for mine. I got every mothafuckin' mind to go ride to this bitch house and kill everything moving in that mothafucka." Heated couldn't begin to describe how I felt. I wanted to kill that bitch and anybody who stood in the way of me doing it.

"Calm down. I wanna kill that bitch just as much as you do but we gotda finish this complicated ass puzzle. She's a piece of it not the whole damn thing. We need to figure out why the fuck this Rice nigga ain't made a move yet." King tried to get me to understand.

I understood what he was saying. I just ain't want to agree with the bullshit. "Nigga, you ain't dumb, King. Why the fuck you think his ass ain't moved? I killed his people, his fam. He's tryna do the same thing with me. First move was Peaches. She ain't die. Then I got shot. I ain't dead. He tryna take what I took from him. Tish ass, though? I don't know what the fuck her problem is. Shid, in my eyes, we got two pieces of this puzzle so it's nothing to kill that bitch. A *why* don't even matter to me."

"I hear that and believe me, I don't give a fuck about—why, either. But I'm gon' make sure we get everybody so don't nobody come back, period. Nigga, this ain't just about you. When my sister was brought in this shit, it got personal. We ain't 'bout to leave no loose ends this time around. Be pissed but be smart," King said. "Let's go, yo boy waving," He pointed out my window toward Mac.

I put the face mask on and threw my hood over my head. We got out the truck and made our way to the house where Mac and Krystal stood at the door. Once we made it there, King walked in first.

"Hey, King, it's been a long time." Krystal said and hugged him.

"Damn, he gets a hug before me?" I asked her while pulling off the mask.

Krystal stood still before she looked at King then to Mac. Her eyes came back to me. "Blaze?" She mumbled slowly.

I nodded my head.

"Oh, my God," she mumbled lowly. I thought she was about to pass out and I went to grab her.

Mac pushed me out the way and took hold of Krystal by the waist. "I got you, sweetheart. Come on, let's go sit you down." He turned her away from us and led her to the living room.

"I think I just might like him. That's some me shit right there." King laughed and followed them to the living room.

I closed the door and made my way into the room with them. The crib didn't look no different from when I last was there. King sat in the recliner and kicked his feet up on the table.

Whereas Mac sat beside Krystal with his arm wrapped around her shoulders. "You good, sweetheart?"

"Yeah, it's like I'm seeing a ghost right now." Krystal's hands rubbed over her eyes and she blinked. "I thought Blaze was dead?"

"Same shit I said. This mothafucka surprising everybody today." Mac shook his head before getting up and walking into the kitchen.

That nigga was crazy. I went and sat on the loveseat across from her. "That's what I wanted everybody to think."

Mac returned a minute later with a beer and a cup of water. "Here, drink that." He handed it to Krystal, then popped the top on the beer and took a long drink.

That mothafucka done got comfortable real quick. I glanced over at King and he shrugged. Again, my head shook as I focused back on her. "Remember everything you told me about Blue and his girl?"

"Yeah, what about them? It's so crazy to be looking at you right now. B, I saw them bury you."

I was not about to explain that shit to everybody. "You saw them bury a closed casket."

"Nuh uh, the way Peaches was crying. You can't fake that emotion. I can't believe I'm seeing you." Krystal's hand covered her mouth and she just stared at me.

"Same shit I said. Baby girl one hell of an actress. Shorty cried so gotdamn hard I felt that shit. Had a nigga feeling bad as hell for her. Then when she ran out the church, she fuck'd me up. My ass got choked up, boss. Shorty fuck'd me up." Mac explained.

"I know. I cried harder for her. She was just so broken." She agreed with him.

"Nah, she thought I was dead too, at first. I'ight, now back to the subject. Blue's girl, you don't know how she looked but you know her voice. Do you think you'll remember it if you heard her again?" I got to the point. If she was able to give me a straight *yeah* and it turned out to be Tish, I was killing her ass painfully.

"Blaze, it's been so long, and I've honestly tried to put all that behind me once I told you. So, I don't know."

Krystal took a drink from her cup. "B, I wanna let that go and leave it in my past."

I could tell from the look on her face she didn't want to relive it but I was going to push her. "All I need is a possible *yes, maybe* or *it could be.* That would be good enough for me." I realized my words meant the same thing, but I was anxious as hell for a *yes*. "You ain't gotda see her or anything. All you have to do is listen to her talk."

She didn't look like she was going to budge.

I licked my lips and ran a hand over my head. "Come on, Krystal, real shit. I'm tryna be nice about this bullshit."

"B, chill." King warned.

"Nigga, shut the fuck up talkin' to me." I looked back at Krystal. I was ten seconds away from choking the fuck out of her ass. "Damn! This bitch got you that spooked yo ass won't even hear her over the phone?" It took me a second to realize I didn't need her to talk to Tish's ass at all. She just had to listen to her talk. "King, give me yo phone." My battery had died a half hour after I left the house.

"All I got is this burner. My shit at the crib." He held out his phone.

"What the fuck I'mma do with it? I don't know Tish's number." I told him.

"Shid, me either. I don't talk to her ass."

I took his phone and called Sam. He answered after the third ring.

"Hello?"

"Aye, what's Tish number?" I got straight to the point.

I heard ruffling in his background, then a door closing. "You're about to call her?" He seemed thrown off.

I couldn't blame him. I would've been the same way when I was persistent about them not knowing I was still alive. "No, I'm about to have King call her right quick." I was blunt about it. He didn't need to know what I was finding out right now. When the time was right, I would tell him everything.

Sam was silent for a minute. He cleared his throat. "What's going on?"

"I'll catch you up on everything at a later time. Right now, though, I need that number."

"I'ight." He read the numbers off to me. As he did, I repeated it and Mac dialed them on his phone. "What you getting into later?"

"Shit, I'm tryna finish this shit up before nightfall and take my ass to the crib." I muted the phone and put it on speaker. "King, call her and set something up. Tell her you throwing a party or some shit for my death, reliving good times or some shit. Krystal, yo ass listen to her talk." I hurriedly told him before getting back to the call. I got up and went to her bedroom so I wouldn't be overheard.

"Before nightfall? Peaches still ain't gave you none, huh?" He laughed.

"Hell no. Her ass on that bullshit. Aye, I need a favor."

"What's up?" Sam was always down to help with no questions asked.

"I need you to find out all you can on a nigga named Rice from The City. When you get everything, hit my line, bet?" If anybody could find some shit out legally, it was Sam's ass.

"I got you. Give me a couple of hours and I'll call you."

"I'ight." I disconnected the line and went back into the room where King had Tish on speaker.

"Yeah, I'mma have a cookout next week at the Rex for my homie. So be there, i'ight."

"I'll be there. King, how Peaches been? I've been trying to reach out to her, but I haven't gotten ahold of her. I tried talking to her at the funeral but her little friend brushed me off and Peaches didn't say anything. But I took that as her being upset about Blaze. Then I went by Mom B's house after the funeral, but she had already left town. I don't know if I did something to her or not. She hasn't even tried to reach out to me." Tish explained to him sounding weary. "Did I do something to her?"

I leaned against the wall of the hallway listening to their conversation.

"No, Tish, I don't think you did shit to her. But after that shit happened with Le'Ron's ass, she stopped dealing with a lot of folks. She wanted to keep her circle small. So, it ain't shit you did. It was just too much shit that was happening and then with her crib blowing up, Tish you can't blame her. Shid, anyone she met in that short time, she stopped fuckin' with." King smoothly told her, but it was the truth.

Peaches had stopped talkin' to everyone that didn't include her circle of friends. Even then, she only dealt with my niggas, except for Sam. She didn't fuck with him, period. Shid, that was cool with me. He was my nigga and all but I still ain't like the slick shit he did when he tried to get at her. Although he told me about it and I beat his ass for it, that shit was still fuck'd up. I had no problems with a nigga going after any bitch I fuck'd with but going after Peaches was the wrong move.

"I guess I understand that. I just didn't expect her to shut me off. We had become real good friends and she has to know I would never do anything to hurt her. It's just crazy she pushed me off the way she did without even telling me. I thought we were so much better than that, you know?" She seemed hurt.

That bitch know she was a fuckin' actress. I couldn't wait to kill that bitch!

King's head tilted to the side and he stared at the phone. I'm sure he was thinking my thoughts. His eyes slid to me and pointed at the phone before he shook his head. "Yeah," was all he said.

I covered my mouth and laughed. He didn't know how to respond to the bullshit coming through the line.

She got quiet, then sighed.

I snapped my fingers at him to get his attention. When he looked at me, I mouthed for him to bring up Le'Ron.

King nodded. "You gotda look at it from her standpoint, Tish. Shid, she thought Le'Ron was a good dude because he looked out for Blaze but look what he ended up doing to her. Man, he beat the hell outda her and made her have a miscarriage. We still don't know why the fuck he did that to her. His ass just disappeared. So shid, I don't blame her for not wanting to fuck with nobody new. What the fuck did Peaches, or Blaze ever do to him."

She made a weird sound as if she had suddenly become irritated. "King, I know Blaze was your boy or whatnot, but that nigga wasn't a fuckin' saint! He's done plenty of dirt to good people. Now I'm not saying Peaches deserved the treatment she got. Even so, what would one expect when you deal with a nigga like him? Yeah, it's fuck'd up what happened to her, but I'm not surprised that it did." She exclaimed.

"Y'all go around doing all types of shit to mothafuckas and expect no consequences at all. Not everybody is scared of y'all. Somebody gon' step up and come straight for you behind the shit y'all do. I mean, every action has its consequences. You should keep that in mind while you still out here." She warned, sounding pissed.

"Did you just fuckin' threaten me?" King snapped into the phone.

Tish let out a laugh. "What? King? Oh, my God. No, I was simply stating a fact, that's all. Dude, you're crazy. You know I love you, King." She laughed.

I could tell King didn't buy that shit and was about to go clean the fuck off. I stepped out the hallway shaking my head at him, telling him to chill out.

He bit into his lip and took a couple of deep breaths. He was mad as hell. "Yeah, I know. I'll hit you later about the party, i'ight?"

"Okay, boo."

King hung up the phone. "Don't say shit." He pointed to me as he started to pace. He walked back and forth several times before he made a beeline for the door.

I got him and grabbed his arm, stopping him. "Yo, hold the fuck up—"

King pushed me hard into the wall. I felt the plaster break as I hit it. "Don't fuckin' touch me! Fuck you mean *hold up*? That bitch just threatened me and you gon' tell me to hold up? B, stay the fuck out my way." He turned to go for the door.

Quickly. I grabbed him and put him in a choke hold. My arms wrapped tightly around his neck. "Nigga, you gon' calm the fuck down. Yo ass ain't about to fuck this up now." After the shit his ass told me in the truck on how I needed to calm down. Now that nigga wanted to trip.

King pulled at my arms, trying to pry them from around his neck as he rammed us backwards into the wall. He put up a hell of a fight, but I wasn't letting his ass go. One thing about King when he got pissed and his mind was set to tear up some shit, it was hard as hell to talk him down. He was stubborn as hell, just like Peaches ass but worse. I wasn't about to fight with that big mothafucka just to calm his ass down. Fuck that. I was putting his ass to sleep so I could think.

Once his fight dimmed, I looked over at Krystal. "Aye, go get me some duct tape or something so I can tie this mothafucka up before he wakes up."

She jumped up to go get what I needed.

Mac sat on the couch, laughing his ass off. "B, how the fuck you gon' tie that man up, though? I say let his ass go and we go handle this bitch. I clearly heard the threat she made. Boss, I'm not good with threats. I'm gonna get yo ass before you can plot or act on a plan to get me. Fuck that. I say we go kill that bitch now." Mac reached on his side and grabbed his gun and cocked it.

I was down to put a bullet in a bitch real quick but King made sense when he said she was only a piece of the puzzle. We needed to put that mothafucka together and kill everybody, so nobody came back.

"We gon' kill her ass but we need to get everybody. Until we know who's all involved, we gotda play nice." I explained to him.

Krystal returned with both duct tape, rope and some handcuffs. My brow rose at the rope and handcuffs. "I didn't know which one would be better." Her face turned red.

I grabbed the white rope and bound King's wrist together then covered it with duct tape. I moved to his ankles and repeated the process. "Baby girl,

300

you can keep yo cuffs. I ain't touching those mothafuckas. But shid, I ain't gon' lie. I'm curious like a mothafucka to know what you doing with those and the rope."

Again, her face turned bright red. "None of your business as to what I use them for. Blaze, don't look at me like that." She laughed before taking the extra rope back. "Whatever, man. Y'all paying for that wall." She pointed to the big hole in the wall.

"We gon' take care of that." I crouched down and reached in King's pocket, getting his money out. "So, you liked to be tied up?" I asked her while counting off a stack. I folded the money up and handed it to her.

"Thank you." She slid the money in her pocket. Krystal didn't answer my question.

"I see you. Yo ass grown now, huh?" I was just fuckin' with her. When all the shit happened with Peaches' crib blowing up, me and Krystal stayed cool. I didn't fuck with her on no play-*play* shit like before, but we were still cool. We would put some smoke in the air or get a drink from time to time but that was about it.

"Blaze, leave me alone." She rolled her eyes at me.

I laughed. "I'm just fuckin' with you. Aye, I'mma need you in on this shit. You might even have to become friends with that bitch. She probably not gon' think you re-member her…" I started to think on just how I was gonna get those two together.

"B, you can't ask me to do that." Her head shook in protest.

She didn't have a choice anymore. "I'm asking you to. Did you recognize the voice? Be honest, did you?" I asked.

"I don't know. It could've been—I don't know. The tone of her voice sounded more mature then it had."

I could see the battle she was having with herself.

She had to suck that shit up because she didn't have a choice. She needed to get pissed that was the only way I could see her going along with it.

So, I brought up the incident that happened to her and made her think about everything that Blue did in that basement. Then with his girl telling him to kill her, I convinced her this was the only way she would be able to let everything go and forget about it.

"Fine, I'll do it. But how am I going to get close to her? It's not like she's going to come to me." She pointed out.

That was the same thing I was thinking. Tish didn't work at the lot no more after the whole Le'Ron thing.

"Give me a few days to come up with something, bet?"

She let out a heavy sigh but nodded her head. "Alright."

Chapter 23

Peaches

It was now five o'clock and I still hadn't heard anything from Blaze or King. I was past worried, every cell in my body was telling me something bad had happened to them and all I was waiting for was the police to contact us. I had cried so much my head pounded painfully, my tear ducts were swollen, and my nose was stopped up. I couldn't think straight.

That was the first time he'd been out and haven't called. It just wasn't like him not when he knew how worried I got. My chest shook as I sobbed.

"Peaches, babe, I'm sure it's nothing. His phone could've died or something. That's probably why he hasn't called yet." Kim hands rubbed my back as she tried to comfort me.

"Yeah, Peach, that could be it. King's phone always dying on him. And he never charges it up. Believe me if King sees my number, he's going to answer. He's always worried about Keema so there has to be a reasonable explanation as to why they're not answering their phones." Ebony insisted, while she squeezed my hand.

"If that's the case, why not go to a damn pay-phone? Or go get chargers, better yet bring they asses home and tell us something. They are so fuckin' inconsiderate, I swear. If something happened and he's dead, I'm going to kill him. He is not to do us like that. We not staying here. We're getting the hell out of this city. And y'all asses dumb if you stay here too. I'm not about to put us through this bullshit." I cried. "Y'all if ain't nothing wrong with him, why wouldn't he call, though?"

Ebony suddenly started laughing. I didn't see anything about the situation funny at all. King or Blaze could be dead, and she finds this funny.

"E, stop it," Kimmy told her.

I looked over at her to see her lips quivering. I was having a hard time finding the humor in any of it. "If you bitches ain't gon' take this seriously, y'all can get the fuck out my damn house. Something could've fuckin' happened and y'all wanna fuckin' laugh." I snatched myself away from them.

Kim hit Ebony and threw a glare her way. "You're right, Peaches. We're sorry."

"The situation isn't funny. I'm sorry for laughing, but I personally don't feel as though something has happened to those two idiots. King proba bly not answering his phone because he don't have it. If he's making moves, he don't carry his phone with him. He leaves it in his car because he don't want to risk losing it. As for Blaze's crazy ass, I don't know how he operates but I don't think nothing happened to him. I'm sorry but that bastard is a lucky mothafucka." Ebony said before she started laughing again. "And yo pregnant ass. Your emotions are seriously messing with you, is all. That's why we're laughing. Peach, I was the same emotional way. You can't help it. I understand that, but babe, breathe and relax. Please." Ebony grabbed her cup off my dresser and tossed the content back.

"Yeah, I'm sure they are. Peaches, clean your face and let's go out there with everybody and enjoy the rest of the day." Kim held her hands out for me to take.

I let out a sigh, maybe my hormones were making me overreact just a bit. But I couldn't help it. Almost losing Blaze a few months ago heightened those feelings.

"I guess I'm just scared of something happening to him again. Everybody wanna use my baby as a fuckin' target mat. He's not invincible and I'm just scared that our luck is running out. And when you out looking for the trouble…" I trailed off as my head shook.

"Come on, let's go get in the pool and take your mind off of this." Kim pulled me off the bed.

"No, y'all gon' 'head. I'm just gon' stay in here for a bit." I sat back on the bed with a sigh.

"No, you don't. Bring yo ass on now, Peaches. Stress is not good for you or my niece or nephew. Come on, we're about to take your mind off of everything for a while." Kim pulled me up again.

Ebony grabbed one of my arms and began to pull me too. "Yeah, mama, stress isn't good at all for my baby. So, move yo ass, Peaches. Come on. And its food in there."

Kimmy burst out laughing. "Let me move because whenever her ass hear food, she go charging for that shit!" She laughed, clapping her hands together.

My eyes cut at her, but I ended up chuckling to myself. "Yo ass ain't funny. Stupid self gets on my nerves."

"She smiles." Ebony poked at the dimple on my right cheek. "Now come on before Mr. Blake pops in here worrying as well. With his little grown ass. I don't know what you gon' do with that boy when he gets older." Ebony head shook. "With his ol' ratting ass. He do know snitches get stitches, right? We need to teach his ass that." Her eyes rolled up in her head.

"Girl, bye. Peaches ain't gon' let nobody teach him anything. She'll fuss at him about it then turn around and have movie night with him a second later. He ain't gon' learn nothing with her ass always babying him," Kim added.

"Shut up and leave my baby alone. He ain't that bad—"

Ebony stopped. "His ass is beyond bad. Ol tattle telling ass."

I started laughing. "So, what. You shouldn't have been doing anything to make him tell on you."

My laughter stopped and I let out another sigh. "Y'all I'm serious this time. If he's okay, we're leaving tonight. I'm not about to deal with this stress when all his inconsiderate ass have to do is call or text me." I fussed. My mind was made up. We were going back to Lafayette.

"Okay, Peach." I could hear the disbelief in Ebony's voice. She didn't believe me, but I was so serious. Blaze wasn't about to put me through this stress. *He better be okay.*

We walked into the living room where Bianca and Marcus sat watching TV. They looked over at us once we came in.

"Are you okay, sweetie?" Bianca sat up straight in her seat.

"Yeah, I'm good. Just worried, is all. It's just not like him not to call or text me back. You know, especially know-ing I worry—" Ebony cut me off as I started to complain once again. No doubt I would've ended up crying again.

"She's cool. You know how it is. Momma with her hormones and all that jazz."

"I figured that much. That's why I didn't go running after her. The boys are good." Bianca waved me off, then leaned into Marcus and started back watching TV.

She got on my nerves sometimes. "I'm about to go check on my babies." I said, referring to Blake and Keema. I left them and went into the backyard. Missy and Blake were in the pool playing, she kept dunking him under the water. "Missy, don't be doing my baby like that." I yelled to her in the pool.

"Girl, he just drowned me!" She laughed as she picked him up once more and dunked him down. She pushed him away from her and hurried to the end of the pool.

I quickly ran to her and pushed her back in. "Ahh!" I screamed as she snatched me with her, pulling me into the pool. Once I came up for air, I burst out laughing. "Damn, Miss!" Grabbing her head, I pushed it under water and then made a quick swim to the end of the pool.

"Nuh uh, Peach." Ebony pushed me back in. "Ah!" She screamed as she came falling into the pool as well.

"How the hell you gon' try to push her back in? Yo ass going in too! The fuck you thinking." Blaze laughed.

I cut my eyes at him. He walked up in here like he hadn't been gone all day without checking in. My eyes soon slid to the brown skin dude with him. I could tell immediately he was younger than Blaze.

"Boon, why is King tied up?" Bianca stood at the back door, arms crossed under her chest with her hip cocked to the side and a scowl on her face.

My brows raised as I looked at him, wanting to know the same thing. I moved to the edge of the pool and got out.

"Boon, why?" Bianca asked him again.

"He had got out of control, so I had to tame him." He shrugged as if it was nothing.

The guy with him laughed.

"Excuse me, Momma. B, I'm about to kill you." King snapped as he rushed out the house.

"Uncle Boon, don't do my mommy like that." Keema's little grown self walked up to Blaze like she was about to do something.

Blaze looked at King then picked up Keema. "Who you think you talkin' to? Huh? I'll throw yo little butt in the pool." He pretended like he was going to do it as he tossed her over the water.

"Ah, stop!" She screamed out a laugh. "I'mma tell you mommy on you." She threatened still laughing.

Blaze laughed with her. "What's up, little mama? You been looking after yo auntie for me?" Blaze asked when I stood next to him.

Keema grabbed his face and pulled it close to hers. She tried to whisper to him. "Yeah and her was crying bad."

Blaze looked over at me then back to Keema. "Why was her crying?" Keema bopped him on top of his head with her fist. The surprised looked that covered his face made me laugh. "Why you hit me?"

"Because you didn't call her. She called you and daddy. Tell her you sorry." Keema grabbed Blaze's face and turned it in my direction. "Say I'm sorry, Auntie Peaches."

"I'm sorry, Auntie Peaches." Blaze repeated.

I bit into my lip and rolled my eyes in order to stop my smile. It didn't help once Blaze's arm went around my waist.

"I'm sorry, Auntie Peaches. My battery died and King didn't have a charger. All he had was a burner and I wasn't calling or texting you from that. You see I came home early, I ain't want you to worry." He pulled me even closer to him.

Again, my eyes rolled. I wanted to be mad longer. I should be, given all the crying I had done.

Blaze head came down and he bit into my cheek as his hand grabbed my butt. "Peaches, you gon' accept my apology?" He kissed my cheek.

"You get on my nerves. I shouldn't." Regardless of my ill feelings for him not calling and checking in, the most important thing was he was okay, safe and in front of me. I stretched my neck up and pressed my lips to his. "Next time you do this, I'm not gon' be too forgiving." I kissed him again and then wrapped my arms around his neck.

"Uncle Boon, you son splashed water in my face. Auntie Peaches didn't whoop him. Can you?" Keema stopped talking when she looked at King. She wiggled out of Blaze's arms and ran to her dad. "Daddy, Blake said he gon' beat your butt. And he splashed water in my face." She fussed.

I started laughing because she was lying. Keema's little butt was determined to get Blake in trouble for splashing water in her face.

"No, I didn't! Sha, stop lying." Blake walked toward us. Once he was close to Keema, he jumped at her.

"Say it in my face, then. My daddy gon' beat your butt. Ugly little boy." Keema snapped at him.

She was gon' get King in a lot of trouble. Keema's mouth was terrible.

"Sha, shut up. Dang you talk too much." Blake snapped at her.

I laughed at them before I tuned them out. "Who's your friend?" I asked Blaze, nodding toward the dude that came with them.

"Oh, this my nigga, Mac. Mac, my girl Peaches." Blaze introduced us.

The dude looked at me smiling. "I remember you." He laughed. "You used to whoop my mans' ass. Have my nigga walking around beat the fuck up." He continued to laugh.

"Mac, shut the fuck up." Blaze pushed him away from us before he looked at me. "You find something funny?"

I laughed. "No, I don't." I looked back at Mac, returning his smile. Blaze must had really trusted him to bring him over to the house. As I thought that, King's visit to Muncie came to mind. That must had been the young dude he was talking about. "It's nice meeting you, Mac. We have lots of food, feel free to get whatever you like. Make yourself at home."

"Thanks, Peaches. Y'all got it smelling good out here." He rubbed his stomach while looking around.

"Gon' make yourself a plate," I waved him toward the table where the food was. Blake walked over to where we stood, going up to Blaze.

"What's good, man? You been looking after yo moms?" Blaze asked him as they did their handshake.

"You know I was—" Blake was cut off.

"Damn B, Lil homie look just like yo ass." Mac looked from Blaze to Blake. A thoughtful look soon came to his face. His head nodded. "I understand now. I respect that, big homie." He shook up with Blaze.

"Yeah," was all Blaze said as he pulled Blake to him.

"I'm about to go get me something to eat." He laughed, then walked off.

Blake turned toward his dad, not saying anything. He reached in Blaze's pockets then pulled out his phone and the money that was with it.

"Boy, what the hell you doing? Get yo ass out my damn pockets—" Blaze's sentence was cut off as Blake pushed him in the pool.

"Ah!" A scream tore from my throat as Blaze pulled me with him. We went under at the same time but once I came up and caught my breath, I hit Blaze. "Why would you grab me?" I splashed water into his face.

He ignored me. "Blake, I'm gon' fuck you up. Why the hell you do that?" He fussed at him. He rubbed his nose trying to get the water out of it.

"Blake, I will knock you out if you push me." King threatened as Blake eased over to him.

"Daddy knock him out." Keema excitedly yelled.

"Don't worry, baby girl. I'mma get him. Aye but you better watch that little smart mouth of yours before I tear yo little butt up." He warned her.

Keema looked over at him for a long while, with her cheeks puffed up. She dropped her head and her lips poked out, Keema then looked up at him through her lashes. "I'm sorry."

"Don't be sorry, just watch yo mouth."

"Okay, Daddy. Gimme kiss." Keema lips puckered up and she gave him a big kiss. She wiggled out of his arms. "Nana!" She yelled running to Bianca.

That little girl was just too damn busy for her own self.

"B, don't think I'm playing. Wait until yo ass get out that fuckin' pool. I'm fuckin' you up." King snapped at him once Keema was out of earshot range.

"I'll be ready." Blaze responded as he grabbed me from behind. He didn't seem bothered by King's threat. "Where you think you're going?" He pulled me from the edge of the pool. Blaze kissed my neck then turned me around to face him.

"I'm still mad, Blaze. You need a backup battery or something. Not calling while you're out ain't gon' work for me." My arms wrapped around his neck.

"Yeah, I hear you." His nonchalant demeanor didn't go unnoticed.

"I'm serious, Blaze. Otherwise, we're leaving—"

"Peaches, shut the fuck up. Damn, I don't wanna hear that bullshit, man. We ain't going nowhere so kill that noise." He kissed me again, trying to shut me up.

I bit his lip, then laughed. "Yo ass get on my nerves." My arms tightened around his neck and my legs went around his waist.

Blaze walked us against the wall. "You wanna go get cleaned up?" His tongue played with mine while his hands slapped my booty.

"Nope, I plan on swimming until midnight. Now go play with Blake." I kissed Blaze again, then pushed him away from me. I turned and pulled myself up on the siding but ended up falling right back into the pool.

"Damn, Peach!" Missy burst out laughing. "That would've been a badass exit if you had of gotten out." She continued to laugh at my failed attempt to sashay off. I was hella embarrassed and Missy's ass didn't have to blast me like she did.

"Shut yo duck lip having ass up! You talk too damn much, big lip ass wench. I'll come over there and smack the shit out of you." Blaze snapped at her while he picked me up and sat me on the edge of the pool. "Fuck her! I got you."

My lips was parted the whole time not believing he just went off on her like that.

Missy stopped laughing and stared at Blaze. Her eyes cut into slits at him. "This why I never liked yo ass. That mouth of yours gon' get you hurt. Keep on here, play with me, Blaze." She reached under her seat and grabbed her bag. "Talk that sweet shit."

"Fuck you, Lips. You don't want it, I promise. Peaches, watch out." Blaze waved me off. I didn't need to be told twice. I hurriedly got up and moved away from the pool.

Blaze pulled off his shirt and tossed it outside the pool. "Aye, King grab her big lip ass." His fingers waved beckoning her toward him.

King was already standing on the side of her. Before Missy could jump up King snatched her ass up so quick. He ran and jumped in the pool with Missy in his arms. King came up for air first. Then once Missy came up, he grabbed the back of her thigh and forearm, lifted her in the air and tossed her to Blaze. He caught her and dunked Missy under.

"Blaze, stop! Don't do her like that." I yelled at him, unable to contain my laughter, however.

"You want some?" he asked.

My head shook fast. "No, I don't. My stomach hurt." I rubbed my belly and laid back on the lounge chair. That was not my fight. I wasn't about to play with them. They never knew when to stop. Those two will have you pissed the fuck off for a week when they got playful in the pool. King and Blaze just didn't know how to act, with their childish asses.

"Ooh, Keema, gimme some." She walked out the house with a Pure Leaf extra sweet tea in her hands. "Come here, Keema." I held my arms out for her. She walked her little self over and let me pick her up. I sat her on my lap.

"Auntie Peaches, what you gon' name the babies?" Keema asked as she handed me her drink.

"I don't know just yet; I don't even know what I'm having." I told her, just now remembered to tell Blaze about my doctor's appointment in a few days.

"Can I have one of your babies?" Her hand rubbed over my stomach.

I didn't know how to respond. My eyes squinted in a confused like manner. "Um...I'm only having one baby—"

"Nuh uh! Uncle Boon, ain't Auntie Peaches having a lot of babies?" She yelled over to the pool and quickly got everybody's attention.

This little girl here. I finished off her tea and laid back on the chair waiting to see what her parents would say.

King gave Keema a look and she quickly hopped off my lap and ran to her momma, tucking herself under her arm. Well, damn, if a look was all it took from King to give her some act right. I needed to learn it, shit. Both Blaze and Blake needed some gotdamn act right.

***

For the next few hours we all sat outside in the back talking. The mosquitoes started to get bad, so the boys started a fire to keep them away.

I sat in a lounge chair laying against Blaze. My arm clung to his while he ran a hand over my stomach.

"Look at Peaches' ass." Kim pointed out.

My brow rose as I looked at her. I didn't understand why she was telling them to look at me. "What?" I pushed myself more into Blaze.

"Y'all should have seen her earlier when neither of you were answering your phone. Baebae, listen, she cried and made threats. Blaze, she was gon' get you. She promised y'all were moving from Gary as soon as you got back. Now look at her ass, all caked up like she ain't made not a threat." Kim laughed at me.

Ebony clapped her hands together in agreement. "I swear she acted a whole ass fool. I personally think it's cute to watch someone else go through those same pregnancy hormones I went through."

"So, you was worried about me like that, huh?" King chimed in sitting on the chair with Ebony.

She cut her eyes at him, then pushed King away from her. "Hell no! And don't you even start thinking that I was because I promise you, I wasn't." She shrugged King off as he tried to lean into her. "Gon' somewhere now."

"E, I don't know why you acting. Y'all need to stop playing and give my niece a baby. I don't know what y'all gon' do with that little girl. Y'all heard her ask me if she can have one of my babies." They had their hands full with that one. I truly felt sorry for them.

"I told her she had to ask her momma about that. Shid, I'm tryna work on my boy but Ebony's ass be acting funky and stingy." King slapped her on the thigh hard.

Ebony whacked the hell out of him in his back. "You play too much."

King turned around to face her fully. He took ahold of both of her wrist, locking them in one of his hands. The other went between her legs as he leaned into her.

"Y'all take that shit in the house some fuckin' where." Blaze snapped at them. As expected, King paid him no mind and he continued to mess with Ebony.

"I'll be back. I gotda go to the bathroom." I unwrapped myself from Blaze and got up.

"I'm coming with you." Blaze hopped up with me.

I stopped walking to look at him. "Why are you coming with me?" My brows raised and my head tilted, waiting on his response.

"I gotda piss. The fuck kinda question is that? Why I gotda have a reason to piss?" Blaze pushed passed me and walked into the house.

"Yo ass know good and well why he going to the bathroom with you. He about to be all up in those guts." Missy linked her fingers and pumped her palms together.

"Miss, shut up with yo stupid ass." Laughing at her, I went into the house. I stopped by the living room to see Keema stretched out sleep and Blake on the floor playing his video game.

I left out and rushed to the restroom. Once finished I washed my hands and walked into our bedroom. Blaze laid stretched out on the bed, watching TV. "Why are you in here?"

"Shit, just thinking." His hands slid into his basketball shorts.

Biting into my lower lip, I stopped myself from laughing. I knew exactly what he was thinking. A hum left my mouth. I kicked off my sandals and got into the bed. "What are you thinking about?" I crawled over to him until I was close enough to straddle his hips.

"Just shit." He shrugged.

I pushed the hem of his shirt over his stomach then pulled him up, removing his shirt fully. "What did you do today? Did you find out anything?"

"Mmhm," he hummed as he untied my swim top. He pulled the string from my neck, releasing my breast. Blaze cupped each breast and held them up. His tongue flicked over my right nipple before he pulled the small nub into his mouth, sucking until it became erect. His head pulled back, letting the little pebble pop from his mouth. He gave my left nipple the same treatment.

A big smile came to my face once I felt his friend poke at my sex. I grabbed the sides of his face and brought it back to mine. My tongue played with his lips before I gave them a peck. "Bae, we have guests. We can't just leave them out there." My tongue curled as I licked his top lip.

"Fuck them, they ain't guests. We're passed all that bullshit."

"Ahh!" A laugh filled scream left my mouth as Blaze suddenly flipped us over. "B, what are you doing?" I laughed as he quickly pulled his basketball shorts down.

My fingers wrapped around his dick, slowly I began to stroke him.

"Yo ass playing. I'm about to get in yo guts before yo worrisome ass son come knocking on the door or one of those irritating as tricks you call friends come looking for you." He pulled my shorts off and tossed them to the floor.

I stood up and kissed his tip but before I could go any further, Blaze stopped me. "We ain't even got time for that. It's been two weeks. I want some pussy. You can suck my dick in the morning." He pushed me back onto the bed and placed himself between my legs.

All I could do was laugh at his seriousness. My hands went to his sides and my legs spread for him. My neck stretched up as I met him halfway.

Blaze placed his dick at my opening and pushed the tip in. His arms went under my thighs, lifting my legs up as his hips started a slow deep stroke. His hips began to roll while he was deep inside of me.

He pulled out, ran his tip through my slit before pushing inside of me only to pull out again. Blaze thrusted back in, fast and hard. My inner muscles squeezed tightly around him as my hips started to roll and grind against him. My nails dug into his sides, my lips parted as his hips slapped into mine, hitting my sweet spot.

"Ooh, sss! Baby, harder!" My mouth went to his chest and kissed the skin before I bit him. My head fell onto the bed as my back arched. "Blaze, oh, my God, baby! Ooh!" I cried out.

Blaze brought my thighs up to my shoulders, picking up the pace as he went deeper.

"Oh, my. No, nooo, ooh…" My hands went to his hips and I tried to push him back as my hips raised. My muscles tightened and my body started to shake. "Ah!" I screamed as I came hard around his dick.

Blaze slowed down to flip me over. He slapped my ass hard as he pushed inside of me. My inner walls squeezed around him as my body continued to tremble. I fisted the sheet and bit into the pillow remembering we had a house full of people.

Blaze pulled out once more, his hand came down on my ass and he thrust deep inside of me. His hips began to slap against my ass. I screamed into the pillow and gripped the sheets tighter. Moan after moan left my mouth but was muffled.

Blaze's hand grabbed my hair and he pulled me into him. My head twisted so my lips could press into his. I gave him a peck.

With one hand fisted into my hair, the other came around to my front, going between my legs. His fingers found my clit and he began to toy with my swollen pearl. Again, I came moaning loudly, causing my sounds to echo through the room.

Blaze's head went into the side of my neck, muffling his grunts and groans. "Ooh fuck, Peaches." He grunted into my neck. His movements became frantic as his thrusting became harder.

My sensitive sex just couldn't take anymore. I screamed as tears left my eyes. The feeling was just too much, but it felt amazing. I wanted him to stop but at the same time I didn't.

"Oh, my God! Blaze, ooh baby! Ah shit! Ooh! Ooh, I love you." I cried out as my inner walls milked him.

"Ah fuck!" Blaze pumped into me three more times before he came. His hands held my mount, holding me to him as his hips jerked against my ass as he released his nut inside of me. Blaze kissed my neck before he made his way to my lips.

Kissing me, he pulled out, then turned me to his front and laid me on my back. Blaze grabbed his dick then pushed inside of me.

"Mmm…" I moaned into his mouth as he groaned.

Unlike usual he didn't move, he just laid there.

I had no problem with that. My arms and legs wrapped around his waist, holding him to me as we continued to kiss.

Blaze broke the kiss and put his head on my shoulder, panting hard. "Damn, Peaches." Was all he could say in that moment.

322

With my arms and legs still wrapped around him I rolled us over. I just laid on top of him. My body was literally tired. I didn't feel like doing anything but stay in bed.

My lips pressed against his chest.

Blaze's hands slowly began to caress along my hot, sweaty skin as we laid in a comfortable silence. It didn't take long for my eyes to become droopy and I fell asleep.

Chapter 24

Peaches

One Week Later

A heavy sigh left my mouth as I waited impatiently to be called in the back to see the doctor. For damn near an hour, I had been sitting there waiting to be called to the back. My frustration levels were already high because I had to come to the appointment by myself.

Blaze pretending to be dead was truly taking its toll on me. I simply hated it. This was now my second time going to the doctor and just like before, he couldn't be there.

My phone vibrated. Blaze's name popped up on the screen and my eyes rolled. "Hello," a tiring breath left my mouth.

"You still ain't been seen yet—turn up here." He instructed someone.

The fact that he could run the streets at any given time of the day or night bothered me. He could do all of that but couldn't come from the dead and be at a freakin' doctor's visit with me. Pissed couldn't begin to explain my feelings. I was on the verge of killing his ass my damn self. I shook my head, ridding myself of those violent thoughts.

"Peaches?" Blaze's called my name loudly.

"I'm sorry, I got caught in a thought. But no, I haven't been called back yet. I'm about to say fuck it and take my black ass home. I'm tired of sitting here and watching everybody go before me. Half of them got here after I did, like damn! How much longer am I going to have to wait? Ugh." I just felt so irritable and uncomfortable.

Blaze laughed through the line. "Peach, you bet not leave. I'm sure they gon' call you back soon. Just chill out."

"I don't find anything funny at all. And how much longer am I supposed to sit here? Damn." I caught myself before I snapped at him. My hand rubbed over my ponytail and I took a deep breath. "What's up, bae?"

"Shit, I was just trying to see what's happening with you. Peach, you know if I could, I'd be there with you, right?" He sounded so sincere. "I don't like this shit no more than you do. But stressing ain't gon' make this no better, you hear me?"

My head nodded because I knew he was right. I just didn't want to accept it. "I know and I'm sorry, but bae, something have to give. I don't like this at all. If we have to drive hours away for a damn appointment just so you can be here with me, then that's what we have to do. I hate having to sit here by myself."

"Yeah, that's what's up. Aye, let me hit you back in a minute, bet?" Blaze disconnected the line before I had a chance to say anything else.

I looked at my phone. *No, this black motha— did he even hear what I was saying? Ugh, I fuckin' hate him! Stupid ass, I swear!*

"Peaches Johnson." A medical assistant called out.

I couldn't wait until I saw his yellow ass. "Here I come." I tossed my phone in my purse and hurriedly went to her. Once we got in the back, she weighed me and then led me to a room.

After she did the normal routine, she pulled a sheet from a drawer. "You can get undressed from the waist down and the doctor will be with you shortly." She informed me before she left out the room.

I pulled my shorts and panties down my hips as the door suddenly came open. "What the fuck?" I quickly pulled my clothes up and spun around. The hooded figure had me snatching my purse up.

"Yo, Peach, chill." Blaze pulled the hood from his head and then held his hands up.

My hand went to my racing heart and I let out a deep breath. "Blaze, what the hell? I just almost shot you." I waved my little baby toward him. I could admit that moving back to Gary while I was pregnant had me always on high alert when I had moves to make.

"No, shit. Why the hell do you have a gun in the doctor's office, Peaches?" He laughed at me. "Man, put that shit up before you go to jail."

I put my gun away, then went to him. My arms wrapped around his neck and I kissed him. "I was going to kill you when I got home. You play too much. Why didn't you tell me you were coming?" My lips pressed against his once more before I pulled back.

"I didn't know if I was going to make it at first. That's why I kept calling yo mean ass." He sat down in the chair and took his hat off. Blaze hand ran over his head then down his face.

"What's wrong?" I pulled my shorts and panties off. After I folded them up, I handed my clothes to him.

"Shit, tired and hot as hell." He reached out and grabbed me, pulling me into his lap. "I don't think I like this shit. Yo ass got to get naked? Hell no."

Laughing, I pushed his head back. "She has to check me out. Wait how did you get in here and how did you know what room I was in?" My head tilted curiously.

He shrugged. "I told you before money will make a way."

My mouth opened and I was about to go off. No, they didn't just let anyone in who waved a dollar. *What if he was a killer trying to kill me?*

"No, she cool, though. I know a friend that knows her. They called in a favor for me."

Truth be told, I didn't care how he got in, I was just glad he was here with me. "Well, I'm happy you're here." I kissed his lips then stepped out of his hold. I sat on the medical bed and placed the sheet over my legs.

Blaze stared at my legs for a long while before he bit into his lower lip. His mouth soon stretched into a smile. *No, he wasn't thinking what I thought he was.* He licked his lips and his eyes met with mine. He stood up and took off his hoody then pulled up his jeans.

"B, get yo ass out. Right now." I pointed to the door.

"Damn, what I do?" He feigned innocent. "How my *babies* doing?" He came to me and rubbed my stomach.

"The *baby* is fine. Blaze, we are not about to do this in here so go sit yo ol horny ass down somewhere." Laughing, I pushed him away from me.

He came right back, stepping between my legs. "You always say that before you let me in." His lips pressed against mine.

I kissed him back but then pushed him away from me. "I'm serious, gon' now."

"I'ight, yo black ass gon' remember this. Ain't no dick for you tonight."

The door opened and the doctor entered. Her lips pursed together as she tried to stop her laughter. She waved her hand then pointed to Blaze. "Do I need to sit you in the lobby?" She asked him as she went to wash her hands.

Blaze laughed. "No, I'm good." He sat back in his chair and grabbed his crouch. He pointed to it and then waved his finger at me. *You ain't getting none*, he mouthed.

I couldn't do anything but laugh at his foolishness. I swear I loved that crazy ass man.

"So how have you been feeling? The doctor asked as she lightly patted my leg. "Lay back for me." She then proceeded to get everything she needed for the Pap smear.

"I'm good considering I hate this morning sickness." I will never understand why they called it morning sickness when I got sick at all times of the day.

"Everyone hates that. Scoot back for me." She finished the pap then disposed of her gloves. "Do you ever feel around your breast for lumps?" She checked my breast.

"Yes, I do." I knew how common breast cancer was. I checked myself consistently.

When the doctor finished her examination, she grabbed the ultrasound machine from the side of the room and wheeled it over. She grabbed a tube then raised my shirt. "This is a little cold." She squirted some gel on my stomach, then grabbed the wand. She moved it over my belly for a few seconds, paused and pointed to the screen. "There goes your baby." She pressed another button and moved the wand around my stomach again. She clicked a few buttons. A few seconds later a whooshing sound echoed in the room. "That's your baby's heartbeat."

"Oh, my God!" My eyes quickly began to water. Last time around, I didn't get a chance to experience this. So, to hear its beating heart and to actually see the little baby inside of me was simply amazing. I wiped my eyes, but more tears continued to fall.

"What you mean one baby? You need to fix that damn thing or shake her damn stomach. I know its two babies in there. Hell no." Blaze told her as he stood on the side of me.

I hit his arm as I covered my mouth. A tearful laugh slipped through my lips. "Bae, shut up, please. There's no twins."

The doctor laughed along as she pointed to the screen. "I'm sorry, daddy, but it's only one baby, one heartbeat."

Blaze's head shook and I pinched him before he could say anything else.

"Would you like to know the sex of your baby?"

"Yeah," Blaze answered before I could. His eyes held excitement as he stared at the screen with one arm folded across his chest while his hand rubbed his chin curiously. He was so focused.

"Let's see, if the baby would just move its leg…" she trailed off as she moved the wand about. "There you go." She clicked another button.

"What is it?" Blaze and I asked at the same time. Looking at each other, we started laughing.

"Congratulations, it's a girl."

"Ah, I got my girl." I squeaked out. I didn't know what I was going to do if I was having another boy. Blake and Blaze was enough. I couldn't handle no more boys.

"Shit, we're about to go broke." Blaze said the stupidest stuff sometimes.

I would never understand him. "Blaze, shut up." I laughed.

He did the same as he leaned down and kissed me.

"I love you." I kissed him again.

"Love you, too, Peaches."

"I'll give you a minute to get dressed." She pushed the machine back and then left out the room.

"I'm actually about to have a baby. This is really happening." I looked at Blaze through teary eyes.

"Yeah, it's really happening." Blaze's lips pressed against mine before he helped me sit up. "Damn, I'm about to have a girl. Two of you. Shit! It's about to be trouble." He played. "Peaches, I'mma need you to stop worrying and stressing over me when I'm out here. That's shit ain't good for y'all so chill the fuck out. I'm going to be good, i'ight?"

I wiped the gel off my stomach with the sheet then tossed it in the trash. "Blaze, we are not about to have that talk here. We can talk when we get home." I put my clothes back on. When Blaze didn't reply, I glanced up at him to see his hand rubbing the back of his neck. "What is it?"

"I need to make a run out to Ohio tonight. If everything goes as planned, then I'll be back tomorrow night. If not, I'll be home in a few days." Blaze said.

Worry immediately set in my body and I knew it showed on my face. I didn't want him to go.

"Peaches, don't give me that look. I'mma be straight. I promise you." He took ahold of my face and tilted my head back. His eyes stared into mine as if willing me to believe that he was going to be alright.

"B, why—"

"Peaches, don't ask questions, just trust and believe me. Can you do that?" His eyes didn't once leave mine.

My eyes rolled up in my head. "I can but I don't want to. Blaze, just be careful."

"I always am." He stopped talking when someone knocked on the door.

The doctor entered and handed me photos from the ultrasound. "There you go. Once you're finished up in here you can go to the front for your next appointment." The doctor was about to walk out until Blaze stopped her.

"Aye, I have a question. Can she still suck dick while she's pregnant?" He asked her seriously.

My mouth dropped to the floor. "Oh, my God, Blaze!" I hit him. "I'm so sorry. You don't have to answer that."

"Yes, the fuck she do. Peaches, shut up. I got this." He pushed me behind him and stepped closer to her. "So, can she still suck dick?"

My hands covered my face and tears ran from my face as I laughed from both embarrassment and his stupidity. He would be the one to ask that damn question. I would never complain about having to come to the doctor by my damn self ever again.

"Yes, she can if she wants to." She shook her head at him before she looked at me. "Good luck." The doctor walked out of the room. Her laughter could be heard from the hallway.

"Blaze, why? I can't believe you." I stepped to him.

"What? I wanted to know." He licked his lips while he pulled me to him. "You gon' suck my dick when I get home?"

I pushed him away from me. "Man, bye. I have to go pick up my baby and get something for dinner. I'll see you at home. Give me a kiss so I can go." I stood on my tip toes and pressed my lips to his.

"I'll eat yo pussy," he said between pecks.

I couldn't do anything but laugh at him. "You gon' do that anyways. Bye, I love you." I kissed him again and then pulled back.

"Gon' 'head. Call me when you leave my mom's crib, bet?"

"I will." I kissed him again then slipped out of the room. I saw the doctor walking into another room. She glanced at me and smiled. My cheeks went hot. He was so gotdamn embarrassing.

***

"Oh, Lord, not another Keema I hope. Hell, she might be worse. She got Boon in her. Damn it!" Bianca stressed playfully.

"Nuh uh, Momma. Keema the way she is because of Britt. My baby is not going to be nothing like that nor will she be around Brittany's ass." I took a drink of my sweet tea.

"So, which one of these can I have?" Bianca picked up the photos from the ultrasound, looking at the four different pictures.

"I don't know, I'll have to ask Blaze and see what he says." I pulled out my phone and called him.

"Why you have to ask him for? This is your baby." She pointed to the pictures, making me laugh.

"It's his too. I'll ask him." I whispered just as Blaze answered the phone. "Hey, bae, I'm at your moms' house now, but we're about to leave in a minute." Bianca held the pictures in front of me. I rolled my eyes showing my slight irritation. "Bae, momma wanna know if she can have one of the ultrasound pictures."

"Hell no! She can't have nan one of them."

I couldn't contain my smile or laughter. I loved the hell out of that man. I knew what he was going to say before I even called. My baby was not afraid to tell nobody *hell no!* Whereas myself, I didn't feel right telling Bianca *no* even when I really wanted to.

"Momma, he said *hell no.*" My shoulders shrugged, my lips twisted, and my head shook as if I felt some type of way about his answer.

"Whose baby is that?" She asked me.

"What she just say?" Blaze sounded confused.

"She asked whose baby was this."

"That's mine. Fuck she talkin' 'bout? Hell no! She can't have no damn pictures. Those mine too. Shit! Peaches, I keep trying to tell you to stay yo baldheaded ass away from her. She gon' get you fuck'd up. Man, take yo ass home." He demanded playfully.

And he wondered where Blake got his attitude from.

"Don't talk to me like that." Laughing, my eyes rolled. "No, seriously, we're about to leave now because I still have to stop by the grocery store and get something for dinner. Do you want anything in particular? Hold on— Blake, let's go!" I yelled out to him.

Bianca spun around and looked at me like she wanted to slap me.

"Sorry." I let out a nervous laugh before getting back on the call. "You know what you want?" I asked Blaze.

"Big mouth ass." He laughed. "I want some tacos, though."

"Okay, I'll make that for dinner then. Well, we're about to get out of here. I'll call you when we make it home." I grabbed my wallet and keys and then went into the living room where Blake sat.

"I'ight, Peaches. I don't have nobody on you so don't be out their long. Get what you need and go to the crib," he warned.

I understood what he was saying. With all the crazy shit still going on and me having Blake, he didn't want to take any chances. After we said our goodbyes and I told him *I loved him* a few times, we hung up the phone.

Bianca walked us to the door seeing us off.

Once we got in the car I pulled off.

"Where are we going now?" Blake asked as he played a game on his phone.

"To the grocery store so I can get stuff for tacos. Is that good for you?" My hand covered his phone.

He looked at me and smiled. "So, what happened at the doctor? Was everything okay?"

My smile grew. He was such a little protector and it melted my heart. My baby always had to make sure his momma was alright. "Yeah, everything's good. The doctor told us I'm having a girl."

Blake turned in his seat to face me. "I could've told you that. I told dad that."

"How would you have known?" My lips twisted and I glanced at him with a questioning brow.

"Because you cry way too much. So, I knew it was a girl, boys ain't that weak, we got tough skin. We Carters." Blake explained.

I came to a stop light and looked at him with my head tilted to the side. "Um, she's a Carter. I'm trying to understand what you're saying but I can't. You have to explain a little better than that." I was certain my baby girl was a Carter. So, for him to say that Carter's have tough skin was crazy. "Wait a minute, I do not cry a lot, first off." I felt offended.

Blake let out a loud snort. "Yeah, you do. Dad could yell at you for something and you'll start crying. You might yell back but you cry. But the baby is a Carter but she's more you than us. You're not a Carter but a Johnson, so that baby takes after you. I never see dad cry. Besides, it's a known fact that boys take after their fathers and girls take from the mommas."

I parked at the grocery store. "Who in the hell told you that?" What the hell was he saying? The baby takes after me? I wasn't no damn crybaby. Yeah since I've been pregnant, my emotions have been heightened but I wasn't always crying. I thought I was very strong.

"I'm just saying if she was a full blooded Carter, she wouldn't be making you sick all the time and you wouldn't cry as much." He shrugged as if it was nothing.

"If she was a full blooded Carter? You're not even a full blooded Carter. What the hell? You take from both the mother and the father."

"My point exactly. It's obvious I took after dad and this baby taking after you. I mean maybe if your last name was Carter, this problem would be solved." He pointed out, then got out the car stretching.

"What?" I mumbled to myself as I caught on to how he just played our conversation. My little man was to gotdamn smart. I found myself laughing at what he just said. I got out of the car and walked around to his side. I hit the alarm button and then wrapped my arm around Blake's shoulder. I kissed the side of his head and laughed.

"My last name doesn't have to be Carter in order for her to be full blooded. Regardless of anything, I am a Carter and we don't need no papers to tell me otherwise. The moment you entered my world that title was mine. Plus, being a Johnson is not bad. We are very strong, we're far from being weak. Have you not met Uncle King?" I questioned as we walked into the store.

"Or Sha, she ain't weak and she's a Johnson. That little girl is crazy. Man, I hope this baby don't be like Sha." He groaned out.

He better stop trying to play my niece. Even though I could admit Sha'Keema was something else, she wasn't that bad. She was a total sweetheart. "Leave Keema alone, she's not that bad."

Blake looked at me with a blank stare. "Yeah, okay."

I laughed at his response. "Shut up, let's get this food and get out of here."

Chapter 25

Peaches

"Blake, run in there and get me an extra sweet Pure Leaf Tea." I handed him a five dollar bill before I started pumping the gas.

"Ma, I can pump the gas for you." He stood by me trying to grab the nozzle.

"I got it, just run in there and come right back out." I instructed as I started to pump the gas. "Watch the cars, Rashad!" I yelled after him as he ran across the lot.

I lifted the latch and let the gas pump itself. A yawn left my mouth and my arms crossed over my chest. I leaned against the car waiting on the tank to fill. I was tired as hell and was ready to go to sleep.

"Peaches?" A manly voice called my name.

I looked over my shoulder and mentally groaned. *Why now?* This couldn't have been at a worse time. *Shit!* I couldn't pretend I didn't hear him because I had already looked at him. And I couldn't jump into the truck and pull off because of Blake.

Blake, shit! This couldn't be the worse fuckin' time.

The man walked over to me with a wide smile.

I forged my smile. "Hey, Joseph."

"Hey, I've been hoping that I'd run into you since I never received a call. I wanted to check on you. How have you been?" He leaned against the car with folded arms, which indicated he was getting comfortable and was ready to catch up.

"I've been good, dealing with everything, you know? What about yourself?" I asked, looking at the numbers on the pump station.

"Like you said, I'm dealing with everything. I still wish I had more time with him, you know? Got the chance to apologize for everything. I've been reaching out to Brittany. I met up with her a couple of months ago and got the chance to talk to her. I explained everything. Every now and then, she'll send me a text or call to see how I'm doing. That's more than enough to me." He smiled as if Britt talking to him made him happy.

"That's good." The pump clicked and I let out a relieved breath. I pointed to the pump then took it out. "That's really good to hear. I don't mean to rush but I really need to go. I have this food in the car and it so hot out here. I don't want my meat to spoil." I needed to be far away from him. I just hoped Blake didn't come out just yet.

"Oh okay. I don't wanna hold you up, but did you move back here?" He looked into the car at the groceries.

"How did you know I didn't stay here?" I was on high alert and suspicious of him because Blaze told me to stay away from Joseph.

"I figured you didn't when I dropped you off at the hotel, but with your bags of groceries, I just figured you moved back." Again, he looked in the car.

"Oh, no I didn't. I'm just hear visiting." I shrugged.

"Ma!" Blake yelled from the store's door.

I ignored him.

Joseph looked up toward the voice.

Shit! "If you give me your number again, we can probably do an early lunch before I leave town if you like." I quickly said, grabbing his attention.

He looked back at me with a smile. "That would be nice, but I'm thinking I should get your number this time. Just in case you lose it." He joked.

"Ma!" Blake called once again.

Joseph looked up.

"Sure!" I said a little too loudly, but it got his attention back on me. "You can save it in your phone."

"Are you okay?" His head tilted as confusion showed across his face.

God, Blaze took after him so much.

"Yeah, I'm fine, just hot." I fanned myself to emphasize being hot. "Your phone."

He looked down at his pockets, feeling them. I took the chance to glance at Blake who was making his way toward us. My head shook in his direction. I didn't want him to come over to us, but he wasn't paying my gesture any attention.

"Oh, my God!" I spoke loudly getting both of their attention. My hand waved in front of my face. "Damn, bee." My hand swatted at nothing, but this time I looked at Blake and shook my head at him.

He stopped in his tracks. His eyes squinted and he slowly started to walk back. Blake's eyes slid to Joseph as he moved back to the door.

"Here it go." He handed me the phone from his breast pocket. Once he gave it to me, he glanced over at Blake. He turned away only to quickly look back.

I tried to hand him back his phone. "There you go, Joseph. I should be leaving in a few days so call soon." I pushed the phone into his hand, but he paid it no mind as he continued to stare at Blake, who had stopped walking.

I hit my car hard trying to get Blake's attention more so then Joseph. I just wanted my baby to go into the store until he left. *Why wasn't he moving?*

"Watch out!" Joseph yelled at Blake.

He jumped out the way just in time as a car flew through the lot and out of the exit. Seeing my baby almost get hit, I forgot about Joseph and I ran to him.

I grabbed his face and quickly examined him. "Are you okay? What I tell you about watching out for these damn cars, Rashad? That car could've hit you." I fussed at him.

"I'm fine. I didn't even see it." That was his argument.

"That's why I said look out for the damn cars. This is still a street, God!" I yelled at him. I could literally see that car hitting him. The images that flashed in my head scared me to death. I pulled him into me and hugged him. "You have to be more careful." My head reared back, and I looked at him again. "Do you hear me?"

"Yeah, I'm sorry." He apologized.

A relieved breath left my mouth. "You sure you're alright?"

Blake tried to shake me off. "Ma, I'm fine. It didn't even touch me."

"Okay, let's go." I kissed the side of his head and wrapped my arm around his shoulder.

"Ma, who is that man?" He pointed to Joseph who was now a few steps away from us. I didn't know how to answer him.

"Is he okay?" Joseph asked.

"Yeah, he'll be fine. Look, we really have to go." I just wanted to get as far away from him as possible.

"Wait. Ma?" Joseph repeated Blake's word. "That's your son?" He asked, staring at Blake.

"Baby, go get in the car. Hurry up." I urged him.

"Ma—"

"Go get in the car. I'm right behind you." I gave him a push. He went on to the car as I instructed. Once Blake was in the car, I went to walk past Joseph, but he grabbed me. His grip on my arm was painfully tight. "Let me go, Joseph."

"That's your son? Blaze's son—"

I cut him off, trying to get loose from his hold but that only made his grip tighten more. "That's not Blaze's son—" I tried to lie.

"You lying little bitch," he shook me hard. "You had his son and didn't think to tell me after everything I fuckin' told you?" The back of his hand raised and came down.

I jerked my arm free and was just about to knee him in the balls as his hand stopped midair and his body started to shake.

"Ma, let's go!" Blake yelled at me.

I stood there frozen for a few seconds watching as my baby aimed a stun gun at Joseph's neck. *I didn't even know he had a damn taser!*

"Hurry up, let's go!" He demanded.

The tone of his voice shook me from my shocked state, and I ran to the car as did Blake. He hopped in the front as I got in and hurriedly pulled off.

"Don't you ever yell at me like that again, do you hear me?" I fussed at him, but he paid me no mind as he texted fast on his phone. I stared at my little man for a long while before looking back at the road. "Blake, where the hell did you get a stun gun from?"

"From my daddy. He told me to keep it with me at all times, just in case. Hold on." He held up his finger as he answered his phone. "Yeah. We were at the gas station... I don't know... He kinda looked like you... Yeah, like you and Momma called him Joseph." Blake ran what he saw to Blaze.

I looked over at him not believing my baby paid that much attention to the situation. Blake looked at me and his eyes roamed over me before he looked away.

"She's okay... No, she's not shaking or crying... He grabbed her and shook her hard so I tased him... No, we didn't call the police. We left him there... Okay. Hold on. Ma, my daddy wanna talk to you." Blake was so calm.

What the hell had Blaze been teaching my baby? "Hello?"

"You straight?" He sounded pissed.

"Yeah, I'm good. A little worried about Blake but I'm good." I didn't know how I truly felt about the situation. I kept trying to shake the more hurt, than angry look on Joseph's face out of my mind. I didn't want to tell Blaze my thoughts because he already made it perfectly clear he didn't want me near his dad.

I didn't want to sympathize with Joseph or put myself in his place, but I couldn't help but to. Maybe it was truly a trick behind him talking to me but deep down inside I felt like it wasn't. My reaction would have been the same as Joseph's if I found out my dead son had a child with the person, I confided in.

"Peaches?" Blaze called my name loudly.

"I'm sorry, B. Can we talk when I get home, please?" I couldn't focus or shake his face from my mind.

"You sure you're i'ight? You ain't hurt or nothing?"

I nodded my head, even though he couldn't see me. "I'm fine, I promise. We'll talk when we get home." I didn't give him a chance to question me again. I just ended the call. Even though Joseph was on my mind, Blake was on it more. His reaction to what happened and how he handled the whole situation scared me. If I was a kid his age, I would've freaked out and ran to get help, not think to use a taser. I glanced over at Blake only to find him looking at me.

"You sho' you straight?" Blake questioned.

I nodded.

Who the hell was this kid and where was my baby? Better yet what the hell had Blaze been teaching him?

Blaze

"Fuck, we gotda hurry up. I need to get to the crib." I told King as I called Bellow.

"What happened?" King asked.

I held up my finger for him to wait a second.

"What's up?" Bell answered after the second ring.

"Aye, fuck that bitch. Head to my crib and sit there until I pull up." My hand ran over my face. I was gon' kill that mothafucka when I saw his ass.

"I'ight, what's good?" Bellow asked.

"I'll catch you up when we meet up. We out in The City so we'll be there in about an hour."

"Bet." Bellow hung up the phone.

"Come on. Yo ass riding, so gon' close this little place up." I pointed around Jerron's office as I stood up. King, Mac and I had been there for a good fifteen minutes before I got the text from Blake.

Joseph done fuck'd up. If I didn't wanna mess with the nigga while I was alive, why the fuck would he think it was cool to keep tryna talk to my folks? Brittany was grown and could make her own decisions now, but Peaches was off limits. I hated he even talked to her. Now he was grabbing on her. I was gon' kill that mothafucka.

"B, what's going on?" King asked me again.

"Peaches ran into Joseph while she had Lil B—"

King cut me off as he walked faster on the side of me. "Is they cool?"

"From what they're saying, yeah. Blake said he shook Peaches, though. I don't like that shit. Why the fuck would he think it's cool to touch her? Aye, gon' 'head and cancel that trip to Ohio. *Fuck*!" We had gotten word earlier that day about Rice pushing some work out in Ohio. I had a little dude out there I supplied. He kept his ear to the ground and put me on to Rice. We lucked up when he called us about his move but now, we were about to miss this chance. *Fuck!*

Even though, I would have someone watching over them while I was gone. I wouldn't be able to focus on the job after that shit. I couldn't chance it. Images of Peaches laying in the hospital a few years back quickly flashed in my mind. That bullshit wasn't going happen this time.

Once we started driving, I texted Bellow to see if he made it there yet. He said he was a few blocks away. I could now relax a bit and get back to business at hand. Jerron and I sat in the backseat. I looked over at him.

"What you find out about yo baby momma?" I cracked the window, then lit a square.

"She still out in the Suburbs about a half hour from here. She's staying with some dude." He took out his phone and started doing something on it before handing it to me.

On the screen was a picture of Macy and some dude. "She looks the same. Who is he?"

"That's the dude she's living with?" He took his phone after I sent myself the photo.

"What about Ace? He with her?" I had to know because when I come for that bitch, I needed to make sure he wasn't around. I didn't want no stray bullets hitting him in the mix.

"No, he don't stay with her. She got him staying with her sister and her dude, JB. Monica don't bother with him unless it's his birthday or Christmas. That's how I found her, from watching him." His hand tightened around his phone.

I could tell he was pissed. "How he's doing?" It's been five years since I saw my little homie. I was most definitely concerned about him.

"He's good. That bitch and her nigga ain't looking after him like they supposed to, though. I done picked him up a few times, took him to the park, shopping and whatnot. They didn't say too much to him about it, though."

I believed Jerron because they didn't seem to worried about Ace when I did the same thing a few years ago. I turned in my seat and looked at him like he done lost his fuckin' mind. "What the fuck is you doing, yo? Do he know who the fuck you are?"

"No, he don't know I'm his dad. He don't even know my real name. So, chill the fuck out. If I'mma take his ass after we kill his momma, he gotda know who the fuck I am. I know what the fuck I'm doing." He snapped at me.

"My nigga, I would beat the fuck out yo hoe ass. You better lower yo fuckin' voice. You bitch ass mothafucka—"

"B, chill out, damn." King called from the driver's seat.

"Nigga, shut the fuck up and drive. I ain't talking to you." I tossed my cigarette out the window.

"Fuck is you talking to?" Ron shot back.

"Yo, I will pull this mothafucka over and put both you bitches out. Don't start that bullshit in here. Damn, you two mothafuckas need to grow the fuck up already, shit!" King snapped before he started talking again. "Ron believe

349

me, I understand you wanna get yo son. But don't get too fuckin' reckless. We don't need you to fuck around and be seen. We got a week and you can have shorty but until then stay away from him and keep yo eyes on that bitch. B, yo ass need to chill the fuck out. He don't want Peaches ass any damn more. That man done already told you that shit. He got a bitch!"

"Aye, watch your mouth with that bitch word. You don't hear me calling yo girl a bitch!" Jerron spat the word bitch out harshly.

King pulled to the side of the road, threw the truck in park and turned around. "Because yo ass ain't stupid enough to disrespect my girl. Now let me hear you refer to her as a bitch." He was pissed.

I started laughing. "Nigga, shut the fuck up and drive. That big mouth trick ain't even yo girl no more. Now, nigga, go. I gotda get back to my pregnant wife." I glanced at Jerron and couldn't contain my smile. When the truck didn't move, I looked at King. "Nigga, go! Fuck you steady looking back here for." I hit the back of his seat.

King looked at me. "I'mma fuck you up."

"Okay, now drive." My fingers waved at him and he started back driving.

"You mothafuckas crazy. Here, B," Mac passed me the blunt.

I took a deep pull. "So, the hit in Ohio is dead. Shid, we can find out where he stay out here and snatch his ass up real quick." Mac chimed in. He had been quiet the entire time.

"I'm working on that now. Sam's getting all the information he can find on this Rice cat." I pulled up the picture I sent myself from Jerron's phone. I sent it to Sam.

"What this babe look like?" Mac asked and I handed him my phone. He looked at the photo, then pointed to the screen. "That's Rice. Wait yo bitch been fuckin' Rice this whole time?" Mac stared at Jerron.

"Who the fuck is Rice?" Jerron looked at me.

I couldn't blame him. He was on a need to know basics only. Shit we could have been had that nigga.

"Who is Rice?" Jerron repeated.

I went to reply as my phone started ringing. "Hold up." Sam's name flashed across the screen. I answered. "Yeah?"

"Why did you send me a pic of Monica?" Was the first thing that left his mouth.

"How the fuck you know her?" This shit was seeming to fuckin' crazy.

"That's one of Tish's friends. B, what the fuck is going on?"

I damn show couldn't talk to his ass or tell him shit until I tied all of the pieces together. "I'll catch you up later." I hung up the phone, staring at it. I didn't want to think Sam had something to do with the shit that was going on but too much shit wasn't adding up.

First, two of the niggas his sister fuck'd with came for me. Second, how the fuck was his sister in the middle and he ain't no shit about it? Third, he knew Monica. I knew

I shown his ass a picture of her a few years back but not once did he say he knew her.

Why the fuck would he wanna do me dirty? It wasn't like he wanted a hood life or status.

I just couldn't believe he didn't know.

"B, what's up?" Mac asked.

I looked from him to the mirror in the middle only to see King staring at me.

"B, what's good?" King questioned. "Who was that on the phone?"

"Sam." I replied bluntly.

"What he say?" King continued to ask questions.

My head shook and my hand ran down my face. "I'll catch you up later." I looked back at Mac. "Hit Krystal's line and tell her I ain't gon' need her. King, I'mma need you to push that party up. We got two days. We can catch Rice on another day. Those two bitches, though, I need to kill them yesterday."

"What make you think she gon' bring that Monica chick?" King asked.

"I don't know but just in case she doesn't, Ron gon' watch her ass. If she don't come, he gon' grab her and bring her to the Mill." I instructed. It was about time we ended this shit.

Chapter 26

Peaches

"**B**laze, you didn't see him. This is not how it supposed to be." My hand rubbed against my forehead. "It's no way Blake is supposed to be carrying a damn stun gun." I just couldn't shake earlier events from my head. It made me feel so bad that Blake was put in such a situation.

"Peaches, calm down. It's not a bad thing that he learns how to use a taser or a gun. I mean if its gon' protect him or you, I don't see why you acting like this." Blaze shrugged like it was nothing.

How could he not see a problem with our baby using those weapons?

"Do you hear yourself right now, Blaze? Blake is eight, *eight*! And you don't see anything wrong with him having a taser or a fuckin' gun? Are you fuckin' serious right now?"

Blaze waved me off as he pulled his shirt over his head. "I was holding a gun when I was his age—"

"Blaze, don't you dare try to compare you to him because your whole living situation was so different. You were practically forced to grow up. Blake don't have that type of responsibility like you did. He has us to look after him. We are not about to throw him in the mix of this bullshit. He's a kid who doesn't need this…" My hand ran over my head as what I was about to say ran wild through my mind.

He stared at me with squinted eyes. I looked away from him. I didn't want to do it but he gave me no choice. "What?" He asked me.

A heavy sigh left my mouth. "I…" I didn't know how to tell him.

"Peaches, what the fuck is it?" He yelled at me.

Again, I let out a deep breath. I looked away from him and focused on my feet. "Blaze, you know I love you more than anything in this world aside from my baby. I get where your head is at with this whole thing but right now, I have to do what's best for Blake and being here isn't it. I don't want to leave you, believe me I don't, but you haven't given me any other choice. Just like you said you'll do everything to protect us, I have to do everything to protect him. You didn't see him today. I don't want Blake to be sucked into your world. He was not scared. He didn't show an ounce of fear at all. My baby is only eight. He should have been terrified that Joseph could have hurt the both of us, but he wasn't." I stressed to him and that scared me. Blake just didn't deserve that. He was only a child.

"I don't want him caught into your world. He doesn't deserve that. I want Blake to live a normal carefree life and living in this city isn't giving him that. I'm not going to ask you to come with us because I already know the answer. Just be careful while you're out here."

Leaving Blaze was the last thing I wanted to do given I had almost lost him. He was everything to me. I loved him with everything inside of me. But I loved Blake just the same and I wasn't about to jeopardize his life over that shit, I couldn't.

From my understanding, they knew nothing about the people behind the hit aside from Monica and they haven't even found her. I had to get my baby from Gary. We were safer back in Lafayette, Blake had a life and friends out there. There, he had no one. My baby couldn't even go outside to make friends. We were confined to a fuckin' house most of the time. This was not how life was supposed to be.

Blaze suddenly let out a laugh. "You good now that you got that off your chest."

My eyes squinted at his humorous laugh. "Blaze, I don't see nothing funny about this. I couldn't be any more serious right now."

"You can say what you want and feel as you may. But yo ass ain't leaving to go nowhere and you damn sho' ain't taking my son." His eyes stared at me hard as his jaws clenched tight.

I stood up and walked to the side of the bed where the two suitcases I packed earlier sat. It wasn't until I grabbed the handles and wheeled them from their spots that he saw them.

"Peaches, you're not leaving this fuckin' house. You really packed yo shit, though? What you gon' leave for another five maybe ten years this time? Then decide you wanna be with me again? Fuck you. I'm doing everything I fuckin' can to make sure y'all straight but that's not good enough, is what you're saying?" He walked toward me. I could tell he was beyond pissed.

"I'm not saying that. And not once did I say I was leaving you."

"What the fuck did you just say, Peaches? You got yo shit packed and you telling me you ain't leaving? What the fuck is you doing then? What the fuck is these then, Peaches? Huh?" He snatched up one of the suitcases and tossed it against the wall, putting a hole in it.

"Blaze, what the hell!" I stared at him like he was crazy. "You need to calm down and lower your voice."

"Fuck you! I ain't gotda do shit. You wanna leave because I'm not gon' be a bitch and runaway? Fuck you, man, and yo ass still ain't going no fuckin' where." He grabbed the other suitcase and literally threw it into the opened closet.

He missed my whole point. I wasn't going to sit there and argue with him when he wasn't trying to hear me. "Blaze, this has nothing to do with you not running away. This isn't about you but Blake's safety. I didn't say it was over between us, either. I'm trying to give my baby a life again. He's not happy here. Blake has to tase folks now? That's not the type of life I want for him. I knew you wouldn't leave this shit alone because that's just you, which is why I didn't bother to ask you to come with us. You want to finish this, baby? I understand that and I'm not trying to stop you. Handle your shit then come back to us, until then we can't stay here."

Leaving our relationship wasn't an option for me anymore. That was the last thing on my mind. I just wanted my baby away from it all.

"Peaches, you're not going anywhere." His tone was final, his mind was made.

My head nodded in understanding. "Okay, Blaze, I don't wanna fight with you over this. So okay." I walked to him and wrapped my arms around his waist. "Baby, I wish you could see where I'm coming from with this but I'mma let it go." My lips pressed against his bare chest then his chin.

He was pissed. He wouldn't even look at me.

My arms left his waist and my hands went to each side of his face. I flicked my tongue over his bottom lip before I kissed it. "Blaze, I love you." I sucked his bottom lip into my mouth.

He pulled his head back. "For real, Peach, I ain't with this bullshit."

My mouth covered his and I pecked his lips. "I hear you." I unbutton his jeans then slid the zipper down. I pushed his pants down his hips. Slowly, I began to kiss my way to his pelvis. My hand slipped into his boxer briefs and I pulled out his dick. My fingers wrapped around the shaft and I began to stroke him as my tongue licked around the rim.

Pulling back, I spit on his dick as I stroked him faster. I took the mushroom shaped tip into my mouth. My cheeks sunk in as I sucked on him.

Releasing him with a pop, my tongue swirled around the rim before I sucked on the tip once more. I took him deeper into my mouth, to the back of my throat, and moaned around it.

"Mmm, shit." Blaze grunted as his hands tangled into my hair. His hips started thrusting.

I gave him free range of my mouth, letting him fuck it as he pleased. When it became too much for me, I'd gave his hips a slight push. I released him and took a deep breath while my hand jerked his dick. I gave the tip a slight squeeze as I sucked on his sack, moaning.

"Ooh fuck!" Blaze pulled me away from his man. He pulled me to my feet and quickly took off my clothes, tossing them every which way. He pushed me down on the bed. He kissed my lips before he went to my breast. His tongue played with my right nipple then the left as his hands slid down my stomach to my pelvis. His hand covered my sex.

My legs stretched wide apart waiting for the invasion of his fingers. My hips raised and rolled egging him to go further.

Slowly he kissed his way down my body until he reached my pelvis. His tongue ran through my slit as his fingers pushed inside of me. Blaze's mouth latched onto my pearl and he started sucking. He pressed down on my pelvic and began to massage my inner walls.

"Ooh, Blaze!" My back arched as I grasped the nape of his neck, grinding my pussy against his face. "Ooh, ooh shit! Just like that, baby." His fingers moved faster as his mouth sucked harder on my swollen pearl. It wasn't long after that my inner muscles tightened around his fingers, milking them.

Blaze quickly left my contracting sex and hovered over me. He brought his dick to my opening and thrust deep inside of me.

"Oh, my God! Ooh," a loud scream left my mouth as my orgasm shook my body.

Blaze's lips covered mine as his hips thrust fast and hard against my own. My moans were muffled by his mouth.

My nails dug into his lower back as my hips grinded against his, trying to match his pace. "Oh, my God! Oh, my God! Ooh!" My moan stretched as my nails dug deeper into his skin. "Ah, ah, shit! Ooh, Blaze!"

His thrust became harder, causing my muscles to tighten and my back to arch. I tried to push him back.

"Nuh uh. Don't go nowhere." Blaze flipped me on my stomach. He raised my butt in the air. Blaze's hand came down on my ass. The sting caused my inner walls to throb faster. His hand came down a second time but harder as he thrust deeper inside of me.

"Ah, ah, Blaze!" I cried. My fist gripped the sheets as the sensation shook my body. The feeling was beyond incredible. I screamed and moaned loudly. I couldn't control myself. "Oh, my God! Ooh, ooh!" The pleasure was so amazing I wanted to cry. "Mmm, ooh!" my ass rolled then grind against him.

Blaze gripped my hair and he pulled me up. His lips came to mine as his free hand went to my pearl. He slapped the swollen nub before he started playing with it.

My orgasm quickly started to build, causing my inner muscle to squeeze tightly around him. I hooked my arm around his neck, kissing him as I bounced fast on his dick, trying to reach that high peak.

My lips pulled away from his, my eyes rolled up and I bit into my lip. "Ooh, I love you so much." I whined out.

Blaze turned us around. His lips played with mine before he kissed me, slipping his tongue into my mouth as it began an intimate dance with mine.

With me now on top, I pulled back from the kiss. I took ahold of his man and brought it to my opening. Slowly, I slid down on him, I came back up only leaving the tip in as my muscles squeezed around it.

Blaze's hips pushed up and he filled me completely.

"Mmm…" My hips rolled before they started a back and forth motion. His hands came to my breast, he squeezed then pinched my nipple as he thrusted up. My feet laid flat on the bed and I started to bounce faster on him. Moan after moan filled the room.

Blaze knees bent and he took hold of my hips, stopping my movement. He started to thrust upwards, fast and hard.

"Aah, shit! Ooh, Blaze!" I grabbed his knees, digging my nails into his skin. "Ah, ah, ah, ah!" My body shook as I came with a loud moan.

"Ah fuck!" Blaze grunted as his movement became frantic. His pelvis jerked as he held me tightly to him and released his fluids inside of me.

Sweat covered our bodies as we laid there panting in sync. Neither one of us said a thing. I was afraid to say anything for fear of giving myself away and I didn't know what Blaze was thinking.

I kissed his chest as my finger drew patterns over the left side of his ribs. Once again, I pressed my lips to his chest before my eyes closed.

"Peach…" His lips pressed against my sweaty forehead and his hands grabbed my butt with a nice firm grip. "Peaches," he shook my booty.

My lips stretched into a smile. "Hm?"

His rough callus hands moved up then down my spine before they returned to caressing my booty. "Don't leave this damn house, you hear me?"

I didn't know what to say, so I didn't answer him. I pretended I was asleep. "Eep!" A little squeak left my mouth.

Blaze's hand tangled into my hair. He gripped it tightly and he jerked my head back, so I was looking at him.

"Yo ass bet not leave this fuckin' house, do you hear me?" He damn near growled out.

My eyes cut at him from the vice grip he had on my hair. "Blaze, I swear to God—"

He cut me off by flipping us over. "I ain't tryna hear that bullshit you about to say. All you have to say is *okay*. Now did you hear what I said?"

I didn't say anything in response. I knew when he went to sleep, I was taking my baby and leaving. I didn't want to lie to him, so it was best I said nothing at all. "Blaze, let my hair go." I grabbed his wrist.

Ignoring me, he took ahold of my right thigh and put that leg over his shoulder. With his grip still on my hair, Blaze pulled my head up and bit into my bottom lip, gripping it between his teeth. He pulled it.

The slight pain caused my inner walls to clench around him. I sometimes hated how my body reacted to him. I wanted to be mad, but I couldn't. I felt him twitch inside of me. My tongue flicked over his top lip.

His head reared back, and he let go of my hair. Blaze pulled out of me then pushed back in. Slowly, he started to build up his pace, going faster. He watched me as he moved.

Lazily, my eyes tried to hold his gaze but with the pleasurable sensation his body was giving mine, I couldn't. I bit into my bottom lip, my hands gripped his sides, pulling him closer as my eyes rolled up before they closed. Once they did, Blaze's lips came to mine.

His hips moved faster, harder into me. The head-board knocked against the wall with every powerful thrust he made.

"Mmm, shit, Blaze." I quickly lost myself in him like I'd done a million times before.

"Peaches, yo ass bet not leave this house. You hear me? Ah fuck!" He grunted out as his pelvis slapped into mine.

I paid no mind to what he was saying to me. I truly couldn't at that moment. All I wanted was to feel that mind boggling high he always brought me to.

"You hear me?" He bit into my bottom lip as his hips rolled. He pulled back and brought his mouth to my breast. His tongue played with my nipple before he sucked the little nub into his warm mouth.

Again, I said nothing as my hips continued to grind into his, loving the feel of him. It wasn't until he pulled out that he grabbed my full attention. *What was he doing?* "Blaze—" I grabbed for him again.

He pushed my hands away as he brought the head of his dick back. His tip went in and again my eyes closed. He pulled out once more.

"Bae, don't do me like that." I reached for him. Now wasn't the time to tease me. I was beyond horny. It seemed like my hormones were in overdrive.

"Did you hear what I said to you?" He pushed deep inside of me again. His movement was slow before it picked up.

My nails dug into his flesh. "Ooh, ooh, ooh! Oh, my God!" My head rolled to the side and I bit hard into my lower lip.

He pulled out of me and began to slap his man against my swollen pearl a few times before he pushed back in and started to drill into me.

I could feel myself reaching my peak. "Ah, ah, ah, ooh! Oh, my God!" I cried out in frustration. "'Blaze, I swear to God." I whined.

"Did you hear what I said?" He questioned.

I didn't know but I also didn't care. "Yes."

"Yes what?" He pushed inside of me.

My inner muscle squeezed around him. "Ooh, yes."

He pulled out. "Yes what, Peaches? You gon' stay here?"

"Yes, I promise I'm not going anywhere."

Blaze's hands cuffed the back of my thighs as he raised them. Once he had my legs in the air, he became relentless.

For the rest of the night he gave me that rough, loving sex that my body craved.

***

I woke up at three in the morning to go to the bathroom.

Once I finished taking care of my business, I washed my hands. It was then that I noticed the t-shirt I had on. Blaze had cleaned me up. A smile stretched across my face, but it quickly faded away as Blake came to mind. *I had to get him away from Gary.* With that thought, I went back into the room. I walked over to Blaze.

"Babe," I whispered his name. He didn't move. I stood in his face for a few seconds longer to see if his eyes would open. They didn't.

I kissed him on the lips then went to the closet. Quickly, I slipped on a pair of shorts and then my gym shoes. My eyes slid to the suitcase then out into the room where Blaze slept. A sigh left my mouth as I grabbed the handle and wheeled it into the room.

I was doing the right thing. I couldn't let Blake be around this.

With that thought, I left out of our room and went to Blake's. I crept inside and woke him up. "Blake, baby get up." I shook him. He didn't budge at first. I shook him harder. "Rashad."

"Hmm?" He rolled on his back, rubbing his eyes while looking up at me.

"Come on, get your bag and let's go." I pulled him up and waited for him to throw on his basketball shorts.

Blake grabbed his duffle bag that I had him pack earlier that day. Once we left out his room, I led us to the living room. As we approached the front door. I stopped once I got there as a worrying ache grew in the pit of my stomach.

I stood by the front door trying to shake that feeling but I just couldn't. A heavy sigh left my mouth before I glanced over at the table. My brows furrowed in confusion.

"What?" Blake asked with a yawn.

"My keys and my purse aren't here. I know I left them on the table, I always leave them right here." I pointed to the table by the door where I always sat my things so I wouldn't lose them.

I thought about my keys and purse being gone. Blaze popped into my head. He knew me all too well. There wasn't a doubt in my mind that he had taken and hid them from me so I wouldn't leave. He knew I had planned on going regardless of his warning.

"I don't know. I haven't seen them. Ma, I'm sleepy. If you don't find your keys, can I go back to sleep?" He stretched as another yawn left his mouth.

I stared at my baby for a while before I let out a heavy breath. "Go back to bed." I kissed the side of his head and gave him a slight push in the direction of his room. Once I saw his door close, I went into the living room and sat on the couch thinking about what I was about to do.

I was actually about to sneak out of the house and take Blake with me regardless of what Blaze had to say about it. My palms pressed against my forehead. I didn't want us around that mess anymore. I wanted it to be over. But sneaking out wasn't the right way of doing it. That would only cause more problems with us.

With a groan, I put my feet on the couch and laid back. A part of me felt like shit as I closed my eyes. It felt as if I was choosing Blaze over the safety of my child by staying. But it was that nagging ache inside of my gut that told me if I left, something terrible was going to happen to one of us.

Whenever I got that feeling, something bad always happened.

Chapter 27

Peaches

"**B**laze, stop biting me." A groan slipped through my lips. My shoulder shrugged trying to get him to stop.

"Peaches." He kissed my neck while his hand slid under my shirt, massaging my left breast.

A slight moan left my mouth as my eyes closed once again. Slowly, I had begun to fall asleep.

"Peaches, wake yo ass up." Blaze's hand slapped my thigh.

My eyes opened and I turned around. He grabbed my arms.

"Gon' somewhere, Peaches." He laughed.

I glared hard at him. "That shit ain't even funny, with yo stupid ass. You play too damn much.

That shit hurt, black ass." My arms jerked in his hands as I tried to get free.

He wasn't letting go.

"Are you done?" His tone was serious, but I didn't take him as such.

The question actually made me mad. "Hell no, I'm not. My leg hurt, it's hot. Why would you even hit me like that, Blaze?" From the tone of my voice and the slant of my eyes, he knew I had an attitude.

"Why the fuck would you try to sneak out of the house earlier this morning after last night?" He was pissed.

The hard look to my face left. I opened my mouth to explain but no words came out.

His hand slapped hard against my thigh again. "Now yo ass ain't got shit to say, huh? Why the fuck—"

"I know but you ain't gotda be hitting me either. I'm not putting my damn hands on you." I snapped at him finally jerking my hands free. Once they were, I hit him. "Yo irritating ass, you get on my damn nerves. If you don't understand why I wanted to leave, then you truly haven't grown up at all. Blaze, I want Blake safe no matter what. That's why I was going to leave." His mouth opened to cut me off, but I held up my finger, stopping him.

"Let me finish. Don't take me saying that as if I think you can't handle taking care and protecting us. Because I know you can and will do everything in your power to keep us safe. But, bae, you will not always be around and having someone sit at the house to watch us isn't always guaranteed. We both know that all too well. I just don't want to take any chances." My shoulders shrugged.

"I know. So why you ain't leave?" He licked his lips as he leaned over me.

My eyes rolled up in my head and I bit into the side of my jaw.

That action caused him to laugh. "Be straight up with me. Why you ain't leave? You knew I was gon' come and beat yo ass?" He joked.

My eyes rolled harder that time. "I knew you was going to come after us. You beating my ass, though? I don't know about that. Blaze." I grabbed his wrist as his hand slipped into the front of my shorts.

He easily shook my hand off as he started to play with my clit. "Nuh uh, keep talking. Tell me why you ain't leave."

I licked my lips before I let out a pleasurable sigh. My hand grabbed the nape of his neck, trying to bring his lips down to mine.

"Nuh uh." Even though he said no, his lips covered mine as his fingers pushed inside of me. Blaze massaged my inner walls as his tongue danced with mine. He bit into my bottom lip then pulled away. "Why you ain't leave, Peaches?"

He was not going to leave it alone. "Because I didn't want to leave you. I thought if I did, something would happen. Mmm."

Blaze's fingers moved faster. "That's why?"

"Mmhm," I moaned.

"That's one of the reasons." His fingers pulled out of me and he got off the bed.

I was beyond confused. "Blaze, where you going?"

He walked into our bathroom. A few seconds later I heard water running.

I sat up on my elbows, watching the door. *Did he have to pee?*

Blaze came back into the room, grabbed his shirt off the bed and put it on before he sat down to put on his gym shoes.

Okay maybe I was reading too much into what just happened, but I could've sworn we were about to have sex. I was so horny. "Bae?" I know I didn't hear a phone ring so he couldn't be going anywhere. I made my way to the bottom of the bed, where he sat. My hands moved over his shoulders. I kissed his neck before pulling the skin into my mouth. "Bae, what are you doing?"

His head turned sideways, and he kissed me. Blaze pulled back and stood up. "Shit right now, but you need to get dress so we can go."

My mouth parted and I pointed to the bed. "What? I thought we were about—wait what just happened?"

Blaze laughed. "You thought I was about to give you some dick?"

I didn't hide my thoughts as my head nodded. "Yes, I thought just that."

Again, he laughed. "You must be crazy. Yo ass tried to sneak out the fuckin' house last night. The only reason you didn't leave is because I took yo keys and shit. Why the fuck would I treat you? Huh? Baby, get ready so we can go." He grabbed his phone and keys then left out the room.

Blaze never turned down sex no matter what. He got on my damn nerves! A loud frustrated scream left my mouth as I fell back onto the bed.

I was so damn horny. My pussy muscles continued to contract as the pit of my stomach remained tight. I could still feel his rough callus hands rubbing against my clit before they began to stroke my inner walls.

I couldn't take it. "Babe! Come here, please!" I yelled out to him. We could have a quickie. I pulled off my shirt and shorts then laid back on the bed. I knew if Blaze saw me naked and playing with myself, he wouldn't be able to resist.

A knock sounded on the door. "Momma, my dad said come out here and tell him what you want. He's not coming in there." Blake replied through the door.

"Is he fuckin' serious right now?" I asked more to myself, but I got a reply from Blake.

"He said yeah. Now put on some clothes." Blake laughed loudly before I heard him running down the hallway.

"Ugh! He gets on my damn nerves. Stupid ass!" I mumbled to myself as I laid there looking at the ceiling. "That's why his momma a trick." I said to myself before I burst out laughing at my childishness.

372

A groan left my mouth. I got up and went to the bathroom to take a quick shower before getting dressed like he asked.

***

Once I was dressed, I went downstairs to the kitchen where my two men were with grocery bags on the table. "Why y'all didn't tell me you were going to the store?"

"Nana went to the store for us." Blake told me. He hopped off the counter due to the nudge Blaze had given him.

"What?" I already knew it was something.

"Before you say no to make lasagna, I really want some and you haven't made it in a long time." Blake pleaded.

I laughed at him before I glanced at Blaze and rolled my eyes. "I'll make you some lasagna. What's this other stuff?" I peeked inside of the bags to see junk food.

"Since we haven't really done nothing together, I figured we could have a family day in. We can watch movies, play video games and play basketball. Me and you against dad." Blake explained excitedly.

He was no longer asking but telling me what he had planned for us to do. I had no problem with it. "I'm down, but you gon' have to guard your dad hard to keep him away from me. He likes to cheat and pull hair."

Blaze spit out his water and started laughing. He looked at me. "Fuck you, man." He wiped his mouth with his shirt. "Stupid ass."

"How am I stupid when you're the one who cheats? I'm just warning Blake of your ways." I smiled at him.

"I know he be cheating and he don't like to pay when he lose. So, we not betting." Blake glared at his dad.

"Shut yo ass up! Y'all ass just don't never win, which is why y'all complaining. Black asses. Come on, it's me and Blake against you." Blaze grabbed the basketball from the back door and snapped his fingers at Blake. "Let's go." He walked out the back door.

"And this is who you want to be with? He crazy." Blake joked.

"Shut up, you act just like him." I laughed as we followed Blaze outside to the basketball court. Blake shook his head then ran over to his dad.

"Come on, Blake, take the ball out." Blaze tossed him the ball. "Peaches, don't get scared. Bring yo ass on." He said, talking shit.

I stood on the sideline laughing. "How is that fair, y'all against me?"

Blaze stopped and looked at me like I was crazy before his eyes dropped to my stomach. "Fuck you mean. Peaches, baby, you got two shorties inside of you. Shid, it's three of y'all against us. How is that right, yo?"

Blake fell on the ground in a fit of laughter. "Played!" He hollered out.

My mouth was just wide open. I didn't know what to say as I looked down at my protruding belly. "Blake, it's not even that funny. And Blaze you get on my damn nerves and just for that, I ain't making shit! Y'all better go to McDonald's for dinner. I don't even wanna play anymore." I tried to have an attitude, but I had to admit the shit was funny as hell. Blaze played too much.

"I'm just bullshittin'." He laughed as he walked toward me.

"No, nope, don't even talk to me. I'm going back in the house." I quickly turned around so he wouldn't see the stupid smile my lips stretched into. "Ah!" I screamed out a laugh as he picked me up and tossed me over his shoulder. "Blaze, put me down!"

"Shut yo whining ass up. You ain't going anywhere but on the court. Crybaby ass." He slapped me on my booty before he put me down. "B, give me that ball."

Blake threw him the ball.

"Here take it out." Blaze handed it to me.

He was serious about them teaming up on me. "Y'all really going to go against me?"

"Yeah, now take it out. Stop all that talking." Blake cut in.

I was shocked because he was always on my team. "Okay, bet. Don't start crying when I win. Anything goes for me since I'm by myself."

"That's cool." Blake agreed, which cause Blaze to look at him like he was crazy.

"Hell no!"

As he was protesting, I ran around him to the basket and shot. "Two, zero. Come on, baby, let's get this game going." I slapped Blaze on the butt and hurriedly jumped away from him.

"Peaches, don't make me beat yo ass." Blaze threatened, making me laugh.

"I'm not worried about you. Come on, baby, take the ball out." I tossed Blake the ball. "Don't forget anything goes for me." I reminded him as I blocked Blaze.

Blaze moved fast and came around me. Blake tossed him the ball and Blaze threw it back. Once Blake passed me, I was about to grab him from behind, but Blaze snatched me up off of my feet.

"Shoot, Blake!" He yelled holding me to him.

"Blaze, yo cheating black ass! Put me down!" I fussed at him but ending up laughing.

"Anything goes, Momma, don't forget." Blake repeated what I said, mimicking my voice.

Blaze burst out laughing. "That's what I'm talkin' 'bout!"

His laughter became contagious and I couldn't help but join in.

***

"Blake, run in the kitchen and get my tea, please, and a bottle of water," I said as I cuddled up against Blaze's side.

"Hell no, man. Yo ass gon' be pausing the movie and running to the bathroom." Blaze fussed. "Blake, just bring the popcorn and come on." He yelled into the kitchen.

"You get on my damn nerves. Stupid self." I rolled my eyes hard before I got up to go get my drinks myself, but before I could really walk away, he pulled me down on his lap. "No, man, gon' somewhere. I'm not even playing." I rolled my eyes at him.

"You ain't even mad so stop frontin'. You just want somebody to kiss yo yellow ass." He laughed as his arms wrapped around my waist.

"No, I don't. Blaze, stop!" I screamed out a laugh as his head went into the side of my neck. Whenever he kissed my neck, it tickled.

"Yo goofy ass, man." He turned my face toward his.

My lips immediately puckered, which made him laugh, but he kissed me, nonetheless. My arms wrapped around his neck as his hand slipped under my top. He began to rub my stomach.

"Man, y'all need to stop with all that cake mess. Dad, don't tell me you turning soft." Blake teased.

Blaze kicked him in the back of his knee making him fall. "Cake that shit and I ain't going soft. I do this only for yo momma. Soft? I bet I can still whoop yo ass. Wanna try me?"

Laughing, I popped Blaze on the arm. "You wrong for that and Blake shut up. You don't know nothing about caking. I love my baby caking up with me."

"I don't be caking, fuck outda here with that shit." He started to shrug me off.

"Nuh uh! Don't do that. I ain't say it. Baby, you never cake. Blake, shut up and watch the movie." I reached down and slapped him on the back of his head.

"Whatever." Blake laughed as he turned toward the TV eating his popcorn.

Once I knew he was into the TV, I turned to face Blaze. "You have to ignore him, he don't know what he's talking about. Soft? Who? Not my hood. Nope, I don't see it." I boasted.

Blaze started laughing. "Ain't that shit real? You a good ass suck up. Yo ass just don't want to get up." He called it right.

"No, I don't." I laughed before I leaned in to kiss him. It wasn't until then that something dawned on me. "Mhm." I hummed as I pulled back from the kiss.

"What?"

"Have you talked to King today?" Since we'd been back in Gary, a day hadn't gone by that King and Blaze weren't together or talked for that matter.

"I talked to him yesterday, I told him what we had planned for the day and I didn't want to be bothered, you know?" He shrugged nonchalantly.

My head slowly shook. "No, I don't know. So, what's up?"

"It ain't shit." He shrugged while continuing to rub my stomach.

He had gotten pretty good with lying, I'll admit. But after years of dealing with him, I could always tell when he wasn't being straight up with me. "Blaze, don't do that. Talk to me."

This time he laughed. His hand tangled into the back of my hair and he pulled my face closer to his. "Peaches, it ain't shit you gotda worry about. I got this; I promise you." His lips covered mine once again. Blaze's hand left my stomach and wrapped around my back. He kissed me hard as he pulled me on my side closer to him.

My eyes closed. Slowly, I began to lose myself in his kiss. Our tongues were going stroke for stroke. My stomach tightened and I moaned into his mouth.

"I love you, Peaches." He mumbled against my lips.

I pulled back and stared at him for a long while. His eyes dropped and he looked away from me. He wasn't able to hold my gaze. That alone told me it was something.

"Blaze, tell me what's up? Did y'all find out anything else?"

"It ain't shit you need to worry about right now. We taking care of everything, I promise. So, don't worry about it or me. I don't need yo stress fuckin' up my babies."

I tried to hold a straight face, but I ended up letting out a light laugh. "Don't try to be funny when I'm being serious."

"I ain't being funny. I'm hella serious. If my babies come out looking crazy, I'm leaving y'all at the hospital. Me and B gon' be out." He joked.

"Stupid ass, shut up." My eyes rolled and my head shook at his craziness. Once my chuckles died down, I let out a sigh. My fingers massaged the back of his neck as my eyes stared into his. "Blaze, if you found out something about this mess, you wouldn't keep it from me? You'll tell me, right?" I had to know because something just wasn't right.

Blaze's face came closer to mine and his tongue flicked over my top lip before he pulled my bottom into his mouth.

I knew what he was trying to do. "B, I'm being for real." I mumbled against his lips. "Blaze, would you stop and be serious for a minute." I was starting to become frustrated, but he wasn't listening to me.

He rolled us over, so he was on top of me. "I'm being serious and it's nothing you have to worry about. You hear me?" Blaze tilted my head back. His mouth played with mine, lightly brushing against my parted lips before his tongue flicked the rim of my bottom then top lip. "Peaches, do you hear me?" He repeated as he wedged himself between my legs.

My head nodded. "I hear you." My neck stretched up, meeting his lips halfway.

His lower body pressed against mine and the kiss grew intense.

Once I felt Blaze's hand grip the crouch part of my shorts and pulled them to the side, I stopped him. "Blaze," I moved his hand from between my legs. I kissed him again, but I turned my head to the side to look at Blake. He was still watching the movie. "We do have a kid in the room." My lips pressed into his once again.

"I'm glad you remembered I was still in the room." Blake turned to face us and laughed. "I hope I don't ever be like this with my girl." He shook his head and turned back toward the TV.

Blaze laughed and muffed his head to the side. "You gon' be worse, especially when she put that wet on you—"

I whacked Blaze hard on his back. *I swear he just didn't care what he said to our son.*

"Ah shit! What the hell you slap me like that for? I just almost knocked yo ass out." He snapped at me.

"Don't be talking about no wet with him. What is wrong with you? I seriously happy we are having a girl. I can't deal with you and your bad influences on my son." I fussed at him.

Blake snorted. "Like you have room to talk. I do hear y'all at night. And just a minute ago, y'all just need to separate."

This time I muffed him. "Go to bed. Talking about you hear us at night. You hear me getting sick." I pushed him onto the floor. "Blaze, get him."

He shook his head and shrugged. "I'm sorry, baby, but I gotda agree with him. Yo ass do be loud as hell." He teased.

"When did this double team start? Blake, you always have my back but now you're being flakey. That's okay, you remember this." I made an empty threat. Regardless of his wishy washy attitude, he was still my little man, no matter what. I sat up and pushed Blaze down on the couch then laid in front of him.

He wrapped his arm around my waist and brought his mouth to my ear. "You gon' give me some tonight?" He bit into the spot behind my ear then kissed it.

"No." I pushed my butt more into him and closed my eyes.

"Peach, you gon' do me like that?" His pelvis pushed against my booty.

I paid his erection no attention, like he had done me earlier that day. I ignored his whispers and grinding into me as the sensation slowly began to put me to sleep.

Chapter 28

Peaches

"Ma, you cheating! You can't be holding me." Blake complained with an attitude because I caused him to miss a shot.

My hands went to my knees and I took in a deep breath. My lungs were burning, I was beyond tired. "Didn't nobody tell you to be that fast. Damn, I'm tired." I dramatically fell down to the ground and laid there.

Blake stood over me laughing before falling down.

My arms caught him before he could land on me. "Nuh uh, Blake, you're not a little baby anymore. You can't be jumping on me like that."

He laid on the side of me, tossing the ball up. "I beat you. Now come on, take me to get some ice cream." He smiled, nodding his head.

I laughed at him as I got up off of the ground. "Come on before I change my mind."

He held his hand out for me. I pulled him up and we walked into the house.

"Go get cleaned up so we can leave." I waved him off and got myself a drink of water. "Shower, Blake!" I yelled out to him. Knowing him, he would put on some deodorant and swear he was clean. After I finished my cup of water, I went into my room and hopped in the shower, letting the cool water chill my heated body.

***

"E, have Keema ready in about an hour." I told her before I waved the waiter over for a refill.

"She'll be ready. All she been talking about was going over there with her Auntie and Uncle Boon. This child been getting on my nerves. Oh, and she won't shut up about your babies." Ebony ranted.

"Leave my baby alone. Girl, that's Blaze's ass got her talking about babies. Regardless of the ultrasound, that man is convinced we are having twins. I'm not playing with him, though. E, I am so stuffed." I leaned back in my chair and rubbed my belly.

"Where y'all go eat at?" She asked.

"We're at Great Wall. I promised Blake some ice cream, but I had a taste for some Chinese, so we stopped by here first." I took a drink of my tea and then let out a sigh.

"Keema, Auntie Peaches said get ready she'll be here in a minute to get you." Ebony told her daughter.

Keema's loud squeak of excitement could be heard through the phone.

"Make sure she has on play clothes because I'mma take them out for ice cream and then to Wicker Park so they can tire themselves out."

"Okay, well let me find this little girl something to wear before she tear up her room. Thanks, Peach. I really need this breather." Ebony laughed before letting out a grunt.

"It's cool. I'll call when I'm on my way." After we said our goodbyes, we disconnected the line. "Are you almost finished." I stopped talking and laughed at Blake's twisted up face. "What? Why you looking at me like that?"

"Why we gotda get Sha? She's worrisome and talk too much. That little girl get on my nerves." He grunted out before finishing off his drink.

"She probably thinks the same about you." I had to admit, Keema's ass was something else. Keema's attitude couldn't be helped, though. She had both King and Ebony running through her veins. That was catastrophic. I could only imagine how she'd turn out when she got older.

"Can we sit down and eat our ice cream?" Blake asked as he looked over the bill.

I snatched it from him. "Boy, give me that. You don't have no money to pay for anything." I cut my eyes at him in a playful manner. "Now why we have to sit there and eat the ice cream? On second thought, I don't know why you won't eat the ice cream here. Shoot, I don't see why I have to drive somewhere else when you have, sparkles, M&M's, seeds, peanuts and cherries all over there. Not to mention three different flavors, chocolate, swirl and vanilla." I licked my lips at the thought of the ice cream. "Blake, go get me some ice cream." He glared and I burst out laughing at him.

"Man, no, we about to go get ice cream from Dairy Queen. Plus, their stuff nasty anyway." Blake complained as he came around to my side of the table and pulled me up.

I laughed because I had something for his grown self. "You right, we're going to stop and pick up Keema on the way." I waved my hand at Blake before he could say anything smart. "Wait, hush, let me call your dad." I pulled out my phone and dialed Blaze's number. After a few rings it went to voicemail and I left a message, letting him know we were leaving the restaurant. Before I could finish the message fully, my line beeped. Blaze was returning my call. I clicked over and answered. "Hey, babe."

"What's up, Peaches?"

"Nothing, I was just calling to let you know we were leaving the Chinese spot. I'm about to take Blake to get his ice cream, then go get Keema and take them to Wicker Park. That's all I wanted." I paid the bill, then waved Blake on.

"I'ight. Call me when you pick up Keema. Peach, don't be out too late. Oh, Bell gon' come pick y'all up around six and take y'all to the apartment for me." He informed me of his plan.

I was confused. "Blaze, why do we have to go there?"

386

"Because that's where I'm staying, and I want y'all there with me. Is that a problem?" He joked smartly.

His playful manner washed away all my confusion. "No, I don't have any problems with that at all." My teeth gripped my bottom lip.

"Oh, shit. I hear it. You tryna meet up?" He hummed into the line.

I started laughing as I shook my head. "No, I'm not. If I didn't have Blake, then maybe. But tonight, mmm, most definitely."

"Oh, you gon' get it, so be ready. I'll be there early too. So be there in the bed naked."

"I promise I will be. Bye, bae. Love you." I smiled to myself shyly. Just thinking about everything we were going to do when he got home. Oh, I was going to be ready.

"Love you too, Peach. Y'all hurry up, do everything then get to the crib. I don't like you out when I don't have nobody following you. So, hurry up. As a matter fact, hold off on going to the park. We can do that tomorrow, bet?" Blaze offered.

My eyes rolled and I wanted to protest but I didn't. I knew how he was when it came to our safety, especially with me being pregnant. It was a surprise he even let us get out of the house, knowing he wasn't going to have anyone trailing behind us.

"Okay, I'll get Blake's ice cream, pick up Keema and then go straight home. Give me a half hour and I'll call you when I get there." I didn't want him to worry about us.

"I'ight, hurry up."

I laughed and looked at the phone. "Okay, bye."

We ended the call and I drove us to Dairy Queen down the street from where we were. Once we got there, we went inside because Blake had to use the restroom.

"Just get me a cone dipped in cherry. And ask them to give me another but in a cup." Blake told me before he ran to the bathroom.

I laughed at that child of mine before I ordered everything, he asked me to plus Keema's ice cream.

"Peaches?"

My name was called in a questioning manner. I knew the voice all too well. I turned around and plastered a fake smile on my face. I haven't seen her since Blaze's funeral.

"Hey, Tish." I greeted her.

Her smile was wide as she walked over to me and gave me a big hug. "Oh, my God. You have no idea how long I've been trying to get in touch with you. I tried talking to you at the funeral. Oh, my God." She hugged me again and then pulled away. "How have you been?"

I laughed and put some space between us. I haven't really seen her since Blake, and I left for Lafayette five years ago. After everything that happened to me behind Le'Ron, I didn't deal with her knowing they used to date. Even though she never did anything to me, I knew how close they were, and I didn't want to take the hate I felt for him out on her.

"I've been good. I can't really complain. What about you?"

"I've been blessed, that's all I can really say." Her smile dimmed a bit. "I didn't get a chance to tell you at the funeral, but I'm sorry about what happened to him and know if you need anything, I'm here for you. I don't know what happened that we fell off, but I would love to start hanging out with you again. I've really missed your crazy self." She pulled me into another hug.

I let out a few chuckles before a little body was wedged between ours.

"Mommy, did you get my ice cream?" A beautiful little brown skinned girl asked Tish before she looked up at me. "Hey, what's your name?" she asked, staring at me with pretty almond shaped eyes.

My heart melted. "Aw, you're so cute. I'm Peaches, what's your name?"

"Linnea Le'Shay Wright," she smiled.

Tish picked her up and placed the little girl on her hip. I could see their resemblance immediately.

"That's your baby?" I asked before I glanced toward the bathroom, hoping Blake didn't decide to come out just yet.

"Yeah, this is my baby." She turned and kissed the little girl on her forehead. "Did you wash your hands little girl?"

"Yeah, see." She put her hands to her mom's nose.

I laughed. "She's so cute." Instinctively, my hand went to my stomach. Just imagining how my baby girl was going to be brought a smile to my face.

"Oh, my God. I knew there was something different about you. How the hell did I miss that glow? How far along are you?"

"Six months." I couldn't contain my smile.

"That's Blaze's baby?" Her hand went to my stomach and she rubbed it.

"Yeah, this is his baby girl." I told her before I let out a sigh.

"I'm sorry. I know how hard it is to raise a baby without their father being there." The tone of her voice changed for a slight second sounding a bit depressed. But just as fast as it seeped in, it was gone, and a big smile plastered itself on her face. "Congratulations. I know you're happy about this especially considering what happened last time." She stopped, talking immediately.

"Excuse me? What did you just say?" I heard exactly what she said, but I didn't want to believe that I had. I hoped I heard wrong. She couldn't have possibly known I had a miscarriage. No one knew besides Blaze, my brother, Mom B and my girls. That was kept between us and out of the hospital files.

"I said congratulations on your pregnancy." Her smile was just as wide as before, but her eyes squinted, and she started to look a bit concerned. "Are you okay? I think you need to sit down. You

390

look like you're about to faint." Her hand touched my fore-head.

I slapped her hand away from me. "Don't touch me. What you mean considering last time? What happened last time?" I asked her ready to jump on her and start swinging.

Her eyes squinted in a confused manner. "The last time? What? I'm sorry, Peaches, but I don't know what you're talking about. You don't look good at all. Are you sure you're okay? Do you need me to call someone? The hospital is right up the street."

What the fuck was this bitch talking about?

"Tishana, I heard what the fuck you said." I stepped closer to her. "I'm the last one you wanna fuckin' play with. Bitch, I heard you. No one knew about that so for you to mention it, you must have had something to do with it." I looked at her baby girl and smiled before my gaze fell back on her. "You should have had him kill me. Now your baby girl is going to know how hard life is going to be without both of her parents." I looked back at her daughter. "Enjoy your ice cream, sweetie." Slowly, I backed away from her before I turned around.

Blake exited the bathroom at that moment. "Ma, that Chinese messed up my stomach." He rubbed his hand over his belly with a grunt. "I don't think I want no ice cream no more."

"Oh, my damn!" Tishana said as she held her cell-phone to her ear. "That's his son."

"Come on, let's go." Grabbing Blake's arm, I started pulling him. I needed to get him as far away as possible. As we walked fast out of the door, I had my phone in my hands, calling Blaze.

"Peaches, wait!" Tish yelled out to me.

I ignored her as I walked to my car.

"Peaches, just let me explain, please! I'm sorry for what happened. You weren't supposed to get hurt." She shouted as she made her way toward us.

Had it not been for Blake, I would've been all over her ass. "Fuck you, Tish. I'll see you," was the only threat I made.

She smiled at me.

That was the last thing I saw before something hard hit me over the head, knocking me out.

***

A groan left my mouth from the pain in the back of my skull. My arms felt so heavy and as a result I couldn't lift them to caress my throbbing head. I blinked a few times trying to clear my hazy vision.

After a few minutes when I was able to focus better, I took in my surroundings. I was in a basement.

"Ma? Momma?" Blake called to me. "Ma?"

I followed his voice and saw him sitting on a couch with two big dudes next to him. When I made a move to sit up straight, Blake stood up ready to run to me. The tall dark skinned dude next to him pulled Blake down.

I didn't know those men and I damn sure didn't know what they were capable of, so I wasn't going to be a dummy and find out. Especially not with Blake being there.

Finally, I managed to roll myself onto my back. I pushed myself in a sitting position. "Baby, I'm fine. Just sit there." I realized at that moment my arms were tied behind my back which was why they felt heavy.

A laugh left my mouth as I leaned against the wall. I looked at my son and smiled at him. "Rashad, whatever they ask you tell them the truth. Okay."

"Okay." His head nodded in understanding.

Again, I smiled at him before I scooted from the wall and leaned forward. My arms raised and my joints popped as I brought my arms in front of me.

One of the dudes jumped up and I raised my hands in a surrendering gesture. "I'm just putting my arms in front of me. Nothing damaging. I'm just trying to get comfortable, is all. It's no point of having my arms behind my back. I can't do anything." I confessed. I didn't have my purse and whatever gun was in there. I'm sure they found it. "Tish!" I screamed for her.

I knew that little bitch was around somewhere. The main thing I wanted to know was why. "Tish!" I didn't get an answer.

"Yo, shut the fuck up with all that yelling. When she's ready to talk, she'll be down here." One of the guys said to me.

I ignored him. "Tishana! Bring yo ass down here! The game is fuckin' over!" I sat quiet for a few minutes, waiting to see if she would come. She didn't. "Tishana! Tish! I know you hear me—" The basement door opened, and I stopped mid-sentence.

"Why are you yelling? I heard you and I was coming. I had to put my baby to bed. Now if you wake her, guess who's putting her back to sleep." She laughed, pointing to me. Tish clapped her hands smiling. "So, what do you want?"

"What—" I started to tell her what I wanted to know but she cut me off.

"I'm sorry, I'm so rude. We have another guest. Lo, go get our guest, please." She cooed before squatting down to my level. "I was really your friend, Peaches, but you hurt me. Regardless, I'm still *your* friend. I got her for you." She smiled wide at me, then stood and looked at Blake.

This bitch was crazy. How the hell I missed all of this was beyond me.

"My God! You look exactly like your father. Handsome little man you are. If you were just a few years older or I was younger…" she bit into her index fingernail, smiling. "We would be together." Tish laughed.

"Tishana, get away from my son—" again my words were cut off.

Tish turned toward me and jumped in my face so fast I jerked back into the wall.

"It's so funny you say that because he's about ten and you've only known Blaze for about five years. So how could you have had his baby?" She bit into her bottom lip smiling. "You couldn't have. Because I would've killed it. Now how he managed to keep him a secret? I don't know. But he's not your fuckin' son."

She slowly traced her fingers from my jaw to my eye before she pulled her hand back and shot it forward. The back of her fist slapped hard against my left eye with such force I fell to the floor.

"Momma!" Blake yelled and shot to his feet. "Let me go! Get the fuck off of me!" Blake screamed, trying to get loose.

"Eep!" Tishana squeaked and stood up. She made her way toward Blake. "Let him go. You have a mouth just like your father." Her hand shot out and she whacked Blake in the mouth. "You're going to watch your fuckin' mouth in my house, you understand me?" She snatched Blake to her with a tight grip on his chin.

My mouth parted and I stared at Tishana. *I know she didn't just hit my baby.* My eyes slid to Blake and landed on his red lip. Without a second thought, I hopped up off of the floor and jumped on her back. We fell to the floor, but I didn't care.

"You bitch!" I screamed as I wrapped my arms around her neck. Oh, I was pissed. "You gon' fuckin hit my son?" My legs locked around her body. I was about to choke the life out of her. God, I wanted to punch her so bad, but my wrist was still tied and bound together. I wanted to hurt her. My head turned toward her face and I bit into her skin. I wanted her to feel as much pain that I could cause.

Tishana screamed, clawing at my elbow and arms as she tried to get free but she couldn't. I wasn't going to let that bitch go. My teeth sunk into her flesh harder until the copper flavor filled my mouth. I pulled my head back and spat the blood from my mouth. I took a moment to look over at Blake. The guy he was wrestling with got tired of tussling with him and punched him in the face.

"No!" I screamed as Blake hit the couch. "Blake!" I cried out his name momentarily loosening my grip on Tish.

She capitalized on my distraction, Tish rolled us over and then got on top of me.

At that moment the guy turned away from Blake and he kicked the man hard in his balls before he dodged to the side of the couch.

I didn't see anything after that because Tish started choking me.

"You crazy bitch! I was trying to help you out and you attack me? I brought you here to apologize to you and hopefully be friends again!" She shouted as she lifted my head up and hit it against the hard floor.

A loud shot rang out in the basement. Tishana froze. So, did I.

I couldn't move. I was scared and in fear that my baby had been shot.

Slowly Tishana's head turned to the side and I peeked around her only to see Blake laying on the floor.

"Oh, my God! No!" I screamed. "Blake!" My hips bucked wildly trying to throw Tish off of me. "Rashad, get up!" I yelled at him, but he didn't move. "Blake, please!" I pulled Tish's neck hard, bringing her face closer to mine. I bit her while rolling us over before I began choking her as I cried.

Tish's fingers clawed at my face. She was bucking violently to get out of my hold.

"Bitch, I'm going to kill you!" I yelled at her. Lifting her head up, I slammed it on the hard concrete floor. My tears blurred my vision as they flowed rapidly down my face.

I needed to get to Blake and make sure he was alright. I took the chance to look over at him only to be met with a hard kick to the face.

Instantly, everything went black.

Chapter 29

Blaze

"We got a problem." Jerron said the moment I answered my phone, sounding pissed and worried.

"What the fuck you mean *we got a problem?* Whatever the fuck it is you better fix that shit." I snapped at him.

"Yo, chill with that shit right now. I lost Monica."

I sat up straight in the passenger seat of King's truck. "What the fuck you mean you lost that bitch? How the fuck you do that?"

"Shit if I know. I followed her to a nail shop and the bitch ain't never come out. I was sitting outside that bitch for two hours until I started seeing mothafuckas leaving out who went in after her. I go inside and that bitch was gone. I went to her crib but weren't no cars at that mothafucka." Jerron paused before he continued. "So, I go to her sister's crib and these niggas packing to leave. I couldn't let that shit happen and let them take my son again."

I knew something happened by the way he said that. "What the fuck did you do?"

"What I had to. They ain't know shit. All they said was Monica told them to pack up. Nann one of them could tell me where she called from or where the fuck they were supposed to go. So, I did what the fuck I had to."

I hung up on his ass. I wanted to kill that mothafucka, but I couldn't be mad because I would've done the exact same thing. "Fuck!" I hit the dashboard.

"What's up?" King asked.

"That stupid mothafucka lost Monica's ass! How the fuck he do that? He got his boy, though." I grabbed a cigarette and lit it. "Fuck! We should've grabbed that bitch a long time ago!" I inhaled and then blew out the smoke.

"Damn." King pulled into Sam's law office and parked.

We got out the car and went inside where he sat waiting on us.

"What's been good?" He slapped hands with King before coming to me. He stared at me then nodded toward the chair. "You ready to tell me what's up now? Or you still holding back, B?" He got straight to the point.

"Nah, I ain't holding back. I was trying to figure some shit out about yo sister." I jumped right into it.

"Tish? What the fuck Tish do?" He seemed confused as to why her name was mentioned.

"I never put two and two together until recently. But every nigga yo sister get with comes after me. That Blue mothafucka, Le'Ron, then this Macy bitch." I brought to his attention. Sam stood leaned against the wall with his eyes squinted, thoughtfully. "Sam, I don't know that bitch. I ain't never even hit her ass. But she's pretending to be a stripper. For what?" I asked him. But before he could respond I held up my finger, stopping him.

"But I send you a pic and you know Macy— wait Monica as you call her. Do you see where I'm going with all this shit?" I walked closer toward him, watching as he processed everything I just said. When I felt that he caught on, I nodded my head. "Exactly."

"Hold up, so what the fuck you think? Tish and I was plotting against you?" I could tell he was offended, and it pissed him off. "Are you fuckin' serious, B? You think I'm plotting against you?" He pushed me hard in the chest.

King stood up and Sam turned on him.

He laughed. "What you gon' kill me? Why the fuck you jumping up for? Huh? You gon' shoot me, King? Huh?" He laughed and shook his head. "This shit is so fuckin' comical right now. You really think I'll plot against you, Blaze? For what, though? Huh? Money?" He laughed. Even though he was laughing I knew he was hurt.

"Is that why? I'm tryna understand this. My nigga, we been boys since we were kids. When our moms ain't have shit, nigga, I was on that block with you tryna get it just like you was. Whatever we made separately, we combined and split equally. How many mothafuckas would do that bullshit? My nigga, you my fuckin' brother. You think after all the shit we done been through together, I would throw it away to plot against you for some mothafuckin' money?" He snapped, pissed as he pushed me again.

"Wait! If it ain't money, what you think I want? Some fuckin' work? If that's the case, I would still be out here hustling like you two old bastards. I left that shit alone because that's not what the fuck I wanted. Yeah, I jump back in when you need me but not for no gotdamn money but because you my fuckin' brother. Why the fuck would I plot against you? Nigga, I'm good, sitting on hella money. So, what I need yours for? Huh?" He snapped before he pushed King back. "Get the fuck out my way."

King looked at me.

I shook my head with a wave of my hand, telling him not to say anything. I watched him pace back and forth for a minute, waiting on him to say something else. When he didn't, I spoke. "Are you done now?"

Sam turned around on me so fast I thought he was about to whoop my ass. "Fuck you, Blaze. Do what the fuck you gon do and get that shit over with."

I walked to his desk and opened up the bottom drawer and then grabbed the bottle of Hennessy before I sat down in his chair. "Aye, King, give me a cup." King went to the sink and grabbed three glasses from the cabinet.

"What the fuck is you doing?" Sam asked, looking from me to King.

"I'm about to pour us a drink." I poured myself a shot, then quickly downed it before I gave them theirs. King tossed his back, but Sam looked hesitant. "Man, drink the fuckin' shot and have a seat."

Once he tossed the drink back, he leaned against the wall with his arms crossed.

"King, he's pissed off." I laughed before pouring myself another shot. I drunk it, then focused on Sam. "Yeah, everything you said is true. You my nigga, my fuckin' brother. For a second the thought popped into my head but you're my fuckin' brother so the idea left immediately. So, this whole rant yo ass just went on wasn't even necessary. I know you my nigga, period. And if you ever call me an old ass bastard again, I'mma beat yo ass, simple as that. Now, when I said *exactly*, I thought yo head was on the fact Tish mothafuckin' ass know all these folks. Think about it." I gave him a minute to think about everything.

"Remember when I told you about Krystal and Blue's situation? How she got my shit and all that? Tish was his bitch at the time. She helped him plot all that bullshit. I ain't tell you this shit until now because I had to make sure. Nigga, that's yo sister. You understand where I'm coming from?"

"Over some work, B?" He didn't seem to understand.

"I'm not fuck'd up about no work. I can always recoup that shit. My nigga she was fuckin' with

Le'Ron when that stuff happened with Peaches and she lost my baby. The shit that popped off at my party, word around is some nigga named Rice was behind that hit. The picture I sent you was of him and Monica. They saying he's Blue's uncle—"

"I can tell you that he wasn't Blue's uncle. His only uncle died in the fire with him and his aunt." Sam told me before he pointed to his desk. "Look in that first drawer and get the case file."

My head tilted and I stared at him. "I don't need to look at it. I believe you. But if he ain't his uncle, then who the fuck is he? And why the fuck is he coming after me?" I shook my head. "We'll figure that out later. But I'm snatching Tish's ass up tonight at this little party King is throwing. Now this is where shit gets hard. She is yo sister and I plan on killing her ass for the shit she did to Peaches and what she took from me. This the only way it's going to end. Sam, you my nigga, my brother but if you get in my way, I'mma do what I have to. But I'm going to kill her." I poured myself another drink and then stood up.

"What's up?" King answered his phone. His brows raised. "No, I ain't talked to Peaches at all today. Hold on." He put the phone on speaker. "B, you talked to Peaches?"

I shook my head as I pulled out my phone to make sure I didn't miss a call or text. "Not since a couple of hours ago. She was supposed to get the kids some ice cream then pick up Keema and go straight to the crib. She was supposed to call me damn near two hours ago." I informed him as I called her.

"I know but she never showed up and Keema is having a fit. I've been calling her, but I haven't gotten an answer.

I called Blake's phone too but nothing." Ebony sounded worried.

I wasn't trying to hear that in her voice right now. "I'ight, I'll find her and when I do, King will hit you back." I hung up on her and then called Blake on his phone while still trying to reach Peaches on mine. I got the voicemail for them both. "Why the fuck y'all ain't answering!" I yelled before ending the calls. "Let me see your phone." I used Sam's office line and called both of them only to get the same response. "Fuck!" I knocked the lamp and phone off his desk.

"B, calm down. Peaches probably took little man and went to Lafayette." King threw out there.

I shook my head in disagreement. "No, she wouldn't have done that. Come on, let's go to the Chinese spot then Dairy Queen on 30." Shit just wasn't right. I knew for a fact Peaches wouldn't leave and take Blake. She had the chance to leave but didn't, so her bouncing now wasn't likely. I started to walk out of the room but stopped to look at Sam. "When was the last time you talked to or seem Tish?"

"I ain't seem Tish in a few years. Once that shit happened with Le'Ron and Peaches, she shut us out. She'll call and holla at me every now and again but besides that, she pretty much stays to herself. Blaze, what reason would Tish have to hurt you? This could all be a coincidence. I know you don't believe in them but come on this is just a little too crazy. Just think about it. B, I can't let you kill my sister." Sam told me.

"Then do what the fuck you have to and I'mma do the same. King, let's go." We walked out his office then made our way to King's car.

Once we were inside, he started it up then looked at me. "You'll kill yo boy?"

"Yeah, if it meant protecting my family, yeah. Ain't no questioning that. They're the only reason I'm here. Now let's go." I turned up the radio ending whatever conversation he was trying to have with me.

My mind was on Peaches and my son. That gutful dreading feeling returned to my stomach, telling me something bad was about to happen. Immediately, my mind went to Peaches laying in that hospital bed five years ago.

I shook my head. I couldn't let history repeat itself.

***

Once we got to the Chinese restaurant, I wasted no time going inside. A picture of Blake and Peaches was on my phone's screen ready to show the hostess.

"Have you seen them?" I asked the older woman at the front desk.

She shook her head *no* before calling over a waitress. "Have you seen them?" she asked in her thick Chinese accent.

The younger lady looked at the screen and smiled. "She left a big tip. They left hours ago."

"Was anyone with her when she left?" I needed to make sure she didn't run into anyone while she was there. But it was no telling who she could have ran into right after.

"Just him." The waitress pointed to Blake's photo.

"Shit, i'ight." I left out the restaurant. "They were here but left hours ago and they didn't see her with nobody. Let's go to Dairy Queen." I told him once I hopped in the truck.

"I'ight, Bell said she ain't at the crib. He said nothing is out of place, their clothes, and shit is still there." King let out a frustrated sigh as he drove. "Fuck!" He hit the steering wheel. "I know this bull- shit ain't starting all over again. Those mothafuckas better have dead batteries. That better be the reason they ain't answering."

I was hoping for the same reason, but my gut feeling was telling me a whole different story. We pulled into Dairy Queen and got out. Once inside, I did the same thing I did at the Chinese spot. "Aye, have you seen them?"

The female cashier glanced at the photo and shook her head. "No, I haven't. Sorry."

The dude next to her was trying to be slick and looked at the screen. I turned the phone his way. "Have you seen them?"

"Yeah, a few hours ago. Her and the little boy just left in a hurry. Did you want their ice cream? She already paid for it, but didn't take it?"

"Do it look like I want some fuckin' ice cream?" I snapped at him.

His mouth opened then closed before he looked at the female cashier. "No need for the attitude I was just asking—"

I cut him off. "Why she leave in a hurry?"

"And I'm to know that how exactly?" He popped slick with a pop of his lips.

I grabbed the front of his shirt and snatched him over the counter. "Yo don't fuckin' play with me. Answer the fuckin' question before I make you the little bitch you're trying to be." I pulled my gun from my hip. I was gon' light his ass the fuck up. I wasn't in the mood for no gotdamn attitudes.

Someone screamed from behind me and it pissed me off. "Scream again, I dare you." I snapped at her before I looked back at dude. "Now why the fuck did she leave?" I repeated my question.

"I don't know. She was talking to some lady and then left out." His voice shook as he answered.

I let him go and put my gun away. "Is this her?" I showed him a picture of Monica.

He shook his head *no*. "No, it wasn't her. She was a bit darker than this lady with blond and black hair."

I found a picture of Tish and showed it to him.

"Yeah that's her."

I hurried up and ran out the place back to King's truck. "Go! Pull the fuck off before they call the police." I was sure somebody in there was going to call the laws. We were in Merrillville too; they didn't play that shit out there.

King pulled off. "What the fuck you do?"

407

"I was trying to find out what happened to them. That little nigga in there said she saw her talking to Tish before she bounced out with Blake. Fuck!" I hit the dashboard, realizing my fuck up.

"If she has Blake with her and she ran into Tish knowing everything we do, she probably took him somewhere safe," King said.

"Fuck! Damn!" My hand ran over my head. "Yo, Peach don't know shit about this. I ain't tell her shit. Damn, I fuck'd up!"

"What the fuck you mean she don't know shit? B, don't tell me you got my sister running around this bitch blind?" King stopped at a light and turned to face me.

"Fuck, I ain't want her stressing so I didn't tell her shit. I ain't tell her nothing." I didn't think to keep Peaches informed because I never let them out the house or unprotected for that matter.

"OnStar her damn car," King suggested.

"Damn, I forgot all about that shit." I grabbed my phone to pull up the tracker.

"You lo-jacked her car?" he asked.

"Hell no, I bugged both their phones." I told him as I pulled up the GPS tracker.

"That shit ain't no good if the phone is off—"

"King, shut the fuck up, nigga. I ain't stupid. Nigga, don't you think I know that? The fuckin' thing ain't in their phones. It's a small fuckin chip on their sim card. So, the phone don't need to be on to track. Just shut the fuck up." I pulled up Peaches phone on the GPS and immediately it put us in route of her location.

The GPS took us on a fifteen minute drive to the mall where we found Peaches car. King parked behind her car and let out a relieved breath.

It didn't feel right to me, though. If she was at the mall, why would she leave her phone in the car? I hopped out the truck and called her number again as I made my way to her car. I peeked inside hearing the tune play. Peaches' phone sat on the front seat with her purse. I looked at the mall then pulled out my set of keys and unlocked her doors.

The smell of cigarettes hit my nose. "Fuck!" I kicked the car hard, leaving a dent in the side. "Mothafuckas!" I was pissed with myself and the mothafucka who took her and my son. I turned on the lights to see if they dropped something. Once I leaned into the driver's seat, I noticed the keys in the ignition.

Seeing her keys eliminated the small hope of them being in the mall shopping. Peaches leaving her phone in the car was possible but to leave the keys in the ignition and lock the doors wasn't.

King and I continued to search the car but ended up not finding anything.

My hand rubbed my head as I tried to calm myself down. I was ready to tear the whole fuckin' city up. I took a deep breath. I couldn't think. My mind flashed with different terrible scenes of what could've happened to them. I couldn't focus, all I saw was them dead.

Those thoughts was fuckin' with me bad. A helpless feeling filled my gut and I got even more pissed. I didn't even know where the fuck Tish stayed, so I didn't have a place to even start looking.

"Fuck!" I punched at the steering wheel. I had no one to blame but myself if something was to happen to either of them. I should've told Peaches everything instead of keeping her in the dark.

"Blaze, where Blake's phone?" King poured everything out of Peaches' purse.

"What the fuck is you doing?" I wanted to punch his ass only because he was close to me. I needed to tear some shit up. I was gon' fuck some shit up!

King ignored me and pulled out his phone. He dialed numbers and held up his finger to me. He stood there as if he was listening for something. King hung up his phone. "Pop the truck." Hurriedly he put everything back in Peaches' purse.

I did as he asked and followed him to the back. "King, what the fuck are you doing?"

He tossed Peaches purse in the truck then grabbed the gas can from the back. "Track Blake's phone. Come on." He tossed the can in the hatchback then hopped in the driver's seat.

I locked up her car then jumped in his ride. With finding her purse and phone I forgot all about Blake's cell.

I pulled up the GPS location for Blake's phone. Just like before it immediately found his device and put us in route to him. A new sense of hope formed in my gut as we left further from the mall.

Somebody done fuck'd up.

They better hope neither of them was hurt.

"We gotda make a stop before we get there." All I needed was my toys.

My body became jittery as excitement filled me.

Somebody most definitely fuck'd up.

Chapter 30

Peaches

A painful, muffled grunt left my mouth as I opened my eyes, blinking to clear my vision. The right side of my face was in so much pain. My eye felt swollen and my head throbbed. I was in a dazed state I wasn't able to register anything around me.

It wasn't until I felt the stroke of fingers caressing my stomach that I became fully aware of what was happening. The cold hands made my belly tighten. I glanced down at Tishana sitting next to me. I saw her lips move but she was whispering so low I couldn't hear her.

I jerked my body and glared hard at her. "Bitch, don't touch me!" I tried to yell forcefully but my mouth was taped.

Tishana smiled at me before she punched me in the face. "You have to be the dumbest bitch I know. Do you not know I could kill you right now? Peaches, you're smart, so you know this. But yet you continue to try and hurt me. Why?" She swiped her thumb over my eye. "You're bleeding."

I jerked my head away from her.

She grabbed my chin and held it tight. "Stop it. Why do you want to fight me?" She placed her ear by my mouth as if she was waiting to hear my reply.

I looked away from her and my eyes landed on a large puddle of blood, then Blake immediately popped into mind. My eyes widened and I began to look around the basement franticly for him.

My body jerked around, and tears began to pour from my eyes. "*Where is he?*" I screamed through the tape, but the words only came out as mumbles to her. I tried to move my arms, but they were taped against my side as were my legs.

I tried to plead to her with my eyes, but it didn't seem to work.

"I want to know what you're trying to tell me so bad. But your mouth is very dangerous, and it hurts me..." She stopped talking once she noticed I wasn't paying her any attention after the first sentence. She followed the direction I was staring at and she waved her hand. "A big ass mess that little boy made. But I'll just paint over it once we're done here."

Tish's words had a muffled sob leaving my mouth. My shoulders shook as my chest heaved up and down hard. I shook my head trying to convince myself it wasn't true.

The large pool of blood wasn't helping my thoughts. My knees folded and I tried to pull myself up to somehow make my way over to the blood.

It just couldn't be Blake's. My heart squeezed painfully, and I fell to the floor crying. My nose became stuffed and I started to choke from my lack of oxygen.

"Shit! It's not that serious, Peaches. He wasn't even your child. Lord, you are so dramatic." She ripped the tape from my mouth.

Immediately, I started to get sick.

"Ugh, that's so nasty." Once I finished, she pulled me away from the vomit.

"Tish, please tell me my son is okay. Please just tell me he's not dead." I begged her.

Tish's eyes rolled up in her head as she tore off another piece of duct tape.

"Tishana, please!" I screamed for her to tell me.

She simply ignored my request and put the tape over my lips again.

"He's not your son. Peaches, you didn't need him." She grabbed a crate and sat in front of me. Her hands came out and she rubbed my tears from my cheeks. "I like you, really like you. And I meant what I said about apologizing. You have to know our friendship was real. You just got involved with some really bad people. I felt terrible about you losing your baby. I know how it feels to go through that and have to be alone. I tried to reach out to you, Peaches, be there for you through it all. But you wouldn't let me. I understood, though, because I went through it. Twice actually and both times almost killed me. Do you now understand why I had you pulled in the middle of this?" She asked me as her fingers continued to stroke my cheeks.

My head reared back, and I stared at her through tearfully squinted eyes. "Why?" I didn't understand what she was talking about.

"Why?" Her eyes cut into mean slits before she quickly composed herself and a faint smile came to her lips. "You asked why?"

My head nodded before my eyes slid to the pool of blood again.

Tish moved in front of my view so I could no longer look at it. "It'll be better if you didn't look at it. It'll only remind you of him. So, focus on me. Okay?"

This bitch was fuckin' nuts. "Why?" I wanted to understand what I did or the people I was involved with did to her that was so terrible.

"Why? That's what I want to know. Peaches, I've been trying to figure that out since I was sixteen, but he never gave me the *why*. He just ignored me as if it never happened." She shook her head.

My head tilted to the side showing my confusion.

"Blaze." She bit into her lower lip as she tried to contain her smile. Tish's eyes seemed to glaze over as she stared passed me.

Now I was even more confused for the simple fact she encouraged me to give him a chance and not to give up

415

on him. Why would she do that? I didn't understand. "What?"

She looked at me. "Hm?" She hummed in a questioning way.

My eyes squinted in a confused manner.

She snapped her fingers. "Oh, I got you. You didn't know about me and Blaze? No one knew about us." Tish shrugged her shoulders. "I was young, and he wanted to keep it a secret from everyone. Especially since him and Sam are best friends. It used to piss me off at first until one night..." her smile widened.

My eyes cut at her hard. That psychotic bitch was doing this because she was crazy about Blaze? That didn't explain why she encouraged me not to give up on him.

"I was staying with Sam for a little while. Blaze crashed at the house after one of their drunk nights. You know how they get. Anyway, that night he told me how he felt. He told me that he loved me." She let out a giggle.

I was so confused. I was sure the blank look showed on my face.

She caught it and rolled her eyes. "What you think you're the first woman he ever loved?" The attitude in her was very noticeable.

I didn't respond but I'm sure my face gave away my true thoughts with its blank stare.

She saw it and jumped up, kicking the crate. "Well, you weren't. He loved me. He may have not said it with his mouth, but his body told me he did. Blaze was in love with me and I loved him. That whole night he let me take full control of us." She smiled again. "I knew he loved it. His eyes stayed closed the entire time as he groaned. He let me do whatever I wanted without stopping me." Her teeth sunk into her bottom lip and again she seemed to daze off.

My brows raised as I played the many different times Blaze and I had sex. He never once let me be in full control of us nor were his eyes ever closed. Blaze loved to watch me as we had sex or made love.

I stared at Tish with a tilted head. I hummed to get her attention. It just didn't make sense to me. The way she was describing her experience just didn't seem real. Hell, it didn't fit Blaze, period.

My lips wiggled for her to remove the tape.

Tish rolled her eyes and walked to me. "If you bite me or do anything stupid, I'm going to kill you."

She ripped the tape from my lips.

I glared at her. "I'm sure your night was special, Tishana, but are you sure it was with Blaze—"

Her hand shot out and she slapped the shit out of me. "What are you trying to say?" She pulled me up, getting in my face. "I know who I gave myself to! Blaze was the first man to ever touch me. Yes, I'm positive it was him." She pushed me into the wall then fixed her shirt. "We spent the whole night together. I held him all night long until I had to sneak out of his room the next morning."

She held Blaze all night?

I don't know who the hell she was with but it damn sure couldn't have been Blaze.

"What happened after that?" I asked her curiously.

"I don't know. That's what I've been trying to figure out. What did I do wrong? The next morning, he completely ignored what we did. I thought he was going to talk to Sam about us being together, but he didn't. I tried talking to him but for some reason I couldn't catch up with him. Everything went back to how it was. I was just Tishana, his best friend's sister. Nothing else and that hurt me. Blaze was my first and he played me. But I guess he didn't want to ruin his friendship with Sam. After that, we barely talked but that wasn't nothing new to me. Blaze was never talkative when he was around me anyways. But then after a few months had gone by, I found out I was pregnant." Her hand went to her flat stomach.

"Blaze was your baby's father?"

"Yes, he was. Peaches you wasn't his first everything. He loved me first. He had a baby with me first. Hell, you didn't even make baby momma number two. Bitch, you're number three. I was here way before you." She snapped at me. Her chest heaved up and down as she panted, pissed off.

"I knew he loved you. I could tell from the way he looked at you and how he picked on you. I knew that, but why did you push me to make things work with him?" I was going to play this game with her. It was obvious Tish wasn't dealing with a full

418

deck and I was tied up, there was no telling what she would do.

She let out a depressing sigh and then sat next to me. "I seriously thought I was the only one who noticed the way he teased me at times." Tish let out a laugh.

She was so lucky I was tied up. As soon as I got loose, I was going to kill that bitch. I was going to kill her over and over again. "What happened when he found out you was pregnant?"

Tishana's smile quickly left and she let out a laugh. "What happened was he accused me of messing around with some dude. He told me I needed to leave these niggas alone and focus on school. Then he gave me a stack. He gave me a thousand dollars to get rid of it." Angry tears fell from her eyes. "He thought I came to him to get an abortion. I wasn't going to do that, though. I was going to keep our baby, but he didn't want to have nothing to do with me. I was so stressed out during the pregnancy I had a miscarriage. Do you know he didn't show up at the hospital?"

"Are you sure Blaze knew the baby was his? Hell, did he even know y'all had sex? Are you sure he wasn't sleep? You said he was drunk, Tishana. He could've been passed out, but his body could have still reacted to you. That just doesn't seem like something he would do. Especially if it's his baby." I glanced around at the sound of a door opening. Immediately, I recognized the female.

What the hell was really going on?

"It was his baby. Do you seriously think I would have sex with him while he's asleep? Point of the matter is he wasn't there when I needed him!" She yelled at me.

I couldn't help but roll my eyes up in my head this time. "You know, Tish, whatever your problem is or was with Blaze should have died years ago. I don't see what the fuck I have to do with anything. Or why the fuck this bitch is here at all." I glared hard at the female standing next to her.

"I need you to hurt just like I had by the hands of Blaze, twice. When Blaze threw me away, I started to make plans. You were truly collateral damage. You see, I wanted Blaze to feel the exact same pain he made me feel when we were together. But I couldn't for the simple fact the nigga didn't care for shit once we stopped messing around."

My head tilted to the side. *Was she serious right now?* After hearing her story, I didn't once get the impression they were fucking around. This stupid bitch took her own gotdamn virginity and used Blaze stupid drunk ass to do it.

The dumb bitch should've gotten an abortion and none of this would be happening. Tishana was in a whole relationship with Blaze and he didn't even know it.

"Tish, I don't understand what you mean." I once again glanced at the woman beside her.

"Because hurting you would hurt him. Killing his baby would kill a part of him. Killing you would have killed him. But I actually like you and believe me, I had no idea you were pregnant at the time. It wouldn't have changed what I had Le'Ron do, but I felt bad. I wish I would have known about his first bastard child. I wouldn't have needed you if

I did. Then again, I would have still needed you seeing as Blaze made me lose two babies. His child and my baby I had with Blue. You never got the chance to meet because Blaze killed him. Now are you starting to understand your role in all this?"

I was over her dramatics. This bitch was simply crazy and whatever her deal was with Blaze should have died by now. She better hope she killed me before I got loose somehow. I didn't care to hear another word she had to say to me. To show her that, I focused my attention on the second female.

"What is your whole thing in this? I know damn well you're not going to tell me you started plotting because Jerron gave me oral sex almost ten years ago? Please tell me you haven't held onto that shit? Then again, you are friends with this psychotic bitch who done had a whole ass relationship with a man that didn't even know he was taken." I looked directly at Tish.

"I know what Blaze and I had was real. Peaches, your words can't hurt me." She smiled, walking closer to me. "But I can crush you again. All I have to do is kill your soul and you're dead. I have already taken one baby from you. No, wait. I've taken one and a stepchild. Do you want me to continue to break you?" Tishana dug her nails deep into the flesh of my stomach.

I bit hard into my lip to keep myself from making any threats.

"Now apologize for hurting my feelings." She dug her nails into my skin even harder as she yanked my head to the side.

I let out a deep breath. "I'm sorry, Tishana. I didn't mean to hurt your feelings." I was pissed about having to say any of that bullshit. "Tish, can I please see Blake?" I pleaded with her, this time sincerely. I wasn't going to believe he was dead until I saw him. She couldn't take him from me. I would never forgive myself if he was gone. And I don't think I would be able to forgive Blaze for bringing us back here.

Images from the past began to flash through my mind. My heart squeezed painfully. What if he didn't realize we were gone? What if he thought I took Blake and left for Lafayette? He could be on his way there now. It would be too late before he realized it.

"Why so you can cry? No. I have to finish telling you my story." Tish waved me off.

I was starting to think she liked to hear herself talk. My eyes rolled and looked away from her. I glanced at the other female who hadn't said a word since she came into the basement.

"Would you stop looking at her?" She snapped at me. Tish rubbed her forehead. "Peaches, Monica. Monica, Peaches. You two have been introduced. Now can I finish my story?" She waved her hand as if shooing Monica away.

And to my surprise she went and sat on the couch without saying a word.

"My second baby Blaze took from me—"

I cut her off. "You had sex with him twice and got pregnant?" Now that I didn't believe one bit.

"No, now shut the fuck up! Blaze had moved on, kind of. I had gotten a new man." That annoying smile once again graced her face. "Blue. He was unexpected but he won me over and made me forget about everything Blaze put me through. He was my everything and we had been going strong for four years." The smile on her face faded a bit.

"Blue was my heart, but he had his flaws. He loved to gamble. He sucked at it, but he was addicted to it. We went to Vegas for the weekend, we eloped, no one knew of course. My momma and Sam hated him, but he was my heart, so I'd rather lose them over him any day. I went with him and we got married." Tish eyes started to water, and she turned away from me.

"The two days we were out there he lost well over thirty thousand dollars. He pissed me off so bad, but I let it go. He promised me he would get the money back, that what he lost wasn't shit but play money. Of course, I believed him. A few weeks had gone by after our trip and he had suddenly come up on some money, a lot of money. I asked him about it and he told me that he was working for his aunt's husband, Rice. A big dealer out in the city. Problem with that was Blue gambled. He couldn't keep money for anything." She stressed with a heavy sigh.

"Rice wanted to move some work over in Gary. He wanted Blue to push it for him. Blue wasn't really a dealer; my baby was a straight up stick up nigga. He would run up in yo shit and hit you for everything. But Rice wanted Blue to make shit happen for him. He threw him some money and he started making plans. The biggest dealer out here was Blaze. The spots Rice wanted were Blaze's territories. Blue didn't really know Blaze. He heard of him, but he didn't know him. He was sure Blaze was going to jump at the deal

Rice was offering." She grabbed the crate and sat on the side of me. Tish let out a depressing sigh.

"Given Blaze and my previous relationship, I knew it was a bad idea. I didn't want Blaze to get jealous about me finally moving on and I didn't want to be disrespectful throwing our thing in his face, you know? I told him about Blaze and his clubs. He only knew Blaze was Sam's best friend, that's it. See he really needed this deal to go through for two reasons. One, we had spent the money Rice had given us and two, that was more money. So, he got his boy, Cornell." She smiled at me. "Yeah, your boy, Cornell, which just so happened to be Monica's baby brother. Anyways, they showed up at the club and pitched Blaze the idea. He shut it down and told Blue to get the fuck out of his club. That night, he and Blaze got into a fight." Her eyes rolled into her head at that.

"Blue wasn't expecting him to shut down the deal, but he did. Now mind you Rice done gave Blue money because he counted on getting double in return if Blaze agreed. Blue's mistake with Blaze was he thought he would jump at the idea of getting more money and because Blaze didn't, he had to think of something else." Tishana's head shook. "Blue and Cornell hit a bank. They came out with a hundred thousand, which they split between themselves. After the bank robbery, they had to lay low for a minute and no money was coming in. Blue was stressing and getting mad about every little thing. I had just found out I was three weeks pregnant and I couldn't bring our baby in this world without nothing. No one knew I was pregnant, and I wanted to keep it that way until I started showing." She continued on with her story.

My eyes rolled into my head as I became bored of her talking all together. Even so, I didn't say anything. I just listened to her talk.

"I didn't plan on working long, it was only until Blue got back on his feet. So, I went to my brother for a job. Brandy, that bitch had a problem with it because I would basically be taking over her job, which she could hardly do. It caused problems between her and him, so he called Blaze for a favor. That's how I started working at the car lot. When I was fourteen, he would let me work there for the summer and everyone after, so he knew I could do the job."

"Now fifty thousand dollars isn't a lot when you have an addiction. Saving is a bitch as well, so the money we were supposed to be putting up to give back to Rice, Blue was spending. We needed to do something quick, we needed money. So, he went to First Midwest Bank to open up an account to basically scope out the place. But he found more, a flirty little slut. Wait one second." She stood up and stretched. "Mikel, can you bring in my guest, please?"

The door opened and the guy she sent out earlier to get her so called guest came back with someone over his shoulder.

Mikel walked over to us and carelessly dropped the person to the floor. A grunt left the female's mouth before a muffled scream followed as he snatched a handful of her hair and pulled her to the wall.

My head tilted so I could get a good look at her face, but it was covered by her hair. I kind of got pissed off by the way he was handling her. Regardless of my ill feelings, I said nothing.

"Now, *this* bitch, I hate." Tish booted the girl in the face twice. The last blow hit the right side of her head hard, causing her to fall into my lap.

"Tish!" I yelled at her before I pushed my knees and shook them slightly. "Are you okay?" My legs moved a bit faster.

She didn't respond. As I shook my legs to get her attention, her hair moved slightly out of her face.

Instantly my legs went still as I stared down at a bruised and beaten Krystal.

Chapter 31

Peaches

I stared at Krystal with mixed feelings. The ignorant part of me wanted to knee her head off of my lap, given the problems she caused. But the logical side knew it wasn't all her fault, in fact it was all Blaze's. He could've ended things with her but he chose to continue to see her.

"Krystal." I tried to get a response, but I got nothing. She was knocked out. I looked up at Tish. "What does she have to do with anything? Is it because of Blaze?"

Tishana's eyes rolled. "Please, this is beyond Blaze. This was the flirty bitch that helped him open the account. I wanted to kill her. Blue saw how she reacted to him and thought if he got with her and made her fall in love with him, he could turn her. Of course, I didn't like the idea, but I loved and trusted my man. I just had one rule and it was that he couldn't fuck her. Anything else could go. Some bitches like

427

a man that would wait for sex and as expected this dumb bitch fell for it."

Tishana snatched Krystal up off of me and started stomping on her. Once she became short on breath, she spit on her and then kicked her one more time. "She started to take him away from me. Blue thought I wouldn't notice but he started liking this little bitch. He always wanted to be with her, had to stay at her house or vice versa. She was cutting into my time with him." She kicked Krystal again.

I was confused once again. "Tish, if he was supposed to make her fall in love with him, wasn't he supposed to spend a lot of time with her?"

She hauled off and slapped the shit out of me. I jumped at her and let out a frustrated growl. My tongue swiped over my lips and I hissed from the split she had made.

"Shut the fuck up! This is my story, so shut the fuck up! You don't know shit. Were you there? Huh? Did you see what was happening?" She yelled in my face. Tish grabbed my neck and squeezed it tightly, cutting off my airway.

The veins in my face felt as if they were going to burst from my lack of oxygen. I tried to wiggle away from her, but it was no use, I was tied up and helpless.

Tish squeezed harder one last time before she let me go. She punched me across the face and then backed away. "You're starting to piss me the fuck off. I know what the fuck the plan was. I told him to do it!" She screamed at me.

428

I fell to the side, choking as I tried to regain my breathing.

Tish paced the floor. She seemed to be trying to calm herself down as she mumbled to herself. After a few minutes of her back and forth walking, she stopped. Tishana pushed her weaved hair over her shoulders and then looked back at us.

"I'm sorry, you just pissed me off. I'm not stupid, Peaches. I know what the job would consist of. But that didn't mean he had to fall for her or cancel dates with me just for her. I was pregnant with our baby and this was how he was doing me. I must admit I acted off emotions when I told him it was time to get the job done. It had been a couple months so if she had fallen for him, then she wouldn't hesitate to give him the information." Tish walked over to Krystal and just started beating her ass. She stomped and kicked her in the face and stomach repeatedly.

"But no, this dumb bitch wouldn't talk! If she did, we wouldn't have had to hit Blaze's spot and Blue would've still been alive! I would have never lost my baby."

She was beating the hell out of the girl. Krystal was already knocked out from the first attack, now she just laid there. Hell, I didn't think she was breathing.

"Because of her, we had to rob Blaze that night for the money to pay off Blue's uncle. That same night we robbed him; he came back. I had just left Blue's house a few minutes prior to drop Cornell off. When I left, he was to kill her and then meet me back at my place. When he didn't show, I called but got the voicemail over and over again. So I went back only to see fire trucks. I didn't know what happened until a few days later when Blaze was arrested."

"Blue's uncle called when he heard about the fire and I told him everything. He was pissed and wanted to kill somebody. Especially when he found out Blaze caused all of that pain for only fifty thousand. He felt it wasn't that serious. He would've given Blaze the money. Hell, he wasn't even pissed about Blue spending all of his money without returning it." She looked at Krystal as she started to stir awake. Tish kicked her again. "I thought this little bitch died in that fire. Imagine my surprise when I saw her with Blaze at the Lot."

She started to beat on Krystal again.

"Tishana, but what does this have to do with me!" I tried to get her attention. Hell, I didn't care for Krystal, but she could have at least given the girl a fair chance. She was going to stomp the poor girl to death, but my yelling got her attention.

"Everything. You have everything to do with it. Because Blaze loved you. And we want to take away everything he loved."

When she said we, I looked over at Monica.

"I didn't know about you at first. It wasn't until Monica saw y'all together in the shoe store. She knew about Blaze but not you. But when she saw your name, she was pissed. You ruined her life. You took Jerron from her. It's funny because she was pregnant as well." Tish laughed. "But she let it go because she moved on and started over. She don't give two fucks about you, Blaze or Jerron anymore. She was only doing a favor for me until you killed her brother that night."

430

"That was self-defense. Now I understand why she's pissed but Tish, Blaze is dead. Why am I here?" That was the nagging question. Everybody thought Blaze was dead so why was I being pulled into that all over again.

"Oh because—"

Her words were cut off as the basement door opened. At that time, Krystal had started to groan in pain as her eyes started to blink open. "Krystal, was Blake in that room?" I mumbled to her, but she didn't respond as she blinked repeatedly. I moved closer to her. I got that she was hurting and in pain, but I needed to know if Blake was in there. "Just knob your head. Was Blake in that room with you?" I whispered again. I got the same answer, nothing. A helpless feeling grew in the pit of my stomach. All I could do was cry.

Why didn't I just take him away from here like I had planned? I would never forgive myself if he wasn't okay. I would rather they killed me as well. I couldn't live with myself knowing I was the reason Blake was gone.

"Tish, can you please just tell me if Blake's okay. I donc heard your story and I'm sorry you went through all of that. I wish you hadn't but that has nothing to do with me and Blake. Just let us go and I'll forget about all of this." I once again pleaded with her before my eyes slid to the tall light skinned man that descended the stairs.

I didn't know what it was about that man but his whole aura screamed danger. With Tish, I could pinpoint her reaction and I knew she wouldn't have hurt me. The man, on the other hand, looked like he wanted to destroy everything in his path.

He glanced at me and smiled before he went to Monica. He pulled her up and kissed her deeply. When he pulled back, he kissed her forehead, then whispered something into her ear. She nodded her head and left out the room, going up the stairs.

The man turned and looked at me before he walked over. "I don't believe you'll forget what has happened to you." He crouched down in front of me, taking ahold of my tied up ankles.

I resisted the urge to jerk away from him.

"Are these too tight?" He patted the tape.

I was hesitant to answer at first, but I nodded my head. "Yeah, they're hurting me."

He hummed as his finger hooked between the gap of the tape. He pulled a knife from his pocket. He flicked it open and cut my legs free. "I wouldn't forget if I was you. To be held this long worrying if you and your boy gonna live or die. No, I don't think you would forget, because if I got free, I'm coming back and killing everybody involved." He said with a smile. "Come here." He grabbed my shoulders and pulled me closer to him. His eyes locked with mine and a sweet smile came to his face as he cut the tape that kept my arms bound to my sides. He helped me to my feet. "I know you're a fighter. Now if I cut your hands free, you're not going to attack me, are you?"

I didn't know what it was exactly, but I wouldn't try him. He just seemed so off. And to be honest, he scared the hell out of me. "No, I won't."

He walked behind me and cut my hands free before he came back to my front. He examined my wrists, looking at the bruised skin. "You need some ice." He looked at Tish. "T, go get Peaches some ice and a wet towel."

"Alright." She said nothing else as she headed up the stairs.

Who the hell was this man? Whoever he was, he knew me.

"Let's go sit down." He led us to the couch were Blake and the other man sat earlier.

I had to ask him, I needed to know. "Can you please tell me if my son is okay, or let me see him? Please? I have to know—"

He waved his hand, shutting me up. "He's fine. He's sleeping, that's a wild little dude. You know he shot my man? But it was his fault. Why would he leave his gun on the side of the couch? Your little man got the gun and shot him. I can't have him shooting my men, so I put him to sleep. I'll let you see him when he wakes up."

A relieved sigh left my mouth at his words. "Thank you…" My words trailed off because I didn't know what to call him.

He caught on and held out his hand for me. "I'm rude. I'm Rice."

Hesitantly, I shook it.

"You are a very interesting person to me. Very brave female. I like that about you. I knew you were something special when you locked Blaze in your bedroom and fought him."

"What?" My body went still. It was only one time that I had locked Blaze in my room and fought him. And we weren't even in a relationship at that time. "You were watching me?"

"Of course, I was. I must admit, at first, I thought it was nothing between you two. And when you shot up his truck, I thought for sure he was going to kill you. That's what I would have done. But he didn't, he kept coming back like a lost mutt who found its owner. I knew then you were the one to break him." He smiled at me.

My face was twisted trying to figure out how he knew.

"The video cameras in your apartment. I know you didn't think Cornell's dumb ass was smart enough to do that. Or had the money or man power to pull that off. True enough, I had everything setup at his place and had him watching from time to time, but it was me mostly." He confessed with a look of satisfaction.

"But why? Wait, it was you that posted that video of Blaze and I—"

"No, that was Cornell's dumb ass. He almost fuck'd everything up when he did that. I was going to kill him myself, but we had to throw a trail off of us. So, I threw him out there instead. I thought Jerron was going to kill him but that dumb mothafucka let Cornell shoot him! What kind of shit is that? And he's the fuckin' hitta!" He barked out a laugh.

"You know about Jerron?"

"I hired him. That was before I found out he was Monica's ex. I found it kind of funny really.

434

Monica hoped they'd kill each other, two birds with one stone. But his loyalty to you proved everything and money didn't mean shit because like a bitch, he confessed everything. That fuck'd us up and set us back. And we had to lay low for a while." His hand stroked along my jaw to the slit on my lip. "Tishana got you good. Tish!" He yelled out to her. It wasn't long after he called her that the door opened, and two sets of footsteps descended the steps.

Tishana and Monica came into the basement. Tish held a baggie of ice and a face towel. Monica had a cup.

"It took y'all long enough. Damn." He fussed before waving them over. Tish handed him the towel. Rice took hold of my chin then brought the wet towel to the corner of my lower lip. He pressed it into the cut.

I hissed and jerked my head back slightly.

"I know you can take a little pain. This shouldn't be nothing to you." The smile he gave told me he was joking. "Baby, give me that cup." Without looking at Monica he held his hand out toward her. She gave it to him, and he held it out for me.

"No thanks, I'm not thirsty." I wasn't taking shit from Monica. That bitch was just too fuckin' quiet for my taste, especially if she felt I ruined her life. On top of that, she was gone way too long just to be getting a cup of water.

"Peaches, drink the water. I wouldn't poison you or give you anything that will hurt you."

I looked at Monica and she looked away. "I'm fine."

He laughed. "I'll drink it first if that'll make you feel better." He put the cup to his lips.

"Don't drink that!" Monica smacked the cup from his hand, and it wasted to the floor.

He looked at her like she was crazy. "What the fuck did you do?" He yanked her to him by her hair. "What the hell was in the cup?"

"Nothing—" She screeched out a cry.

Rice smacked the shit out of her. "Bitch, don't fuckin' lie to me. What the fuck was in the cup?" He repeated viciously, slapping her again. The hit was so hard blood started running from her mouth.

"Cyanide!" She cried, folding up to protect her face.

Now I saw why she hardly said anything. At the same time, I had to stare at her like she was crazy as well. *Cyanide? This bitch was seriously trying to kill me.*

"You're going to kill me over a mistake that Jerron made when he was younger. Something that happened only once and something he told you about? I didn't ruin nothing. He didn't even tell me about you. Damn! You two are some sick bitches!" I snapped at both her and Tishana.

There was no way in hell I would ever trip over a man that hard. Especially, not to the point I was going to try and kill the next female.

I didn't even know about her ass. Shit, kill Jerron's ass not me.

"I had one thing I asked you not to do. I simply said no one was to touch her. Did I not fuckin' say that? And you're about to fuck everything up because yo fuckin' ex cheated once. You stupid bitch. I'll fuckin'—" He had Monica by the throat and pinned against the wall. Whatever he was going to say or do he caught himself. Rice let Monica go. "I'll deal with you later. Get the fuck out my face before I do something I'll regret later." Rice pushed her away from him and she wasted no time running up the stairs. "Mikel," he called the same guy from earlier.

Mikel came out of the room and Rice whispered something in his ear. With a head nod, Mikel headed up the stairs.

Rice came back over to where I was and sat beside me. "I'm sorry about that. Some women just don't listen. Tish, can you go get her something to drink."

"Okay," she nodded and left us alone.

Now I understood why Tishana wasn't really trying to hurt me. She must have been scared of him as well. Tish knew he wasn't wrapped too tight.

"I'm sorry about that. I specifically told them not to touch you. Tish got a pass. I saw what you did to her." He shrugged nonchalantly. "Monica though, that wasn't called for. But she has played her part, now I have no need for her."

"Rice, you seem like a straight up man. I honestly don't see the point of me and my son being here. Blaze is dead, so why is this still going on?" I had to know. "Le'Ron had told him it wasn't going to stop until he stopped hustling or was dead. He's gone now, so why are we getting pulled back into this mess? His territory is open to anyone."

Tishana returned and handed him the water. He stared at her then the cup before he took a sip. She didn't

437

flinch. He smiled at her. "Thank you. Now, give us a minute." Rice dismissed her. Once she left out the room, he handed me the cup. "Drink it."

With a heavy breath, I took a sip of the cold water.

"To answer your questions, Le'Ron was a dummy and believed anything that came out of Tish's mouth. Remember I told you, Cornell fuck'd up so I had to throw shit off. Let me ask you this. Do you think it was a coincidence your boyfriend found all of that information at Cornell's apartment? You think it was by accident he found photos of Monica and her son's birth certificate there? Think about it, I hired Jerron, he failed. Cornell started fuckin' up. Monica didn't want me to kill her brother and she's my girl, so I respected that. But that nigga was doing some dumb shit, like getting with your friend for instance. That was dumb as hell. Shid, he had already put himself out there. The logical thing in my eyes was to make it seem like it was him." He explained with that same nonchalant shrug.

"Peaches, this was never about drugs. I don't give a fuck about territory. I don't live in this fuck ass state, so I don't care who has what corner. That was just another throw off to yo nigga. Yes, he's dead now. It felt so good to watch that whole thing play out. Now you're being pulled into this shit because when yo boyfriend started that fire, he killed the only person I loved in this world. I wanted to kill you and let him watch me do it so he could know the pain of how it felt to lose the only thing that matter to him in this world. That night of his party, you were my target. I was shooting to kill you, not him. I wanted that fuck ass nigga to hold you as your last breath left your body. But he would never feel that now. But you know how it feels to have that taken away from you. I saw you hold him in that alley. You didn't want to leave him. That's how I wanted him to feel. That'll never happen now."

He licked his lips as he seemed to fade off into a distance.

"I didn't know Blue meant that much to you. Tish made it seem as if you were going to kill him for money that he owed you." I didn't think he loved Blue to that extent, but I guess he was family.

He let out a laugh. "I didn't give a fuck about Blue. He was a fuck up and that mothafucka couldn't hold money. I knew this before I gave him the money, so if I wanted the shit back, why the hell would I give it to him? I gave him shit because he did favors for me sometimes and I looked out for him. He brought little niggas my way and I put them on. That's about it. You misunderstood me. My wife was in that house the night Blaze killed everybody in that bitch and set it on fire. I didn't even have a body to bury. I wanted you in the same condition, unrecognizable. I must admit Le'Ron did a number on you, but he could've done better. You was still alive. You are a very lucky mothafucka, I'mma give you that. I've tried just about everything and you're still breathing. The bomb in the garage, how the fuck y'all walked away from that shit is beyond me. The night of his party, yo ass walked away with only a bullet to the shoulder and a fuckin' graze. You're a lucky ass bitch." Again, he laughed.

"I'm not going to put all the blame on Blaze. He retaliated the only way any hood nigga would. He was in the right on this. Had it not been for Blue and Tishana, my wife would have still been alive to this day. Everybody that was involved is going to pay. I needed Tish because she knew Blaze. She was in love with that nigga." He stood up and stretched. "Tishana, come here for a sec." He called out to her.

A few seconds later, Tish came walking down the stairs. "Yes?"

"Peaches, I meant that literally, everyone will pay. She brought me you, so she paid for it to be easy and fast."

"She paid for what to be easy and—aah!" A scream left my mouth and I jumped from my seat.

Rice pulled his gun and shot Tishana twice in the head. Once she hit the floor, he walked over to her and let off two more into her chest. "A painless death." He tucked his gun in the back of his jeans and then turned back to me. "You wanted to see your boy, right?"

I stood there frozen not knowing what to say. He was talking so normally. I just wasn't expecting him to kill her. After she helped him set everything up, he just killed her like she was nothing.

"I'm not going to shoot you. I promise. Do you want me to get him for you?" he asked me, calmly.

"Yeah, yes, I wanna see him." I was scared out my mind. I didn't know what to expect from that man. "Are you going to kill us?" I asked him, not knowing where our fate lied.

The look he gave me seemed as if I had offended him. "I would never kill a kid. He ain't done shit to me."

"Neither have I." I blurted without thinking.

"True. Mikel!" He yelled for his friend.

Mikel must have been the only other muscle because his name was the only one being called. My eyes slid to his back where his gun was tucked. If I could get his gun, then we would be fine.

Before I could think of a plan to take his gun. Mikel and Blake were coming down the stairs. Once Blake saw me, he snatched away from Mikel and ran straight into my arms. I held him tight as tears fell rapidly from my eyes.

"Are you okay? They didn't hurt you, did they?" I took ahold of his face and my eyes glanced over him. He only had the one bruise on his cheek from earlier.

"I'm good. You okay?"

That made me cry harder. There was no way my baby should have been asking me that question, ever. My head nodded as I wiped my tears. "I'm fine. We'll be fine. I love you—" My words were cut off as something hooked tightly around my neck, cutting off my airway. I couldn't breathe.

"No! Let her go!" Blake screamed while he made a grab for me, but Mikel snatched him up and held onto him.

My hands clawed at the leather strap that was choking me.

"Calm down, little man. We gon' have our day." Rice told Blake as he pulled the strap tighter. "I told you I needed someone to feel like I did. Blaze is dead, so the next best thing is a child. When he gets older, he'll come for me. And

I promise to kill him quick so it's painless." He whispered into my ear. "Stop fighting and sleep." His lips pressed into my temple.

The strap tightened even more after that. My eyes felt as if they were about to pop out of there sockets, as well as every vein in my face felt like they were ready to burst.

"Let her go! Momma!" Blake cried and screamed as he fought wildly in Mikel's arms. "Please, just let her go! She didn't do anything. Please! Momma, please!"

My eyes closed and my body went limp. The sounds around me started to slowly fade out.

Everything went black.

Chapter 32

Blaze

It took us damn near two hours to get to this hick town. The GPS led us to a secluded house. It was two cars parked in the yard. Once King parked, I hopped out with Mac right behind me.

"When we get in this bitch, ain't no questions asked. Drop the first mothafucka you see." Once we made it to the door, I kicked that mothafucka as hard as I could. The door swung open. As soon as we stepped in the house, all I heard was Blake yelling.

He was literally screaming, that sound hurt my damn soul. Never in the six years since I had Blake had I ever heard him scream like that. I ran to where the sound was coming from. I was about to throw the door open, but King stopped me.

"B, you don't know what the fuck is down there. Or how many guns down in that bitch. Mothafuckas will start shooting and he'll get hit. Creep that bitch open." He explained in a whisper.

His calm demeanor always pissed me off, but he made sense. I snatched my arm from him and slowly opened the door.

"She didn't do anything! Please! Momma, please!" Blake cried.

I got in a crouched position and looked down the stairs. First thing I saw was Peaches on her knees, her body was limp. That was all I needed to see. I couldn't see the nigga's face, but I had a clear view from his neck down. My gun cocked and I shot twice.

He released the strapped he had around Peaches neck, causing her to fall to the floor. I wasted no time running down the stairs. I shot the dude twice more and he fell to the ground.

King was right behind me. He shot twice at the dude that was holding Blake. The first shot missed whereas the other hit him in the shoulder. He yelled out in pain and let Blake go.

My son hit the floor, covering his head, like I'd taught him plenty of times over again.

The dude reached for his Glock and King's .9mm ripped as did mine. We lit that mothafucka up.

He fell backwards onto the couch. His lifeless eyes were void and looking to the ceiling.

"Blake." I called his name and went over to him.

"Dad," he threw himself at me.

444

I held my son tight before I let him go and looked him over. "You i'ight?"

Blake pulled away from me. "Yeah, but he was choking Momma." He went to Peaches and pulled the strap from her neck.

"Fuck! Peaches." I pulled her up to me, slapping her cheek. "Peach, come on baby girl. Get up." I slapped her cheek harder. I couldn't do this shit again. I wasn't about to lose her behind this bullshit.

"Blow in her mouth. Give her CPR." Blake's finger went under her nose. "She's not dead."

"Blake, shut up, i'ight?" I pointed toward the stairs. "Go sit down."

"Dad, she's breathing."

I put my face next to hers and heard the faint sounds of her breathing. I let out a relieved sigh. I didn't know what the fuck I was going to do if I had lost her. I would have never been able to forgive myself knowing all of that could've been avoided had I not brought them back to Gary. They were safer without me.

Peaches took in a deep gush of air before she started choking. Her hands went to her neck as she coughed hard. After several long minutes, her breathing returned to normal. Immediately, she began to frantically look around.

"Momma!" Blake ran over to her and threw himself into her.

"Oh, my God! You're okay." She cried, holding him to her.

"Blake, let her breathe. Get up."

He ignored me as they both embraced each other.

Once those words left my mouth, Peaches looked at me and started crying harder. "I love y'all so much." She said as tears ran down her face.

"You good, Peach? The babies good?" I looked her over before my hand went to her stomach.

Those mothafuckas was never leaving our house again. I couldn't take this shit.

"My throat hurts, I'm shaken up but we're good." She held me and Blake once more before she pulled back. A scared look crossed her face. "Where's Rice?"

"He's dead. You don't have to worry about shit anymore. It's all over, Peaches." I kissed her. I knew this was what she wanted.

"The upstairs is clear. It's a dead bitch in the kitchen but besides that, ain't shit moving," Mac said as he bounced down the stairs with two cans of gasoline from the car.

"B, ain't this yo girl?" King asked, pointing at a body laid out on the floor.

I picked Peaches up bridal style and walked over to him, with Blake at my side. I stared down at the body. "Damn, is she dead?" I looked at Krystal.

King crouched down to check her. "No, she's breathing. Barely, though. They beat the fuck outda shorty." His head shook and he scooped her up.

"Damn, shorty." Mac pushed Krystal's hair out of her face. He was about to grab her but stopped and grabbed his gun.

Footsteps came down the stairs and we quickly turned toward them. Sam came into the basement.

"What the fuck you doing here?" We left his ass back at his fuckin' office.

"I followed y'all. I wanted to talk to Tish—" His words fell short as his eyes landed on her dead body. "No." He went to his sister.

"Rice killed her. He said since she brought me him, he didn't need her anymore." Peaches explained to him. "She helped him with every move. It was never about drugs, he wanted Blaze to hurt like he had, same with Tishana. She wanted you to feel how she felt when Blue died, same with Rice. His wife died in that fire and he blamed you, Tishana and Blue for it." Peaches laid her head on my shoulder.

That night I killed Blue was a blur. I only remembered bits and pieces of that night.

It was time to put this shit behind me.

"Clean this bitch up." I told them before I looked at Sam. My nigga looked like he was hurt. "You good?"

"Hell no. How am I going to explain this to my momma?"

"I don't know, but we need to get out of here." I nodded toward the stairs and King headed up them. "Blake, follow yo unc out." He did as I said. Once they were upstairs, I looked at Sam. "What we doing? We taking her and burying her back home or is she staying?"

"How am I going to explain this shit?" he asked again.

"I don't know, but I'm with you on whatever you do." I assured him.

Sam shook his head, looking down at Tish. "Let's go." He turned and headed up the stairs.

Mac started throwing gasoline over the bodies. Once we got to the top of the stairs, he was about to strike a match.

"Wait, Tish's baby girl is here." Peaches got out of my arms.

I looked at Sam and he shook his head before I looked at Peaches like she was crazy.

"Tish ain't got no kids, Peaches." Sam stopped to stare at her.

"She does. A little girl that's five. Linnea!" Peaches called out.

"Peaches—"

"Shut up and listen. I met the little girl earlier." She yelled again.

"Wait! They did all this shit while a baby was here?" I asked her not wanting to believe that bullshit.

"Yes, she told me I was going to wake her baby up when I was calling her." She told me before she opened a door that led to a set of stairs. Peaches took the steps by two.

I stood at the bottom, not believing they had a kid there that entire time.

"I got her." Peaches came bouncing down with a shorty in her arms. She went to Sam with the sleeping little girl. "Sam, tell your momma a good story about Tishana leaving, but she wanted y'all to look after the baby." She told him as she looked down at the little girl.

"We didn't even know Tish was pregnant. Damn, this shit is fuck'd up." Sam exclaimed pissed off.

"That's because she didn't want y'all to know. Tish wasn't all there mentally. She put up a good front, but she was mentally crazy." Peaches let out a breath. "Her name is Linnea Le'Shay Wright. Here." She gave the little girl to Sam.

Once she handed the kid to him, we left out and got into our separate cars. It wasn't long after that the house went up into flames.

***

When we got back to Gary, King dropped us off at the crib and then left. Neither Blake nor Peaches said a word the entire ride home. I could tell they were both shaken up about whatever happened in that basement. Especially Blake, the whole ride home he just laid under Peaches. I was going to have to find out everything that had happened down there but for right now, I wasn't going to bug them. They looked hella tired, so I was going to let them rest.

That night Blake slept in our room; he did not want to leave Peaches' side at all. I didn't fuss or snap like I normally would have. Instead, I let him sleep in there.

Two Weeks Later

Blake had slowly started to become his old self again. After Peaches told me everything that had happened in the basement, what he saw and what he had done with shooting that man, I now understood why he was so shook up.

They told me about Tishana saying Peaches wasn't his momma. That pissed me off and I wished like hell I could've killed her my damn self.

We never lied to Blake about Peaches being his birth mother, he knew. He just didn't acknowledge it because she never treated him bad. He admitted that it hurt him to hear Tishana say it but in every sense, Peaches was his mother. Blake said he forgot she wasn't until it was said. He barely remembered Leslie, which was a good thing to me. He did vaguely remember her mother because of how mean she was to him.

Blake told Peaches no matter what anyone said, she was still his birth mother.

The one thing I couldn't wrap my head around was the fact Tishana thought we were in a relationship when she was younger. It was hard to believe that because she was always quiet around me when she was a teen. As for us fuckin', I didn't remember that shit. But at that point of my life if I was drunk it was no telling. And if she claims I got her pregnant I had to be fuck'd up because I never hit a bitch raw when I was aware of what I was doing. I do remember giving her money to get an abortion, but I didn't know shorty was mine. She never even implied that it was. Then again even if Tishana had of told me I wouldn't have changed what I did.

Now that everything was over, I was happy as hell. I now saw what Peaches meant when she wanted to leave and go back to Lafayette. I wish I hadn't stopped her because Blake wouldn't have experienced none of that bullshit. He was too young to be dealing with my mess, but I felt they were safer with me then off on their own. I explained that to Blake and he seemed to understand.

He was just mad with himself that he couldn't do anything to help his momma.

Everybody had loosened up about the situation. Even though Krystal had taken a hell of a beating, she was good. A few broken ribs, a broken nose and a dislocated shoulder but she was healing. Mac had been looking out for her. I knew he wasn't going to leave her alone, which was fine by me.

Peaches said she was glad Krystal was okay, but she didn't want me to deal with her. I was cool with that. I'd rather lose her than to not have Peaches.

After that bullshit happened, I thought we needed to blow off some steam and just chill.

I called my moms' over to throw some stuff on the grill and called Peaches' ghetto ass friends over along with hitting up Sam, Bell, the twins and Mac.

Later that day...

"Uncle Boon, go get your son. He get on my nerves and that little girl over there won't let me play with her doll. Can you go take it from her?" Keema came and sat on my lap as she rolled her eyes at Linnea. I just prayed my baby girl wasn't shit like Keema's grown ass.

"Keema, go in the house and get a doll. How you gon' bully her and take her stuff?" I asked her.

"She not sharing. I let her play with my toys. Hold this. Nana!" She gave me her doll and ran to my moms'.

"King, I'mma whoop her little ass." I pointed to Keema, not thinking she could hear me.

She stopped talking to my moms and looked at me. "Uncle Boon, who you gon' whoop?" Her little hands went to her hips.

"You." I pointed to her again.

"You want me to make you plate?" she asked me.

I burst out laughing. "Yeah, make me a big plate."

"Okay!" She went back to talking to my momma.

Peaches came over and sat between my legs. "You better leave Keema alone." She leaned into me with her lips puckered up.

I kissed her like she wanted. "Man, that little girl grown as hell. She gon' be real pissed when I tag that ass in real life." I knew I was only talking shit. I wouldn't touch her. I was a sucker for that bad ass little girl.

Peaches grabbed her long beach towel and put it around her waist before she straddled my legs, wrapping her arms around my neck. "I love you." She kissed me again.

"You gon' fuck around and get in trouble out here." My hands went to her ass and I pulled her up on me.

"How much trouble would I be in if I did this?" She bit into my bottom lip before she licked my top. Peaches pulled back and brought her mouth to my ear. "What about this?" She bit into my lobe before she kissed down to my neck.

My hand tangled in her hair and I pulled her head back. "Peaches, you better stop. I got on shorts."

"You gon' spank me if I don't? Mmm, you know I like that shit." Peaches hips rolled before she grinded into me.

My dick got harder.

"Mmm, there he go." Her lips pressed against mine as her hand slid between our bodies. Peaches' hand went into my shorts and she took hold of my man.

"Peaches, why you playing?"

"Can I sit on it?" She whispered, licking my bottom lip.

I picked her up and jumped in the pool.

"Ah!" Peaches screamed loudly making my ears ring. Once we came up from under the water, she hit me. "Ugh, why would you do that?" She hit me again.

I laughed and pushed her against the side of the pool. "Because yo ass was hot and needed to cool off. Yo ass was straight about to pull my shit out and sit on it." I laughed at her.

She let out a whine. "Wasn't nobody gon' see. Besides, you could've taken me in the house, threw me on the bed and had me screaming my lungs out."

My brows raised. "Really now? Tell me more."

She started laughing. "See you playing and I'm serious." Peaches brought her mouth to my ear. "Bae, I am so horny. Let's sneak off for about ten minutes?" Her nails dug into my shoulders as she bit into my earlobe.

I was tempted like a mothafucka but with these kids here, her friends, my moms, and my niggas, we were bound to be interrupted. Especially with Blake's cock blocking ass around. I wasn't about to set myself up for that bullshit. It was only going to piss me off. And ten minutes damn sho' wasn't gon' be enough time for me. "Who the fuck you think gon' last ten minutes?"

She gave me a pointed look. "You."

"No, the fuck I ain't. I'mma be in that shit for at least an hour, beating." My hips pushed into her emphasizing me beating her pussy up.

Peaches let out a loud snort before she pushed me away from her. She turned around and got out of the pool. "An hour my ass. You ain't held an hour round in months. Everything been about ten/fifteen minutes. I'm starting to think you just too old to be tryna beat." I could tell she was mad. That mothafucka did not like to be turned down but would hold out on my ass for weeks.

I laughed at her. "Maybe so. We probably need to play around a bit. Try out some new shit." I joked in a serious tone.

Peaches stopped walking and looked back at me. "I will kill you and that new shit. Don't play with me, Blaze." She rolled her eyes hard before a thoughtful look covered her face.

Oh shit. I shook my head already knowing she done thought up some bullshit.

"Have you been looking around? Is that why you ain't been tryna have sex lately?" Her arms crossed over her chest as she cocked her hip to the side.

"Lately?" This mothafucka was crazy as hell. I was jumping on Peaches ass two/three times a fuckin' day, not even including the earlier mornings when I would wake her ass up to fuck. I didn't have a chance to think of no new shit because she had my ass hooked.

"Yeah lately," she countered.

"Shut the fuck up! Lately was about two hours ago."

She looked at me like I was crazy. "So—Ah!" Peaches screamed as King pushed her into the pool.

"Cool yo hot ass the fuck down. That's why yo ass pregnant now. Fast ass trick. Oh shit!" He cussed as Blake shoved him in the pool.

"That's what you get for not watching yo back." Blake fell out laughing.

"Nuh uh, Blake don't push my daddy! Uncle Boon, you better get you son." Keema fussed, walking up to Blake.

Blake picked her up and then tossed her in the pool. "Sha, you talk too much!"

Keema came from under the water and swam to the side. Her eyes were wide as she tried to regain her breathing. I grabbed Peaches and tucked my head in her neck, trying to hide my face as I laughed.

Peaches elbowed me. "That's not funny, Blaze."

Shit if it wasn't. I was cracking the fuck up. Keema soon started crying and I laughed harder.

"Blake, I'm about to beat yo ass." King threatened.

"And I'm helping." Ebony chimed in, getting out of her seat. Blake took off running.

"Hold her." King gave Keema to Peaches then hopped out the pool and chased Blake with Ebony.

"Auntie Peaches, can you whoop him." Keema's shoulders shook as she cried.

I tried to stop laughing but I couldn't. That was some shit I would have done. Blake definitely had it honest. He was my son.

"Uncle Boon gonna get him for you, okay." Peaches assured her.

"Okay. When you babies get here?" Keema switched the conversation quick.

"In a few months." Peaches said, laughing.

"Uncle Boon, can I get on your back?"

I stretched as I laughed once more. "Come on, baby girl." I turned around and she got on my back. Peaches went to leave but I grabbed her back to me. "Where you going?" I picked her up. "Keema, hold yo breath." I took us under water.

For the rest of the day, we all just played around in the pool before me, my son and my niggas started playing ball.

"Don't be having my baby out there betting either!" Peaches yelled from the lounge chair.

We all looked over at the girls before getting back in our little circle. We looked back at Peaches, who was watching us like a fuckin' hawk. "Two each. Give Sam yo money when we go in the house." I whispered to them.

"On what we whispering, though?" King whispered to the group. "She ain't my damn momma. She got one kid over here."

"Shid, I saw her fight him once. So, I ain't giving you shit until she's gone." Mac said in a hush tone.

"What he said." Bell, Khyree and Khalil agreed with Mac.

Sam scratched the back of his neck. "I don't know. She done got meaner."

"Y'all some punks. She a girl." Blake jumped in, shaking his head.

"What that mean? That mothafucka crazy. I wouldn't try her. She done shot at me once." Bellow told Blake, shaking his head.

"Me too. Her bullet grazed my ear." Sam told him, showing the light pink mark on his ear. "Shid, she done beat yo daddy ass so many times, I lost count. And she tased yo uncle too. B, yo momma crazy and she pregnant. She's 'bout twice as worse."

Blake looked over at Peaches and then back at us. "We'll just give you the money when we get in the house." He walked away from the circle and went to get the ball.

"Why y'all tell him that shit?" I asked them, laughing.

"Shid, he needs to know his moms crazy as fuck." King shrugged.

I looked over at Peaches to see her already staring my way. She smiled and waved.

Yeah, that mothafucka was most definitely crazy, but I loved the fuck out of her.

Epilogue

Peaches

One Year Later

I stood in a chair hanging the *Happy Birthday* banner over the sliding back doors. Once I finished, I threw the balloons onto the covered pool.

A lot had changed over the past year. My family had grown closer and as bad as I wanted to leave Gary, Blaze made me realize we couldn't always run away from our problems because they would eventually catch up to us, like his past mistakes had.

I understood what he meant and now that everything was over, I agreed to stay in Indiana. Especially with his businesses he had out here, I figured it was best. Blaze said we could move if I really wanted to. I did want to get out of

459

this state, but I knew he didn't want to leave. At the end of the day, where we were didn't matter to me as long as we were together, and our family was whole. I'd live anywhere to keep that.

"BJ, get over here!" I yelled at my son as he tried to make a quick dash for the back door. I stood there for a second, laughing to myself at his bowlegged self. Still chuckling, I sat the decorations down on the table and went after him. "BJ!" He fell to the ground but got right back up, wobbling to the door. Quickly catching up to him, I swooped him up in my arms. "Where are you trying to go?" I asked before tickling him.

My baby burst into a fit of laughter, which was contagious. I kissed his spitty mouth before I wiped it with my fingers. "Where is your daddy?" I asked him before putting him in the playpen. As soon as he got in there, he started crying. "Nuh uh, little boy. I'm not going to hold you." I laughed at his spoiled self. He stood up and held his arms out for me. "No." My head shook as I went to the table to get his sippy cup. "Here you go." I gave it to him, but he threw it to the side before he fell back on the soft mat, crying.

I stood there looking at him, not believing he was acting like that on his birthday.

"What's wrong with my baby?" Joseph asked, coming from out of the house.

"Y'all got him spoiled as hell. That's what's wrong with him." I fussed. They did my baby so wrong. They sat around holding him, then left his spoiled self for me to deal with. "Don't pick him up."

Joseph ignored me and grabbed his grandson. "Peaches, stop being mean." He came over to me and kissed my forehead. "How you feeling?" He sat on the lounge chair with BJ on his lap.

I rolled my eyes at him before going back to setting up the purple and black party decorations. "I'm good, sleepy but good." I sat the cups on the table then glanced back to see Joseph handing BJ some chips. "Joseph, do not give him those Cheetos. He's gon' make a mess." I fussed but again he ignored me. Instead he took a napkin and tucked it in the front of my baby's shirt. My eyes rolled but I ended up smiling no less.

It was nice to see Joseph interact with his grandson. It had been seven months since we welcomed him into the family.

We ran into Joseph one day at the grocery store. Blaze was ready to kill him because he remembered my and Blake's last encounter with him. He was in full protective mode and the fact we were in a store didn't matter to Blaze one bit.

Joseph explained his intentions wasn't to hurt or scare us. He was just surprised to find out his son had another part of him in this world. And he was hurt that I didn't tell him. He also explained how the night after he found out about Blake that he relapsed, which he hadn't done in over five years. He just couldn't carry the burden of knowing his son had never forgave him or that his grandson would never know him.

Me being the sensitive punk I was, I cried for Joseph. Only because I saw that broken look in his eyes, and I felt worse knowing he relapsed.

After that run in with him, Blaze told me to stay away from his father. He simply didn't trust him. I don't know what happened within that weeks' time between the two of them, but Blaze brought Joseph to the house and reintroduced him to us. He had been family ever since.

I looked over at BJ to see he had Cheetos all over Joseph's white jeans. "Joseph, look at your pants."

"Peaches, sit down and shut up. They only pants." He waved me off before giving BJ some juice.

"Whatever you say, Joseph." I started blowing up the balloons.

"Ma, we about to ride up the street, i'ight?" Blake called from the door. He was about to slide the screen closed. Blake was ready to take off.

"Blake, hold on. Who is we and up the street where?" I waved him to me only to see Ace slide out from behind him.

Where did he come from?

"Hey, Ace. When did you get here?" I asked him. After everything went down, Sam helped Jerron get full custody of Ace. With Monica not showing up to a trial hearing, it was easy. Ace seemed to be happy with his new living situation. Of course, Jerron was spoiling him rotten for the times he missed out on.

"Hey, Peaches," he came over and gave me a hug then kissed my cheek. "My dad just dropped me off."

Why would he just drop him off without telling me? I looked at Blake with a raised brow.

"Ma, can Ace spend the night over here?" He looked just like his damn daddy.

I rolled my eyes at him. It was too late now. "Ace, you can stay over. Blake will get the guest room ready for you."

"I told you she wasn't gon' trip." Blake told him.

I cut my eyes at him. "What y'all trying to do?"

"Just go up the street." Blake vaguely answered.

They were up to no good. I could tell. Those two together were trouble. You would have thought they were brothers with the way those two acted.

"Y'all can help setup then ask me. Come on, we got people on the way over here."

"People? That's family. They can help setup. You help them." Blake complained.

Ace started blowing up balloons. "I got you, Peaches."

My lips pursed together as I pointed at Ace. "Why you can't be like that?"

"He just sucking up to you, is all. You my momma. I don't have to do that. But you know I love you." He kissed my cheek, then went over to where his granddad sat. "What's up, Joseph. BJ, you fresh, huh?" He fist bumped his granddad. "Dad gon' have a fit when he see him. He got Cheetos everywhere." Blake pointed out, picking up his baby brother.

"That's between him and Joseph. I don't have nothing to do with that." I shook my head.

"Ugh, he stinks." Blake's face turned up. "Here." He held BJ out to me. "He just messed up my stomach."

"You are so damn dramatic. Give me him and help Ace." I took my son from him, then went into the house to change him. Once we were in his room, I took off his bottoms and gagged. "Ugh, where yo daddy at?" A whine left my mouth as my stomach turned.

BJ laid there smiling hard with all eight of his teeth showing. Laughing, I changed his stanky butt, then picked my baby up. "You smell good now, don't you?" I talked to my baby, laughing. "Give mommy kisses." My lips puckered up. BJ grabbed my face and gave me a kiss. His little lips popped as he did.

"Where my kiss at?" Blaze asked from the door.

I looked at him and smiled. "Give mommy kisses."

Blaze walked over and leaned down toward me. I dodged sideways and kissed my baby girl before looking to her dad. "I was talking to Brianna not you."

"Oh, it's like that?" Blaze leaned down and kissed me. He stood up straight and looked at his son, smiling. "What up, man? You been good?" Blaze held out his fist.

BJ little fist pounded his dads before he started reaching for him.

We swapped babies. I took my baby girl from him and kissed her fat cheeks.

Blaze was right when he said I was having twins. I was beyond surprised. Blaze was excited because he knew. He even had the nerve to call the doctor dumb as fuck for not listening to him.

The doctor went on to explain that BJ was hiding behind Brianna. And since their heart beats were in sync, there was no way to tell that it was another baby in my stomach.

Even though I was surprised and wasn't expecting another baby, I couldn't have been happier. I loved my twins to death and beyond.

Blaze DeShawn Carter Jr. aka, BJ and Brianna Alexis Carter aka Bria or Bri-Bri, completed our dysfunctional family.

I honestly thought Blake wasn't going to like the babies, but he was the opposite. Blake was just as happy, and he was a great big brother to the twins.

"Where y'all been at?" I asked him as he wrapped one arm around my shoulder.

"Bri-Bri and I had to do a little shopping." He smiled a crooked smile.

The muscles in my face went straight. "What you get?"

"She picked it out, not me. What you mean? How you gon' blame that on me. Bria said daddy that one." Blaze explained before looking at his baby girl. "Didn't you, Bria?"

Brianna's arms went out for him to get her. She wrapped her arms around his neck and tried to push BJ off of him.

"Bri-Bri, you better stop it." I said in a stern tone of voice. She was always doing him like that. Couldn't nobody be on Blaze without her trying to fight them.

Her bottom lip quivered, and her fat cheeks puffed up, her shoulders started to shake before she started crying.

"Peaches, I'mma beat yo ass." Blaze snapped at me, pushing me away from him. "Sssh, it's okay Bri-Bri. Mommy gon' make me kick her ass for yelling at my baby." Blaze cooed.

"Really, Blaze?"

"Yeah, really. You ain't gotda take that tone with her. Yo ass acting like she knows what she's doing." He fussed at me.

My mouth opened and then closed. "You better be glad you holding them." I walked away from him. "Gon' fuss at me like I'm his damn kid. Boy…" I fussed as I walked out the back door.

"Auntie Peaches!" Keema yelled for me as I stepped outside.

"Hey baby, what's up?" I picked her up giving her a big hug. Linnea was right behind her with her doll.

"Hey, Auntie Peaches," Linnea spoke, giving me a hug. "Can we spend the night at your house and play with the babies?" she asked in her cute little voice.

"Hell no!" Blaze said from behind me. "No, y'all can't spend the night unless you sleep outside." He shut it down quick. "Go find who brought you here and stay with them." He waved them off.

I loved my nieces as if they were my own, but those two girls together were hell. I just couldn't take it. The last time they stayed the night, one of them colored all over the walls and blamed Blake before saying the twins did it.

Ever since then, Blaze's answer was *hell no*. When they asked me, I sent them his way. I was a sucker and would say yes but not anymore.

"Blaze, don't be mean." I pretended to scowl him.

"Those two little girls are demons together. Hell no! I got a daughter now and they asses can't be nowhere near her. Hell no." His head shook as he held the kids.

I looked at Brianna play with his ear as she slowly started to fall asleep. My eyes then slid to Blake who had just pushed Keema down before taking Linnea's baby doll. My eyes glanced to my youngest son who was eating his fist.

They all had Blaze flowing through them and he had the nerve, no the audacity to talk about somebody's kids?

"Did you forget how Blake was when he was younger than them? Look at the twins now. Dude, don't say anything about nobody's kids when ours are just as bad. Give me her, she's about to go to sleep." I grabbed Brianna and her eyes open. She pulled away from me and turned more into her dad. "Forget you too, little girl. Come on, BJ." He came to me with no problem. "Give mommy kiss." He gave me a wet kiss. When he finished, I stuck my tongue out at Brianna.

She started crying as she reached for me. I laughed. "See what I mean? Give me kiss, Bria." She gave me a kiss and then laid back on her dad.

Blaze's arm went around my shoulders and he pulled me to him. "She acts just like you. Stuck up and spoiled." He joked.

"I am not spoiled or stuck up." My lips pursed together as I playfully rolled my eyes at him.

His head tilted to the side. Blaze's smile slowly faded, and he stared down at me for a long time not saying a word.

I didn't know why but my cheeks turned hot and I looked away from him as that giddy feeling formed in the pit of my stomach. I glanced back at him and my eyes rolled. His facial expression didn't change a bit. "What?"

"I love the fuck out of you, Peaches." He told me with that same serious face.

I didn't know why but it was something so different about the way he said that from the way he normally did. I didn't know exactly what that something was, but I was scared. Something wasn't right. "B, I love you too." I pushed BJ up on my hip.

Blaze's eyes slid to him then back to me. His eyes dropped for a second as he seemed to fade into his thought.

"Babe, what's wrong?" My hand caressed his forearm getting his attention.

"Ain't shit wrong. I mean, I'm good. I love the fuck out of you, though. I mean that shit. I done told you this many of times before, but I don't think I really knew what it meant or felt like until right now. Seeing all this shit right here," his hands waved around us. "Looking at my kids that you done gave me, you accepting my son and making him yours. You ain't have to do that shit. It ain't too many females out here that would have done half the shit you did or continued to ride with me through all this bullshit. Especially with you getting hurt behind my fuck ups. Most mothafuckas would've bounced a long time ago." He explained.

"When that shit happened with Le'Ron. You ain't have to stick with me after that. You had no ties to me at all, but look at you Peaches, you're still here. You done gave me two kids and never asked for shit since we've been together. You never asked me for shit, ever. This been fuckin' with me hard lately because it seems like I'm the one always asking for shit. I can't remember one time you actually told me no and if you did yo ass never stuck to it. I remember you telling me at the beach—*how do you know what place is for you if you never left where you're from?*" And *"Don't claim what's not for you when you haven't given any place a chance."* He quoted what I said to him over six years ago.

"True to fact, I never gave nothing a chance because I didn't care about shit else. A hood is what I am or was. I never expected to be no damn father. Hell, I didn't know what it meant to be a dad or a family man because I never had that. Regardless of not knowing, I'm finding myself not

469

wanting to be anything but a family nigga. Shid, I never expected to live this long, and I think if it wasn't for you, I wouldn't have." His head shook as he stared down at me with a serious expression.

"Now what I'mma do is give you the chance to ask me for anything, anything you want and if I can I promise on my life, I'mma give it to you. Think about it now. I done put you through a lot of shit. If you could ask me for anything, what would it be?" His fingers stroked the back of my head as his face lowered, coming to mine.

I stood on my tip toes, kissing him. It never failed how random Blaze would be and leave me completely speechless. I didn't know how to respond.

Blaze's hand tightened in my hair and he pulled back, laying his forehead against mine.

My head tilted and my lips played with his. I couldn't help how he made me feel. I was in love, helplessly. And regardless of what I'd been through while dealing with him, I wouldn't change it for the world because in the end, it gave me everything I always wanted.

He had given me my three babies and I had him. I couldn't ask for anything else.

"Peaches, you better stop before you start some shit." He bit at my top lip, then sucked on my bottom.

I smiled at him before kissing him again.

"Tell me what you want. Price don't matter."

My eyes rolled up in my head at that. "Blaze, what I wanted you couldn't buy me. And I couldn't tell you what I wanted because it wouldn't have been real at the time. Now it is and I have everything I want and need."

His brow raised. "What's that?"

My smile widened. "Baby, all I wanted was you in the beginning. Now I have you and three beautiful, healthy kids. I have everything I need, and you've given that to me." My hand ran over Brianna's ponytails as I kissed Blaze Jr. on the head. I looked over at Blake and then back to him, smiling. "You, Blake, BJ and Bria are all I want and need. I'm happy." I told him honestly. I couldn't ask for anything else.

"That's it? You don't want to move from Gary? Move to a bigger house? You don't want a new car? Nothing? Just us?" He questioned with a disbelieving stare.

I laughed as my head nodded. "Yes, none of that matter to me. Just y'all."

"I love the fuck out of you, Peaches." He laughed before he kissed me.

"I love you too, Blaze." I laughed again but harder. His reaction was too funny. It was like he was expecting me to say something else instead of what I said.

"Peaches, marry me."

I couldn't stop myself from laughing.

Blaze stopped laughing. "I'm dead ass serious, Peaches. Marry me."

My laughter died down; only little chuckles left my mouth as I took in his serious expression.

"What?" The smile on my face slowly left as his words started to settle in.

"Peaches Monique Johnson, will you marry me?" He repeated.

I looked around the backyard to see everyone looking at us. But I just didn't know. I had to admit I was hella slow sometimes but only because I never knew when it came to Blaze. He was so random at times. I didn't know when to take him serious.

I leaned closer to him. "Blaze, I don't know if you're being serious or playing right now. So, if you're not serious, stop please." I whispered to him.

That made him bark out a laugh. "Baby girl, I'm dead ass serious right now. I have never been so serious in my life. You said all you wanted was me and the kids. The kids already yours, now I'm giving you me. This yo shit, remember?" He reached in his pocket and pulled out a box, then opened it. "Will you marry me?"

He was serious? Oh, my God!

"You're serious?" My eyes were wide as I stared up at him, shocked.

He thought that was funny. "Yes, dead serious. You gon' marry me or not?"

I laughed out an excited squeak. "Yes, yes! Oh, my God." I didn't even look at the ring as I pulled him to me. "You're serious."

"Yeah."

I looked at my girls and we started screaming. I didn't know what else to do besides that. I never expected Blaze to ever ask me that question.

"Peaches, where you going?" Blaze pulled me back to him.

"I got to tell the girls." I told him excitedly.

"They heard me plus they're about to watch." He laughed at me.

"Watch what?"

He ignored me at first as he waved Ebony and Kim over. "Get them," he handed Ebony Brianna.

Kimmy grabbed BJ from me.

"Watch what, Blaze?" I asked him as he pulled me to him again.

"Us, getting married."

I'm sure my confusion showed on my face. "When?"

"Right now. What's a better time or place to get married besides right here with our friends and family?"

"Are you serious?"

"Yes, Peaches, I'm serious." He laughed again.

I looked down at my yellow and purple sundress. "Okay. Wait! I don't have a ring."

"Don't worry about that. I told you we went shopping earlier." He grabbed my hand and brought me to the pool. "Reverend James," Blaze called to an older man I hadn't noticed sitting at the table until now.

Where in the hell did he come from? I glanced at Blaze. How long had he been planning this? And on the twins' birthday, no less. "Blaze, when did you plan this?" I whispered to him.

"Yesterday. I woke up that morning thinking about it. And figured why not. Neither of us is going anywhere, time has proven that. I'm in it for the long haul. Are you?"

"Why would you ask me that stupid question? Yes I am." I stood on my tip toes and kissed him.

"Let's do this then." Blaze beckoned the man over. "Yo, Blake come on. You my best man."

Blake jogged over to us. "You're a Carter, now we are officially complete." He hugged me.

I laughed at Blake as I hugged him tightly. That was what he wanted, he told me that a while ago.

Reverend James stood before us and started. "Dearly beloved, we are gathered here today…"

***

Once the ceremony was over the party was in full swing. Blaze and I had the twins and Blake in the middle of the pool, dancing on the plastic floor as the water flashed different colors beneath us. We laughed and danced all night long with our friends standing around dancing with us.

I must admit we had been through so much during the past few years we'd been together. It was times I wanted to say forget it and walk away completely with no regrets. But I could never seem to stick with it.

Blaze was most definitely bad for me, but he was also my perfect match. I couldn't have asked for a better soulmate or go through hell with any other person besides him.

We were both broken at one point in time and it took us finding each other to mend our pieces perfectly back together.

Blaze was my everything. He made me complete as I had done him.

I stared at him and my kids, I couldn't help but laugh as I remembered the times we fought constantly and the time I told him I would never date him because of who he was, *a hood.*

Now look at us. The both of us were head over heels in love, grown with three amazing kids and for once in our lives, carefree.

For the life of me, I couldn't find an ounce of regret from the time I had met him to now. I wouldn't have done anything differently.

I sat BJ down and wrapped my arms around Blaze's waist. I stood on my tip toes, smiling hard and wide, kissing him through my smile.

He picked me up and I laughed, wrapping my arms around his neck and my legs at his waist.

"Blaze De'Shawn Carter Sr., I love you so much."

"Peaches Monique Carter, I love you with everything that's me." His hands tangled into my hair and he kissed me deeply.

I never knew the meaning of *A Dangerous Love* until I fell in love with Blaze. It took everything I went through to make me truly understand *The Price of Loving a Hood.*

With the cheating, beatings, losing my baby, having my house blown into pieces, nearly losing my *husband* and having my son witness such brutality was a lot to go through, but I still gained so much more.

My wonderful life and beautiful family.

Now I could live, love hard and cherish every waking moment with my kids and husband with no regrets.

The Price of a Dangerous Love was so well worth it in my eyes.

The End!

Carter's Babies
Delivery Scene

"**P**each, sweetheart, you gotda push." Blaze coached as his hand ran over my sweaty forehead.

My eyes cut hard at him as my teeth grind together. I wanted to hit him so bad. But I was tired and sleepy. I had been in labor for over ten hours. My baby girl just wasn't ready to come into the world yet. I was giving my all in every push, but she wasn't coming out.

"Peaches, come on man, you gotda push." Blaze repeated.

Pain shot up my back and I let out a loud grunt as I squeezed Blaze's fingers hard. "I am pushing. Why would you put me through this? I swear I hate you!" I growled at him.

Blaze kissed my forehead and laughed. "I know. I love you too. Now push, I'm ready for my baby to get here." He spoke excitedly as he kissed me once more.

I bit into my bottom lip as I squeezed his hand even harder as I pushed.

"Ah shit, Peach! Man, let my damn hand go." Blaze pulled his hand from mine.

"Just get out! I don't wanna see you right now! Oh, my God!" I screamed as I grabbed his shirt. I pushed hard once more before I flopped down on the hospital bed.

"You doing good, Peaches. I want you to take a deep breath for me then give another big push like the one you just did. Can you do that for me?" Doctor Thomas asked.

"No I can't. She's not coming." I cried. I was ready for those contractions to stop. I wanted this baby out of me. Hell, I wanted to be out of my own damn body.

"Yeah she can. Peach, you gotda do this—"

"Blaze, shut the hell up talking to me! Get out! Momma, make him get out!" I pushed him away from me. He wasn't making me feel any better. I was in this fuckin' situation because of him. Another contraction hit and I grabbed Blaze back. "Ooh, no don't leave me! It just hurt so bad."

Blaze looked at me and started laughing. "I got you, baby." He told me before he looked at the doctor. "You ready for her to push again?"

"Yes, I need you to give me a big push now." The doctor instructed.

My head shook. I just didn't have it in me to push any more. I was so tired.

478

Mom B laughed at Blaze then came over to me. She grabbed the face towel from the table and wiped my sweaty face. She then picked up the cup of ice chips and put it to my dry lips. "Here." Momma put it in my mouth. "Peach, I know you're tired, but you have to push for us. Okay?"

I let out a huge sigh, then sat up slightly. With Blaze's hand gripped tight, I started to push. Once I couldn't push anymore, I fell back on the bed, panting heavily.

"That was good I can see the head. Come on give me one more." The doctor urged.

"You can see the head?" Blaze questioned as he walked away from me. He went to where the doctor was. "Oh shit! That mothafucka right there too. Hell nah!" Blaze sounded shocked as he stood there looking at my coochie.

"One more push, Peaches." The doctor said.

I let out a deep breath then started to push again, giving it everything I had. I felt my baby leave my body before I heard her joyous cry.

There was a loud thump following my baby's cry. "Did you drop my baby? Is she okay?" I shouted. I couldn't see anything passed the blue sheet that covered my propped up legs.

"Girl, no she didn't drop the baby. It's the damn daddy that dropped. I don't know why he took his dumbass down there." Bianca fussed.

"Blaze dropped?" I tried to look down, but I didn't see him.

Bianca started laughing. "Yes! His ass fainted when the baby came out."

I didn't get a chance to respond as the nurse brought me my baby.

"Congratulations on your baby boy." She handed him to me.

"A boy?" I mumbled as I looked down into my baby boy's light brown eyes. I was shocked but happy because that was my baby. I had him. "You're a boy. You're so beautiful." I kissed the top of his head. "Mommy loves you so much." I couldn't believe this beautiful being just came out of me. He was what Blaze and I created. My fingers stroked his face before I kissed him again. As my lips touched his forehead another pain shot up my back. "Oh, my God! What is that?" I asked.

"What's wrong?" The doctor asked as the nurse took my baby.

I just had the urge to push. "I have to push! Oh, my God!" I grunted out as I pushed hard.

"Oh! It's another baby. I can see the head. Keep pushing."

I leaned forward and pushed. Again, I felt my baby leave me.

"It's a girl!" The doctor announced excitedly.

"Two babies?" Twins? I said to myself. I looked over at Blaze who was now in a chair still passed out.

I could not believe I just had twins. And Blaze knew this entire time.

***

"I told you dumb mothafuckas she was having twins. Y'all need to buy new fuckin' equipment!" Blaze fussed at the doctor, but he was so excited about the twins.

All I could do was shake my head at him and apologize. "I'm so sorry for him. It's a condition he has." I hit Blaze in the arm. "Shut up, please."

He laughed, then leaned down to me. His lips pressed into mine. "I love the fuck out of you." He kissed me again.

I laughed into the kiss as I wrapped my arms around his neck. "I love you, too, Blaze, way too much."

"You ready for some more? If you keep popping out twins, I'll have my team within a year." Blaze smiled down at me.

"Get away from me. I love you but this is it for me. I thought I was about to die." I shook my head at him. I wasn't having no more kids.

"Fuck outda here with that. You are having some more that's already been decided. As soon as I get back in there you gon get pregnant." He bit into my lip before he started kissing me.

All I could do was laugh as he cut off my reply. For now, I would let him think whatever he wanted, but I was getting my ass back on birth control. I was taking a break from sex that was a sure way I knew I wouldn't get pregnant.

Blaze climbed in the bed with me.

Immediately the last thing I thought went out the window. Cutting sex off from Blaze was simply a no go.

A clearing of a throat interrupted us. Blaze pulled back and squeezed on the side of me. My eyes cut at him. His big ass could've went and sat in a chair. We were tight as hell in the bed.

Bianca walked in the room with the nurse and the twins. "Boon, get out that bed. You cannot be in there with her."

"Who gon' tell me to get out the bed?" He asked his momma before he looked at the nurse.

She looked like she wanted to say something but thought better to keep her mouth shut. I was so glad she went with the latter.

The nurse turned her focus to me. "Do you plan on breastfeeding or formula feeding?" She asked me.

I shrugged Blaze off my shoulder. "I want to do both." I told her as I reached for my babies who were still nameless. "Momma, pass them to me."

Bianca ignored me as she cooed over the twins.

"Okay, do you know how to breastfeed?" The nurse asked.

I shook my head no. "No, I don't. But I watched some videos which I think should be kind of easy to follow."

Again, she looked at Blaze and I started laughing. "Babe, get out the bed so she can show me how to feed the babies."

Blaze looked at the nurse with a raised brow before he laughed at her. "Scary ass. Man, come show her."

The nurse came over and showed me the position the babies needed to be in and how I should cradle their heads. She then grabbed my baby girl and brought her to me. One by one she showed me how the babies should latch on when I go to breastfeed them. My baby boy didn't waste no time latching on to get his milk.

I started laughing at him as did Blaze.

"Yeah, that's my son. He don't need no instructions. Ain't that right, Lil B?" He asked him.

My brows raised at that. "Lil B? We already have a Lil B—"

Blaze shook his head as he cut me off. "We gon' have two of them. We got, Lil Blake and now we got a junior, Lil Blaze." He explained before he grabbed our baby girl. He didn't even let her finish feeding. "What's up, Lil Mama? What's yo name gon' be? Huh?" He asked her. A cute lazy smile came to her small lips as milk slid from the corners of her mouth. Blaze wiped her mouth with a bib before he leaned down and kissed her. "Peach, what you think about Brianna? She looks like a Brianna."

Not once would I have thought this would be us. Just thinking about how Blaze was when we first got together. Never in a million years did I think I would actually be having kids with him. Hell, or have him by my side as he named our babies.

The feeling inside of me couldn't be explained. I was beyond happy. No words could do that feeling any justice.

"Blaze Jr. and Brianna are beautiful names." I smiled at him before I beckoned him to me. "I love you so much." He has blessed me with three beautiful kids. That alone made me fall deeper in love with him.

Then again, I didn't think *Love* truly expressed how I felt about Blaze. He was everything I could ever ask for. He was the only man for me.

My Blaze, My Hood, My Addiction.

He was simply… *My everything*.

I couldn't wait to start our new life together.

The End!

A Dangerous Love 8 Continuation:

A Love Like Ours

Available On Amazon

Made in the USA
Columbia, SC
25 November 2023

27101514R00271